It Could Be Anyone ...

"What are your procedures for a situation like this?" the Captain asked in a whisper.

"Truthfully? I've never been in one."

"Never?" He was incredulous.

"Usually I chase a killer when they have a place to run. I've never backed one into a corner like this and not known who it is. Most often they make a mistake and I make a capture. In this situation, who knows what he'll do? His behavior is escalating, there's no doubt of that."

"Why do you think he's killing?"

I frowned. "I don't think it's random. There's more going on here than three murders."

A beat, and then, "What do you mean?"

"I can't tell you until I know everything. But there is definitely a reason for the killer's method."

He grew furious. "This is my station, Tanner. I demand to know —"

"I can't tell you. It's as simple as that."

"Why? Because the Council sent you? Because you're the best at this job?"

"Because frankly, Captain, you could be the killer."

He looked down and saw my hand on my pistol. His jaw dropped. "You're serious."

"Absolutely."

THE FURNACE

by

Timothy S. Johnston

Copyright © 2011 Timothy S. Johnston
All rights reserved.
ISBN: 1466276657
ISBN-13: 978-1466276659

> We are lost! They have thrown us into the furnace,
> without rations, almost without ammunition.
> We were the last resources; they have sacrificed us ...
> Our sacrifice will be in vain.
>
> Sergeant Paul Dubrelle,
> Verdun, 1916

2401 A.D.

Part One: Orders

Investigator's Log: Lieutenant Kyle Tanner, Security Division, Homicide Section, CCF

Certain death approached.

It had stalked me for days, always just a step behind, but I had thwarted its every attempt. Skill, foreknowledge, and perhaps even luck had aided in my escape. Unfortunately, even the best Investigator couldn't have avoided events on that damned station once they were set in motion, and it had taken me too long to discover the truth. *SOLEX* was now gone — destroyed in the final carnage — but hopefully I had eliminated the danger within.

Now, however, a new threat rose on the horizon.

Unconscious and alone in space, my body spun like a rag doll, limbs nearly sheared at the torso. It took ten minutes for consciousness to return, and when it finally did, I longed for the darkness to take me again. My head ached and my body felt like it had been through a twelve round prize fight. The acceleration had been brutal, but I had made it. My neck hadn't snapped, my brain hadn't turned to jelly, and my lungs hadn't collapsed. I had withstood g-forces that would have killed most people.

But I had no choice. I had to run.

I shook the cobwebs from my head and winced in pain as I did so. The status display inside my helmet indicated nominal function across the board — yet another surprise. The temperature was in the high-normal range, but that was expected at this distance from Sol.

I craned my neck to look toward the sun, but could no longer make out the debris that orbited at just five million kilometers. The separated station components now drifted on unplanned and unknown trajectories, their interiors baked into oblivion, the dreadful cargo they carried cleansed forever. Now, hurtling through space in only a vacsuit taxed well beyond safe tolerable limits, I knew I was in grave danger. I had only a weak comm, and transmitting amidst the radiation emitted from the sun was like shouting into a hurricane. No one could ever hear, especially Mercury, still sixty million kilometers away.

Dammit! I had survived this far, I told myself angrily. I couldn't let it end this way.

I swallowed nervously and licked my cracked lips. The mass driver had done its job well, but my velocity was only three kilometers per second. My oxygen readout indicated that only three hours remained. The extra canisters I had thrown into the driver with me each held four, which gave a grand total of fifteen hours. I groaned as I did the simple math in my head; I'd only get a hundred and sixty-two thousand kilometers before my air ran out.

My throat was sandpaper, my tongue swollen against clenched teeth. I had long since depleted my water supplies, but in the grand scheme of things, its importance was negligible. The poor radio, the lack of water, the diminishing oxygen — none of these held a candle to the true danger.

The radiation.

My exposure was rising fast. Alarmingly so. At this distance from Sol, I could only withstand it for a few hours. I had now been out in empty space, the sun's massive fury blazing at me unblinkingly, for a quarter of an hour. Even though I was moving away from it, the punishment my suit had to deal with was just too much. My speed wasn't nearly enough.

Not by a factor of a thousand.

Unfortunately, I had sabotaged my own ship and all the escape pods as well. I had only hours — maybe *minutes* — to say my prayers, call for help, and record what had happened to me on *SOLEX One*. I had to let the authorities know who had killed all those people — myself included.

I thumbed the button on my wrist and began to record my story.

— Chapter One —

I filed the capture warrant at 1300 hours; fifteen minutes later, I marched from the hotel that had been my home for the past four months. The guy behind the counter scowled at me as I pushed through the lobby and stepped out into the tunnels of the city. It was a typical reaction; people didn't much like the military in this district. A scowl was the least I would get today; mostly I heard muttered comments and sometimes, if the guy was brave enough to take me on and receive a beating, he'd spit. I was used to it. I could even understand, to a point. A lot of officers in the CCF were cold and heartless. They didn't give much thought to people's feelings, and if anyone got in their way, look out.

I'm a little different though. I'm in the military, sure, but a Homicide Investigator can become conditioned to death, gore and pain, and as a result we can sometimes grow more sensitive to what people are going through these days. I've seen some of the worst crime scenes imaginable: corpses skinned, decapitated and hanging upside down, limbs and eyes and a variety of other parts missing. There's a lot of fluid in the human body. I've waded through feces and blood and urine, ankle deep, and examined the crime scene while taking notes like it was an ordinary day. I've faced the victim's family afterward and attempted to explain what had happened. Doing so taught me to be sympathetic, and without that, this job would have killed me years ago. That's why, even though I'm in the Confederate Combined Forces, I don't really deserve the rap others in the military get.

In the tunnel outside the hotel, deep beneath the surface of Mercury, I found myself shoulder to shoulder with the surging masses who made their way to work, play, or wherever people went on this godforsaken planet. I threw a glance at the rock ceiling a few meters above my head. Who the hell could live underground like this for more than a few days? It boggled the mind.

I garnered a few more dirty looks on my way to The Gates of Hell, but I had long learned to ignore them. Checking my datachip reader, I studied the map of Mercury's underground warrens. Off in a distant corner, pretty much as deep as you can get, was the place I wanted. A dusty, grimy little tavern, a shit hole from what Flemming had told me. Full of shady figures, criminals and kingpins, it was the last place a respectable person would be found. If it hadn't been for Quint Sirius, I'd be on my way back to Earth.

I scowled. Quint Sirius. He had killed the best — and only — friend I had.

Michael Flemming was also a Homicide Investigator. There weren't many of us, considering the population in the system. As a result, we were forced to work alone, traveling from job to job, planet to planet, and station to station as needed. We never partnered up; there's just too much damn work and not enough people who can see through the lies and deceptions like Flemming and I could. When the opportunity presented itself, however, we had sometimes conferred with each other on our cases, providing helpful advice and opinions.

Flemming had asked for my help on his most recent case. Someone had raped and murdered a young woman named Tara Silvers. After questioning everyone related to the crime, he wasn't close to pinning a motive on a single person.

And so I took his files, read his notes, looked at the facts objectively, and finally determined that the killer he was after wasn't there. Flemming simply hadn't found him yet.

That was sometimes the case in our line of work. Usually it was one of the first people you looked at. Someone in the immediate family. The closest 'friend.' The guy who found the body. The neighbor. But on occasion he was so far removed, so distantly related, that it just took longer to get to him through the usual methods. I had once spent a month looking for the killer of an elderly woman on Mars, and had grown exasperated after such a long and fruitless search. And then, purely by chance, I stumbled upon something in the lady's personal belongings that directed me toward an old acquaintance — an enemy who had let his anger simmer for *two decades* before he finally acted. And I had found him purely by chance.

The recruiters in Security Division said they'd seen something in me. Intuition. Luck. Hunches. Perhaps all that played a role. Who knows.

I had studied Flemming's investigation reports and skimmed right over Quint Sirius. He didn't stand out at the time, but two days later I realized he was the one. Unfortunately, by the time I told my friend, it was too late. Sirius had either killed him or put out the hit.

The Gates of Hell had a gaudy fluorescent sign over the entrance: red flames licked upward and partially obscured the name in rapid flashes. The G wasn't even lit; it had probably burned out long before.

I removed the pistol from the holster strapped to my thigh, straightened my black CCF uniform tunic, and stalked through the hatch.

It was dimly lit inside and I paused for a few precious seconds as my eyes adjusted. It might have been a mistake, but I figured the uniform would prevent troublemakers from doing something *too* stupid.

There weren't many people inside, just a few scattered patrons who nursed drinks at round tables. There were some hooded glares, and a couple of outright hostile ones as well. I scrutinized them as I searched for Sirius.

The bartender in particular stared at me with narrowed eyes. "We're closed," he finally growled. "Get out."

Ah. The usual resistance to the military. I was used to it by now; you had to be, in this society. We controlled nearly every facet of life, including the legal and justice system, and it was bound to draw scorn from the civilian population. I kept my voice flat as I responded. "I'm not here for you."

"I don't care, bud. Out." He pointed to the hatch, displaying a stubby finger and a thick, knotted arm. The guy was big, stocky, bald. Branding up and down both biceps, piercings everywhere. He flexed his muscles as I measured him up.

I marched toward the bar. "I couldn't care less what you want right now."

"You think that pistol scares me? You got no business here."

His type wasn't uncommon; I'd dealt with them on many occasions. Scary to look at, tough talking, but when push came to shove they were too slow to fight the good fight. Age, alcohol, brainstim, and a variety of other vices had done a lifetime of damage.

I holstered the pistol. "How about this? Come out from behind that bar and we'll settle it, right here."

He stared at me as he considered. "You'll be back with your buddies when I beat you. Or you'll pull the weapon. No dice."

I spread my arms wide. "Scared?"

He scowled. "Of what? A little guy like you?"

I shrugged and simply studied him silently.

"What are you trying to goad me for?" He bared his teeth. "Get lost."

I threw a quick glance around the establishment during the exchange. There, in a dark corner, lurked a skinny guy in a dirty white t-shirt. Quint Sirius. I had studied the bar's floor plan; I knew there was only one way in and out. If this bartender wanted to make a fuss, let him. I'd make an example of him right in front of the exit. Quint could watch; it would make capturing him that much easier. In fact, already he eyed me intensely, perhaps curious as to why a CCF officer was in The Gates of Hell.

The bartender was growing angry. I could see the thoughts churning through his head. He knew I was determined not to march out empty-handed. Finally, his furrowed brow flattened, he moved around the bar, and stepped forward. "All right then, let's —"

I took a huge step, turned to the side, and struck out with my left fist. It sank into his Adam's apple and he stumbled back with a gurgle. I twisted in the other direction and brought my booted foot savagely into his knee. A sickening crack and he hunched over with a groan. He clutched his shattered kneecap.

Less than two seconds had passed.

"You bastard," he wheezed in agony. "You tricked me!" Saliva dribbled from his lips as he stared at the contorted leg grasped in his hands.

I snorted. A typical response from a loser. I wasn't a fantastic fighter by any means, but I knew that taking the initiative and presenting a fiercer, more intense front made up for a lot. That, and the fact that he was in such a sad state had practically guaranteed my victory. In another twenty years, I realized sadly, things probably would not go so well for me. Take advantage of it now, I often told myself. One day you'll be too old for field work.

"Bullshit," I snapped. "I challenged and you accepted. Now you can limp to the hospital."

He glared at me for a second before he flashed a glance at a man seated directly beside me. In his eyes I saw a hidden order ...

I spun and drew my pistol. "Enough. Stay there and put your hands on the table." The man — already partly out of his chair — slowly lowered himself, fists clenched in anger. I shook my head. Why couldn't they accept the outcome and just be done with it? "Quint Sirius," I yelled. "Get your ass up here."

From the back I heard a scuffle and the scrawny man stumbled forward against his will. Obviously the tavern's other clients wanted me — and therefore Sirius — out as soon as possible.

He fell before me and looked up from the dusty floor. The grumbling behind him had intensified; he knew he was in trouble. At that moment, he had no friends in The Gates of Hell. "What do you want?" he spat.

"I'm here to serve a capture warrant."

"On what charge?"

"Murder."

He blinked. "That's ridiculous! I —"

"Save it," I growled. "You killed Tara Silvers and Michael Flemming."

His face grew pale, but he managed a quick laugh that sounded more like a squeak. "I don't even know those people."

I gestured with my pistol. "Get up, let's go. I don't want more trouble."

"Do it, Sirius." The bartender was now in a chair, his ruined knee still clutched in his hands. "Get out now, and take the goon with you. And don't come back."

"No problem there," I said.

Sirius jerked his head from side to side. "I didn't do nothin'," he cried. His eyes darted about in search of a friendly face. "Someone, help me! Don't let him take me — they'll torture me! Kill me!"

"Torture is too good for you," I said. I looked at the faces that surrounded us. Perfect. I had angered them greatly, but they had no particular love for the man at my feet. I was going to get out of this with my health — and my pride — intact. "You're on your own, Sirius."

The bartender snarled, pointed once more to the hatch.

Sirius looked like a frightened little girl. It brought a smile to my face. Justice for this one would be sweet.

I brought the lanky murderer — all hundred and thirty pounds of him — to CCF headquarters, booked him into the brig, and tried to resist the temptation to beat him to a pulp. A murderer was bad enough, but this guy had killed the only friend I had.

The cell was a small chamber with a narrow bunk and a steel toilet. There were no other amenities, not even sheets. I had to carry in a stool.

He stared at me defiantly, but there was no mistaking the look in his eyes. He knew his odds were diminishing by the second.

"You killed Tara Silvers," I said without preamble. "And when Flemming found out, you killed him too."

"Nonsense," he sneered, putting on an air of righteousness that was more act than truth. He had regained some of his confidence, but I knew it wouldn't last.

"It was in your file. When Flemming questioned you the first time, you claimed you'd never met the girl."

"I hadn't. I don't —"

"But when I reread it I realized you'd been on Mars."

He looked instantly suspicious. "Yeah. For a spell. It was —"

"Three years ago. You were there gambling and drinking. The same old shit you always do. Right?"

"I was working!"

"Sure you were. And meanwhile you were causing trouble and getting yourself arrested."

He hesitated for a moment. "No. I never got —"

"CCF records state you were fighting. It was a brawl that you started, Sirius, in a sleazy tavern. The usual rock you're found under."

It was always the same for his type of lowlife, and as a result they were simple to track and easier to catch. They never gave up carousing, it was in their blood.

"Bullshit," he retorted.

"You can't argue with military records. It's as plain as day."

"I — I — there must be some mistake."

"Nope. You were on Mars. You got arrested, and in custody, you met the girl."

He shot to his feet. "No way! I told you —"

"You took an immediate disliking to her. She rubbed you the wrong way somehow."

"She wasn't in the brig with me!"

I paused. "Oh. So you *were* in the brig?"

"I ..." He trailed off, eyes shifting as he thought furiously. "No. I wasn't. I told you that."

"Right. So there you were in the brig with everyone else who'd been fighting, and Tara Silvers was also there for some other minor offence." I didn't want to say that it was prostitution; she was dead and cremated. There was no sense furthering her disgrace. "Something happened between you two. What was it?"

"I never met her. I told you —"

I plowed on, trying to keep him off balance and on the defensive. Make the facts seem strong. Don't stop pushing. Be confident. No hesitation. "The records don't lie. You had business with her."

He shook his head violently. "No way, man."

"And something happened. Something went wrong. Maybe you couldn't get it up —"

"Bullshit!" he screamed. "Bullshit!"

I suppressed a look of satisfaction; I was close. Some sort of dysfunction had prevented this little weasel from performing that night. "So you couldn't do it, and maybe she laughed. Maybe she made a comment or something. Whatever it was, it drove you nuts."

"You're making wild guesses right now, asshole!"

"But you were in that brig, right? You already admitted —"

"No I didn't!"

"So you felt insulted by her," I continued, ignoring his protests. "It stuck in your craw. Who knows. But three years later, here you are on Mercury. Hanging out in the usual dives. And surprise, surprise, who should you see but Tara Silvers. Maybe you spoke to her, maybe you tried to do her again. Or, maybe you tailed her one night, found out where she was staying, and when no one was watching —"

"You're insane, man!"

"— you broke into her place and killed her."

Sweat beaded his forehead. He didn't like my train of thought, that was for sure. Maybe I was dead on, or maybe just a little close for comfort. Whatever the case, it was obvious he had killed her. He was acting damn jittery, and he had already lied to me.

"This is all conjecture," he fumbled out. "None of it's true."

"People saw you two in the same bar the night she died."

He frowned. "There were lots of people in the bar that night."

"Flemming questioned you about her. You said you'd never met her."

"That's true!"

"Lie. It escaped his notice. Mine too, for a bit. But security arrested both of you, the same night on Mars, three years ago." I stood. "There's the connection, Sirius. You lied about knowing her. It tells me you killed the girl, here on Mercury."

His eyes were frantic. Pleading. "Just because I say we never met?"

I shrugged. "Sure. You lie about that, you lie about other things, right?"

His eyes fixed to mine for a long moment before his expression abruptly sagged. "All right, all right. Look, sure, we met. But it was just for a minute or two. We chatted in the brig, on Mars, like you said. But that was it — nothing else happened!"

He broke, just like that. Too easy. Things had snowballed out of his control, and here he was, back in a cell.

"You killed Flemming when you realized he might connect the two of you."

"No way," he protested again. But he just wasn't as fervent as he had been a minute earlier.

I leaned forward and stuck my nose right in his face. "Got ya," I whispered. "The penalty is execution." I grabbed the stool and marched to the hatch. The guard stepped aside. He was glaring at Sirius, his distaste clear. He knew the man was guilty of murdering a comrade. Even though Flemming was an officer and he a lowly grunt, he knew he had to enforce the line that connected us all, otherwise the civil disorder that always lurked just below the surface would emerge with a vengeance. When I stepped through the hatch, I knew what would happen in that cell. So did Sirius — he had that sad look of a beaten animal.

"Think of Flemming when you die," I said as a parting shot.

I heard him whisper something under his breath, too quiet to make out.

"What was that?" I asked, oddly curious.

He dissolved into tears. "I'm sick," he managed between sobs. "I need help."

Despite myself, I swallowed past a lump in my throat. I didn't want to see my captures act like ... like ...

I shoved the thought aside as quickly as it had come.

I left the room and didn't look back.

—

I slammed open the doors in CCF headquarters, oblivious to the stares that followed me. I marched past everyone without seeing them; I could hear their muttered comments filled with jealousy and perhaps even some criticism. They knew who I was; I had heard it all before.

A seeming eternity later the exterior hatch slid aside and I thrust myself out into the dark tunnel.

My heart pounded.

I couldn't help but blame myself. Had I put the pieces together sooner, had I read the facts correctly the first time, Flemming and I could have issued the capture warrant two days earlier. What had happened to me? Why hadn't I seen it?

Why had I failed Flemming?

—

Ten minutes after I left CCF HQ, I received a page on my reader. A single beep called my attention and I reluctantly moved to answer it. "Damn," I muttered. No rest for the weary. I didn't even get a day to relax before the next job. I hit the receive button. "Kyle Tanner."

"Tanner, how'd it go? Did you get that little punk?" It was Lieutenant Commander Bryce Manning, head of CCF Security Division on Mercury. That placed all military police and nearby off-planet Investigators under his direct authority. His face looked up at me from the tiny screen.

"I got him. He's in custody. And you already know that or you wouldn't be calling."

"Yeah, you're right." He paused. "Listen, I just got a call from Earth. They want you for a job."

I stopped in my tracks. "They asked specifically for me?"

"Your reputation, obviously."

"Doubtful."

He snorted. "Listen, even I'd heard of you before you got here. You're uncanny."

Not all the time, I wanted to say. "What is it?"

"Not quite sure. They've asked me to send you to a place called *SOLEX One* Command Group. I've got the directions, it's here on Mercury. Swing by my office and I'll —"

"What is *SOLEX?* A ship?" He didn't respond. "Who exactly called you?"

He cleared his throat and looked off camera for a moment. "Someone high up. That's all I can say right now. Come on over and I'll fill in the details."

The screen went blank.

Shit. Another mystery, which meant another murder. One day it would get to be just too much for me, and I'd quit this damn job.

It's too bad so many people thought I was so good at it.

— Chapter Two —

Bryce Manning was my contact on Mercury. He dispatched the Homicide Investigators in this sector of space, and sometimes, in exceptional cases, sent them as far away as the outer reaches, beyond even Pluto. Out in deep space, however, shipboard military personnel and local colonial governments took care of their own problems — under the laws of the Confederacy, of course.

I had been all over system. I wish I could say I'd seen the sights on Ceres, investigated Valles Marineris on Mars, and gone orbit diving on Venus, but I couldn't.

On Ceres I had investigated the death of a wealthy widow. Her brother had cut her into pieces and mailed them all over the system. He was a mad and bitter guy.

On Mars I had looked into the death of a CCF Captain who had disappeared while on leave. A prostitute had killed him in a jealous rage and left his body on the surface in a tattered vacsuit and a shattered visor.

On Venus I had captured a serial murderer hunted for years. It was my most famous catch: the guy, nicknamed The Torcher — or *torture*, a play on words the media thought was pretty clever — burned each of his victims for twenty-three minutes. All seventeen cases. No one knew why; crazy people don't often make sense, and I didn't much care. I caught the guy, brought him in, and seven days after his guaranteed speedy trial he was just a bad memory.

They execute the vast majority of killers I capture. That's just the way it is; I don't give much thought to it. The evidence is usually hard to come by, but once I've found it, there's no arguing their way out of it. They're all guilty, every last one.

Some people might think hunting killers is a glamorous occupation; me, I just thought of it as a job. I did it well and I derived satisfaction from it, but I'm no different from the guy who maintains the hyperspace engines on a Colony Ship, or the guy who shovels shit on a pig farm in Utah. It's all the same.

I moved my hand over the scar on my left thigh, a reminder The Torcher had left for me during the difficult capture. I'd kept it as a reminder of how dangerous the job could be. A warning to never let down my guard.

I jumped a high speed track, sat wearily, and thought about Quint Sirius. I should have at least roughed him up. Maybe even killed him myself, but it just wasn't my way. The guard probably had some fun, then later the proper authorities would execute him. But it wouldn't be vigilantism; it would be after a trial and a review of Flemming's file.

There wasn't a lot to see as I rode the track through Mercurian rock. It was all dull, lifeless tunnels with veins of iron, nickel, and copper lacing the smooth surfaces. The station where I exited was just as bad: a long, barren, featureless cave where passengers could board and disembark the vehicle. I shook my head. Mercury.

—

Bryce was a good enough sort. He took his job seriously, but sometimes was a little too military for my tastes. He respected my abilities and usually laid off the military protocol when I was around, which suited me just fine. But to others he would bark orders, demand salutes, and practically humiliate new recruits. It wasn't my style, but at least he followed regs and didn't mess around with my investigations. Pretty soon he would send me to another colony in-system, and I would report to a different contact.

He flipped me a salute as I entered his office. He was overweight and had three chins, but still managed to stand as I entered.

"Lieutenant Kyle Tanner," he said.

"Hello, Bryce." I sat in front of his desk and stared at the maddening little model of the solar system that sat there, forever spinning. Along with the Oort Cloud and the Kuiper Belt, Pluto was included in most models of this type — for nostalgia's sake — and every time it and Neptune crossed orbits there was a tiny squeak. After thirty of them it was enough to drive you crazy. Bryce had probably listened to it a hundred thousand times or more, and it didn't seem to faze him.

"Good work on Quint Sirius."

"I just hope he gets what he deserves," I muttered.

"Of course he will. What else do you think will happen to him? He killed two people, one of them an officer in the CCF. His trial is in three days."

"Do you want me to —" I began.

"No. You're going to *SOLEX One*."

"Never heard of it until today. Where is it?"

He exhaled and pointed to the model that undulated on his desk. "Here."

I peered past his finger. "The sun?"

A chuckle. "Just about. It's an energy generating station, orbiting pretty much as close as we can get. Five million kilometers. It's gathering solar energy, massive quantities of it, converting it to microwave form and beaming it outward."

My heart sank. I thought Mercury was bad. This was worse. Remote as hell, nowhere to go, and on a station with a small complement of crew that included one killer. Not an ideal situation, to say the least.

"Where are they sending the microwaves?"

"Right now to a single satellite orbiting Earth. It's a feasibility test. When this phase is over there will be a thousand of these things orbiting the sun, beaming microwaves all over system. It's cheaper than fusion and totally clean. Just a little dangerous for the people who work the collectors."

"Must be." Five million kilometers. Sounded insane to me. Here on Mercury the daytime temperature got up to seven hundred Kelvin, hot enough for rivers of tin and lead to flow freely on the surface. And Mercury was fifty-eight million kilometers from the sun. *SOLEX* was one-tenth that distance.

"And," Bryce continued as he tapped a few keys on his reader, "there's been a murder."

"Why am I not surprised?"

"Ha, ha," he barked sharply. "Good one." He wheezed for a few seconds, then spent a couple more trying to catch his breath.

"So what happened?" I asked, prompting him to hurry.

"I have orders here from CCF headquarters on Earth. They asked for you."

"Why me?" I murmured.

"I guess they haven't forgotten your work with The Torcher. Word is the Council Members themselves are looking closely at this one."

My jaw dropped. "The Council? Why would they be interested in this?" The Terran Confederacy's ruling body usually had more important matters to deal with, like seeding colonies and maintaining peace.

"Who knows. Maybe one of their relatives is on the station. Hell, maybe it was the victim."

I sighed. "Damn it, Bryce. I hate other people interfering —"

He held a hand up. "You won't have to worry about that, trust me. *SOLEX* is so remote that you'll essentially be on your own up there. No one coming or going. There aren't many ships with heat shields that can take that stress." I shot him a pointed look, but he had seen the question coming. "*SOLEX One* CG has access to a small ship with a shield that'll get you there just fine."

"*SOLEX One* CG?"

"The Command Group for the station is located here, on Mercury. Maybe that's why the Council requested you."

There were other Homicide Investigators on Mercury they could have called. I stared at the sun on Bryce's desk. I had seen a lot of places in the solar system, but nothing that equaled this. It seemed more dangerous than he let on.

"Don't worry," he said, noting my discomfort. "It can't be that bad. The station's personnel have been there for months now."

I tore my eyes from the model. "Do you have the file?"

"No, just the orders. The file is at the Command Group a few tunnels away. Here are the directions." He gestured to a scrap of paper on his desk with some scribbles on it. "The Commander there will tell you everything you need to know." He stood abruptly and saluted. "Good luck."

I got to my feet and returned the salute wearily. "Who do I report to when I'm done?"

He frowned, hesitating. "Me, I guess. Back here."

"Very well."

I turned and left his office.

"Watch your back, Tanner!" he yelled when I was ten meters away.

"Thanks," I muttered. I couldn't think of a worse assignment.

SOLEX One Command Group was simply a couple of rooms carved from the rock — like all other places in the city — with monitors on the walls that displayed information related to the station's energy production. One showed a schematic of *SOLEX*: it was essentially a series of cylinders, two massive solar panel arrays, and a transmitter that beamed microwave radiation and FTL signals outward. Seemed straightforward enough.

The floor of the main room had large rectangular tables covered with papers and files. When the hatch slid open, a man in a uniform with Lieutenant Commander's insignia stepped forward to greet me. "Are you the Investigator?"

"Lieutenant Kyle Tanner, Homicide. Nice to meet you."

The older man grimaced. "Actually, I wish I never knew you." He noticed my expression and shrugged. "Sorry. Sometimes I'm a little crass."

I was well aware that the very reason I entered people's lives meant a complication of a violent nature had occurred. No one ever welcomed me. It was something Investigators had to grow accustomed to, or they turned bitter as time passed. And being resentful of life was the last thing I wanted — especially when I dealt with death every single day. "Don't worry," I said finally. "A lot of people say that when they meet me. I actually find it amusing."

His expression turned contrite. "I'm Jase Lassiter, in charge of the Command Group."

"A military installation, obviously. I didn't know that." Bryce had said the person in charge was 'Commander,' but he had neglected to supply the rest of the rank.

"Yes. It's surprising, isn't it? Most people think our government would rather stick with fusion, which is proven and reliable."

"I figured it would be a private enterprise trying this out, yeah." In fact, the Council was notorious for farming out this type of thankless endeavor to civilian companies, simply because the CCF had better things to do. Perhaps this station was more important than I had initially thought.

"Well, the Council is actually looking forward for a change. They know energy collectors like *SOLEX* are better in the long run."

"Tell me about the station," I said as I studied my surroundings.

"It's been running with fifteen people. Six officers, four scientists, and five crewmen. I'll give you a bio on each."

He'd anticipated my request. "Good. Who died?"

"One of the crew." He led me to the schematic and pointed out the obvious features. "The Engineering Corps built the station in Venus orbit. Took roughly eighteen months. The energy-microwave converters were the most expensive components; the heat shield next most."

"How does the shield work?" It could get damn hot at only five million kilometers from the sun. Vacsuits had to withstand incredible temperatures, and ordinary ones weren't rated for places much hotter than Mercury.

"It's a bright ceramic that reflects a great deal of shortwave energy; as a result the station's albedo is incredibly high. About point nine nine. The ceramic also has to take intense heat for several decades at least. The temperature where *SOLEX* orbits is about fifteen hundred Kelvin. This shield is very effective, providing it covers the entire station. If it's compromised by a meteor, for example, the crew has to get it repaired quickly. They always monitor the shield."

I knew the basics of course. Space itself had no temperature. It was vacuum. However, in direct sunlight an object that absorbed the sun's radiation would heat enormously. In the shade the temperature would be freezing. It was an interesting dichotomy of space that had given original pioneers some troubles in designing the first vacsuits. The Apollo suits, for instance, from way, *way* back, had to withstand temperatures of -180 to +150 degrees Celsius. And that was just the range in Earth orbit. Closer to the sun where *SOLEX* was, the difficulties of living and working in space were magnified a thousandfold.

"Okay," I said. "Tell me why I'm here."

His face fell. "A report we received from our doctor on the station, Lieutenant Lars Malichauk. It caused a major ruckus when we got it, let me tell you." He stopped abruptly and just stared at the dusty floor.

"And?"

"Well," he said finally. "I'll let you read it. It speaks for itself."

He led me to a small room, within which was a tiny steel desk. On it was a lone black folder.

"You can read that hard copy, but leave it here when you go," he said. "I'll upload the entire thing to your reader."

Lassiter sealed the hatch. I sat, and with some trepidation, opened the folder. I had an uncomfortable feeling about all this already. At the time I attributed it to mere paranoia. Now, however, I'm not so sure.

The first page had a picture of the victim, Crewman James Chin, a young Asian man who smiled affably at the camera. The next couple of pages contained Malichauk's report. I read it, interest growing as I turned each page. Finally, I flipped the last one.

I looked up to see Lassiter staring at me from the hatch.

"You've got to be kidding," I said.

— Chapter Three —

Ten minutes later I was on my way to the largest spaceport on Mercury. It was a massive cavity in the planet's crust, carved decades earlier to make room for the burgeoning population. Clearly marked berths sectioned the rock floor; within each, ships were either parked or preparing for departure. Airtight umbilicals connected the ships to an underground warren of tunnels. In the ceiling of the spaceport — at least two hundred meters up — a large opening permitted the passage of landing or departing vessels. The immense cave was fully open to vacuum, but its location under the surface prevented the sun's radiation from penetrating, except for the hour when the sun was at its zenith. It made work around the ships more manageable.

The ship was there, already prepped and ready. Equipped with the heat shield, it would take me directly to *SOLEX*. It would remain docked at the station until I had finished my investigation and caught the killer.

I didn't have many possessions, just a small bag with a couple of items for hygiene and a change of clothes. The good thing about being in the military was that I didn't have to invest much thought into what I was going to wear — it was the same thing every day: the black, pressed, crisp uniform of a Confederate Combined Forces officer.

The CCF had been my life for sixteen years; I had enlisted just prior to enrolling at the academy. My parents had died when I was twelve, and afterwards, I'd moved to Seattle to live with my uncle. He was a requisitions clerk in the CCF, and I often ended up spending time at the local base.

While the military provided me with a top rated education, my recruiter noticed something in my profile and psych test results: apparently I had a highly analytical mind with an innate sense of deduction, human psychology, truth detection, and even hunches. It was enough to trigger some alarms, and as a result, at age twenty-three, I found myself placed in the Security Division of the CCF, Homicide Section.

There was no civil police force in our society, the military had taken over that duty. In fact, it had taken over practically everything else, too, from the media to education. There were a lot of naysayers about the turn society had taken, and generally the more vocal ones seemed to disappear rather suddenly. I didn't question where they had gone, but I figured they must be in camps somewhere. Either that or dead.

—

Departure Control placed me at the head of the queue, and my ship, so tiny it didn't deserve a name, only a license code of six numbers and three letters, started its countdown. The airlock connector withdrew and disappeared underground. I looked up through the cave's opening to the massive fireball that burned a mere sixty million kilometers away.

"Next stop, hell," I murmured.

—

Liftoff went smoothly. Our intrasystem drive, called *gravtrav*, simply reversed the pull of gravity to provide propulsion. We could amplify it enormously to allow travel at tremendous velocities. We could also reverse the process, grab onto nearby stellar bodies — often more than one — and increase their pull to provide the speeds needed for solar travel.

The same process also permitted artificial gravity on board a ship. An acceleration of five gees could shorten distances enormously, and meanwhile the crew would never feel more than a constant single gravity. It was this ability that had opened up the solar system to colonization.

In distant space, past the gravity wells of any nearby stars, gravtrav would simply not function. There we used hyperspace drive, which allowed our ships to slip out of normal space and pass through massive distances in significantly less time. The hyperspace drive was useless if there was a star too near; its gravity field interfered with the process and prevented travel.

Gravtrav had allowed us to settle the solar system, but it was the hyperspace drive that had given us the stars.

—

Two hours out from Mercury, I opened Lars Malichauk's report that detailed the death of James Chin on board *SOLEX*. I read it again, but this time only skimmed it for the most important details.

> Report Filed by: Doctor Lars Malichauk,
> Lieutenant, CCF
> Report Location: *SOLEX One*, Close Orbit,
> Sol
> Date: 12 June, 2401
> Report Type: Murder (?)

The question mark after 'Murder' had immediately struck me as odd. Why was Malichauk unsure of the cause of death? He was a doctor with decades of experience. If it was indeed murder, someone must have concealed it expertly.

> At approximately 1300 hours on 11 June, James "Jimmy" Chin was engaged in an EVA activity outside the station. He was performing routine maintenance on the solar collectors ...
>
> ... At 1315 hours, Jimmy transmitted a call for assistance. Something had compromised his suit. For the exact transcript, you can ...
>
> ... We recovered the body at 1400 hours. Decompression was immediately determined as the cause of death. There was a tear in his suit; it was impossible for one man to seal. A sharp instrument of some sort was responsible. I placed the body in the freezer and planned to perform the official autopsy the following day at 0800 hours.

I stopped there. According to military regs, medical personnel performed autopsies on every single death that occurred in space, no matter the cause. It was a matter of maintaining protocol, even when the death wasn't suspicious. There was nothing odd about what Malichauk had done, except perhaps waiting eighteen hours for the procedure. I'd have to check with him on that.

... At approximately 0815 hours the following day, I removed Jimmy's corpse from the freezer. I immediately noticed that the body's head and hands were missing. Someone had used an extremely sharp cutting instrument. There were no other signs of tampering, no injuries other than those consistent with death by decompression ...

... I am filing this as a possible murder report, though I am unsure if the actual death was intentional. Surely tampering with a body is immoral and against regs, but it is perhaps not associated with Jimmy Chin's death.

I closed the file. The report intrigued me; already I had numerous questions. First, who had been on the EVA with Chin at the time of the accident? When working outside a ship or station, crew *always* paired up. It was perhaps the strictest regulation related to EVA's. If Jimmy's suit ripped, a partner could have sealed it for him. Instead, the man had died. Had Malichauk simply failed to mention Jimmy's partner? Or, had the Captain disobeyed regulations and allowed a man to go EVA by himself? It was unthinkable, but possible, I guess.

Despite these issues, an even bigger question remained: why had someone felt it necessary to remove the corpse's head and hands?

I spent the rest of the trip studying the CCF dossiers on the officers, scientists, and crew of *SOLEX*. Nothing stood out as being abnormal. All the personnel had passed their psych tests, none of them had criminal pasts — though a few had spotty records — and there hadn't been any problems leading up to Jimmy's death, which is something that often preceded a murder of the type that was unplanned, or occurred in the 'heat of the moment.'

So there was nothing out of the ordinary. Surprise, surprise. It didn't matter though; people were often far different in real life than they were on paper. I knew that when I questioned them I would find something. A little squabble that Jimmy had had with someone. A debt he owed. A fight over some liquor.

There was always something.

—

Six hours later I approached *SOLEX* and prepared to dock. The sun had become so intense that the auto-dimming viewport was now nearly opaque. The star's outline was visible, but only barely against the backdrop of starless space. I could see huge tongues of fire that lashed out, almost as if the sun swatted angrily at my pesky little ship — an insect that dared invade its territory. The surface was a burning maelstrom; eddies and currents of pure hell rolled across the star ceaselessly.

The ship's heat shield had held up remarkably well. I had made a point to keep the dedicated shield display in my field of view constantly during the voyage, but all systems registered in the green. It was perfect.

I stared at the temperature readout incredulously: fourteen hundred and ninety Kelvin. Damn. The people who lived and worked at this station must be *very* tough individuals. Imagine being outside in a vacsuit, beyond the heat shield designed to protect human life. It bordered on insane.

High speed particles that radiated from the sun were another danger in space, but it was something we'd long since learned to deal with. It was another example of technology mimicking nature: the Earth's magnetic field intercepted and redirected these particles to both poles and created the unforgettable auroras seen at higher latitudes. I had seen it once or twice as a youngster in western Canada. Ships and stations like *SOLEX* used the same principle: powerful artificial electromagnetic fields surrounded our vessels and protected us from solar radiation. I just hoped the ship could withstand it this close to the star.

Had the pressure of living in this remote, dangerous environment finally gotten to someone? Had a crewmate snapped under the strain? Was Jimmy the unfortunate victim of someone's silent, secret, psychotic break?

I shrugged the thought aside. Nonsense. There would have been warning signs and a variety of other indications. Neither the Captain nor the Council Rep had reported anything unusual on *SOLEX*. Of course, they could have covered up that type of escalating behavior, but it was unlikely. Both Manfred Fredericks, the Captain, and Brick Kayle, the Council Rep, were solid CCF officers. They would have notified the Command Group if the crew had started to act odd.

I would just have to dig a little when I arrived; that's what I was good at, after all.

—

SOLEX grew larger as the autopilot brought me in under gravtrav. It was exactly as the schematic at Mercury CG had shown: a series of connected cylinders, the huge solar collectors, and the antenna and transmitter that beamed its invisible microwaves to Earth. The incredible brightness of the station momentarily startled me before I recalled that the ceramic heat shield reflected much of the short wave solar radiation.

On either side of the connected modules was the broad expanse of a solar array, each two hundred meters long and comprised of a steel mesh grid and dark panels that shimmered in the starlight.

The ship coasted into the docking bay and the huge door sealed soundlessly behind me.

SOLEX One
CCF Solar Experimental Facility #1
Microwave Conversion Study/Close Orbit — Sol

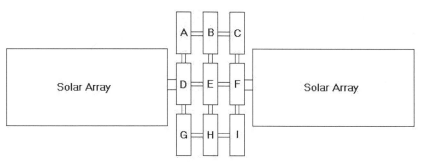

0 20 40 60 meters

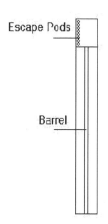

Station Components:
Module A: Life Support/Engineering
Module B: Officers Module (OM)
Module C: Common Mess/Clinic/Command Center
Module D: Microwave Conversion Module (MCM)
Module E: Crew Module (CM)
Module F: Scientists Module (SM)
Module G: Docking Port/Bay
Module H: Storage
Module I: Storage
Module M: Mass Driver

Officers: 6
Crew: 5
Scientists: 4

Project Initiation: 7 Oct. 2400
Project Duration: Unknown
Project Status: Nominal; Output: 12 034 MWe
Command Group: Mercury
CG CO: Lt. Cmdr. J. Lassiter, CCF
Captain: Lt. Cmdr. M. Fredericks, CCF
Design: Lt. S. Ramachandra, CCF

Part Two: Investigation

**Investigator's Log: Lieutenant Kyle Tanner,
Security Division, Homicide Section, CCF**

I checked my oxygen reserves for the thousandth time and groaned inwardly. I had become compulsive about it, studying the readout every few seconds as if it would make a difference.

It didn't.

Only thirteen and a half hours remained.

I had managed to open the innards of the suit's communit, but it had proven more difficult than I'd hoped. The unit's transmitter was omnidirectional, which severely limited its range. I knew I had to change it to unidirectional and extend its capabilities if I was going to have any chance at all. It would mean aiming manually toward Mercury and hoping that the sun's radiation wouldn't block the signal. But once again, a one-in-a-million thing if it actually worked. I didn't even know where Mercury was in its orbit. I had guessed when to fire the mass driver. Hopefully I was at least in the ballpark.

I also needed to increase the power to the comm, if at all possible. I couldn't risk frying its circuits, but a little extra power could only help.

I sighed in frustration. I couldn't believe my predicament. I turned my head and brought the sun back into view. My suit's interior temperature continued to rise; pretty soon the coolant layer would cease to function altogether. When that happened, I'd probably have only minutes left.

The throbbing in my shoulder had also proven to be a huge distraction; trying to manipulate fine tools with gloved hands was hard enough, but doing so with an injury made things even more difficult.

I snorted. I couldn't catch a break. The problems kept mounting.

As soon as I thought it, a series of coughs wracked my body, and when I finally managed to reopen my eyes and see through the tears, my chest tightened in sudden terror.

There was blood on my visor.

The internal bleeding had started.

— Chapter Four —

Two people greeted me at the airlock hatch: Captain Manfred Fredericks and Lieutenant Shaheen Ramachandra. Fredericks was a middle-aged man with salt and pepper hair and an angular, weathered face. His eyes — which exuded confidence — seemed older than his forty years; his smile showed an affable side that I immediately liked.

Shaheen was the Station Systems Officer and the Chief Engineer. I couldn't help but stare at her. She was East Indian with long, straight hair and delicate features. Her lips weren't full; rather, they were slim and pressed tightly together. Her figure was incredible — it was obvious even under the black uniform — but what really captivated me were her blue eyes. Bizarre to see such a thing on a woman from her part of Earth. It was unique and exotic.

"Lieutenant Kyle Tanner, Homicide," I said after a second.

She tried to suppress a smile. "Who else would you be?"

Startled, I studied her for another moment. She had spoken with a British accent. "I guess you don't get many visitors," I finally managed.

"Indeed," the Captain said. "You're only the second person to arrive since we started this little experiment." He gestured toward a hatch. "This way to your quarters."

The starkly lit corridor was uncommonly narrow; the three of us couldn't walk side by side. It was awkward carrying on a conversation as we marched through the station. The tight partitions meant to contain atmosphere in case of a hull breach would permit only two of us at a time. The steel grating rang with each step; the polished bulkheads cast fuzzy reflections. We passed a sign that said *Module D*.

"I'm sorry I had to come," I said. "I know this sort of thing is difficult." I frowned inwardly; introductions in these awkward situations were always the same.

The Captain shot me a sideways glance; his look held a hint of annoyance. "It is. I hope you can find the answers quickly." The comment held an obvious suggestion: *Finish and leave as fast as you can.*

I hesitated. "It's quite a mystery you've got here."

Shaheen said, "I'm sure you can solve it. The Torcher was a tough one, but you got him."

"You know about that," I muttered.

"Doesn't everyone?"

"Unfortunately."

The Captain watched the exchange with interest. "I'm hoping it's just a little vandalism. Bizarre, yes, but —"

"Someone died, Captain."

"Call me Manny." We rounded a corner and ascended a steep ladder two levels. "The death was accidental. What happened afterward was unfortunate, but doesn't mean it was murder."

I remained silent. I hoped he wouldn't object too much to my presence on *SOLEX*. Sometimes my investigations caused a lot of tension, which could in turn hinder communication. Getting people to feel free to come speak with me was an essential part of the job, and I couldn't risk jeopardizing that.

Shaheen noticed my discomfort. "Don't worry about Manny. It's his command, after all. He's just upset —"

He pierced her with a glare. "Don't analyze me. You don't know that."

"Sure I do," she said, oblivious to his irritation. She turned to me. "Look, we've been living together for nine months now. It gets pretty intense. We see each other at our best and worst, and I know Manny pretty well. He's bothered by what happened to the body."

I absorbed that. "No matter what you think, Captain —"

"Manny," he said again.

"— someone on board this station is pretty sick. Don't you think it's best that I find this person, murder or no?"

He stopped abruptly and turned to me. "Don't get me wrong, Tanner. Of course I want to know what happened. I just can't believe there's a murderer here with us."

"It's pretty frightening," Shaheen added.

"I'm hoping it was a prank of some sort," he continued.

I had dealt with his attitude on many occasions. He simply didn't want to believe that someone he had worked with for almost a year was capable of this kind of crime. But the fact was that someone here *had* done it, and we needed to remove that person from *SOLEX* as soon as possible. The crew's hold on survival this close to Sol was tenuous. They needed to be at their best at all times. "Anything's possible," I said in a flat voice.

"Just don't come into this thinking it's murder right off the bat," he said with an edge.

Shaheen read my expression. "He's not new at this, Manny. He's good. He got The Torcher."

The Captain fixed me with a cold glare. "Finish this as quickly as possible. Then get out."

We locked eyes for a long, hard moment. I sighed. So much for good relations.

I had only a few minutes to orient myself with my cabin — which according to the sign on the hatch was located in Module B, Level Three — before I had a visitor. It was Lieutenant Junior Grade Brick Kayle, the station's tall and muscular Council Rep.

"But don't hold that against me," he said with a grin after introductions. His Australian accent was enormously likable, but I reminded myself that even killers had friends. "He seemed so normal," they'd say. "He kept to himself. He was a nice guy."

"Why would I hold it against you?" I asked, even though I already knew the answer: as the station's *political officer*, it was his job to keep his eyes and ears open at all times, to search out dissension among the personnel. A careless comment could result in arrest and prison, or worse. People generally disliked Council Reps.

"You know," he said in a sheepish tone. He gestured to the symbol on his uniform — the warship and galaxy of the Terran Confederacy's political organization.

"Don't worry, I work for them too." I shrugged aside his worry with a wave of my hand. "What can I do for you?"

"I'm here to escort you to the officer's mess for dinner."

I glanced at my watch. Damn, time had passed quickly. I hadn't eaten in hours; I was famished. I threw my pistol and holster on the bunk. Although it was technically part of my uniform, I didn't want to intimidate people by walking around the station armed. A distant part of my mind screamed at the decision, but I overrode it perhaps a tad too casually.

It would turn out to be a huge mistake.

"Is Council Rep your only duty?" I asked as we started for the mess. I already knew the answer, but wanted him to talk openly as much as possible.

"Nah. I'm also the Scientist Liaison."

Jase Lassiter at the Command Group had said there were four scientists at *SOLEX*. Brick's job was ensuring that they had all the necessary supplies and equipment for their studies. The scientists had to inform CG of each experiment through requisitions and paperwork; Brick made sure everything got done with minimal disruptions.

"There are four of them here, right?"

"Exactly. They're always hidden away in their labs, looking at the only thing there is to see outside. Taking measurements, testing theories, and so on."

As we moved through the corridors, I realized how dangerous being here really was. The sun, only five million kilometers away ...

The killer, possibly within arm's reach ...

And I on my own, as usual.

"You've been here nine months now," I said, continuing the small talk.

"It's tough, I won't deny that. Everyone goes a little stir crazy now and then." Realizing what he had said, he suddenly stopped in his tracks and looked at me. "Don't get me wrong — I'm not implying that one of us is crazy enough to kill someone!" He brushed a hand through his blond hair. "Sheesh. I'm just a little nervous talking with you, Tanner. Don't mind me."

He showed an enormous lack of protocol in the way he addressed me. I outranked him, and yet he called me simply by surname. I certainly wasn't a stickler for protocol, but he seemed to act a little *too* calm for my liking. It was almost a facade. Then again, he had served here for nine months and probably felt at ease with the other officers. I remembered that even the Captain insisted on using his first name; perhaps I was reading too much into it.

We continued toward the mess in silence. Eventually he said, "Jimmy was a great guy. Everyone loved him. I can't believe someone did that to him."

"You mean the murder?"

"I mean cutting his head and hands off. Who the hell would do that?" He shook his head.

"A lot of things don't make sense at first, until you ask the right people the right questions."

He looked at me. "Well Tanner, I hope you're good at your job. I want answers too."

The officer's mess was the most ornate room I had seen on *SOLEX*. It was still all metal and plastic, but someone had attempted to give it a little class: there was a Monet print hanging directly beside the long table, a few fake flowers, and even a curtain that hid a viewport.

"Don't let it get to you," Shaheen Ramachandra said. She walked toward me with a drink in hand. Her blue eyes were fixed to mine. "Here, this one's on me."

I accepted it graciously. "Don't let what get to me?"

"There are no viewports. It bothers people at first. You'll get used to it."

I frowned. "What about that?"

She looked at the curtain and grinned. "Fake. Behind is just more bulkhead."

"Oh — the heat shield." I recalled that it had to cover every square centimeter of the station. An opening — even a small one — could spell disaster.

A slim, jittery man with dark features appeared at my side. He had an old, lined face and jet black hair. It was a curious combination. "Hello, Lieutenant. I'm Lars Malichauk."

Ah. The doctor who had filed the report. I had many questions for him, which he must have realized. "Pleased to meet you."

"It's nicer to meet you. We don't often get new people here."

"When we do," Shaheen said, "we like to have a little celebration."

I gestured at the table. "That's quite a setup." There were candles and even glassware, as opposed to the usual steel dishes.

A voice from behind: "Don't get your hopes up. We're only eating standard rations, that's all we ever have."

Captain Fredericks had entered the mess and marched straight over. He smiled cordially, evidence of his previous displeasure gone. Or, perhaps just concealed well.

"Hello, Captain," I said, wary.

"Manny," he reminded me. "Please, no more 'Captains.'"

"You didn't have to do anything special for me."

"Nonsense. You're the first new person we've seen in a while. We have to acknowledge that fact."

Malichauk's face twitched. "Indeed. It gets a tad wearisome talking to the same five people at dinner every day."

"But I thought there are also four scientists and five —" I halted abruptly. "Four crew, I mean." I cringed at the slip, but nobody seemed to care or notice.

"Sure. But we never see the scientists. They're always locked away studying the monster out there."

"You must give them checkups now and then."

"Once a month. Other than that, they're a very shy group."

"And the crew?" I pressed.

"Busy manning the station. Shaheen sees them more than I, she's the Chief Engineer."

I pursed my lips. This was odd. "And you never see each other? Three separate groups of people who never socialize? What about dinners? Lunches?"

"Lars overstates things somewhat," Manny said. "We all see each other quite often. The reality is that Lars is the one who's isolated, not the other way around." He raised his hands as the doctor opened his mouth to object. "Oh, come on now — you do seem to lock yourself in your clinic often enough."

He chuckled. "Maybe. But I'm trying to get out more."

"Most of us eat together in the common mess at lunch," Shaheen supplied. "Except the scientists, who seem to always be working."

I mulled that over. "What do they do at dinner?"

"The crewmen eat together and have an end-of-the-day briefing, and the scientists do whatever it is they do." She laughed. "The officers eat together here, in the officer's mess."

Manny watched me with narrowed eyes. "Is this just curiosity? Or investigation?"

I shrugged. "Both, I guess."

The hatch slid aside and two others entered. The first was a tall, broad-shouldered black man. He had closely cropped hair — almost shaved — and sharp, chiseled features. The second was a slim, fragile-looking woman in her fifties with blond streaks in graying hair.

"This is my First Officer," Manny said with a gesture to the man. "Lieutenant Commander Avery Rickets."

I offered my hand. "Kyle Tanner." Generally in the military we were to offer salutes to other officers, but this was clearly an informal situation — and an informal outpost. I still had qualms about it, but squashed them for now. I had learning to do. I had to understand this place.

"And Belinda Bertram, Information Officer," Manny continued.

I shook the woman's hand and glanced at her insignia. Lieutenant Junior Grade. "Nice to meet you."

She looked at me skeptically. "So the Council thinks there's trouble on their precious station, do they?"

"Oh don't start that, Bel," Brick drawled. "You gotta admit, we have to find out who cut poor Jimmy's head and hands off."

"That we do," Avery Rickets said. His voice was deep and melodious.

"Did you investigate at all?" I asked the Captain.

He looked startled. "Of course! I didn't get anywhere though. No one knows when it happened exactly, so alibis don't really matter."

I turned to Malichauk. "You can't tell when the body was ... tampered with?" As I recalled, it happened between the time he left the clinic at the end of the day and 0815 hours the following morning.

"No. It happened after death, so it's quite impossible."

"Surveillance?"

"All camera feeds went offline during that period."

My jaw hit the deck.

"You see?" Manny said. "Not a single person — not even myself — has an alibi that lasts twelve hours. Any one of us could have done it."

I filed this important information away for later. I wanted to talk to everyone individually, to corroborate stories separately rather than share them here. The others looked uncomfortable; they shifted nervously as they stood around me. A change of subject was in order.

"How's the station holding up?" I asked.

"Fine," Shaheen answered. "But being this close to the sun puts a lot of stress on the equipment."

"Five million kilometers," Brick added.

I said, "You know, Jase Lassiter —"

"First class asshole," he spat.

"— at *SOLEX* CG," I continued, noting Brick's response, "said the temperature of an object in space here is fifteen hundred Kelvin."

"That's right," Shaheen said with a nod. She shot a look at Brick and a crease appeared between her eyebrows.

"But reentry to Earth creates temperatures of up to four thousand Kelvin. Those heat shields can handle it okay." In fact, technology to withstand such temperatures had been around for centuries, even since the pioneering era. It was something about the station that still confused me.

"Right, but reentry only lasts a few minutes, and the shields are two inches thick. Our shield here is paper thin and has to last for decades. There's a big difference."

My eyebrows rose. "Impressive. Who designed it?"

"You're looking at her," First Officer Rickets said. "Our very own Shaheen Ramachandra did it. She also supervised the eighteen month construction phase."

I turned to her. "What else can you take credit for?"

She looked embarrassed. "Nothing else, really."

"Oh, pah!" Doctor Malichauk scoffed. "You'll be getting the Nobel, Shaheen. You also designed the radiation shield."

"No, I didn't," she objected. "We've had that ever since we colonized the inner planets. I just upgraded it for the greater radiation this close to Sol."

I looked at her in a new light. Who says a beautiful woman can't be brilliant as well? I studied her blue eyes as she and Malichauk began a lengthy conversation about the dangers of long term radiation exposure. Her gaze flicked to me once or twice; she had noticed my scrutiny. Embarrassed, I turned to Belinda Bertram.

"Anything new in the world of information?" I asked the station's Information Officer.

She raised a glass to her lips. "Very funny. You probably know more about what's going on in the system than I do. This station is *so* damn remote."

Her title meant that she was in charge of all communications off the station; she was also the science officer. They probably didn't need one with four solar physicists also present, so I assumed she had a lot of time to spare. Before I could ask her about it, Brick Kayle cut in.

"So," he injected in his Australian accent, "can you tell us about The Torcher?"

I sighed. Damn. I'd never live that down.

—

"So he actually set his victims on fire?" Belinda asked, screwing up her face as she bit into her rations. We now sat at the table, our meal illuminated by candlelight. In the background I could hear a concerto by Chopin.

"After they were dead, yes." I tried to hide my fatigue.

"Come on, Bel," Brick said. "You haven't heard about The Torcher?"

"He's this century's Jack the Ripper," First Officer Rickets said. "And our visitor is the one who caught him. He's famous."

"Who, The Torcher? Or Tanner?" she asked.

"Both."

"Really?" She looked shocked and even a little disgusted. "Famous for catching a killer?"

"Indeed," Manny said.

"Curious. I didn't know there could be such a thing. Not to offend," she added quickly.

"Don't worry about it," I mumbled. "Frankly, I wish there wasn't such a thing either."

Brick studied me with a raised eyebrow. "Fame can get to you, I hear."

I growled inwardly. His obvious attempt at analyzing me was insulting. I didn't need him making gross implications about my psyche. Despite my anger, however, I smothered my reaction and tried to be civil. "It's just that ..." I trailed off. It was hard to express why it bothered me. I understood that The Torcher was well known everywhere in the Confederacy, and that as the man who had captured him I was famous too. But it didn't thrill me.

"Surely you must understand that you have talents other people appreciate," Malichauk said.

I nodded. I did understand that. But there was something else, too. Like the time in Tokyo when the reporters made me a celebrity briefly while I investigated the politician's death. It just annoyed me now. I didn't want notoriety anymore — just peace and quiet while I did my job. "I can't really explain it," I said.

An uncomfortable silence fell over the table. Finally, Shaheen spoke. "Well, this is a time to thank Kyle for coming to help us. Maybe we should change the topic."

I met her eyes. *Thanks*, I signaled silently.

We continued to eat our rations as conversation picked up again. This time, the officers spoke about the latest vid entertainment, the scientists on board, and the station itself. I took the opportunity to study my food as they pointedly stayed away from topics involving The Torcher, killers, and Jimmy Chin.

— Chapter Five —

The following day I rose early, intent on beginning the formal interview process with *SOLEX's* inhabitants. I grabbed a bite to eat in the common mess; there was no one else around. The station was fairly large for such a small complement; apparently the equipment needed to convert solar energy to microwaves and beam them to Earth took quite a bit of space.

The schematic of the station was easy to locate on my reader; Jase Lassiter had uploaded it for me during my brief visit to the Command Group on Mercury. There were ten large cylinders called *modules*. Nine of them were located in a three by three grid pattern. Superimposed over these, the tenth was as long as three of the other modules combined, but also more narrow. I brought up text labels for the station components and studied the schematic's details intently.

The letters A through I designated the nine cylinders. Each consisted of three levels, called One through Three. Sounded simple enough: Module E, Level Three would be the uppermost level of the middle cylinder. Tunnels on Level One of each connected all nine cylinders.

The tenth module — the long narrow one — was unique. I peered at my reader. "Module M," I murmured. Weird. By their notations, the next cylinder should have been Module J. I zoomed the schematic in on M and discovered a slim passageway that traversed its entire length. The label read, "Mass driver." Ah. A magnetic slingshot that could launch metallic objects at extremely high velocities. Usually they were for transporting cargo or industrial material, but it was also common for colonies in deep space or dangerous locations to use one to propel escape pods in case of dire emergency.

I brought the schematic back to original size and examined the individual components. Module A held the life support and environmental machinery, B the officer's quarters, and C the 'community' cylinder with the command center, the clinic, the common and the officer's mess. Module D was the microwave generating machinery, E the crew's quarters, F the scientists' labs. Module G was the docking port. H and I were dedicated to storage: food, water, equipment and so forth. Attached to the station were large solar arrays, each two hundred meters across. The sheer size of the collectors had astounded me during my approach to *SOLEX*.

There wouldn't be a problem navigating around the station. I had been in places a lot more convoluted and had always managed. *Gagarin Station*, located at the Lagrange point between the Earth and Moon, for instance, had been a nightmare. I had chased a suspect for hours through the underground labyrinth of tunnels, and succeeded only when he fell and injured himself scaling a reservoir wall. Fortunately, witnesses called the accident in and the local CCF Commanding Officer directed me to the scene.

SOLEX's size was surprising. It could hold three times the crew complement of fifteen easily. It would seem it wasn't solely dedicated to converting solar energy to microwaves; despite my previous assumption, that equipment only utilized one station module. It was something I would have to look into.

I finished my breakfast and decided to first interview Doctor Malichauk. I had a number of questions about his report, and I also wanted to look at Jimmy Chin's body. According to the schematic, the clinic was located in the same cylinder as the mess — all I had to do was go up to the second level and I'd find him.

The corridor was typical of any CCF operation: aesthetics served no functional purpose. Everything was bare metal, steel grating, and dull plastic. The only somewhat comfortable area I had seen was the officer's mess, but even that was plain by military standards.

I approached the clinic hatch, hit the toggle, and stepped inside.

Malichauk had deep lines on his old, craggy face, but a thick head of long black hair contradicted his elderly appearance. It was a bizarre look: his face appeared ancient while his hair seemed to belong on a much younger man. In my dossier he seemed like a one time magnificent doctor who was now just a recluse serving out his final days in any out-of-the-way post he could find. He had become a loner, happy to be left to himself. His eyes seemed tired.

When I entered, he was puttering around taking an inventory of the medicines held in a locked cabinet with transparent doors. On a table in the corner was a datachip reader; I picked it up as he finished. Invading someone's privacy was hardly an important consideration when there was a killer on the loose. A journal article shone brightly on the display. The title was a mouthful: *Myosin VIIa and Vezatin Protein Production in Cellular Biological Processes.*

"A little light reading?"

He turned. "Just some research."

I moved to a chair and glanced at my notes. It was important to speak to Malichauk before the others because he had written the report that had begun this process. As the first person to examine the body, he had a great deal of knowledge that I needed, whether he knew it or not. I also had some questions regarding Jimmy's death — questions I wanted answered before I spoke with the Captain.

"Do you have a few minutes?" I asked.

He looked wary. "I guess."

I paused for a beat and studied the man's expression. He didn't seem to be overly interested in speaking with me. If he had nothing to hide, it was an odd reaction. Then again, he might just be nervous. "What can you tell me about Jimmy's death?"

"You read my report," he said. "What else do you need to know?"

"Let's go over it from the beginning. From the EVA."

"I really don't know the details. You'll have to ask Manfred or Rickets, whoever was in the command center —"

"I will. But I'm curious what you know of it."

He sighed. "Very well. Jimmy was doing an EVA —"

"How long can someone stay outside here?"

He seemed annoyed at the interruption. "Eh? Oh, I guess ninety minutes at the most. After that, radiation exposure overcomes you."

"Is it cumulative?"

"Yes and no. We have medication we administer after each EVA. It helps reverse the damage, but not completely. Our regs say that no EVA will exceed the maximum time per day, provided the person receives treatment after each one. The total allowed time for EVA is a hundred and fifty hours. After that, maximum exposure has occurred."

"Meaning?"

"No more EVA's allowed."

"Can the person stay in space?"

"Of course. We're completely protected inside our ships and stations. Just no more going out on space walks."

"What about the magnetic radiation shield? Doesn't it protect people out on the hull?"

He nodded. "To an extent. Without it the exposure time would be much less."

I consulted my reader. I had Malichauk's report open, but shielded from his view. "Go ahead," I prompted. He wasn't very forthcoming with information, that was for sure.

"The EVA began, as I understand it, at 1300 hours. Fifteen minutes later he reported a rip in his suit."

"Your report doesn't mention how that happened," I said.

"I know, because we never found out."

"Who was with him at the time?"

He eyed me. "You'll have to ask the Captain. I don't know."

"But someone was with him, surely." He shrugged and didn't answer. I tried a different tact. "Your report says the body was retrieved forty-five minutes later."

"At 1400 hours, yes."

"Who recovered it?" I hoped the answer to the question could help solve this particular mystery, but of course he was too perceptive to be tricked.

His eyes narrowed. "Ah, now you're trying to be smart with me, Detective."

"Lieutenant, or Inspector. How so?"

"Obviously the person who recovered the body would have been the one partnered with Jimmy."

I shrugged. "Perhaps."

"Well, I'm not sure about that either. All I know is that two crewmen brought the body here just after 1400 hours."

He was covering for someone, there was no doubt about it. "Very well. Tell me about the body."

"Have you ever seen death by decompression?"

"Of course. It's the sixth most common method of murder."

"Really?" His eyes seemed to light up. "How interesting. And the top five?"

"Knife, pistol, poison, strangling, and a fall from a lethal height."

He looked surprised. "That's quite a list."

"It is. So I take it Jimmy showed all the signs of decompression."

"Yes. Eyes bulging. Ocular liquid drained. Ear drums burst and bloody. Dermal capillaries broken. His skin looked like a roadmap. Tongue swollen and protruding. Intestines pushed out the anus." He stopped abruptly and looked at me, perhaps concerned he was being overly graphic.

"I've seen it before, many times. Don't worry about me. What happened next?" This was one of the things I was most curious about.

"I put the body in the freezer and —"

"Why?" It was actually a stasis field; it didn't actually *freeze* the bodies.

"To preserve it before the autopsy, of course. You know I have to do one after every death. Regulations."

"I know that, Doctor. But what I'm curious about is why you didn't perform the procedure immediately."

He looked uncomfortable. "Well, the cause of death —"

"I think I know the regs better than you, Lars." I shot him a pointed look. I had to know them front and back because I frequently worked in military environments, especially since banks, schools, corporations and factories were all under CCF control.

He shuffled his feet. "We're so remote here ..."

"You thought no one would notice."

He threw his arms in the air. "Look, I couldn't predict what would happen to the body. No one could."

"There's a reason for the regs. You're facing disciplinary action regarding this."

"Out here, so far from everyone else, I guess it didn't seem that important. We didn't immediately think it was murder, you know."

"It's so no one can tamper with the body before it's been examined."

"Well I —"

"Did the Captain know you waited?"

"I don't know." He looked away from me again. "You'll have to ask him."

Interesting.

45

I stood and paced the clinic slowly. Malichauk eyed me uncertainly. He seemed to regard me as an enemy, someone who dared intrude on his own private existence here on *SOLEX*. He neglected the fact that we were both in the military, and that I had complete jurisdiction here as the Investigating Officer of a homicide. I could ship him off to CCF HQ on Mercury in an instant if I felt he needed *incentive* to speak.

"So what was so important that you didn't examine Jimmy immediately?" I asked.

"Research," he snapped. "I don't know. Reviewing charts."

I cocked my head. "Researching what?"

"New medicines. That sort of thing."

"Whose charts?" I persisted.

"I do have patients here, you know." He had grown irritated, his face was flushed. He wasn't trying to hide it though, which a guilty person would do.

"What time did you leave the clinic?"

"At dinner. Around 1800 hours."

"Let's move to the following morning. Tell me what happened."

He tapped the table with his fingers. "How much longer?" he grumbled. "This is tiresome."

"As long as I want. I'm here under CCF's highest authority. As an officer in the CCF, you're obligated to answer my questions. If you were a civilian it would make no difference." I forced a smile. "Let's be civil, Lars. I'm just doing my job. Please answer my questions and I'll leave you alone. Surely you must want to know what happened to your crewmate." After all, the incident had occurred in his clinic; the mutilation should have incensed the man.

He moved to a stool and lowered himself onto it. He seemed to deflate. "I guess I should apologize. I'm not accustomed to being interrogated. And I do feel terrible about what happened. You're right, of course — I should have done the autopsy immediately. I didn't, and now we'll never know what happened."

I bristled at the word *interrogate*, but shrugged it aside. "I'll discover the truth, don't worry. I just don't want you to make it harder for me."

"Fine," he said, but still didn't seem completely willing. I waited, but nothing more came.

"The following morning ..." I prodded.

"I grabbed a coffee from the common mess. I came here and got the instruments ready. I was going to use that table, right there."

"Do you have an assistant? Someone to help?"

"Are you kidding?" he snorted. "Not enough crew to warrant help." He gestured behind me to a narrow opening in the bulkhead that disappeared into a partially hidden chamber. "I went back to the freezer and pulled open the drawer. I found Jimmy minus two hands and a head."

I rose and marched into the tiny alcove; Malichauk followed close behind. There were three small hatches on one side of the room, all stainless steel. "Which one?" I asked.

"On the left."

"Open it."

He paled. "Why?"

I frowned. "So I can see the body, of course."

He grew immediately nervous. "Ah ... that won't be possible."

My brow wrinkled. "Why not?" I said, suddenly troubled. He better not have —

"I jettisoned the body that day."

My mouth hung open. "Say again?" It was a ridiculous development, criminal in itself. To dispose of the only physical evidence available? It was obstruction of my investigation at the very least, not to mention potential incompetence — something the military did not tolerate.

"Don't worry," he said, trying to mollify me. "I took some pictures. I'll upload them to your reader."

I shook my head. "Doctor, you of all people should know the importance of examining the victim's body for evidence. Why the hell would you do that?" I paused. "You realize what this looks like."

He lowered his head. "I guess it makes me look guilty. I just didn't think."

"You can say that again."

His face seemed drawn; he was clearly embarrassed. He opened his mouth to speak, then immediately closed it. He knew there was little he could say in his defense. He glanced away, then back again, and realized by the look in my eyes that he had to say something. Anything.

"Look," he finally managed. "All I can say is that I didn't think it was murder. The death appeared to be an accident. I jettisoned the corpse like I would any other."

"Unless foul play is suspected."

"I didn't really think —"

"For Christ's sake, someone cut his head and hands off!"

"But his death was an accident! That happened afterward!"

"So you think. But you don't know for sure, Malichauk. It's my job to find out, and you've obstructed evidence, which is a crime."

He looked at the deck morosely. "I know. I'm sorry. It wasn't smart. I already admitted that."

I watched him in silence for a long moment. No matter how upset I got, nothing could change what had happened. What was done was done, as they say. Malichauk looked guilty, but I knew that he wouldn't have made himself such an obvious suspect if he had in fact killed and mutilated Jimmy. I decided to move on.

"When did you begin to think it was murder?"

"Excuse me?"

"Your report. It said you thought it might be murder."

"Ah. The Captain suggested it after we saw the body, so I put it in."

"Do you agree?"

"I'm not sure. I didn't think so at first."

I paced the small enclosure, thinking. Manny had recommended the murder notation despite his assertion to me that it was just an accident with some possibly unconnected vandalism afterward. At least he had acted professionally with the report. At the very least, someone had to look into it, and he had recognized that.

"Tell me about the body," I said, now resigned to the loss.

"Whoever did it severed the head at the C-two vertebrae. The hands just above the thumb. He or she used an extremely sharp instrument."

"Laser?"

"No burn marks."

"Serrated edge on the knife?"

"No, it was very sharp, the cuts weren't jagged."

"Scalpel?"

"Longer. At least six, eight inches."

"Why do you think it was done?" I asked.

He grunted. "How the hell would I know?"

"I'm asking for conjecture. Why would someone —"

"Because they're sick," he snapped. "I don't know."

I paused. "I'm a Homicide Investigator, Lars. Do you know why someone would tamper with a body after death? Other than sexually, I mean." He frowned but didn't respond. I continued, "There's only one reason. The killer is trying to hide something."

The questioning continued for another hour. Malichauk grew more annoyed as the session dragged on. I didn't get the impression that he deliberately delayed the autopsy, but it seemed to me that he was trying to conceal something.

I just couldn't tell what.

Killers tamper with corpses to hide evidence, unless it was for something sexual. I had mentioned that to Malichauk. I had seen similar things in the past, and those cases always turned my stomach. I would now have to review the entire crew's history, looking not just for criminal activity, but abnormal sexual behavior in their psych profiles as well.

It gave me something to go on, for if the mutilation was indeed for something of that nature, it meant the missing parts were probably still on the station.

— Chapter Six —

The Captain was next on my list of people to question. There were numerous things I was hoping he could tell me — inconsistencies regarding regulations being foremost on my mind. However, before I did that, I needed to get to know Jimmy a little better.

Understanding that Crewman Chin's closest friends would most likely be from among the crew, I stalked over to Module E. I hoped to find a colleague of his to chat with, to try and come to a better understanding of his life here at *SOLEX*.

I passed through the scientists' cylinder on my way and found a cluttered mess on the deck in the corridors: equipment, computers, old circuit boards, fiber optic cables, plasma and holo screens, broken stools and desks, various cables and electrical components. It was typical of scientists so engrossed in their work that they cared little about cleanliness and order. The four at *SOLEX* probably loved it here; they had orbited closer to their object of interest longer than any manned satellite had before. They had unlimited access to the sun; they could watch it endlessly if they wanted, study it every hour of the day, day after day. It seemed like madness, but I couldn't pretend to understand what the scientist's mind is like. I shook my head as I stared at the deck.

A hatch slid open and a skinny, middle-aged Asian in a lab coat stepped into the corridor. He had an armful of electronic components that he unceremoniously dumped on the deck. He kicked the little pile and mumbled something under his breath.

"Problem?" I asked.

He looked up, startled. "Who the hell are you?"

"Lieutenant Kyle Tanner. Who are you?"

Understanding slowly dawned on the man's features. "Ah, of course. Please excuse me. I'm still waking up. I only got two hours of sleep and haven't had my coffee yet. Of course Manny told us you were coming. It just slipped my mind." He looked at me for a minute in an awkward silence. "Oh, sorry." He thrust out his hand. "I'm Reggie Hamatsui, one of the scientists here."

Really? I thought. *Could have fooled me.* He had a thin neck and closely cropped hair. His Adam's apple protruded and bobbed as he talked. I had to fight to keep from staring at it.

"I was just on my way to the crew module," I said.

"You're going the right way." He smiled and another silence ensued.

"I'm here to investigate Jimmy's death."

"Yes, yes. A very sad thing. Tragic. Do you really think it was murder?"

"I'm going to find out." I peered past him into a cluttered lab that made the corridor look spotless.

He noticed my gaze. "Want to look around?" He gestured inside and a grin split his features.

"Of course." Never turn down a chance for information. One of my mottos.

I stepped past him and entered a different world. Charts and pictures of the sun plastered every vertical surface. There were so many that I could barely see the bulkheads. Benches and tables were everywhere, all covered with papers and folders. There didn't seem to be organization of any sort. There were at least seven computer monitors in view; on each I could see either a graph or a close view of the sun. Flames churned about its surface and flickered in seemingly slow motion. It was almost hypnotic.

"My specialty is atmospheric dynamics," he said.

I frowned. "The sun has an atmosphere?"

"Of course! It's not like Earth or Venus, to be sure, but it does have one. We call it the corona."

"I've heard of that. I didn't know it was the atmosphere."

"Yes. The structure of the sun is fairly straightforward." He led me to a nearby diagram. "It has a core that generates incredible energy. Ten percent of its mass is located there. The immense pressure from the layers above actually causes fusion there. The temperature is sixteen million Kelvin."

"Fusion of hydrogen into helium, right?" It was all coming back to me, though slowly — primary school science.

His eyes sparkled. "You bet. Four atoms of hydrogen combine to form one atom of helium and an emission of neutrinos and energy. It's that energy that produces all the heat and light. The next layer is the radiative zone. Here all the core's energy moves to the outer layers. This occupies about eighty-five percent of the sun's radius, and technically includes the core."

"I see." I wasn't so sure I needed this lesson. I tried to change the topic. "Did you —"

"The next layer," he said, on a roll now, "is the convective zone. The motion of gas occurs here in convection currents like we'd see in any fluid. It's just trying to move heat out into space."

I didn't really have time for all of this. I'd accepted his invitation hoping to get a look at what he was doing and where he worked, but this was a little much. "I think —"

"The surface comes next. We call that the photosphere. It's only about six thousand degrees Kelvin, which is relatively cool. It's here that sunspots occur, which are cooler areas of the sun's surface, only about four thousand Kelvin. We actually have a scientist here totally devoted to studying sunspots — Lingly."

"How interesting," I murmured, wearily submitting myself to this unnecessary lecture.

"Solar prominences occur here, which are bright clouds of gas that form above the sunspots and follow the sun's magnetic field. They're really quite fascinating. They last days to weeks. A large prominence is what we call a flare. They only last minutes to hours, and this material can actually escape the sun's gravitational pull. When the burst of ions hits Earth, it can cause a lot of trouble, let me tell you."

"Not to mention what it would do to us," I muttered. Reggie seemed single-minded in his quest to teach me about the sun. His Adam's apple was going like crazy. I studied the lab in more detail as he wore on. Nothing seemed overly unusual — it was just incredibly disorganized. I remembered back on Venus I once marched right into a suspect's apartment and caught him with the murder weapon in plain view. He'd been getting ready to dispose of it, and I had somehow entered a minute before he'd done so. It was insanely fortunate; it was one of those things that happens once in a career and never again. Nevertheless, I looked around for the eight inch blade used to sever Jimmy's head, but of course saw nothing. Regretfully, I turned my attention back to Reggie.

"— but don't worry, we're fully protected here," he was saying. "We have Shaheen Ramachandra to thank for that! She may be an officer, but she's a scientist at heart, let me tell you."

"So I —"

"I haven't gotten to my area of study yet."

"Your area?"

"Yes, the atmosphere, remember? The corona. It's just past the chromosphere, the layer above the photosphere. The density decreases there, but for some reason the temperature actually *increases*."

"I thought it decreased out from the core."

"Yes, it does, until it gets to the corona, where the temperature suddenly surges upward! It reaches about *two million Kelvin*, where it was only six thousand at the surface. It's most peculiar. There are a lot of scientists studying this phenomenon, but the four of us here at *SOLEX* are the lucky ones. We have an astounding amount of information and data coming in every minute from our sensors. We're hoping we can solve this mystery, once and for all."

That, at least, was interesting. A mystery that needed solving. I could relate to it. In many ways scientists and Investigators did the same thing, only my area involved a hell of a lot more gore and pain. Despite my better judgement, I asked a question. "What's your theory?"

He looked guarded. "Ah, there are already many. I am reticent to tell you mine until further study. But rest assured I think it'll stun the astrophysics community."

Great, I thought. The only information about the sun I was interested in, and he refused to talk about it.

"You don't look too impressed," he said, studying me.

"No, I —"

"You have to understand that this increase occurs over only two hundred kilometers! It's a very small distance to have such a drastic change in temperature. The sun is full of intriguing riddles." He pointed at a nearby chart and continued without even taking a breath. "As I mentioned, the sunspots are another item of intense curiosity for us here, although it's not my area. But there is talk of sending a probe to the surface to monitor conditions there! Imagine, landing a probe on a sunspot!"

"Really. That is fascinating." Yawn. For him to be so intelligent, reading body language seemed impossible for him. If given the opportunity, he would probably fail miserably at my job, despite the similarities in what we did. He was socially inept, like most scientists I had come to know in my travels.

"How did you get picked for this post?" I asked, steering him in a direction that suited my investigation.

"We applied. There was a long selection process, interviews, and so on. They studied our research and published works. The other three scientists here are really quite good."

"I'm sure you're good too."

"Well, I don't know about that." He grinned. "I'm just thrilled to be here!"

"You never feel nervous?"

He looked quizzical. "About what?"

"The heat, radiation. The danger." I studied him as I said it. I stressed the last word to see if he'd react in some way.

"Oh no. Our station is quite safe. The heat shield that Shaheen invented is remarkable. We've been here nine months with no problems. I don't foresee any trouble."

"That's not quite true, sir."

He frowned. "What do you —" He stopped abruptly. "You mean Jimmy's death. Yes, that was sad. But it wasn't because of our proximity to the sun. It was an accident."

You can't be sure of that, I thought. The stress could have been just too much for someone. "Did you know him?"

A sigh. "Just casually. You know, I said hi to him in the mess, but I don't often eat there, so it was just now and then."

I marched to another display and pretended to show interest in the structure of a solar prominence. "Are you familiar with EVA procedures?"

"I think that's the officers' responsibility, not mine."

"What I mean is, are you familiar with them, generally?"

"Not really, no." He looked puzzled. "Why do you ask?"

"Just curious. Can you tell me any more about Jimmy?" He shook his head and didn't respond. "Perhaps things you heard from your colleagues ... rumors, that sort of thing." Still nothing. "Any problems here at the station? People getting stressed, fights and so on. Anything of interest?"

He pursed his lips. "Really I wouldn't know. I'm kind of secluded here. I spend most of my time in F. I don't see much of anyone else on a regular basis. Just my three colleagues. Only thing that bothers me is the CCF asking for reports."

His mention of 'F' threw me off, until I realized he was referring to the cylinder where the scientists worked and lived. I pointed to a small hatch set into the bulkhead. Stenciled red warning labels had attracted my notice. "What's that?"

"Ejection chute for hazardous waste. All the labs have them, as well as the clinic."

I moved back toward the corridor. "Thanks for your help. I may be back."

His face brightened. "The sun can be incredibly fascinating. I'd be happy to answer any questions you might have."

My smile was forced. Weird guy. I wondered if all the scientists were so ... *obsessed*.

—

In a cramped lounge in the adjacent crew module, I found a woman sitting by herself and drinking a mug of coffee. She was staring at a datachip reader in silence. I recognized her from *SOLEX's* personnel dossier. She looked up as I entered and watched as I approached. I introduced myself and she nodded in recognition.

"The Captain informed us you were coming. I hope you find who did this terrible thing to Jimmy."

"You're Aina Alvarez, right?"

"Yeah. Call me Anna, everyone else does." She was in her twenties, short and stout and not exactly attractive. More muscled than chubby, she had a pug nose and dark, serious eyes. Her hair was pulled back severely. Her skin was olive and betrayed her Chilean Mestizo heritage.

"You were friends with him?" I asked. I skipped all preliminaries; making small talk when the crew already knew why I was there would be tactless and embarrassing. Besides, as an officer, I wasn't supposed to be friendly with lowly NOM's — or those who were *Not Officer Material*. They had their world and we had ours; the only reason I was currently in theirs was to investigate a crime.

She looked around the room and lowered her voice a notch. "Great friends. Yeah, you could say that."

"How great?" It was obvious from her tone, but making assumptions was one of the worst things an Investigator could do when questioning a witness. We needed it all laid out on the table, plain and simple.

She narrowed her eyes. "Let's just say *very*, if you get my meaning."

I filed that away as potentially important information. Spouses, lovers, and immediate family members were the guilty party to a premeditated homicide eighty percent of the time. "He confided in you," I said, not missing a beat.

"Yeah. He was a special guy. I'm going to miss him."

"Did you two ever argue?"

"The odd time. Nothing major. Just about petty stuff."

I studied her closely. She seemed sincere. People in relationships always argued, it came with the territory. She wasn't trying to hide anything.

"Did he have any enemies? Anyone who could have done this to him?"

She looked puzzled. "No. A disagreement here or there. Nothing major."

"With who?"

Her brow crinkled. "Once with Lieutenant Kayle, our esteemed Council Rep."

That would be Brick Kayle, the Australian I had met the night before. "About?"

"Money. Kayle owed some money to someone, and Jimmy lent him some. He never repaid the full amount."

Of course. Money. There was always something. "Who did Kayle owe?" I asked.

"No idea."

"Why did Jimmy lend it to him?"

"I dunno." She scratched her head. "You know, it's weird. To a certain extent Jimmy did it because he was just a nice guy. He was like that. But I think there was more to it than that."

"Such as?"

She shrugged. "The fact that Kayle is an officer. Jimmy was just a Private First Class. I think he may have —" She suddenly looked apprehensive. "Say, is this, you know —"

"Between us, yes. Unless it has something to do with his death." People often hesitated to speak freely unless they thought it was in confidence. I'd lied to her, of course, but didn't much care about it. It didn't matter to me if someone's feelings got hurt in the process of finding a killer.

She bit her lip. "Good enough, I guess."

"You were saying?"

"The fact that Kayle is an officer. I think Jimmy may have felt obligated, or even threatened."

I perked up at that. "You think Kayle threatened him?"

"I don't know for sure. But Jimmy seemed a little stressed after Kayle first approached him."

"When was that?"

She pursed her lips. "I guess two months ago, give or take."

I made a note of that before I continued. "How are things here on *SOLEX*?"

She rolled her eyes. "Boring. We orbit the sun endlessly. Every day is the same: maintain some machinery, move some cargo for the scientists, get some supplies from the storage cylinder. Same old shit."

"What about the people here?"

"I guess they're okay. I don't really know some of them."

"The officers, right?"

"Yeah. I chat with the scientists sometimes while I'm doing stuff for them. But they're so involved in their work that getting to know them is difficult. But they're better than the officers, who just like to give a bunch of orders. It's the same everywhere, I'm sure."

"What about the crew?"

"Well there's only five of —" She stopped suddenly and looked embarrassed. "Sorry, I'm still doing that. There's only four of us now, and we live in the same module, so yeah, I know them pretty well."

"Any problems between anyone?" Possible tensions and squabbles between coworkers were of critical importance for any murder case. There hadn't been much in the official reports, but it didn't mean nothing had happened. Manny or the First Officer just hadn't reported such instances.

"Not that I know of." She pondered the question for a beat before something suddenly occurred to her. "Say, Jimmy did mention something once. It seemed really strange; I wasn't sure if he was pulling my leg or not. He was a real prankster."

"A fight or something?"

She paused. "Not really. At least, I don't think so." She thought for a moment. "He told me he was doing some maintenance on the life support systems. Routine stuff. You know, there's a lot of equipment keeping us alive. Our air and water are only part of it. There's also the recycling system, which is extremely important. All our water passes through the recyclers, as does our solid waste. Galley garbage too. It's all used again, mostly. Ninety percent of it, anyway. Then there's the carbon dioxide. Levels are always building; we have to keep them down."

"So what did he see?" I pressed, anxious not to receive another lesson.

"He said that behind one of the carbon dioxide scrubbers — which are actually pretty damn big — he saw two people doing something suspicious. It was dark, he couldn't make out their faces. Just from the way one of them kept looking around, Jimmy said it seemed odd. Like the guy was worried someone would see."

I'd heard this one a million times. "Something sexual?"

"No, that's the weird part. One of them was on the ground, slumped against the scrubber. Jimmy said he looked unconscious. The other was standing over him, grabbing him around the arm, and just holding on tightly. Like he was trying to steady him, only the guy was already on the deck." She shook her head. "Jimmy was standing in a dark corner, by the water filters. They couldn't see him."

"How long did he watch?"

"More than five minutes. Neither man moved much, just the guy who kept looking around."

I frowned. I definitely had *not* heard this one before. "Did Jimmy tell anyone else?"

"He told an officer a few days later. I don't think he got anywhere; he acted a little weird about it afterward."

"Who did he tell?"

She shrugged. "Didn't say. I asked him what was wrong. I could tell something was bothering him. He said he had to make a decision about something, but refused to say what."

I paused and mulled the story over. Did it have anything to do with his death? "Can you show me where this happened?" I asked her.

"Sure, but remember I wasn't there. I only know what Jimmy told me. But I'll try my best."

—

Anna led me to the upper level of the life support cylinder — Module A. It was similar to my cabin in that the bulkheads curved together toward the center of the ceiling. They were probably double- or triple-hulled, with insulation, wiring, equipment and ducts running between the different hulls. The deck had numerous openings where pipes and ducts led downward to the lower two levels. I looked through one opening, but could see only darkness below. There was an odd echo as well; anything we said seemed to float back to our ears a second later, distorted and hollow. It was disconcerting.

It was difficult to make anything out in the enclosure due to the low light level. The only illumination came from display panels on the equipment. I asked Anna why it was so dark.

"Doesn't make sense to light a non-living area."

"What about someone who needs to do some work?"

"Oh. We have portable lights we just plop down next to the system we're working on."

"Did he have one with him the day he was here?"

"Dunno." She led me to a machine through which large ducts passed; it was clearly something for the station's atmosphere. "This is one of our scrubbers. According to the story, the pair would have been right here."

"And Jimmy?"

She peered into a far corner. "There are the water filters. He was over there."

I marched to the indicated location. There were plenty of shadows to lose oneself in. I crouched in the corner. "Can you see me?"

"No," Anna said. "Not at all."

I got back to my feet and approached her. "Thanks for showing me this. If I have any more questions, I'll find you."

"Okay." She started to leave, hesitated, then turned back to me. "Say, remember what you said? This wouldn't go anywhere unless —"

"Unless it had to do with Jimmy's death. I haven't forgotten."

"Good." She spun on a heel and left the compartment quickly.

I glanced around the dark surroundings. Just a few hours of questioning and I finally had some suspects on my list: the person Jimmy had seen subduing the prone man in the life support module, the officer Jimmy had told about the strange incident, and Brick Kayle, who had owed Jimmy money. Not bad for a morning's work.

— Chapter Seven —

I ate lunch in the common mess. All the officers were present, as well as most of the crew. The scientists were absent. They were apparently having a working lunch. Every day, according to Brick, was a working lunch for the scientists.

Avery Rickets, the First Officer, introduced me to the crew. He led me to the table where they sat scowling at their plates; they didn't look up as we approached. "This is Godfreid Grossman, Larry Balch and Bram O'Donnelly," he said. "These three plus Anna are the ones who really keep the station running."

Grossman was stocky, bordering on fat, with big arms and a long, handlebar moustache. Balch was his opposite: tall and skinny with thin biceps and a long neck. Veins protruded up and down his arms, blending in with a tattoo that stretched the entire length of his left arm. Bram O'Donnelly was an older man, stout, with a full red beard to match his hair. He chewed his food slowly as he watched me.

I nodded to them. "Nice to meet you."

"It's too bad Anna's not here," Rickets continued. "I could have introduced you."

"I met her earlier," I answered. "I also spoke with one of the scientists, Reggie Hamatsui."

"Great. Reggie is a nice guy. Did you interview him?"

I snorted. "Yes, but he was more interested in talking about the sun."

"Typical. They're all so preoccupied with it."

"I'm getting a little sick of that," Bram O'Donnelly said. "Whenever I'm in Module F all I hear is those four talking about solar electromagnetic field this, fusion temperature that, missing mass this, and all sorts of other bullshit."

"How'd you end up at *SOLEX?*" I asked as I studied his angry expression.

"I didn't request it, you can bet on that."

"What was your previous post?"

"Venus. Wasn't great, too much damn work and not enough free time, but it was a damn sight better than this."

Captain Fredericks grinned. "Come on, Bram. It's not that bad." To me: "Bram is perhaps the most negative crewman I've got."

The pair began to argue in earnest. Bram criticized everything from the work schedule to the recent death of Jimmy Chin. Manny, on the other hand, had a smile on his face and chuckled with every critique. I'd seen Captains in the CCF who, like my contact Bryce Manning, were fanatical about military formality and protocol. Manny obviously wasn't one of them. In fact, here he was allowing one of his crew to openly complain about everything related to *SOLEX*, including its officers.

Rickets noted my expression and leaned toward me. "Don't worry, they do this every day. They're actually good friends; knew each other back before either of them were in the CCF. I think Manny had Bram transferred here."

Leaving the two to their disagreement, I turned to Larry Balch and Godfreid Grossman, who were now engaged in an animated discussion at the end of the table. Every now and then one of them glanced in my direction. It was obvious that I was the topic of conversation.

"What's the problem?" I asked.

Balch grew immediately silent and stared at his food. Grossman said, "Jimmy was a friend. That's all. We were wondering how your investigation is going."

"Fine," I said in a noncommital tone. "Just started. Were either of you two out with him during the EVA?"

I noticed their eyes flick to the Captain and back to me. "No," they both said.

Their expressions were too rigid. They were hiding something.

"Who was?"

They looked at each other, got to their feet, and left the messhall without another word.

—

Manny remained in his chair as the others filed out. Bel Bertram and Shaheen Ramachandra cast a curious glance at us as they departed; they were the last to leave.

"I have a few questions for you, Manny."

His expression was grim. "I expected you would."

"Who was on the EVA with Jimmy?" I said without preamble.

He exhaled and looked remorseful. "I suppose it would come out in the end. I knew it would, especially after what happened to the corpse. But let me say this: my officers and crew were under orders not to disclose what happened. It's my fault, not theirs."

So it was true, after all. "Why was Jimmy outside by himself? It's —"

"Against regulations. I know."

"A severe misjudgement on your part."

His face looked suddenly haggard and drawn. "You probably can't understand — you've never lived in a place like this for as long as we have. It gets to you, the loneliness, the isolation. The constant danger being so close to Sol. It's hard to maintain protocol."

"I noticed Bram earlier. Hardly any military formality there."

"We're friends. It's not like that with everyone."

I bristled at that. Although I wasn't a stickler for military protocol, I knew it was absolutely necessary to maintain discipline in severe conditions and remote locations. Once military people started to act like civilians, the more basic emotions churned to the surface and caused all sorts of trouble. The Captain should *never* let military formalities fall to the wayside.

"Go on," I pressed.

"*SOLEX* is isolated from the Confederacy. No one comes and goes. Every day is as mundane as the one before it. There's little for any of us to do, except the scientists." He hesitated. "I know it sounds like I'm making excuses."

"You could say that." In fact, boredom could be extremely useful. Life in the military generally consisted of long stretches of nothing but routine training punctuated by moments of sheer terror. Survival depended on one's ability to deal with a crisis, and your mental state — hardened by training and even learning to deal with boredom — determined who lived and who died. I simply couldn't believe that Manny didn't understand that. He was a Captain in the CCF; he wouldn't have ascended to the rank without accepting and in fact *appreciating* it.

"It really is difficult out here," he was saying. "Regs falter a bit. We get a little more informal. One day they're not saluting, and you don't care because you understand the stress everyone's under. Then the crew's efficiency scores drop, but you don't do anything because they're doing the best they can in a tough situation. They didn't ask to be here. Someone assigned them to this post. Then, before you know it, you're bending regulations beyond what's normal or acceptable. And the funny thing is, you don't even really notice."

"Until someone dies."

He grimaced. "Yes. Jimmy must have been too careless outside. He slipped up." The guilt was clear in his features. He had a spotless record, and it was a shame that a mistake ended in a fatality. There was nothing I could do to help him once I filed my report. His career would be over.

He eyed me. "I know. I'm through. There's no getting around it."

"I'm sorry. I can't help you."

His smile was sad. "Just find out who cut Jimmy's head and hands off and get them out of here."

I knew he wasn't angry with me; he was just under tremendous pressure. I empathized with the man, I really did. I wish I could have overlooked what he had done, but doing so would mean disobeying regs — the very mistake Manny had made. I just couldn't do it.

"Can you answer a few more questions?" I asked.

"Shoot." He got up to grab another coffee, returned with a steaming mug.

"Did Jimmy ever make any odd reports to you?" According to Anna, he had told an officer about the assault in life support. I didn't yet know which one.

He pursed his lips. "Not that I know of. Nothing comes to mind. You mean with the station?"

"No, with the personnel."

"No."

"What if he told another officer? Would you know about it?"

"I guess it depends how weird it was."

I paged through my notes, dwelling for a moment on Doctor Malichauk's statement. Manny sipped coffee. Finally I asked, "Why didn't you order the autopsy immediately?"

He sighed. "I figured Malichauk would do it."

"Did you punish him for not doing it right away?"

His expression turned gloomy. "No."

I shook my head. Yet another regulation disregarded. It was a clear indication of a lack of formality that resulted in escalating problems. For me in particular, it meant the loss of the corpse and a potential wealth of physical evidence.

"What was he doing that was so important?"

"I asked him. He never gave a concrete answer."

Absurd. If that happened anywhere else in the Confederacy, the officer in question would be in the brig for weeks.

"Tell me about Lieutenant Brick Kayle," I continued.

"Brick? He's a decent sort. Kind of loud and outspoken. You know the type. They speak their minds and don't care what anyone thinks."

"Odd for a Council Rep to be like that."

"Oh, he never talks about the Council. He's not fanatical about that."

"Any personal troubles?"

"You'd think someone that opinionated would have problems with others, but I never heard of any. Everyone seems to like him." He paused. "Except *maybe* Shaheen. I thought something might have happened between them, but I'm not sure what."

"Are they seeing each other?"

"Not that I know of."

I digested that. "When I first arrived, you said I was only the second person to come to *SOLEX* since operations began. What did you mean?"

"We had one other person come, four weeks ago. A crewman stationed here, Jarvis Riddel, cracked up. He couldn't take the pressure. Kept screaming about the radiation we were taking, the heat burning us up, a solar flare taking us out, and so on. He went crazy. Doctor Malichauk recommended his removal. Command Group on Mercury sent a replacement and Riddel went to a hospital."

"Who was the replacement?"

"Godfreid Grossman. He wasn't happy about coming here, let me tell you. He's complained to everyone about it on several occasions."

I hadn't known that. There was more going on here than the official reports stated; they never told the complete story. "Where is Riddel now?"

The Captain's face fell. "I guess you wouldn't know. He's dead; it happened on Mercury."

———

Back to my quarters to study notes before I continued the interviews. I had only formally questioned four people: Doctor Malichauk, the scientist Reggie Hamatsui, Crewman Anna Alvarez, and the Captain, Manny Fredericks. Still ten more to go.

Hitting the hatch control, I stepped into the cabin. It was dark. I frowned; the light should have come on automatically. I fumbled for the switch and an instant later someone tackled me. I skidded sideways along the bulkhead, tripped over my own feet, and crashed to the deck. The impact had caught me off guard and I found myself crunched up on my hands and knees. I spun frantically and tried to see something — *anything* — but it was useless. The cabin was utterly black. The hatch had slid shut and cut off the only source of light.

I grabbed for my pistol, but realized with a jolt that the holster wasn't strapped to my thigh. I had removed it the night before and hadn't put it back on. It was on the deck next to my bunk. I dove toward it, landed on my stomach, and slid two meters across the smooth metal. Arms outstretched, I scrabbled frantically for the pistol. Where the fuck —

A crash and the guy landed right on me. I yelled in pain and whipped my right elbow backward. I connected with what I hoped was a kidney and heard a yelp. I tried the other elbow, hit once, then felt a blow across the back of my neck.

I saw stars.

Forcing myself to my knees — thanks to all the pushups I do — I twisted savagely to the side. His grip loosened measurably, but he didn't fall off. I tried to spin him the other way —

— and felt a sharp pain in my lower back. It seared through my body like a phosphorus bomb. The blade penetrated deeply. It moved almost in slow motion and nearly protruded out my front it was so long.

With a sudden burst of energy that comes from desperation, I flung myself backward and crushed him against a bulkhead. He grunted and finally lost his grip.

I swung angrily and connected with a wet thud. I ducked, threw another punch, ducked again, and kicked right in front of me. Miraculously, I landed every blow. I ducked and bobbed and came up with an elbow. It was a vicious strike, meant to shatter teeth and break jaws, but this time I hit only thin air.

Something cracked against the side of my head. It wasn't a fist or an elbow, it felt more like a wrench. I collapsed to the deck and my head drooped to the cold steel. I was blacking out. I felt a hand — powerful and sweaty — grasp my forearm. It began to apply pressure.

A whole lot of pressure.

—

The dizziness almost overwhelmed me, but through it a powerful image surfaced: it was Jimmy Chin, who stood in silence in a dark corner of the life support module and watched as one man gripped another's arm. I didn't understand what he had witnessed; all I could reason at that moment through the fog was that I was experiencing it firsthand.

It was impossible to move. I attempted to kick with my right leg, but succeeded in only moving my foot a fraction of a centimeter. The guy was heavy.

The assault shouldn't have surprised me. After all, I was investigating a murder, and a killer on the run almost always considered eliminating the Investigator to prevent capture. It had happened to my friend Flemming back on Mercury, and it had almost happened to me when I tried to bring in The Torcher. Despite that, this situation was beyond me. The struggling had stopped, and all he was doing was holding my arm in utter silence.

I relaxed to gather my strength. If he assumed I was unconscious, I might catch him off guard. A minute passed. Then another. Still the pressure mounted. I could smell his ragged breath. It was sour like after a night carousing and puking.

A feeling that something dangerous was happening surged within me. Somehow I knew I had to stop this. I yanked my arm sideways abruptly and his wet grip slipped off. I had caught him by surprise. I arched my back, raised my right leg, and kicked with everything I could muster. I connected with something soft and heard a gasp.

Trembling with exertion, exhaustion and pain, I rose to my feet and stumbled back, thankful for the brief reprieve. I reached out and grasped the bulkhead to steady myself. Suddenly, the hatch slid open. In the flash of light admitted from the corridor, I could make out only a dim silhouette as he bolted from the cabin. The light seemed so intense — or perhaps I was just accustomed to the inky black of my quarters — that I squinted involuntarily. When I reopened my eyes, the hatch had slid shut. He was gone.

I lunged at the controls and leapt into the corridor.

There was no one there.

—

The arm he had been clutching was slick with blood. I could see his handprint and the indentation of his fingers in my flesh. Back in my quarters, in the lavatory, I held it under cold water and watched the swirling red spiral down the drain.

To my amazement, there was nothing wrong. No cuts or scrapes. There might be bruising, perhaps, but nothing more. The blood must not have been mine.

It took me another minute before I realized my left side and pant leg felt damp. I looked down and my heart thudded in my chest; he had stabbed me in the back during the altercation. I was bleeding profusely.

—

I managed to get to Doctor Malichauk's clinic under my own power, but practically collapsed as I passed through the threshold.

"My God, man!" he yelled as he saw the trail of blood I left behind. "What the hell happened?"

"Attacked ..." I barely managed. The clinic tilted crazily. I saw Malichauk run toward me, arms outstretched.

Everything went black.

—

A few hours later, I awoke to see Shaheen, Manny and Brick studying me with worried expressions. Malichauk stood behind them, examining his reader.

"He'll be okay," he was saying. "The blade nicked his liver, which is why there was so much blood. I injected some priority nanos that have repaired the damage. They're on their way to his bladder now."

"Who the hell attacked me?" I managed to groan. The pain was intense, but I was more embarrassed than anything. I shouldn't have removed my pistol, which I had done as a courtesy to the inhabitants of *SOLEX*. But to hell with social graces. I couldn't afford to slip up again — the stakes were now too high.

"We were going to ask you the same thing," Manny said.

"Surveillance?" I muttered.

"Turned off," Shaheen said. "Either a glitch or on purpose."

"Couldn't be a glitch," Brick said. "It's happened twice already. Too convenient."

I remembered that the surveillance cameras had mysteriously malfunctioned earlier. I hadn't gotten around to questioning anyone about it yet.

"Shaheen," I said as I struggled to my elbows. "Who has access to that system?"

"Practically everyone but the crew. The scientists don't, but they're smart people. They could figure it out."

"I don't have access," Malichauk said.

Great. That only eliminated five people out of fourteen. And the four crew could easily have learned the system; they'd had nine months to study it.

"I'm going to have to look at it when I get out of here," I said.

"I can do that," Shaheen offered. "I'll try to have something for you within the hour."

I studied her for a moment. Could I trust her to give me an honest and thorough answer? She seemed sincere, but you never really knew in my line of work. Nevertheless, I couldn't escape the fact that I didn't know enough about *SOLEX's* systems; I'd need someone's help to decipher the security protocols.

"Sure," I said finally. "Let me know as soon as possible."

"Tell us what happened," Manny said to me.

I exhaled. "Went to my quarters after speaking with you. Lights were off. Before I could get them on, someone tackled me. We struggled. I got stabbed. I managed to fight him off and he ran."

"All in the dark?"

"Yes. Never got a good look at him."

"Someone wants you dead," Brick said, grave. "I wonder why."

"Go figure."

"One thing's for sure," Shaheen said. "This isn't just a simple prank." She looked at the Captain. "I know you were hoping for the best ..."

He frowned. "I guess we can't go on thinking that now. Someone murdered Jimmy, and the same person tried to kill Tanner."

My thinking exactly. I stared at the four people in the clinic with me. The killer might be here, just waiting for the right opportunity. Waiting for me to walk into another dark cabin, unarmed and vulnerable ...

"Did you hurt him?" Brick asked.

"I don't know. Got a few punches in, but ..." I leaned back, stared at the ceiling, and pondered what had happened. The fight had been so sudden, so intense, but I had no idea what had really happened. He had hidden in my cabin and waited with the lights off ... for how long? How had he —

A thought suddenly occurred. "Is there night-vision equipment anywhere on *SOLEX*?"

Manny's brow furrowed. "Not that I know of. But you can purchase night-vision glasses anywhere —"

"My point is, why would someone bring them here? Unless they knew they'd need them."

Shaheen looked dubious. "Are you sure he had some?"

"Fairly certain. After the hatch closed, he knew exactly where I was. Jumped right on me. And when I hit him, I thought I felt glasses."

Brick said, "Then all we have to do is find —"

I shook my head. "No. Whoever it is will be too smart for that. He'll plant them in someone else's belongings."

There was a long silence as they stood around me uncertainly.

"What next?" Malichauk asked finally.

I twisted sideways, testing myself and my injury. I nearly yelped from the sudden stabbing sensation in my back. Damn. It took a minute to catch my breath. Then, "How long until I can get out of here?"

"Morning. The nanos have repaired the damage, but we need to give it a little rest. The nerve endings down there are still reacting to the shock. Relax a bit here. You'll be safe."

He was referring to microscopic machines that could do miraculous things like repair wounds. Every manufacturer had a different name for them: nanobots, nanomachines, nanites, and nanolites to name just a few. The generic name was simply *nanos*. They'd revolutionized medicine and engineering a thousandfold; their inventor had received the Nobel in both areas fifty years earlier. They weren't intelligent and couldn't replicate — despite the efforts of our most brilliant engineers — but they had saved countless lives.

Mine included.

A cold chill coursed up my spine. Regardless of what the doctor had said, I no longer thought I'd be safe anywhere on the station. "I'll need my pistol," I said. "It's in my cabin."

"I'll get it," Brick said. He left the clinic and was back in two minutes. He looked grim. "Not there. It's gone."

Damn. The bastard had taken my only weapon.

— Chapter Eight —

I passed the night fitfully. The pain faded quickly, but the wound remained itchy and uncomfortable. It kept me from falling into a deep sleep. Or, perhaps it was the knowledge that someone wanted me dead. I sometimes wished I could just live a normal life. Eat, work, sleep, then repeat for a lifetime without stress and without worry.

Ha. Fat chance. No one's life was like that, especially in the Confederacy's current political state. I would have to endure this situation until I found the killer. As always, there were no other options.

A few years earlier I had nearly died in the line of duty. The case was in Tokyo; someone had killed a high ranking politician and I received the call. It was late at night and no one with more experience was on duty at the time.

Only twenty-three, fresh out of the academy, I had just started my career as a full Investigator. Tokyo was my first post, but I didn't stay long; as is usually the case, murder investigations take you all over the system. I only spent five months there before I followed another one out to Neptune. But while on Earth, that one was definitely the biggest I had.

I investigated passionately. I threw myself into it with a vigor that I don't think I've had since. I knew it was a case that could make my reputation in the Security Division of the CCF. What can I say? I was young and reckless. The media scrutiny was intense; reporters camped out on my doorstep right from the start. I hardly slept. The pressure irritated me, and it only grew worse as time wore on.

Perhaps my ideals were a little different then from now. I don't much care about my reputation anymore. I just want to catch killers. I've seen so much death and suffering that I only want to make something right in this crazy galaxy. But back then I'd wanted it all: fame, money, a fast ship, recognition. Everything a young kid could dream of.

Someone put a price on my head and I found myself in great peril while I tried to put the last pieces of the puzzle together. In the end, I exposed eleven senior politicians in Japan of dealing brainstim. The Council's punishment was harsh; they didn't tolerate such activities in the Terran Confederacy. They imprisoned the guilty for life.

But what it boiled down to was that I hadn't been prepared going into the investigation. I didn't see the threat that was right before me. I had been on the verge of exposing some very powerful people, and of course I should have expected trouble. I was inexperienced and a little brash, and it had almost ended my career.

At the time I promised myself that I wouldn't let it happen again. Now, over a decade later, I cursed myself inwardly. I should never have let the pistol out of my sight.

—

When Malichauk gave me permission to leave, I stalked straight to Shaheen's quarters. They were in the same module as my own, just a few hatches down the corridor.

"Come on in," she called, and I stepped inside. She was entering a report into the station's computer system. She stopped typing and turned to me. "How do you feel?" There was concern in her voice.

I growled in response.

"I was going to come by the clinic first thing. Lars let you out early."

"He had trouble keeping me there."

"Difficult patient?"

"You could say that."

She gestured to a small chair in the corner. "Have a seat."

I lowered myself gingerly and winced at the slight discomfort in my back. She watched silently for a beat. Then, "I looked into the security systems. I tried to come by to let you know yesterday, but Lars wouldn't let me bother you."

"What did you find?"

"Someone's accessed them. Wasn't a fluke, or a glitch, or whatever. I told Manny and he went nuts. He wants to have a meeting with everyone and raise hell."

I shook my head. It wasn't a good idea without me there. "When I have more answers we'll have the meeting. Did you find out who did it?"

"I can't tell. The logs —"

"Aren't you the Station Systems Officer? The Chief Engineer?" I cringed at the comment; I had snapped at her. I didn't mean to come off as unappreciative, I was just frustrated.

She didn't seem to notice. "Someone erased the logs expertly. No trace of who did it. I'm entering the report for Manny right now."

I considered the news. "How much time is actually missing from the recordings?"

"The twelve hours around Jimmy's death and mutilation. All feeds including external ceased, as well as warning alarms that indicated a problem. A three hour period yesterday is also gone."

"Exactly when the attack occurred," I murmured. "I'm going to have to check everyone's alibi."

"Manny had Avery — First Officer Rickets, that is — already do that. Only Brick and Katrina were together during that time. They corroborated each other's stories."

"Katrina?"

"Katrina Kyriakis, one of the scientists. She's an electromagnetic field physicist. Brick is the Scientist Liaison, as well as our political officer, so it's natural that he would have been with her."

"What about the other twelve people?"

"No one has an alibi, myself included. We were all doing our own work."

I frowned. "Seems natural enough for the scientists, but no one saw anyone else?"

"It's a pretty big station for fourteen people, Kyle."

I had noticed that *SOLEX* seemed large for the number of people living there. I raised an eyebrow.

"This is only temporary," she said. "After we're done the trial period, if everything checks out, we'll get a larger crew. We could hold fifty here without much trouble. It's no wonder no one saw anything."

I pondered that information. The list of suspects for the attack on me was almost as long as the list of suspects for Jimmy's murder. Things weren't getting easier — they were becoming more complicated.

She was still watching with those blue eyes. They were mostly light with darker flecks. Juxtaposed over her exotic features, they were almost hypnotic.

"You noticed the eyes," she said.

"Hard not to," I admitted, a little embarrassed. "How'd you get them?"

"I'm from Mumbai. My parents thought they were both full-blooded Indian. When I was born with these eyes, it caused a lot of confusion in the family." She laughed. "Actually, that's putting it mildly; everyone went apeshit. You see, the color blue is a recessive gene. It means both parents have it in their family. And being East Indian ..."

"Not many have blue eyes."

"No. But the British once occupied my country. So —"

"You have British blood."

"Yes, on both sides of my family. At some point in the past, centuries ago now, both my parents' families must have had a mixed child. No one in my family knew about it. When I was born, however, it suddenly became pretty obvious."

"Were they ashamed?"

She looked startled. "Oh, no. Not at all. I just represented a piece of the past that no one knew about."

"And the English accent?"

She finished entering the report with a quick jab at a key and moved her chair closer to mine. Her figure was hard to hide, even in the black uniform. She was probably a woman who got whatever she wanted in life just from her good looks. Not to say that she wasn't smart too; her engineering expertise was clearly unparalleled. She had invented the heat shield that protected us and had upgraded the magnetic shield that funneled the sun's high energy particles away from us. Doctor Malichauk had stated that Shaheen would win the Nobel Prize; he was probably right.

She said, "My eyes made a big impact on everyone around me while I was growing up. Even me. When I was ready to go to university, I wanted to get away from India, to explore more of Earth. To travel. I chose Oxford University in England. In a way, I guess you could say that I followed my eyes."

I grunted. "Good story. Interesting history."

That took her aback. "Look who's talking! You get to travel the entire system, catch killers, and get justice for families who have suffered terrible loss. You're the guy who caught The Torcher. Everyone knows that."

I shifted in my chair. "I don't really like talking about that. I thought you understood."

A surge of regret passed over her features. "Sorry. I do."

"You understand that I don't want to talk about it. Not the reason why."

"Of course I do. You enjoy working alone. You don't want to get close to too many people. Maybe it was something that happened when you were younger. Who knows. But you are dedicated to your work. You want to catch people who have broken the law and put things right. Help people who have been wronged. You don't appreciate fame because it cheapens what you do, and you understand that your notoriety is a result of people's suffering." She paused for a beat and pointed at my face. "Close your mouth before a bug flies in."

"How'd you figure all that?"

She shrugged. "It's natural. You're a good person. A moral person. No one who's like that could appreciate fame brought on by the death of others."

I knew she was brilliant, and obviously her knowledge included not just science and engineering, but psychology as well. It seemed that she had a new surprise for me every day.

—

I found Manny in the station's control center monitoring systems. He looked up from a reader as I entered.

"Feeling better?" he asked.

"Much."

"I still can't believe what happened, Tanner. I was thinking of assigning you someone, say Brick or Rickets, to stay with you at all times. Until this is cleared up."

I chewed it over before throwing the idea out. "No, I'll be fine. My guard wasn't up, that's all. I do need something, however."

"Anything."

"A new pistol." I scowled. "Mine seems to be missing."

—

I decided to review the officer's records in more detail. I'd given them a cursory glance on the jumpship earlier, but had realized with perhaps my first feeling of trepidation that this case might be somewhat more difficult than most. I had a hunch that perhaps there was something in those files, somewhere, that might shed some light on things.

Manfred Fredericks, Captain, CCF, had an impeccable history since his first day in the service. He had served on a variety of CCF vessels, including a Colony Ship in the outer reaches and a number of posts throughout home system. There was nothing in the file to indicate hostility or repressed anger toward anyone on the station. He was calm, cool, and collected by every account — a perfect officer in the CCF.

Until his violation of regulations that got Jimmy killed, that is.

First Officer Avery Rickets had enrolled as a young cadet in the Canadian western provinces. He had been eight years old at the time. Serving in the cadets first, he moved into the CCF Youth before he finally joined the CCF at age eighteen. He was a driven officer. He sought challenges and tough assignments. He had distinguished himself as a Junior Grade Lieutenant at the age of twenty when all of the officers on the bridge of his ship — *The Raptor* — had died during a decompression emergency. Rickets pulled on a half-helmet amidst the chaos and took control while exposed to space *in only his CCF uniform.* The word dedication came to mind when I read his file. Astounding.

Lieutenant Belinda Bertram had a fine record. There was no sign of ambition or drive — she requested quiet postings with little challenge — but otherwise she was a good officer. She'd never make Captain, but she was competent. There had been no problems in her past.

Doctor Lars Malichauk had an interesting history. His early records reminded me of Avery Rickets. He was an outstanding biology student who moved into medicine, published in many journals — too many to count, actually — and even worked on the team that developed the vaccine to Crayle's disease that had sprung up in the mid twenty-third century. Following that triumph, he had worked as — my eyes widened momentarily as I read this — personal physician to the Council Member from Venus for a period of five years. Following that, he moved around the system and worked at smaller, quieter, and out-of-the-way outposts as Chief Physician. He had finally ended up in the middle of this mess on *SOLEX*.

I already knew about Lieutenant Shaheen Ramachandra, and what I didn't know I could have guessed. A brilliant schoolgirl, university student and engineer, the CCF had recruited her with promises of working on the biggest and most important engineering challenges in the galaxy. She was indeed in consideration for the Nobel Engineering Prize for the creation of the station's heat shield. Any thought of her being responsible for a violent crime seemed outrageous.

Lieutenant Brick Kayle had a spotty record. There were a few notes about his being late reporting to duty, and even one report of failure to show for an entire shift! Otherwise, he was competent and seemed to want to impress his superiors, despite his minor flaws as an officer. There was nothing else of note in his file.

Frustrated, I put the reader aside. The officers seemed to be exceptional in most regards. Whatever was going on at *SOLEX* was elusive, like a thread too thin to grasp. I knew I just had to keep looking. Eventually I would find something.

I had spoken to everyone but three of the scientists; I decided it was finally time to talk to them. I marched to Module F and soon stood in the cluttered corridor where earlier I had met Reggie Hamatsui, the atmospheric dynamics specialist. There were three other hatches there. I approached the nearest and, after a quick rap on the steel, entered the lab.

An elderly black woman looked up from a computer screen. "Who the hell are you?" Her round face was hard.

"Excuse me, I'm Kyle Tanner."

Her features relaxed after a moment. "I'm sorry," she said. "I had forgotten. You're here regarding Jimmy Chin's death."

"His murder."

She looked surprised. "Really? Have you determined that now?"

"Seems pretty clear."

"And now you're here to question me?"

"Just to find out if you know something that can help." I smiled to put her at ease. "It's only routine, don't worry."

"Well, I don't really have a lot of time."

"Won't take but a minute."

She sighed. "Very well. But do you mind if I keep working while you ask your questions?"

Damn. Another overly preoccupied scientist. Get her talking about the sun and she'd probably babble for hours.

"No, I guess not," I said.

"Shoot." She turned back to her computer.

"You're Sally Johnson."

"Right. Solar physicist."

"How well did you know Jimmy?"

"Not well at all. I don't really know anyone on this station but the other scientists and Lieutenant Kayle. He's the Scientist Liaison. He gets us what we need to research the sun and tries to keep the CCF off our backs."

I frowned, wondering what she meant by that. "I don't understand."

"Well, it's a military project, you know. Power generation and so forth. They're only allowing us here to research because our associated universities put up some cash. They want to know what we're doing at all times."

That seemed normal, I thought. After all, it was their station. "Your universities are helping fund *SOLEX?*"

"Well, a minor amount of money. I guess Jase Lassiter at Command Group figured we'd offset the cost a bit. Anyway, as a result they're constantly interfering."

"Do they think you could make an important discovery or something?"

She shrugged. "Maybe, but I don't really know what we could find that would be of any interest to them. We're mostly interested in the huge temperature increase in the corona. Temperature shoots up from six thousand to two million Kelvin in only two hundred kilometers! It's an —"

"Did you ever hear anyone talking badly about Jimmy?" I asked quickly. The incident with Reggie was still fresh in my mind; I needed to keep the investigation moving forward, and not spend an eternity here listening to details about the sun.

Her expression showed irritation at being interrupted, but she answered anyway. "Never. Everyone liked him. He was a practical joker. Made people laugh."

"Ever see any hostility on the station?"

"No. Just us scientists having the usual squabbles. Katrina, for instance, is always arguing with Reggie. He often monopolizes the instruments and takes scheduled time away from the others."

I asked her where she had been during the assault in my cabin.

"Doing research," she said. "Here. Same as always."

"Ever see anything ... weird? One person maybe accosting another?"

She looked up from her work. "What do you mean?"

"I don't know. Someone grabbing another person. Maybe forcefully."

She thought for a long moment. "No. I've never seen anything like that here."

—

The next lab belonged to Katrina Kyriakis. She had been with Brick during the attack in my quarters. She was in her forties with short brown hair, a thin neck, dark eyes, and aquiline features. She had an elegant beauty; definitely not what I would expect of a scientist.

Or a killer.

"Hello, Inspector Tanner," she said as I entered. Her eyes were penetrating; they seemed to size me up and instantly evaluate my characteristics and manner. She had a perceptive and intelligent aura about her, as if she knew more about me than even I did. She was a far cry from Reggie. I felt uncomfortable under her scrutiny.

I grunted. "Finally, a scientist who knows who I am."

"Don't feel slighted. Of course Captain Fredericks told us all you were coming; my colleagues were probably too engrossed in their work to remember."

"You got it."

"Well, I'll answer any questions you have. Jimmy was a great guy. I miss him."

The lab was the same as the others. Similar equipment, displays, and furniture. I searched for a place to sit before settling on a short bench attached to some sort of scanner. She continued to watch as I squeezed between some books and pulled out my datachip reader.

Everyone so far had stated how much they liked Jimmy. His death was unfortunate and now even more mysterious. He didn't seem to have any real enemies — except *perhaps* Brick Kayle. "Did you know him well?"

"No. But sometimes I ate in the common mess at lunch. I saw him fooling around with the others. Putting vinegar in coffee, mousetraps in cutlery trays. That sort of thing. It was fun."

"Even the officers enjoyed it?"

"Yes."

I asked her the same questions I'd asked Sally Johnson: had she ever seen anything weird on *SOLEX*? One person accosting another, and so on. She stared at me, puzzled.

"You mean an assault?"

"In a way."

She pursed her lips. "Can't say that I have."

"Where were you yesterday between 1400 hours and 1700 hours?"

"Chatting with Lieutenant Kayle. Have you met him? He's our liaison. Tries to keep the CCF off our backs."

I frowned. She was the second person who'd said that now in an hour. "How does the CCF bother you?"

She snorted and rolled her eyes. "They are constantly demanding reports on our work. But that's not so bad. The strange part is that they want proof! They want to see our computer logs, our sensor logs, our rough research work. It's been getting worse lately."

"Why is that odd? They're funding this project."

She looked pained. "It's just damn weird, and a pain in the ass to boot. I've been on many research projects, on a number of different stations. No one's ever asked for so much access to my work. All the other scientists will say the same thing if you ask them."

"You've been on other military stations? Or just ones funded by them?"

"Both. I'm not really sure why they're so interested in Sol." She shrugged. "It probably doesn't mean anything. It's just an irritant."

I turned my reader off. "That's it for the questions today. If I have anything else ..."

"Feel free to come by. I welcome the interruption, trust me." She grinned as I stepped away from her and left the lab.

Hmm. A relatively normal person for a change. She hadn't even talked about the sun.

The last scientist — and the only person on *SOLEX* I hadn't yet met — was Ling Lee, the sunspot physicist. She was Chinese and very pretty. I'd heard Reggie call her 'Lingly,' so I assumed that was the name she went by. She wore the requisite white lab coat, was thin — but not necessarily fit — and had black-framed glasses. She had the same attitude shared by Sally Johnson: I'm busy, don't bother me.

After the introductions were over, she said, "How long will this take?" I almost took a step back from the bluntness of her statement. Clearly she wasn't interested in social graces.

"Just a few minutes." I smiled to ease her tension. "Can I come in?"

She seemed to step aside reluctantly. Her lab was just as cluttered as Reggie's. Pasted to the bulkheads were posters and diagrams of the sun's structure. There was one whole section devoted to sunspots. I spent a few minutes studying them as Lingly straightened up her work area and found a place for me to sit.

My eyes flicked over the diagrams and I quickly absorbed the information. Sunspots were darker areas of the sun's surface that were only four thousand degrees Kelvin, two thousand degrees cooler than their surroundings. During sunspot maximums the sun put out more energy. At these times the Earth's atmosphere actually expanded and led to increased drag on close orbiting satellites. Skylab, an old satellite from the pioneering days, had crashed to Earth partly because of the sunspot cycle.

Lingly looked up and noticed what I was doing. "Fascinating, isn't it?" She sounded contrite, as if realizing how rude she had been only minutes earlier.

"Sure."

"It's my area. I've now spent more than half my life studying sunspots."

"Reggie suggested you were thinking of landing a probe on one."

She laughed abruptly. "He's a daydreamer. The surface isn't solid."

"But the temperature isn't too bad. You could design a heat shield for it, couldn't you?"

"Sure, for short periods of time. But don't forget that the corona's temperature is two million Kelvin, and the ship would have to pass through that. But what would it land on?" She shook her head. "No, there'd be no point. We're close enough here that I can do all the research necessary. You don't have to actually be on the thing to study magnetic fields."

"I see." I sat on the stool she had cleared for me. A pile of circuit boards, datachips, and papers now littered the deck around its legs. I went through the requisite questions and got all the same answers. Nothing out of the ordinary, no assaults, Jimmy was a nice guy, etcetera.

And then something interesting happened: she went on the offensive.

"Do you really think someone murdered him?" she asked. "I thought he died on an EVA. It was an accident."

"Someone cut his head and hands off. That person was trying to hide something."

"What could that possibly achieve? We already knew Jimmy was dead."

"He wasn't trying to hide the identity. There must have been something else."

She cocked her head. "But how do you know that?"

"There's no other explanation." I shrugged. "You see, this whole Investigator rap is pretty easy. It's simple deduction."

"But you don't actually know anything!" She glared at me. It seemed accusatory.

"No, but I know what it's not." I paused. "I also know someone attacked me yesterday."

She suddenly seemed embarrassed by her outburst. "Yes, I heard. I can't imagine anyone here being so violent."

I frowned. "Even after Jimmy lost his head and hands?"

"I see where you're going with that. But Jimmy was already dead."

"So you think it was a prank too."

"It's a possibility. But I do know this: cutting a dead person's head and hands off is a hell of a lot different than murder."

She was taking the same line Manny had originally. She didn't want to believe that there was a cold-blooded killer living on the same station as her. In a flash of insight, I suddenly realized why Lingly was behaving this way: she was scared. It was quite clear now. She didn't want someone else in the lab with her.

I gingerly stepped over the debris on the floor and moved to the hatch. "I'll catch whoever's responsible for this, murder or no," I said to her. "It's only a matter of time."

She remained silent as the hatch closed behind me. The chances of her being responsible for events on *SOLEX* seemed unlikely at best. Still, some people kept their inner demons closely guarded; tremendous will power kept them suppressed. Only in private did they emerge. No one, including colleagues and friends, ever knew about them, until the pain and hate and violence eclipsed everything else.

Then it was time to deal with them on their own terms: violently.

I marched out without another word. Their conversation was interesting, but they hadn't really said anything important. Clearly nothing that would indicate guilt. I'd certainly keep my eyes on them, but unless they said or did something a lot more incriminating, it would be rash to act until I knew exactly what was going on. Something Grossman said had piqued my curiosity though: he had referred to Jimmy's locker. Maybe I could find something of interest there, other than the suit.

The airlock staging area was well labeled and easy to find. A line of benches divided the room neatly in two, half-helmets hung from hooks, and lockers stretched along an entire bulkhead, each clearly labeled. At Jimmy's I threw the hatch aside and pulled out the crumpled vacsuit. In the lower back, far from where he could have patched it, was a rip four inches long. I fingered it absently. A knife or a sharp cutting tool hadn't made it; it was too jagged. It was small enough to patch. It didn't have any blood on the edges.

I pulled out my datachip reader and snapped a few pictures of the tear. Once finished with the suit, I examined the locker thoroughly. There were pictures of relatives and friends on the door, including three or four of the family dog. A baseball cap, a deck of cards, and some old socks were the only other items.

He had been a pretty nondescript guy.

I sat on the bench that faced the row of lockers and considered what I had found. The suit suggested it *had* been an accident after all. But if so, why tamper with his body? Why try to kill the Investigator? It still made little sense.

I stared at Jimmy's locker for a long time.

The crew slept in a common cabin in Module E that was long and narrow and illuminated with rows of harsh fluorescent lights. Each crewman had his or her own private space equipped with a few shelves, a trunk for personal items, and a small wardrobe to hang clothing. Jimmy's bunk and space had been left untouched. After I learned Malichauk had disposed of the body, I had been worried about Jimmy's belongings. Thankfully, I saw a completely normal space with the label 'Chin' stenciled on the edge of the bunk.

I spent an hour going through his things and found nothing out of the ordinary, except for one item: a pair of night-vision glasses.

I can't say it surprised me. In fact, I had predicted this very event: whoever had attacked me knew the glasses would incriminate him. In order to avoid detection, he ditched them where the blame could fall on someone else — in this case, a dead man.

Clever indeed.

At noon I entered the common messhall. The entire complement of *SOLEX* was present, including the scientists. I studied them silently, dismay setting in as I realized that they all sat with colleagues from their own sections.

The crew were together at the farthest table. Anna Alvarez, Bram O'Donnelly, Godfreid Grossman, and Larry Balch spoke quietly, their heads bowed as if sharing a story they wanted kept secret. They couldn't have looked more suspicious if they had tried. There were no smiles; just dull mutters in a distinctly annoyed tone.

The scientists were also together. Sally Johnson, Reggie Hamatsui, Ling Lee, and Katrina Kyriakis were discussing the finer points of the sun's electromagnetic field. Surprise, surprise.

At the third occupied table were the station's officers: Manny Fredericks, Bel Bertram, Brick Kayle, Lars Malichauk, and Shaheen Ramachandra. They looked up as I entered and motioned for me to join them. I did, but immediately decided to sit with the crew at dinner, and with the scientists at the meal after that. I wanted to get to know all of them. I would also try to rotate seating arrangements as much as possible.

I scrutinized everyone. A bruised cheek, a black eye, or a fat lip could easily give my assailant away. I was sure I had gotten a few solid hits in during the altercation. Unfortunately, the fight had left me mortally wounded, otherwise I would have examined everyone immediately.

There was nothing out of the ordinary. It didn't surprise me: a simple injection of priority nanos could easily fix any damage overnight. The knife wound to my liver only the day before was proof of that.

I ate lunch quietly and listened for anything unusual. There was nothing.

Back to the life support cylinder to reexamine the location in more detail. Anna's story of the assault that Jimmy had witnessed seemed odd, to say the least, and after the same thing had happened to me, I knew I had to have another look. The fans that droned everywhere on the station were louder here, punctuated by the odd creak and strain of irregular heating on the station's hull. I shot a look over my shoulder at one point, worried that someone was watching. But when I looked, there was no one there. Just shadows. They twisted along the curved ceiling bulkhead and obscured access panels, ducts, and pipes that led from the lower levels. The deck was a thick grate; I could barely see the equipment below due to the poor lighting. In fact, I could hardly see my hand in front of my face.

A couple of strong work lights, courtesy of Shaheen, helped immensely. I set them up around the carbon dioxide scrubbers, got to my hands and knees, and searched for anything out of the ordinary.

I found it almost immediately.

A dark irregular spot the size of a peanut. Shadows from the scrubber had hidden it earlier, but it was easy to see now: dried blood on the thick steel grate of the deck. It was pure luck it had landed where it did. Some of it had probably dripped down through the openings to the lower levels.

After I snapped some photos from different angles, I used a razor to gingerly scrape the droplet from the deck. I cut it in half and placed each segment into a tiny evidence bag. A sense of satisfaction coursed through me; it was my first real breakthrough since I had arrived.

In the clinic, Malichauk held the bag up to the light and peered at its contents. "Blood?"

"Yes."

"Whose?"

"That's what I want you to find out, Doc," I said, " but keep it quiet."

"Give me a couple hours." He moved to a counter and fiddled with some medical equipment. "Could take some time. It looks old."

I watched him silently and suppressed my immediate reaction. I didn't want the personnel to be wary around me, but still, his lack of effort pissed me off. I departed before I said something I might regret. I needed his cooperation, not his anger.

The investigation was beginning to pick up steam until I interviewed O'Donnelly, Balch, and Grossman, crewmen who all claimed to know nothing about Jimmy's death. They were tightlipped and uncooperative, but that didn't necessarily imply guilt. A lot of people in the military, especially grunts, or NOM's, hated officers. They had their own way of seeing things and didn't care what the ranking authorities said. So they grumbled one-word answers and didn't offer any information unless asked.

First Officer Rickets was next. He knew Captain Fredericks had disobeyed regs, but hadn't pushed him very hard about it. For the record, Rickets felt guilty and in fact knew the CCF could hold him partially responsible if a tribunal ever occurred.

He seemed a decent sort. Very prim and proper, he answered my questions willingly in stiff military formality. He wanted to know what was going on as much as I did. He wanted Jimmy's death put right.

Although technically he outranked me, I was here under the Council's direct authority. That guaranteed all Investigators the respect of a ranking officer, to ensure inquiries could continue unhindered.

"Avery," I asked him in the officer's mess, "did Jimmy Chin ever approach you about something he witnessed in the life support module?"

He looked surprised. "You know, he did."

I perked up immediately. "Really? What?"

"Something about two people having some sort of altercation. One grabbing another or something. I didn't pay much attention."

I frowned. This was odd. He should have followed regs, but like the Captain, he seemed to waver when it came to protocol. But while Manny's deviation from regs was visible — his playful banter with O'Donnelly was evidence of that — Avery's outward behavior seemed to be proper in every regard. To ignore a reported assault didn't seem consistent. "Why didn't you deal with it?"

He shrugged. "It could have been anything. No one was hurt; I checked afterward. No complaints. Nothing."

"Did you tell the Captain or any of the officers?"

"No."

I stopped the questioning for a moment and reflected on this piece of information.

"He was a good guy," he said, fixing his eyes to mine. "He didn't deserve what happened to him."

"How is life on *SOLEX*?" I asked, switching gears. "Have you noticed any other problems here?"

He looked puzzled. "Such as?"

"Fights, arguments, that sort of thing. Escalating behavior of any sort."

"No, not that I can think of. Just that one incident that Jimmy reported."

"Do you like it here?"

That startled him. "Well ..." He shifted in his chair, uncomfortable. "I've served on some great vessels. War vessels, if you get my meaning. Doing important things. But this ... it just seems so *ordinary*. I'm not sure why my superiors assigned me here."

"Are you bored?"

He snorted. "Nah — that comes with the territory. I guess I'm just wondering who I pissed off to get this assignment."

I thought for a minute before I made a sudden decision. "If it's any consolation, your record is flawless. Nothing out of the ordinary. There are no complaints or reprimands. You're probably just here for a short rotation as part of your training. I get the sense that they're grooming you for command."

His face seemed to light up, his worry eased. "Thanks for saying that. I appreciate your candor."

I finished the interview and sent him on his way. He was a genuine person, interested more in his career than with causing trouble. My gut instinct told me that he had nothing to do with this mess.

Shaheen and Bel Bertram had nothing new to offer. The lack of information in this case had grown frustrating. My initial optimism after finding the droplet of blood proved to be short lived. I felt I could crack the case eventually, but timing was crucial. I couldn't wait for another attempt on my life, or worse, on someone else's.

In addition, the pressure Bryce had placed on me by mentioning that the Council was involved didn't help matters. Interference of any sort was distracting, which is one of the reasons regs dictate all others to accord the Investigator the respect of a ranking officer. The meddling of those who tried to influence my decisions created the worst kind of situation for a proper and unbiased investigation.

Another annoyance was the distance between the crew and officers on the station. The crew didn't want to talk. So far Anna was the only one who had been of any real assistance.

But my interview with Brick Kayle shed some light on things.

I found him in his quarters reviewing the latest requests from the Command Group on Mercury. He didn't seem pleased; I could see the stress and anger on his face as soon as I entered.

"These damn guys are always asking for reports on the scientists," he said with a scowl. "I'm telling you, I've never seen anything like it."

His official duty was Scientist Liaison, but he was also the Council Rep for the station. Every ship, media office, school, hotel and bank — the list could go on forever — had someone operating as a Council Representative. They were constantly on the lookout for treasonous talk and dissidents. Freedom had mostly disappeared in our society, but in my eyes that wasn't necessarily a bad thing. The old empire was permissive and liberal; crime soared and morals had all but disappeared. I had no problem with the Council strong-arming all facets of society, but a small minority did. As a result, the military created the position of Council Representative; officers were selected carefully and became watchdogs for the government. It was possible that some people here had a grudge against Brick because of it.

A thought suddenly occurred: what were Jimmy's political leanings? Did he have a problem with Brick? That, combined with the issue of an unpaid debt, could have snowballed into something violent.

I brought my attention back to the interview. "Why do they want so much from the scientists?" I asked.

"Beats me. It's just so much pressure, and it places the scientists under a lot of stress too. Katrina and Sally are getting ready to rip me a new one. I'm not the one demanding all these reports, mind you, but as the one who actually has to ask for them ..." He ran a hand through his hair. "It's exasperating, that's all."

"Mind if I sit?"

"Sure, right here." He gestured to a chair and I lowered myself into it.

"Ever have a problem with Jimmy?" I asked.

He laughed heartily. "You get right to the point, don't you?"

My expression was wry. "Why waste time?"

"Sure, I understand. The answer is no."

"What were his political views?"

He looked thoughtful. "You mean because I'm a Council Rep? You think he was anti-Council?"

"Occurred to me."

A shrug. "He never said a bad thing about the government. Not to me, at least."

"What about to someone else?" People generally suspected Council Reps of spying on the people around them, perhaps even recording private conversations to use as evidence at trial.

"I don't spy on people," he said in a flat voice. His eyes were piercing.

I ignored his anger. "Have you ever had a problem with anyone on the station?"

"No, but I'm sure some people have a problem with me. Can't blame them, really. I'm used to it."

"Who in particular?"

He thought for a minute. "I'd say two of the crew, Grossman and Larry Balch. Also one of the officers, Bel Bertram."

"What did it amount to?"

"Oh, nothing much. A look or two. A sneer. Snapping at me in anger. That's about it." He slapped his knee. "But then there's the scientists. They're ragging at me all the time."

"About all the reports?"

"Yeah. I try not to get too upset. I know it's nothing personal. And I'd be just as upset as they are, trust me."

I consulted my reader. Here we go. I was about to reveal my only real motive for the crime. I had to be careful. "I'm curious about something, Brick. You asked Jimmy for money a while back."

His lips instantly pressed into a thin line and he examined me in a tortured silence. It was an abrupt transformation.

"How much did Jimmy lend you?" I asked, ignoring his body language.

"Fifty thousand," he growled after a beat.

I blinked. "That's a lot of money. What did you need it for?"

"Why is it important?"

"I heard you never paid it back."

"That's a lie!" he snarled. "I gave all that money back."

"That's not entirely true, is it? And you know what?" I leaned forward. "That's motive, Brick."

His features grew harder. "I asked him for a loan and I paid him back. That's it." I remained silent as he fidgeted. He was clearly uncomfortable with the direction the interview had gone. "I'm not talking about it anymore," he muttered under his breath. He spent a minute pretending to go over reports on his reader. I just stared. Finally, "What? I said I'm not talking anymore."

"Failure to cooperate implies guilt, Brick."

"I'm not guilty. I didn't do anything to Jimmy. I liked him, he was a nice guy. I hated how he died and what happened to his body, but I didn't do it."

I studied him and tried to decipher his outburst. He seemed to be telling the truth, but his refusal to answer didn't look good. I got to my feet. "I have one more question before I go."

He seemed to deflate, perhaps realizing how his behavior had made him look. His expression turned to one of regret. "Sure. Go ahead."

"What's your beef with Jase Lassiter?" Earlier, when I had mentioned the name, Brick had called him an asshole. I noted it at the time, but hadn't yet asked about it.

He was eager to answer this one. "He's a prick. All these requests for reports, he's the one responsible. He sits there on Mercury, in charge of our Command Group, and all he does is order me to produce more paperwork! What's the use?"

"That's it?" There was something more, I was sure of it.

"Well ..." He stumbled slightly. "There's Shaheen."

Ah. "What about her?"

He looked away, embarrassed. "I put some moves on her, a couple of months ago. She turned me down flat. She's one beautiful woman, let me tell you. I was hoping we'd been out here long enough, and that she'd be ready to move on, but I was wrong. Anyway, I heard he wasn't the nicest guy. A little abusive."

"She's seeing Lassiter?"

"Yup. She was, at least. She doesn't talk to me much anymore. They might be over, I don't know. Either way you cut it, the guy's a jerk."

I turned my reader off. "Okay, I'll leave you alone for now. But remember this: until you answer my questions about the money Jimmy lent you, you're my number one suspect."

He stared at me, mouth agape, and I stalked from his quarters without another word.

—

After the interview with Brick, I went to see Reggie Hamatsui, the scientist. I spoke with him for about two minutes, and he seemed incredulous as I told him what I needed. Afterward, however, he agreed to my request, and I gave him the other half of the blood droplet that I had found in the life support module. Five minutes later I had the results that I had come for.

There was something going on here bigger than anyone had thought.

— Chapter Ten —

The site of a murder is the most important location of any investigation. A host of physical evidence often remains following the crime, which can often result in a swift capture. In other cases, serial murderers stage the scene and manufacture evidence that may or may not be useful. They sometimes leave clues meant to point the Investigator in the right direction, and it can evolve slowly into a game of cat and mouse that the killer inevitably loses. It's usually just a matter of time before capture. Famous catches involve chases that last for months or even years, though those are extremely rare nowadays. In such cases, it is the game that the killer is after — his test of wits against the lead Investigator's. I had wondered whether the killer had manufactured this situation for such a purpose, but the answer was still a long ways off. I needed to know more about the original accident that had started the chain of events on *SOLEX*.

It was necessary to examine the location where Jimmy had died, but I'd waited until some of the interviews were out of the way. My original suspicion that it was actually an accident — and not murder — further lowered the importance of going outside the station. Now, however, there was no more putting it off.

The Captain assigned Shaheen as my partner, then gave me a couple of quick instructions before going EVA: I had to remain tethered to my partner and the station at all times; I had to set my alarm to remind me when to return; and I had to report to Doctor Malichauk immediately afterward for medicine to counteract the radiation exposure. All three rules were essentially non-negotiable at *SOLEX*, and I noticed Manny shoot me a glance as he ticked them off on his fingers. Perhaps it was the look in my eyes that got him, or maybe it was his own conscience.

Shaheen stood next to me in the airlock. I listened to the pump as it cycled. "How many hours have you accumulated?" I asked as I shifted nervously from foot to foot in the small enclosure.

"Twenty-five, so far. Not too bad." A hundred and fifty hours was the total allowable, according to Malichauk. "Close your visor," she suggested with a grin.

Embarrassed, I snapped the shield over my face and the airlock hatch slid open. I gasped and took an involuntary step back. The scope of the scene was fantastic; I almost couldn't comprehend what I was seeing. Flames and tongues of fire roiled over the sun's surface, weaving about like wheat in a windy field. It was thirty times larger than as seen on Earth! A solar prominence arced near the star's north pole; the flare was a small one, but I knew it was more than ten times the size of Earth. I looked at my wrist readout and saw the temperature soaring. Three hundred ... six hundred ... eleven hundred ... thirteen hundred ...

"My God," I muttered. It stopped climbing at close to fifteen hundred Kelvin. The vacsuit I wore, slightly thicker and more reflective than normal, was also equipped with a skintight coolant suit of the type that hadn't been worn for centuries. It could handle the temperature for a limited time. It was the radiation that was the danger. I had a warning label that changed from green to red as the levels built. When it reached critical exposure, it would display crimson and an alarm would sound in my helmet.

I turned and studied the station around me. It was magnificent. The series of nine connected cylinders, coated in gleaming white ceramic, floated serenely against the backdrop of inky space. The mass driver module above the cylinders ran the entire length of the station, and the microwave dish attached to Module D projected like a crow's nest high above the facility. The orange glow of the sun flickered over everything, glittering like a devilish ghost in the night.

I swallowed. Being outside *SOLEX* was part magical and part nightmare, and I wasn't yet sure which had the greater effect on me.

With an effort, I turned back to Shaheen. We hitched our tethers to a safety rung on the hull and swung out of the airlock.

"This way," she said.

We grabbed the rungs and pulled ourselves along the docking port cylinder and over to Module D. We reached a strut that connected the starboard collector array to the station and clipped our tethers to a recessed eyebolt in the hull.

"What's this?" I asked. "I've never seen anything like it before."

"We can't spend too long out here, so speed is of the essence." Her voice sounded tinny in my helmet. "This bolt is in a track that runs the length of the collector's support structure. We can get out there faster this way."

She pushed a button on her suit's control panel and the eyebolt began to move. Our feet dangled behind as it dragged us along. The two solar collectors were simply *massive*. Each was two hundred meters long, constructed of ceramic-coated steel struts and shimmering solar panels. If the struts were the skeleton of the collector, the panels were its flesh. The eyebolt moved along a track in the central strut that stretched the length of the collector. I floated above an array of solar panels the size of *two football fields*, and there was another one of equal size connected to the other side of the station. Incredible.

Within minutes we had traversed the entire collector. It would have taken us an hour of spacewalking to achieve the same feat.

"Jimmy was out about as far as you can go. I can't believe he didn't have a partner."

"Don't hold it against Manny," she said. "He knows what he did was wrong. He's broken up about it; I can tell."

"Someone died because he didn't follow regs."

She snorted. "Regs. Sometimes they work, sometimes they don't. You can't have standardized regulations for every place in the entire Confederacy! Imagine using the same ones here at *SOLEX* as some colony light years away."

I scowled. "Come on, Shaheen. You can't deny that EVA's are standardized for safety. Never go out alone, it's drilled into us right from training. If anything, EVA regs should be more rigorous here."

She huffed but didn't respond.

"You don't agree?" I pressed.

"I guess. I just feel bad for Manny. Don't mind me."

Do you feel bad for Jimmy? I thought, irritated.

She pointed to a nearby electrical access console. "That's it there. We got a warning light on that panel. It could have been anything from a short to a localized failure in the heat shield to what it really was."

"And that was?"

"The sensor failed; Jimmy had to replace it."

I'd had the notion that the warning had been deliberate in order to lure Jimmy outside the station. The idea, however, was ludicrous. First, it meant the killer knew Manny would assign Jimmy, and second, it meant the killer knew the regs would be cast aside and that Jimmy would be on his own.

We were at the edge of the collector, drifting near a precipice that overlooked the incredible furnace below. A waist-high console abutted a narrow rail that ran the length of the edge. "Where was he when he reported the rip?"

She gestured at the console. "He'd just finished working on it."

I removed my datachip reader from a thigh pocket and snapped a few pictures. I looked back at the station; my visor depolarized immediately as I turned from the sun.

Something suddenly occurred to me. "Surveillance was gone during the accident, right?"

"For twelve hours."

"So if the cameras stopped recording just before the accident —"

"Which they did."

"— then they should have been back on at about 0100 hours that night."

"Seems right."

"So we know that the mutilation of the body must have occurred between the time that Malichauk left the clinic at dinner until 0100 hours that night. A seven hour period. It couldn't have occurred while Malichauk was still in the clinic."

"What's your point?"

"The Captain said no one could have had an alibi during a twelve hour period. But what about a seven hour one?"

"So?" She sounded puzzled.

"Well, did Manny even check for alibis? Maybe he just assumed. Perhaps I can narrow the suspects down. My list is pretty big right now," I admitted, embarrassed.

She was unconvinced. "Sounds weak."

"Well, it's something, anyway." I turned back to the sun and watched the immense ball of fury in silence. It was unnerving. The scale was almost impossible to accept. All the mass in the solar system could be placed in there, with lots of room to spare.

I tore my eyes from it with difficulty and looked at the radiation indicator on my wrist. It was now light yellow. "Let's get out of here," I murmured.

—

Checking in with Malichauk after the EVA, I showed him the tab from the vacsuit and he smiled.

"You didn't take too much, don't worry," he said. "What did you think of it out there?"

"Daunting."

"Being so close to Sol?"

"Yes. Ever been out?"

"Not here."

He prepared the medicine — just a few tiny pills — and I popped them in my mouth. They were bitter, but thankfully went down easily.

"Did you figure out whose blood that was?" I was referring to the droplet I had found in the life support module.

He turned to me, a perplexed look on his face. "Are you trying to test me or something?"

My brow creased. "No. Why?"

"Because I couldn't make a match."

I paused, startled at his answer. "What do you mean?"

"It was old blood. It could have been here since construction."

I pondered that for a long moment. Then, "You think it's from a construction worker or an engineer?"

"Probably. It doesn't belong to anyone here, that's for sure."

—

I decided to check everyone's alibi for the period when Jimmy's body was in the clinic's freezer and surveillance was down. The time was from 1800 hours to 0100 hours, during which Malichauk had been off doing something else rather than performing the autopsy. Most people had gone to sleep — or back to their cabins, alone — at 2200 hours. Before that, the crew had socialized together, the officers had socialized together, and the scientists had studied the sun by themselves in their respective labs. No one had an alibi; Manny had been correct.

Still not much progress, but at least it was worth a try.

—

It had been a busy third day on *SOLEX*. I kept to myself at dinner, spoke to no one, but I watched the personnel closely. Everyone was there again, including the scientists, although they grumbled a bit about being taken away from their work.

The other officers shot a few looks at me, no doubt wondering how the investigation was progressing. They thankfully held their questions.

After the meal, I marched straight to my cabin with the intention of falling asleep. I removed my new pistol, which I now carried everywhere I went, and placed it under my pillow. Sleep didn't come quickly, however. I couldn't stop thinking about Jimmy Chin and how he had died.

I listened to the murmur of the ventilation fans and considered everything I had discovered since arriving at *SOLEX*. I had a single piece of physical evidence, but Malichauk had jettisoned the rest of it. I had nothing else to help me. Nothing except ...

The body.

The thought reminded me of the pictures Malichauk had taken of Jimmy's corpse. I had forgotten about them. I sat up in the darkness and fumbled along the side table for my reader. It was never easy viewing the remains of a grisly death, and Jimmy's body was no different. The signs of decompression were all there: the cracked and bloody skin, the intestines spilling from the anus, the flesh blackened from freezing and/or burning. Someone had indeed removed the head with an incredibly sharp blade — perhaps the very one used against me. The hands were missing; I could see the white knobs of the radius and ulna that protruded from the stumps.

I studied the next set of pictures intently. They showed the back of Jimmy's torso and legs.

I lay back in my bunk and listened to the fans in the darkness. It took two more hours for sleep to come.

— Chapter Eleven —

The next day there were two murders.

Anna Alvarez, while retrieving some supplies for Sally Johnson, the solar geophysicist, discovered the bodies in a cargo bay in one of the supply modules. She couldn't tell who they were at first, because their heads and hands were missing.

I called an emergency meeting in the common mess. Reggie Hamatsui, the Japanese scientist, and Bel Bertram, the station's Information Officer, didn't show. People stood about uncertainly, perhaps torn between anger at the death of two of their friends and the fact that one of them was a killer. I noticed that they had put space between one another and watched their comrades with narrowed eyes. A few had even put the bulkhead at their backs, perhaps in understanding of exactly how dangerous the situation really was.

One of them was a killer.

We were completely isolated.

And worst of all, I hadn't exactly filled them with a sense of security.

Lingly, the Chinese scientist, cleared her throat and said in a trembling voice, "But why would someone do this?"

"It doesn't make sense," Katrina said. "No one's had a problem with anyone else on the station."

"Now come on," Sally snapped, clearly angry. "You and Reggie fought all the time about access to the station's sensors."

Katrina's eyes flashed. "Now just a —"

"Hardly a reason to kill someone," Manny said, trying to defuse an imminent fight. He glared at Sally. Katrina looked like she wanted to say more, but another look from the Captain stopped her too.

Shaheen eyed me. "There doesn't seem to be a reason for any of the deaths, including Jimmy's."

"I haven't found anything concrete," I responded, "but there usually is."

"You're just a typical officer," Godfreid Grossman growled. "You'll try to pin this on a NOM. I know how it works."

"I'll pin it on whoever's responsible," I said.

"Right." His eyes were piercing.

Anna spoke up. "Don't insult him just because he's an officer. He's trying to help Jimmy."

The other scowled but didn't respond.

I ground my teeth in frustration. I wished the crew would stay silent unless spoken to, as on every other military installation, but this was obviously a unique situation. I had to allow some latitude, as did the Captain, but if the insubordination continued, I would have to deal with it.

"All right," Rickets said. "What do we do?"

He deferred to me, even though he was the First Officer. He knew this was my area of expertise; for him, these were uncharted waters.

"I need to examine the bodies," I said. "We'll have to move them to the clinic."

Manny pointed at Larry Balch and Grossman. "You two can do that."

"Aye, sir," they answered immediately, but neither looked happy.

I said, "I'll need to spend an hour going over the crime scene first. That cylinder is out of bounds until I say otherwise." Manny grunted approval. I continued, "When I'm done, I want to question everyone again. Stay here in the common mess until that time. No one leaves."

There were a lot of unhappy looks, especially from the scientists, but no one objected.

"Why wouldn't someone just get rid of the whole body?" Katrina asked. "Why just the head and hands? What's the purpose?"

"The killer is trying to hide something," Brick said.

"What?"

"Who knows?" Malichauk muttered. "He's probably just sick."

Silence fell over the group; they were terrified. It wasn't just Lingly anymore. That might be a good thing, however; I knew that they could become hypersensitive to any perceived danger, and that meant it would be more difficult for the killer to make his next move. He would either pull in his head like a turtle and refuse to draw attention to himself, or, he would make a mistake.

"I promise to find who did this," I said.

"You've been trying for four days now!" Grossman blurted. "What have you been doing?"

"Mister Grossman!" Manny barked. "He is a lieutenant in the CCF, and you will afford him the required courtesies! Is that understood?"

He withered under the Captain's glare. "Aye, Captain."

The crewman was behaving with more hostility than I had seen since my arrival. News of the murders had affected everyone differently, but the most marked change was in Grossman.

I turned to Manny. "I'll let you know as soon as I've examined the crime scene and the bodies."

"Hurry up," he whispered. His worry was clear; the personnel were being pushed past normal extremes. He and I both knew it was important to retain control over them at all times, otherwise chaos would take over — a situation the killer could conceal himself in with little difficulty.

I marched to the cargo bay and the two bodies. Balch and Grossman accompanied me; both turned pale when they saw the carnage within. I ordered them to wait outside until I was done, and to keep each other in sight at all times.

It was obvious the murders had occurred here. There was blood all over the deck, liters and liters of it, but no trail led into the cavernous bay. I searched the surrounding area for the weapon with no luck. It could be anywhere on the station by now.

Bel Bertram's corpse was on its stomach with arms outstretched. Her legs were crumpled under her torso and her uniform was stained dark. Reggie was on his back, one arm folded haphazardly across his body. His legs were twisted together on the deck; the right one looked broken. Blood pooled at the severed neck, collected under his body, and ran in a stream toward a nearby drain. It merged with blood from Bel's body before it dribbled into the station's recycling system.

There were no boot marks in the blood, no sign of the murderer at all. The crime scene was clean. The guy was thorough and smart, that much was certain.

I snapped multiple pictures of the cargo bay and the bodies. Then I called Balch and Grossman to move the corpses to the clinic.

The two crewmen laid the bodies on adjacent procedures tables; the corpses were now naked and pale. The sound of blood dripping into the catch basins under each table was disturbing and brought home why I was at *SOLEX*. Three deaths now, two of which had occurred right under my nose. It didn't look good; so far my investigation had produced more questions than answers.

I sent Grossman and Balch back to the common mess. I wanted the entire station's complement together, watching each other, until I was done.

I bent to my work. Thankfully, the previous eleven years had desensitized me to this sort of thing. Disembowelment, decapitation, torture, and mutilation no longer affected me. These weren't people anymore, they were just meat. There was no more pain, no more suffering. That was all done with. The only thing left for me to do was to locate the person responsible for the bloody messes I scraped off the streets and decks of the places I traveled.

The killer had dismembered both Reggie and Bel. That much was clear. But more telling were the knife wounds in their torsos. Here were two obvious examples of murder — not just mutilation after accidental death.

Bel had a knife wound in her upper back. The blade was probably the same one that had severed their heads and hands: eight to ten inches long, not serrated, very sharp. It had penetrated her heart and killed her within moments. She'd probably been stabbed, fell face down on the deck, then dismembered in her dying seconds. Her still-beating heart had managed to propel some blood from her carotid artery onto the deck a meter in front of her. There was no evidence of a struggle: the killer had approached her from behind.

There were two knife wounds in Reggie. The first was in the lower torso. His small intestine was severed and the intestinal contents had spilled into his body cavity. Had he survived, it would have caused massive infection. The second wound was in his chest. The knife had penetrated deep into his heart. What was most interesting about Reggie, however, were the knife wounds on both his forearms. If his hands had still been attached, I would have seen slash wounds on the palms, I had no doubt of it.

He had fought back. He had seen his attacker. He'd watched Bel die, had probably backed away, terrified, then belatedly realized what was happening. He'd attempted to defend himself, but unarmed and scared, he hadn't had a chance.

There was nothing else of interest in or on the bodies. No illnesses, abnormalities, or distinguishing characteristics. Using the diagnostic computer, I placed the time of death at 0630 hours that morning. Less than three hours ago.

I took multiple photos of both bodies, front and back, and moved them to the freezer.

I grabbed Shaheen from the common mess and Manny approached to ask about the situation. I shrugged him aside with a grunt. It perhaps wasn't the most tactful way to treat the Captain of the facility, but his curiosity could wait for now. There was work to be done.

Shaheen and I marched to the station's command center; she peppered me with questions the whole way. I remained tightlipped. She shot me a sideways glance, huffed once, then said no more.

We soon entered what was essentially *SOLEX's* bridge. Control consoles ringed the small enclosure; they displayed vital station statistics and the status of the environmental systems, power generation, the continuous microwave beam to Earth, artificial gravity, and so on. Multiple display screens showed views outside the station, the sun visible in most of them. It was so huge that I couldn't see beyond it; the entire globe of the fiery star filled each screen. Orange sunlight flickered around the command center like firelight.

"I want to see the surveillance in that cargo bay," I said.

Shaheen went to the nearby security console and called up the datafile. She tapped on the keyboard for several minutes before she frowned in consternation. "No luck. It's been shut off."

As I expected. "For what time period?"

"From 0600 hours until now."

I blinked. "It's still off?"

"It's been shut down permanently, Tanner," she said, fixing me with her blue eyes. "Whoever did this knows our systems well. I can't get it back on. Surveillance is gone."

Back in the common mess, I ordered everyone to the far bulkhead where I could keep a watchful eye on them. The scientists moved quickly without objection. The officers were a little more hesitant, but did so to set an example for the others. The crew, on the other hand, collectively grumbled under their breath as they slowly shuffled into position.

I didn't speak until their backs were against steel.

Finally I said, "The killer attacked Bel from behind and she died quickly. Reggie fought back but didn't have much of a chance. They died this morning at 0630 hours. I couldn't find the weapon, the hands, or the heads." I studied them silently for a minute, watching their expressions change as they absorbed what I had said. Most registered shock, then anger or fury. Grossman and Balch were still pale and didn't show much expression other than sickness after what they had seen.

Lingly spoke up. "How could someone get rid of ... of ..." She trailed off.

"The body parts? There are a number of places. They could be in the garbage chutes right now." They cringed at that; knowledge that human remains were now part of their recycling system was a pretty foul thought. "The killer could also have ejected them into space."

"But how?" Anna Alvarez asked.

"The scientists have ejection chutes in their labs." I turned to Lingly. "Of all people, you should have known that."

She looked stunned at being singled out. "I guess so, yes, but I just associate those chutes with hazardous materials! I couldn't imagine stuffing a human head —" She choked off the thought.

"There's one in the clinic too," Malichauk said in a meek tone.

Of course I knew that, Reggie had told me two days earlier. "There is indeed," I said, watching the doctor. "But there isn't a chute big enough to get rid of the bodies."

"There's the airlock."

"Too difficult to drag them there. Messy."

"Are you suggesting a scientist did it?" Sally snapped. "Just because the labs have ejection chutes?"

I searched the faces that glared back at me. I had clearly incensed Sally, Katrina, and Lingly. I raised a hand to calm them. "I didn't say one of you did it. I said *someone* could have used those chutes to dispose of the ... parts."

"We don't lock the hatches to the labs, Tanner," Lingly said. "We never have."

"And I never said you did." Their anger slowly subsided and I sighed. "Look, someone on this station is guilty. I'm not going to accuse anyone until I know for sure who it is."

I gestured for Manny to accompany me into the corridor where we could speak in private. He looked shaken up. Sweat beaded his forehead and he seemed pale.

"What are your procedures for a situation like this?" he asked in a whisper.

I winced. "Truthfully? I've never been in one."

"Never?" He was incredulous.

"Usually I chase a killer when they have a place to run. I've never backed one into a corner like this and not known who it is. Most often they make a mistake and I make a capture. In this situation, who knows what he'll do? His behavior is escalating, there's no doubt of that."

"Why do you think he killed Bel and Hamatsui?"

I frowned. "I don't think it was random. There's more going on here than three murders."

A beat, and then, "What do you mean?"

"I can't tell you until I know everything. But there is definitely a reason for the killer's method."

He grew furious. "This is my station, Tanner. I demand to know —"

"I can't tell you. It's as simple as that."

"Why? Because the Council sent you? Because you're the best at this job?"

"Because frankly, Captain, you could be the killer."

He looked down and saw my hand on my pistol. His jaw dropped. "You're serious."

"Absolutely."

He stared at me in shock for a minute before he finally backed down. "I guess you are." He exhaled. "So what do we do?"

"You're the Captain, you're still in charge. The orders must come from you or we'll lose control. They're all scared, you can see that."

"Yes."

"We can't let them fall apart." I leaned forward until I was an inch from his face. "I'm on the right track, I can feel it," I said. "You have to trust me."

A long moment. Then, "Okay," he muttered. "I'll follow. But you better figure out what the hell is going on, and fast. Now, what do you want?"

It's true that I had never been in a situation like this before, but the procedures seemed obvious. "Pair them up. Never let them separate. Tell them to keep an eye on their partner at all times. Let them go about a modified work schedule. All meals continue together, here, in the common mess. All free time too. At night we'll confine them to their cabins and lock their hatches."

He blinked. "Do you think that's enough?"

I hesitated. "We have no other choice."

—

I let Manny spell the rules out to his people. They mostly accepted what had to be done, all but Grossman, who continued to complain.

"These rules are his, aren't they?" he snarled.

"They're the rules you're going to follow, *Crewman*," Manny said in a flat, angry tone. "And that's enough of that." Grossman stopped talking, but this time didn't fall back so meekly. He stared at me for a long while; I pointedly ignored him and tried to concentrate on my thoughts.

We ate lunch together. The mood was like death. You could hear a pin drop as we consumed our rations in silence. I sat with Sally, Katrina and Lingly, the three remaining scientists. After a few minutes, they began to talk about Reggie. What a nice man he had been, and so forth.

"How often did you two argue?" I asked Katrina.

She glared at me. "Don't look for motive where this is none. And that's just stupid. Sure we had differences, but I was in the right every instance. He constantly ran into my allotted time. That would make anyone mad and cause any number of arguments. But it's not enough to kill one person, let alone two. Or three!"

I nodded. "I agree, actually. I'm just asking you to be honest with me about your feelings."

Her nostrils flared, but her tone calmed somewhat. "Well now you know. He pissed me off sometimes, but I'm going to miss him. This is horrible."

"We're all going to miss Reg," Sally said, touching her arm.

Lingly said, "Tanner, did he — I mean — did he die fast? Was he in pain?" She blanched when the other women turned to her. "Is that wrong for me to ask? I'd feel terrible if he suffered."

"He didn't suffer," I said. "He fought back bravely, but died quickly. He felt pain, but likely for only a few seconds." His killer had probably been strong, I wanted to add. Just like the guy who had attacked me. Whoever it was, it was no woman.

—

Afterward, still in the common mess, I pulled Rickets and Manny aside. "What was Bel Bertram doing in the supply module at that time?" I asked. I could believe that Reggie would be there; the scientists were always grabbing equipment for their experiments. But the crew were still waking up then, so Reggie had probably gone down by himself to get what he needed. But why had Bel Bertram been there?

Rickets pulled out his reader and punched up the officers' duty schedules. As First Officer, he doled out the weekly assignments. "She was supervising the storage inventory today; been doing it for the past couple of days. She probably wanted to get an early start."

"Perhaps. Or maybe she was involved in something dangerous."

"Ridiculous," Manny said. "Belinda? Involved in anything other than her duty? Not possible."

Rickets said in his deep voice, "I agree, Tanner. Bel went by the book. She frowned on non-regulation activities."

"Like sending a man on EVA by himself?"

There was a long pause while Manny glared at me; his face burned red. "For the record," he grated, "she took me to task every time I broke regs."

I studied his eyes and realized instantly how crass the comment had sounded. Perhaps I was being too harsh with him; there was no need to dwell on his mistake, and bringing it up was petty. "Sorry," I said. "I really am." I needed to focus my attention on the killer, not on decisions the Captain now regretted.

He looked angry, but gave me a curt nod anyway. "No harm done."

Another short and uncomfortable silence ensued and eventually Rickets cleared his throat. "It's possible she was just in the wrong place at the wrong time."

I turned to him. "If that's so, then Reggie was the intended victim." And if that were the case, then I must have been closer to the truth than I realized.

—

The notion that Reggie might have been the target encouraged me to go have another look around his lab. Malichauk, the person partnered with me, tailed me on the way to Module F.

"What are we doing down here?" he asked in a quiet voice. He seemed jittery, looking this way and that. He kept falling behind while sending darting glances over his shoulder, then had to take a few quick steps to catch up. I kept my back to him as I marched quickly along, but I made sure to keep a hand on my pistol, just in case.

I found the usual clutter inside Reggie's lab. I looked around and almost immediately located what I was after: the blood sample I had given him two days earlier. I gestured to the other side of the lab and told Malichauk to search in that direction.

"What am I looking for?" he asked.

"Anything out of the ordinary," I muttered.

"But I don't think there's anything important here," he said as he rooted around a work bench. "It's all solar stuff."

I grabbed Reggie's notes and the blood sample — now pressed between microscope slides — and shoved it all in my pocket. I scanned the entire lab thoroughly, but found nothing more of interest.

"Let's go," I said.

"Where?" He looked at me, confused and unsure about what I was doing.

"Back to the common mess." I needed to review these notes.

—

I removed the papers from my pocket and spread them out on the table before me. The only other person in the room was Shaheen Ramachandra, who I'd asked to help interpret Reggie's work. I'd sent Malichauk back to the clinic with Shaheen's partner, Brick.

"What are we looking at?" she asked as she studied the papers.

"Reggie's notes about some blood that I found in life support."

She looked perplexed. "Blood? What was it doing there?"

I related the story Crewman Anna Alvarez had told me, about how Jimmy had witnessed the bizarre altercation in the darkness of the module.

"Sounds really odd," she said, her brow creased.

"You're telling me." I didn't mention that during the attack in my quarters, my assailant had done the same thing: gripped my arm with incredible pressure for no apparent reason. I flattened the papers on the table. "Let's see what we've got." I had taken the precaution of removing the sheet that indicated whose blood it was; no need for her to see that just now.

She skimmed the papers quickly. "Looks like there's a missing page. It might have told us who the blood belonged to."

"Hmm," I murmured.

She flashed a look at me before she continued. "This is weird. Reggie found a nano in the blood drop. A single nano."

"What kind?" I asked, startled. "Medical?"

"No ... according to this it's a nano of a type he's never seen before."

I scowled. "Come on. It must be one that's used frequently on the station. What are they used for here?"

"Injuries, mostly. When you were stabbed, for instance, Lars injected you with priority nanos. They travel to any wounds in the body, repair them, then migrate to the bladder and leave naturally. Malichauk also would have nanos in his stores for tumor elimination, organ transplants, vision correction, and so on. The medical uses are limitless. But that's not what's strange. This is not a medical nano."

"An engineering one then."

"We use them for manufacturing processes, true, though not here. But this isn't one of them either."

"Then what is it?"

She pointed at Reggie's writing. "'Completely foreign technology,' he says."

I absorbed that. "And it was in the drop of blood I gave him?"

"Yes."

"Completely foreign," I repeated.

She looked at me with fear in her eyes. "Tanner, what the hell is going on here?"

Part Three: Infection

Investigator's Log: Lieutenant Kyle Tanner, Security Division, Homicide Section, CCF

The patch on my wrist had turned orange. My exposure was building. Soon too much damage would be done; already I was bleeding internally, and I knew the effect would magnify enormously in just a short amount of time. My options were limited; the sun was bearing down on me, frying me with its enormous heat and radiation, and here I was floating in the void wearing only a vacsuit with three spare oxygen bottles.

Oxygen! My heart thudded in my chest as I realized that only a few seconds of the suit's original supply remained. My alarm had already sounded; somehow I had missed it. Was my hearing going now as well? I grunted in frustration and switched all alarms to visual; I couldn't miss the flashing light inside my helmet unless my sight went too.

I sucked every last breath I could from the bottle, straining even after the oxygen monitor read zero. As my lungs heaved in agony and my sight began to grow dim, I quickly attached the vacsuit's auxiliary hose to my first spare, fingers fumbling slightly with the valve. The fresh air filled the helmet and I inhaled tremendous gulps. Belatedly, I realized I might have just made a mistake. I should have made the transition smoothly, without the need to take in such huge breaths. Ultimately, I had probably used more oxygen than I saved. Shit.

I was now officially down to twelve hours, but it wouldn't matter with this radiation; I probably wouldn't make it to the next bottle unless I did something fast.

Something was tickling the back of my mind about the radiation. Something about the oxygen and the radiation ...

I needed some sort of shield, something to keep the high speed particles from damaging too much flesh. A sheet of lead would be nice, but of course I didn't have that. All I had were a few tools, a currently dismantled communit, and some spare oxygen bottles.

Some spare bottles ...

Of course! I wanted to kick myself; I couldn't believe I hadn't thought of it as soon as I launched from *SOLEX*.

I yanked the cord and hoisted the oxygen tanks up to chest level. I tore a tether from my thigh pocket and strapped the canisters together, side by side. The nylon material was thin but sturdy; I wrapped it around the top of each, wrenched it tight, then did the same at the bottom of each. The tethers were long and useful for any number of emergencies, but I doubted vacsuit manufacturers had ever predicted this.

At last I finished and looked at my creation in appreciation; I had connected the bottles into something of a raft. It was about a meter long on two sides, and half that on the other two. It was just large enough to protect me from some of the dangerous solar wind. The canisters weren't lead, but they'd have to do.

The skintight refrigeration suit constricted me so much that it was difficult to move. It took great effort to pull my knees up; I couldn't believe the original astronauts had actually worn something like this in a place as cool as Earth orbit. I finally managed to poke my feet into a loop I had left in the tether that bound the bottles. It was like a single large snowshoe made of three stubby pipes. Straightening my legs, I pushed the shield 'downward' and placed it between myself and the sun. I bent at the waist to look and ...

It blocked most of the star from view. Holy shit. It had worked. Well, better than empty space would, at least.

I'd bought myself some more time. Now I just had to get this damn communit working.

I turned the recorder back on as I continued to work on the transmitter. "The discovery — "

— Chapter Twelve —

— of the nano threw a wrench into the entire investigation. Should I continue with the belief that someone was killing for the traditional reasons: personal gain, revenge, or hatred? Or was something else going on that I hadn't anticipated? Something completely alien and therefore impossible to predict? It might be impossible to decipher the clues, because they simply didn't fit into pre-established paradigms. It was a tricky predicament.

Could anyone solve this? Could Michael Flemming?

I sighed in the darkness of my quarters. Michael Flemming, dead because I took too long to see a simple connection between two people. Ever since his murder, I hadn't felt right. It had thrown me off, made me question myself. And if I failed to make the connection here on *SOLEX*, there could be more deaths. I had narrowed the number of suspects down, but it was impossible to watch everyone all the time. If I took too much longer …

Then I'd be to blame. Again.

—

It was the day after the discovery of Reggie, Bel, and the nano. I had needed time to digest the new information, the new deaths. I met with Shaheen in her quarters before the work day began to see if she could help with the problem. I knew one thing was certain: I had to learn more about the nano. Why was it in the drop of blood? What was its purpose? What category was it: medical or manufacturing? How much did Reggie know, and was that the reason he was killed?

He had included a microscope photo and a few words below it scrawled in red letters: *"Nano in blood? Unknown type. Completely foreign technology."*

"That's it?" I asked as I looked at the notation.

Shaheen flipped a few of the pages. "Most of this is about his solar research."

"Yeah, I just grabbed a bunch of stuff near the blood sample." I looked again at the photo. "Why the picture?"

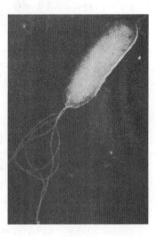

She peered over my shoulder. "It's a bacterium."

"Recognize it?"

"I guess ... but what would he be doing with a picture of bacteria?"

It was cylindrical with tiny filaments that trailed from one end. I thought back to my days in academy biology; they were called *flagella*. The bacteria used them for locomotion.

She said, "He found a nano in the blood but didn't photograph it."

"This bacteria must be more important than the nano."

It all seemed fishy. I gave the blood sample to Reggie to match for me. Apart from doing that, within it he also identified a nano and a bacterium. Something about this knowledge got the man murdered.

Excluding myself, there were now twelve people on the station. One was a murderer, killing not for his own reasons, but now to protect his identity. The closer I got, the more dangerous he would become. It was nothing new for me, but I couldn't let collateral damage get too out of hand.

I looked at Shaheen from the corner of my eye. Asking her to help no doubt put her in incredible danger. Part of me wanted to ignore the feelings that had stirred inside me. Another part needed her help to solve the mystery. She knew more about the station than I, and I needed every possible advantage over the killer. She would also be able to help me decipher this new problem.

"I need access to the station's medical database," I said finally. "I need to find out what kind of bacteria that is."

"Sure, no problem. We can go anywhere, really. Your reader can access the station's network. You can stay here."

I discarded the idea almost immediately; I felt it would be better to be on my own turf.

"My quarters," I said.

She flashed me a coy look. "Really?"

"Don't worry, I won't try anything. Jase Lassiter seemed like a nice guy." I referred to her relationship with the leader of the Command Group on Mercury. Brick had told me about it earlier, during his interview.

She appeared startled. "How'd you find out about that?"

"It's my job, Shaheen." She looked like she wanted to say more, but held her tongue.

I made sure to lock the hatch behind us. Allowing someone access to our personal space was now out of the question; it was too tempting a target for the killer, who could do anything from planting incriminating evidence to laying in wait, hoping to kill again.

As it currently stood, the pairings were: me and Shaheen, Officers Manny and Rickets, Officers Brick and Malichauk, Crewmen Grossman and Balch, and O'Donnelly and Aina. The three scientists, Sally, Katrina, and Lingly, were together. It wasn't a perfect system; the killer could still take out his partner and move on to dispatch others as well, but it was the best we could do. I assumed the three scientists would be safe, but other than that, everyone else could currently be in danger.

In my quarters, we accessed the medical database and called up the information file on *Bacteria*. It was huge; gigabytes of information scrolled rapidly across the screen.

"This is too much," I said. "I just want to know what bacterium Reggie photographed."

"Okay," Shaheen said. "I'll bring up the gallery." The screen immediately filled with images and she peered at them intently. "According to this, there are essentially three shapes of bacteria. You've got the rod, the ball, and the helical. Which one is ours?"

I glanced at Reggie's photo. "Rod."

"That narrows it down a bit," she said. "But there are still thousands of types here."

"Can we just have the computer compare for us?"

She snorted. "Good idea. I should have thought of that." She snapped a photograph of the image on the paper and hit a few keys on the reader. "It'll take just a ... there it is."

I eyed the results. "It says there's no match. How can that be?"

She shook her head, perplexed.

I frowned. No matter how many pieces I put together, the puzzle kept getting larger. I rarely came up against such a difficult case. Usually the clues were all there, and I just had to connect them to the killer and track him down. The capture was the most difficult part. But this mystery had me confounded. It had me off balance and fighting to bring some sort of meaning to all this. If only I could talk to someone about it ...

"I want you to find out what bacteria that is," I said finally. "It's important in some way."

"What about the scientists, or Malichauk? He's the doctor."

"I don't want more people knowing about this. Besides, you're pretty smart, I guess."

"*You guess?*" The corners of her eyes crinkled. She watched me as if I were a lab rat in an elaborate experiment. Then her features grew serious again. "What's hurting you?" she asked in a soft voice.

That took me aback. "What do you mean? I've recovered from the attack."

"You're pretty intense. Quiet. Maybe that's how you work, but I think there's more to it than that."

"I'm like this when I work. You have to be."

"Do you have to separate yourself from your emotions?"

"Sometimes. Some Investigators do. They're so distant they're as cold as the killers they're after. They're like robots. Their relationships don't last long."

"But you're not like that."

I shrugged. "I've learned to separate myself, but only at the necessary times. You need a bond with the victims and the families in order to do the job properly. I need emotion. It's the way I work."

She hesitated, then, "There's more to it than that."

"You said yourself I liked to work alone. You were right."

"Why is that?"

I paused and wondered how much I should tell her. I didn't want to reveal too much about myself, especially in the middle of an investigation. However, as I looked into her eyes, I found it difficult not to answer. "I guess when my parents died, I learned to like it that way. I had to."

"Defense mechanism."

I grunted. "You don't pull any punches. And I have to say this, you're damn perceptive. You would make a good officer in Security Division."

"Homicide Section?"

"Don't get too cocky. Maybe traffic or guard duty."

She punched me in the shoulder. "You ass."

I pulled myself to my feet. "Keep working on that —"

She put a hand on my arm and kept me from leaving. "Wait a minute. You didn't answer my question."

I blinked. "I still don't know what you're talking about. I've gotten pretty close to you. Closer than with any other woman for longer than I can remember."

She pursed her lips. "It's not that. With the others. You're withdrawn."

I paused. "You know, you should have been a psychologist."

"You're just realizing that now?"

"No. You had me pegged two days ago, in your quarters. Dead to rights."

"I know I did. I did study psychology, if it matters."

"Along with starship engineering?"

"And electrical engineering, yes. A little computer engineering too."

I shook my head in wonder. She was almost *too* perfect.

"What are you thinking?" she asked.

"Nothing." I sighed. "You're right, of course. There is something bothering me." How exactly could I tell her that my incompetence had killed a guy? A CCF officer. I was here on *SOLEX* to protect people; I couldn't allow them to lose confidence in my abilities. And yet Michael Flemming was in my thoughts, when he shouldn't be.

"Go on," she prompted. "It's okay, really." I couldn't help but notice that her hand was still on my arm.

I clenched my teeth. "I'm not sure I —"

"Go on," she repeated. It seemed like an order.

Staring at her in silence for a moment, I decided to bite the bullet. I told her the entire sordid tale about Flemming and Sirius. I stared at the dull bulkhead behind her and hardly took a breath during it. When it was over, I held my head in my hands. "It was my fault. He was my best friend. Really the only one I had. And now ..." I trailed off.

There was a long silence. Finally, Shaheen said, "You won't believe me, but it's not your fault. You saw something that Flemming didn't. It sounds harsh, but it was his failure that killed him, not yours. You don't have any responsibility —"

"Dammit I do!" I yelled. She jumped back and stared at me in shock. "Don't you see that he was the only thing I had that bordered on normalcy? He was my last connection to what it means to be human!"

She waited a beat before, "You feel alone."

"I prefer working alone, you know that," I snapped.

"But still, everyone needs someone at some point."

I got back to my feet and stalked to the hatch. Leaving her was against my better judgement, but I felt too exposed. Raw, like an open wound.

"Keep working, Shaheen. Let me know when you've found something. And don't leave the cabin — I'm going to lock the hatch for your protection."

There was no looking back as I left. I regretted my coolness immediately; I knew she had just tried to help. Still, it was difficult to open myself up to a stranger.

As I marched from the cabin, I stumbled across Bram O'Donnelly and Anna Alvarez in the corridor. They were near the ladder that led to the levels below. They pushed by me without a word.

"What are you two doing up here?" I growled at their retreating backs. The module we were in was *Officer's Country*. Our quarters, gym and recreational facilities were located there. The two had no reason to be here, unless of course there was some sort of work to do. If they were just passing through, say on their way from Module A to Module C, then they would be on Level One where the tunnels connected the modules. Our quarters were on Level Three, the uppermost level of the cylinder.

I repeated the question.

They stopped at the end of the corridor and turned to me. "Work," Bram said in a flat voice. "Malfunctioning ventilation fan."

"Where?"

"First Officer Rickets's quarters," he sneered. "Anything else you need?"

I dismissed them and they continued on their way. Great, just what I needed. I'd half expected their hostility; after all, the only reason I was here was because of the murders. I was the only outlet for their anger at Jimmy's death. It didn't bother me because it came with the job, but I didn't want to exacerbate it needlessly. Worse, however, was that Anna hadn't seemed sympathetic at Bram's outburst; I had hoped she would at least treat me with respect, especially after helping me earlier, but her expression had been fixed and cold.

—

I left Shaheen alone for a few hours to research in private. I hoped I hadn't hurt her feelings, but something she'd said had bothered me somehow, and I wasn't quite sure what it was.

Checking the time, I was shocked to see that it was almost lunch. I returned to the common mess where Manny and Rickets conferred quietly over a cup of coffee.

"Kyle," Manny said. "How's it coming along?"

"Interesting," I responded as I grabbed a cup for myself. I didn't want to say too much to him; the fewer people in the loop the better. I knew that as the Captain he might want to know everything, but in the end he would understand my need for secrecy.

"Where's Shaheen?"

"Researching."

He eyed me and considered what I had said. Rickets spoke up. "I thought we were to remain together, in pairs."

"I confined her to a cabin. She'll be fine. I sealed the hatch."

He grunted and didn't look at all happy. "Why can't you tell us how the investigation is going? You could be putting people in danger by not telling them what you know."

I paused and watched him thoughtfully. I couldn't blame him for being terse with me, but there was a limit to how much I could take. "You may be right," I said finally, deciding to reason with him. "But it might also give the murderer important information. It could give him the upper hand."

"You're saying —"

"No. Not that you're the killer. But you *could* be. Or if someone overheard us talking, or you talking to someone later." I shook my head. "It's too dangerous to talk about openly, Avery. Just relax and let me do my job." I knew he was an officer who went by the book, and when things happened in the military that were contradictory to everything he knew and loved, it bothered him. It was a completely natural reaction in the current situation.

"But —"

"He's right," Manny interjected. "Don't interfere. It'll be over soon."

I glanced at the Captain and gripped my steaming mug tighter. I hoped he was right.

―

The others soon entered the mess and sat to lunch. Manny addressed them before we began and tried to reassure them. The scientists in particular seemed most concerned; they were unusually quiet as they ate. No talk about the sun for a change.

I ate in the subdued silence. Rickets kept trying to say something, but stopped himself every time. He was still clearly frustrated. I ignored him.

Finally, Brick tried to engage me in conversation. "How many murders have you solved, Tanner?"

I cringed at his choice of topic, but decided to answer anyway. Some conversation was better than none. I shrugged. "Eight hundred."

He looked shocked. "So many?"

"I've been in Homicide Section for eleven years. There's a lot of crime in the system."

The Council generally doesn't admit to how much crime there really is. They sanitize and monitor the news, and suppress knowledge about the true state of society. They didn't want people to lose faith in them, and I could understand that philosophy to a point. However, knowledge is the best defense against crime, and when people simply didn't know the truth, it made it all that much easier for criminals to prey on the weak. It was wrong of the Council, but they would never admit it.

Brick continued, oblivious to my slip, "You're young to have solved so many. Then again, your reputation preceded you here; you must be good."

"Who knows. I'm thirty-four; I've been doing this since I was twenty-three."

"How long does it usually take to solve a murder?" Malichauk asked.

I understood the unstated question: *How long will it take for you to solve this one?* Inside, I felt angry with myself. Three or four days was the realistic answer, but this case was different. I didn't want them to know that, however; I needed to be the picture of a calm and collected Investigator, one who'd seen it all before. So I lied. "No more than a week," I said.

"Every time?" Brick said.

"It varies."

"Can you tell us about one? It might be ... interesting." He looked around at the others.

People perked up at the question. As much as I hated discussing the suffering that I saw every day, I understood that they needed some kind of distraction.

I resigned myself to the inevitable. "The Torcher is my most famous capture, I guess."

"You caught The Torcher?" Sally gasped. She hadn't been with us the night I had arrived, when the others had first asked about it.

I nodded. "As you know, he traveled the system and took his victims in distant locations. He kept them on board his private ship for up to three months."

"What did he do with them during that time?"

I frowned. "Torture. Abuse. Everything, really. It was terrible what those people had to endure. Death, when it finally came, was a blessing. I wish I had caught him sooner." I noticed Grossman say something to his friends. They grumbled and looked at me pointedly. O'Donnelly grunted and made a crass comment of some sort. The others laughed.

"And you were on the case?" Sally said. "Why did they give it to you?"

I tore my gaze from the crew. "I guess I had this reputation ... I'd solved a couple of cases earlier that others had a hard time with." I sipped my coffee. "Anyway, he killed them during torture, then burned them. He let them all burn for twenty-three minutes, then he left the bodies — charred and unrecognizable as human — on the colonies and stations he visited."

She looked disgusted. "Why twenty-three?"

"No one knows. He was a serial killer, psychotic like most of the rest. People try to understand them, but you can never predict who will become one or why they do the things they do."

Brick said, "I thought abuse as youngsters, bad families —"

"Sometimes that's the case. But there are also a lot of people who grow up in hardship to become good, contributing citizens of the Confederacy. It's difficult to generalize."

"How did The Torcher grow up?" Katrina asked.

"Actually, he had a good family on Gagarin Station who treated him well. He had an education. No one really understands why he did it."

"But I thought he —"

"Some people have written books about him, tried to theorize why he did it. What the twenty-three minutes meant and so on. We captured and executed him, that's what's really important."

"Don't you think it's important to understand a killer, to be able to predict when it could happen again?" Lingly asked in a meek tone. People turned to her and she avoided their questioning eyes.

"Of course," I responded. "But my point is we can't understand everyone."

"Like our situation," Katrina said.

I exhaled. "There's reason behind this. There must be. I don't think it's random, like The Torcher's victims. There's a connection here somewhere." *I just have to find it.* "One of you knows, and soon I'll know too."

Silence fell once again and I turned to my meal. Eventually it grew too great for Crewman Grossman to endure. He threw his fork down and rose to his feet. He fixed me with a glare that could melt lead. "Has it occurred to anyone else that *he's* the killer?" He looked around the messhall. "Jimmy's death could have been an accident. The mutilation occurred *after his death*. Then this guy shows up, spouting off about how he's going to solve this *murder*. Then three days later we have two more bodies! He's keeping us occupied while he kills us one by one!"

"That's preposterous," Manny said. He could have stopped the outburst in a second, but had decided to debate him rather than order silence. I'm not sure I agreed with his decision, but there was little I could do. "Jimmy lost his head before Tanner arrived. Reggie and Lieutenant Bertram lost theirs *after* he arrived. The method is the same. The killer is the same. It can't be Tanner."

Katrina said in a calm voice, perhaps deliberately trying to soothe Grossman, "Maybe you can tell us what you know so far, Lieutenant."

"I'm sorry," I said. "I am investigating every lead. When I know the truth, so will you."

"But you could fill us in on what you've discovered so far."

Beside me, Manny sighed. "He can't, people. It would compromise his investigation. You'll have to accept that, as I have. Let's just continue with our work, and hopefully this will all be over soon."

They weren't happy, but it stopped the argument. We finished our meals in an anguished silence.

"They can't take much more of this," I said to Manny after lunch.

"That's for sure. I'll do my best to keep them in order, but you have to hurry."

"I can't rush it. The pieces have to fall together naturally." I hesitated. "But I understand what you're saying. I'll do my best."

I remained in the messhall long after Manny and Rickets had left and considered what had happened. This was just a taste of things to come. It would get a lot worse as the hours — or days — dragged on.

I had to figure this thing out, fast.

— Chapter Thirteen —

After the exchange with Grossman, I followed Manny and Rickets to the command center and reviewed the security situation with them. The killer had locked out all the station's cameras; presumably he had accessed the system just prior to murdering Reggie and Bel the day before.

"However," Manny said, "there's a chance it might have been shut down *after* the murders."

"Then whoever did it would have had to erase the video to just before the killings," I said.

"That's right. The same thing might have happened with Jimmy's death."

I thought that over. "What you're saying is, Jimmy died outside, the crew brought his body in, and Malichauk put it in the freezer. Then the killer accessed the security program, shut off the system, *erased the tape to the point just before Jimmy's death*, then went and cut off his head and hands. As a result, we are still unsure if it was accidental or not."

Rickets said, "But why erase the tape of Jimmy's death if it was an accident?"

"Strategically, it's a good offense." Whoever was doing this was intelligent. They knew exactly what to do to keep me off balance and on the losing side of the contest. I could only hope that at some point, and hopefully soon, I would learn something that would tip the scales in my favor. Once I had that, it was just a matter of time. It was locating that critical piece of evidence that was the problem. I may have already found it, but unless Shaheen could help, it was useless.

The importance of that droplet of blood was incalculable.

"You're saying the killer wants us confused," Rickets continued.

"Think about it. If you don't suspect the death is a murder, you won't be on the lookout for a murderer, will you?"

"I see what you're saying. But there's no doubt about that fact anymore, is there?"

"Not after he killed Reggie and Bel. But it did work, to an extent. Even Manny here thought Jimmy's death might have been an accident and the mutilation of the body a prank."

The Captain scowled. "Unfortunately, you're right. It tricked me."

Until the discovery of the two new bodies, I had come to the conclusion that Jimmy's death was an accident. Now it seemed likely it was a murder after all. There was no doubt about it — the killer was good at this game.

"Is there any way to recover a video that's been erased?" I asked. I knew the killer wasn't that dumb, but if there was a chance of retrieving it, I had to know for sure.

"I doubt it. But I'm not the Station Systems Officer. That's Shaheen." He shot me a pointed look.

"I've got her working on something right now." I sighed and took a moment to study my surroundings. The video screens cast flickering orange firelight around the cabin; it was more than a little eerie.

"Hey," I said. "How are those cameras working?"

"Those aren't security cameras. They're not tied into the system."

"Are we recording those images?"

"No."

An idea suddenly occurred: perhaps we could use them for the security system, adapt the program for them? I would have to ask Shaheen about that, too.

A light began to flash on the Information Officer's console. Rickets moved to it.

"Incoming FTL transmission," he said. He pushed a button and an elderly face appeared on the screen over the console. He wore a lab coat and had white hair. He also had a puzzled expression on his face.

"This is Doctor Higby from Mariner Hospital on Mercury," he said. "I received a message three days ago to contact a Lieutenant Tanner. Sorry it took me so long. I've been busy."

Rickets peered at me. It took me a second or two to realize who this man was. When Captain Fredericks had told me about the crewman who had left *SOLEX* due to mental instability, I had grown immediately curious. When I learned the man had died on Mercury in the mental ward, I became even more so. That man was Jarvis Riddel.

Four weeks earlier, Riddel had left *SOLEX* and CCF HQ had shipped Godfreid Grossman in as his replacement. It was the only transport on or off the station since *SOLEX* began operations nine months earlier. When Manny told me about Riddel's death, I'd asked him to contact the charge doctor and have him call with the complete story. After the attack in my cabin and the two new murders, it had slipped my mind. Now, however, the call had arrived. The expression on Higby's face made sense. He had no idea who I was.

"I'll take it at a private station," I said to Rickets.

He gestured to a console in the corner. "Use the ear jack if you want."

I sat at the indicated station and inserted the ear piece. The screen illuminated at his command and Doctor Higby appeared.

"I'm Lieutenant Kyle Tanner, Homicide. I need to ask you a few questions about one of your patients."

He nodded. "Go ahead."

"Four weeks ago you received a patient named Jarvis Riddel. He was a crewman here at *SOLEX*. Apparently he suffered something of a psychotic break. The Captain sent him to you on Mercury."

A look of understanding replaced the one of bewilderment. "I remember the case well. The man was very sick when he arrived."

I leaned forward. "What can you tell me?"

"When he got here he was heavily sedated; the transport had been rough. Riddel had been hallucinating, screaming about being burned alive, the radiation, and so forth. It's a pretty tense situation where you are, I understand."

I grunted. "Go on."

"I slowly lowered the dosage during the first few hours. He was still paranoid, mind you, but easier to control when we convinced him he was no longer in close proximity to the sun. We had to be careful not to let him see any outside views. We had to keep his room cool as well."

"How long did treatment last?"

"Well, the funny thing is, he got better all of a sudden. Very quickly, in fact."

I frowned. "How so?"

"He arrived in the morning. By late afternoon he was noticeably better. By evening, he was calm, relaxed, and lucid."

"Did the meds do that?"

"No, I was *reducing* the meds, which were just relaxants. I didn't really do anything at all."

I did a mental calculation. "So within, say, twenty hours of leaving *SOLEX* he was completely fine."

"Before he died, yes."

Two dead crewmen meant that there was a possible connection between them; it was an obvious assumption. I needed more information about the circumstances surrounding Riddel's death.

"Some gentlemen from the CCF came for him that evening," he continued. "I told them he wasn't in any condition and so on, but they ignored me. I had no choice, I had to cooperate. They took Jarvis away, and it was the last time I saw him alive."

"He died in their custody?"

"Yes."

"Did you try to contact these men or their superiors?"

"Sure, just as a matter of routine. I was concerned about my patient." He paused. "That's when I found out."

"They didn't tell you how he died?"

"They said it was a heart attack."

"What are the chances of that?"

He pursed his lips. "Well, he *was* under a lot of stress on *SOLEX*. Most of it mental, but that does translate into physical stress as well. Increased heart rate, blood pressure, and so on. It's not inconceivable."

Still, the doctor had said he was calm and relaxed when the men took him away. Had they tortured him to find out ... what, exactly? What did he know that was so important? As usual, this case was creating more questions than it answered. I reached out to terminate the connection.

"Wait a minute," he said. "I haven't finished yet."

I froze. "There's more?"

"Indeed. When I found out, I demanded the return of the body. After all, I was the physician in charge. I wanted to see the body and determine the cause of death."

"Let me guess, they wouldn't let you —"

"Quite the contrary. You see, I have quite a bit of pull in the Confederacy." He paused and, while chewing his lower lip, watched me silently. It was almost as if he were debating with himself about whether to disclose something important.

"And why's that?" I asked, growing exasperated.

"My position. Let's just say some of my patients would rather knowledge of their stays in my ward remain private."

"Oh." In other words, he had treated high-ranking officers who had mental illnesses and wanted it kept secret.

"I couldn't get Riddel back, but I got permission to go view the body at CCF headquarters here on Mercury."

"And what did you find?"

"Oh, the corpse seemed perfectly normal ..."

I sat up straighter, suddenly anxious.

"... except that its head and hands were missing."

—

"*What?*"

Startled at my outburst, both Manny and Rickets turned to me.

"Yes," Higby continued, "the body was missing its head and both hands! I've never seen anything like it."

"And what did they tell you?" I asked, excited and confused by this news.

"No one knew anything. They said the people who took him from my hospital weren't from Mercury, they were from Earth. After Riddel died, they examined him, removed the head and hands, and shipped out an hour later."

"No mention of why they did that?"

"None whatsoever."

"Do you think they killed him?"

"I wouldn't know."

This development was, frankly, stunning. I hadn't anticipated it. The mystery had begun well before my arrival. Four weeks before, in fact.

"Thanks Doctor Higby," I muttered. "You've been a great ... help, I guess."

The elderly man grunted. "If you need more information, just call. And if you find out why they did that to his body, please let me know."

We severed the link and I sat there for several minutes, too stunned to speak. The Captain and First Officer watched silently with odd expressions on their faces. They had heard only my side of the conversation, but no doubt were intensely curious about what Higby had said. They were aware he was a doctor at the hospital where they sent Riddel. They were probably trying to add this piece of the puzzle to their own mental picture of what was going on. Thankfully, they knew not to ask me what he had said. They knew I wouldn't tell until I had either solved the case, or until I could learn something new by revealing the information.

I sat there for a long time and stared at the blank communit.

— Chapter Fourteen —

Before long there was another signal, this time from Shaheen. She was still down in my quarters, researching the bacteria Reggie had discovered.

Her face appeared on the screen. "Please come here immediately," she said, breathless.

"You've found something," I whispered.

"Get over here right now."

The image turned blue; she had broken the connection. As I stalked from the command center, I passed a very perplexed Captain and First Officer. Rickets in particular looked like he was about to burst from curiosity.

I blew by him without a word.

—

"What is it?" I asked as I entered the cabin. She sat poring over Reggie's papers at the metal table. The picture of the bacteria shone brightly on her reader. I noticed that a smaller window had been opened on the display: it was a closer view of the organism's interior. I peered at it momentarily, but didn't know enough biology to note anything of interest.

She looked up from the mess on the table. "I've made some important discoveries, Tanner." She didn't show any anger at what had happened earlier between us; she had either forgiven me for my outburst or ignored what had occurred.

I sat next to her. "What have you found?"

"This bacteria ... the computer has been unable to find a match, but there's good reason for that." She stood and began to pace. "What do you know of exponential growth?"

Her question threw me off. "I ... I guess the same as most people. Two, four, eight, sixteen, and so on."

"Basically that's true, yes. But there's so much more. It's frightening, really."

My forehead creased. "Exponential growth?"

"In certain circumstances, yes. No, no — wait. Hear me out before you start asking questions, okay?"

I shut my mouth and kept the numerous questions — like what exactly this had to do with murder — inside for now. I fidgeted uncomfortably. Withholding important questions about the case was actually more difficult than it seemed. I now understood exactly how the command staff felt.

She continued, "Something increasing in numbers by exponential growth can grow enormously fast. Faster than most people can comprehend, really."

"Like that bacteria?"

"Hush. I said no questions. Now picture this scenario: imagine taking a sheet of paper like this." She pulled a standard-sized page from the table. "Now let's fold it in half." She did so. "Now, what if I did that a hundred times? Would you believe its thickness would be that of the radius of the known universe?"

"Bullshit."

"It's true. Its thickness would be twelve billion light years."

I shook my head. "Maybe if the paper were a thousand kilometers thick to start with."

"No, I started with the assumption that the paper was point one millimeter thick, the common size."

I stared at her, not completely comprehending. I was an instant from halting the discussion when something inside made me stop. Instead, I waited in silence.

"Look," she said, stern. "I didn't make this up. The idea was first published a long time ago. Every time the paper is folded its thickness doubles." She picked up a pen and began scrawling figures on the same piece of paper she'd demonstrated with. I watched as she drew a table with three columns.

Fold #	Thickness in pieces of paper	in km.
0	1	$.1 \times 10^{-6}$

She moved back to admire her handiwork. "Okay. That's before the folding begins. The paper is only one sheet thick, or point one millimeter."

"Got it," I said, still dubious.

"Now let's begin folding." She added more figures to the table, as well as a new column.

"What's that?"

"Shut up and watch."

Fold #	Paper Thickness	in km.	
0	1	$.1 \times 10^{-6}$	one sheet
1	2	$.2 \times 10^{-6}$	
2	4	$.4 \times 10^{-6}$	
3	8	$.8 \times 10^{-6}$	pencil lead
4	16	1.6×10^{-6}	
5	32	3.2×10^{-6}	cardboard

"Okay," she said. "I just folded the paper five times. It's now thirty-two papers thick, or three point two millimeters. About the thickness of cardboard. Got it?"

I noted that the thickness in kilometers also doubled with every fold: from point one to point two to point four and so on. It seemed correct. "Sure." I still failed to see how she could reach the radius of the universe by doing this only a hundred times, but had decided to humor her.

"Actually, in reality we wouldn't be able to fold it much more. The maximum you can fold a piece of paper is about eight times, but let's assume we can." She continued to fill in the chart; my amazement grew with each iteration. She'd skipped forward to fifteen folds.

Fold #	Thickness in pieces of paper	in km.	
15	32 768	3.3 X 10^{-3}	3 meters, height of one building story
16	65 536	6.6 X 10^{-3}	
17	131 072	13.1 X 10^{-3}	
18	262 144	26.2 X 10^{-3}	
19	524 288	52.4 X 10^{-3}	
20	1 048 576	104.9 X 10^{-3}	one hundred meters

"Here we are at twenty folds," she said. "It's now over one million pieces of paper thick, or one hundred meters. Agree?"

I nodded. "I'm following so far." While folding the paper seemed harmless at the beginning with two, four, eight pieces and so on, by the time she was into the thousands the increase seemed to happen pretty damn fast. "You hit a hundred meters sooner than I thought you would. A lot sooner."

"I'm skipping ahead here," she said as she continued with the chart. She had to widen the columns for the larger numbers.

Fold #	Thickness in pieces of paper	in km.	
30	1 073 741 824	107.4 X 10	Edge of Earth's atmosphere
50	1 125 899 906 842 624	112.5 X 10^6	one hundred twelve million kilometers
60	1 152 921 504 606 846 976	115.3 X 10^9	twenty times distance of Pluto from the sun
70	1.2 X10^{21}	118.1 X 10^{12}	11 light years
85	3.9 X10^{25}	3.9 X 10^{18}	four times the diameter of our galaxy
100	1.3 X 10^{30}	126.8 X 10^{21}	12 billion light years

She stopped, put the pen down, and looked at her handiwork. "See? At a hundred folds, it's hit twelve billion light years!"

I studied her chart, not fully understanding where the numbers had come from. "I'm not sure I believe this. A hundred folds and it's twelve billion light years across?" I paused. "You jumped ahead quite a bit. I can't tell if that's accurate."

"There's a simple formula you can use." She wrote it below the table.

Number of paper thicknesses = 1 x 2^g

"The 'g' in the formula represents the generation, or the number of folds," she continued. "You can see by plugging in a hundred for g — meaning folding the paper a hundred times — the result is exactly as I've shown." She looked at me for a minute. "Or try this. Just plug it in for fifteen folds, see if it follows what I've done."

Picking up her reader, I used the formula to calculate the thickness of the paper for fifteen folds. Sure enough, I got 32 768 paper thicknesses.

"Now to calculate the actual span in kilometers, you have to multiply that number by $.1 \times 10^{-6}$, or point one millimeter."

I did it and got three point three meters. I checked it with her chart. "Seems to work."

"Of course it does." She gave me a sly smile. "Still don't believe me?"

I frowned. "Not yet. What does the two mean in the formula?"

"That's the doubling notation, meaning that with every fold the paper doubles."

"How do we know the radius of the universe is twelve —"

"We don't. In fact, according to Einstein space is curved, so if we traveled right across the universe we'd actually pass the 'edge' and reemerge where we began."

I scratched my head. "I think I heard that in school once. But where'd the twelve billion come from?"

"Well, if you accept that the Big Bang occurred twelve billion years ago, and the light from that explosion — which is traveling outward at light speed, of course — represents the farthest extent of the universe, then —"

"The radius can only be twelve billion light years."

"Yes. Give or take."

I leaned back and exhaled. It meant it would take only one more fold to reach the entire width of the universe!

"What if I told you that, according to Reggie's notes, the bacterium in the photo could double every thirty minutes?" she asked.

"But isn't that normal?"

"Of course. Perfectly normal." She began to pace once again. "You know, in India we have a funny little tale. I'd like to tell it to you."

Before I could respond, she had started the story with even more enthusiasm than before. I folded my arms and listened quietly, wondering what all this had to do with the bacterium found in the drop of blood, the three murders — or possibly four now, if I included Jarvis Riddel — or this godforsaken station.

"I'm not sure about the source of this story, no one is really. But it's common in India, and in China as well, for that matter." She looked up at the ceiling as she recalled the memory. "Once upon a time, a raja in India required his people to turn over the vast majority of their rice in return for his protection. He stored the rice for himself and the nation's nobility, and left the people barely enough to survive. When drought hit, however, they begged the raja to give them some rice. He refused. One day, he decided to have a banquet for his court and called for food. A young girl followed the caravan that brought the rice from storage. She collected in her skirt individual grains that fell to the ground. To her great distress, guards captured her for stealing and brought her before the raja. There, she claimed that she had merely picked up the rice in order to return it. Upon listening to her story, the raja decided to reward her for her efforts.

"He was shocked when the girl asked not for a meal, or meals for a week, or for a month, but simply for one grain of rice on the first day, two grains on the second, four grains on the third, and so on. Every day the rice allotment would double. He decided it was a meaningless reward, but agreed nonetheless.

"So the girl collected her first grain and left the raja's presence. The next day, she came for her two grains. Each day she returned for her rice. By the seventh day she received 128 grains. In two weeks it was 16 384 grains — still not a huge amount. But by the thirtieth day it was a billion grains and the raja himself ran out of rice!"

I snorted. "Funny story. The Chinese one is the same?"

"It involves a bet, I believe. Using a chess board. Put a single grain of rice on the first square, two grains on the next, and so on. By the time you get to the sixty-fourth square, the amount of rice is so phenomenal that it ruins the emperor."

The sixty-fourth square would be equivalent to over two months in the Indian version of the story. I used Shaheen's formula to calculate how many grains of rice that would be. The number I got was ridiculously huge: an eighteen followed by eighteen digits. "What comes after quadrillion again?"

"Quintillion."

"Holy shit. I don't think they'd all fit on the chess board."

Shaheen grinned. "No, they wouldn't."

I sighed. "Look, I don't know why you're telling me all this. The bacteria —"

"Doubles every thirty minutes."

"But that's the same as every bacteria, isn't it?"

"They vary. E. coli, for instance, doubles every twenty minutes. But keep in mind that the rate depends on a few things. No predators for one. Another would be an unlimited amount of raw materials for division to occur." Her forehead crinkled in thought. "No limiting factors would be another, as would the assumption that growth is constant. Luckily for us, bacteria can't grow forever. Human bodies and pools of stagnant water confine them; resource availability limits their numbers, and so on."

My patience was wearing thin. The importance of all this was still lost to me.

"There are many other examples of exponential growth," she continued. She still showed no evidence of slowing. "An atomic bomb, for instance. Each uranium atom that undergoes fission produces neutrons, which then split more uranium. The number of neutrons increases exponentially for as long as the uranium lasts.

"One example that has interested engineers like myself the most is Moore's Law."

"Moore's Law?" I repeated. "Haven't heard of it."

"As a Homicide Investigator, I'm not surprised. In 1965, Gordon Moore co-founded a computer chip company called *Intel*. He said that the number of transistors on a chip would continue to double every eighteen to twenty-four months. In essence, he said computer processing power would double every two years."

"Was that the case?"

"For decades, definitely. In the next forty years transistor counts went from twenty-three hundred to fifty-five million." She noticed the look on my face. "I'm not really a dork, we learned about this in engineering school. It's pretty famous."

"If you say so."

"It is. Now shut up. Eventually, circuits in old-style computers became thinner and thinner, allowing Moore's Law to hold true. But there was a problem with that: the chips kept getting hotter and hotter. They'd overheat and overload. And the circuits could only be so close because electrons can literally jump from one path to the other and short-circuit the chip. The separation limit was twenty-five atomic layers of silicon."

"Atomic layers?"

"Twenty-five atoms of silicon separated the printed circuits."

"Oh."

"So Moore's law found a way around it."

"You say that like the law is a living thing."

"In a way it is," she replied. "Human beings needed faster computation power to keep the economy thriving and technological innovations coming. So they changed the conductor from aluminum to copper. That allowed them to use thirty percent less power. Then they used gallium arsenide instead of silicon as the separator and increased speed by forty percent. But even as engineers overcame the heat and materials problem, there was a limit to computing power: you can't shrink the chip forever. A circuit cannot be thinner than an atom."

"So Moore's Law came to a halt?"

"Hell no. That's when we switched to neural networks." She paused to take a deep breath. "Then there's also the example of Thomas Malthus, who compared the stock of food supplies on Earth with the growth of populations —"

I exhaled in a rush. "Dammit, Shaheen! What does all this have to do with the bacterium Reggie found?"

"I was getting to that."

"It's taking a damn long time!"

She looked at me and grinned. "Sorry. Simply put: he found a nano in that blood sample."

I stared at her, openmouthed. "But I already know that. He wrote that."

"What I mean is, the picture is the nano. It's not bacteria."

I still didn't understand. "What?"

"*Completely foreign technology*, Tanner, as he wrote. It's a *biological nanomachine*, capable of replication. And it does so at an exponential rate."

—

A long moment passed as I digested what she had said. It didn't make sense. Nanos couldn't replicate. They were tools used by human beings, and they had finite life spans. The medical variety did their job and then were lost forever, expelled by the human body through natural processes. The engineering variety performed their functions until they exhausted their internal power supply. Scientists had been trying to create a replicating nano for decades, but it had proved too difficult to achieve; they predicted it would remain so for the next fifty years at least.

"Shaheen," I said. "He found bacteria in the blood. He took a picture of it! He made a comment about a nano, but didn't include a photo, and there's no other evidence of it."

"But he did include a photo." She held up the picture that Reggie had taken. "This is it. It may look like bacteria, but it's actually a nano."

I looked at it: a rod-shaped bacterium with flagella trailing from one end. It couldn't be manmade. Still, deep down, I realized there must be a reason why the computer couldn't classify it, and it had every known bacteria in its database.

"Look at this." She pointed to the enlarged picture of the bacterium. "See those black squares inside the organism? The computer couldn't match it with the database because of those. I enhanced the picture, and got this." She pulled up a stylized diagram of the bacterium's interior. I leaned in, squinting.

"Those look —"

"Mechanical! Yes. Tanner, someone has fused a biological organism with a microscopic computer processor!"

"But not really," I protested. "It's bacteria."

"True, but I'm assuming it's being controlled. Think about it: the flagella on the bacteria provide movement. The bacteria can multiply, and perhaps the processor would be duplicated in the division as well. So yeah, it's biological, but it's probably taking instructions from that processor. It can't do everything our nanos can, like destroy tumors and so on, but it's revolutionary! Scientists haven't come close to getting them to reproduce." She paused for a beat. "This one can."

Skeptical would be an understatement for what I thought of her theory at that point. "So what exactly do you think it can do?"

She shrugged. "I have no idea. It's a mystery."

"Can you find out? Decipher the processor's code? You're an engineer."

She looked doubtful. "It's microscopic. I wouldn't have the first idea. Whoever made it would have the necessary machinery, I'm sure."

"But can *you* do it? It's critical, Shaheen."

She sighed and thought for a long moment. "I'll try."

I frowned as I noticed a look pass over her features. "What is it?"

"I'm just wondering why it grows exponentially. The numbers increase incredibly fast, as I've shown, but why? What number are they trying to reach? And more important, for what purpose?"

The question hung in the silence between us.

—

I left her alone to try and solve the problem. Maybe it was just an aberration, something in that blood that had nothing to do with the mystery. And what about Jarvis Riddel's death on Mercury? How did that fit into all of this?

I knew I had no choice but to let Shaheen continue to study the nano and hope she could find something. Other than that, there was nothing else to do but wait for the killer to slip up.

All her talk about exponential growth. Moore's Law and grains of rice and folds of paper. In all likelihood, her ideas were probably just wishful thinking. She was an engineer who saw what she expected to see because of her training. She *knew* about nanos. She probably wanted to see a replicating variety because it had eluded the greatest scientists' abilities to create one, despite their best efforts.

Then again, I thought with a shudder, what if she was right? Who could have created such a thing? And why?

— Chapter Fifteen —

The station's communit came to life and Avery's voice pierced *SOLEX's* mostly empty corridors and cabins. It was a call for me to go to the clinic, and when I arrived, I found Brick Kayle in a chair in the corner, watching as Malichauk puttered about sorting files and equipment. The two were currently partners, which, judging from Brick's expression, he was not happy about. It kept him from his work with the scientists, or, perhaps more importantly, it kept him from his duties as Council Rep.

Malichauk marched to a locked refrigerator, removed a key from his pocket, and unlocked the door. He placed a vial within. He locked the door and returned the key to his pocket.

"What was that?" I asked, curious.

He turned to me. "A vial of —"

"No, I mean, in the fridge there. Why the lock?"

"Oh, there are some items that, if freely obtainable, might disappear from the clinic if I wasn't careful. Some biological samples, addictive drugs, and so on. As the doctor here — and the only one within fifty million kilometers — I have to monitor its contents."

There was a small hatch just past him covered with warning labels set into the bulkhead. I knew immediately what it was: the hazardous materials ejection chute. There was a lever beside it to purge the contents through the chute and out to space. It was probably where the killer had dumped Jimmy's head and hands after *removal* from his body, I thought grimly.

Malichauk was staring at me and I pulled myself back to the present. "I got a call to —"

"That was me," Brick said. "I wanted to talk with you." He shot a glance at the doctor, as if he wanted the conversation private. He gestured to a chair beside him. "Have a seat."

I hoped this was what I had been waiting for: a confession of sorts about the money he'd borrowed from Jimmy Chin.

"I wanted to explain about the money," he said finally.

Bingo.

"I'm listening," I said.

He licked his lips. "There's no easy way to say it. It might hurt my position here as Scientist Liaison, and as Council Rep for that matter, but I don't want to impede your investigation. I don't really think it'll have any impact on it, in fact, but I want you to know I'm being truthful with you." He stopped talking and simply sat there, quiet.

I waited, but nothing further came. "I'm not sure what you want from me," I said, confused.

He shifted in his chair. "I'm curious whether this information will find its way to the Captain or into my file."

A minute passed as I considered what he'd said. He wanted assurances that the CCF would not discover his secret, whatever it was. In the end, I decided it would be best if I gave him the same promise I had given Anna. "If it has to do with Jimmy's death, it'll have to come out. If it's unrelated, I'll try to keep it quiet."

He pondered what I had said. Finally, "Well, I guess it's the best I can get." He made a poor attempt at a smile before allowing it to fade into a look of remorse. He cleared his throat, then, "In short, I have a bit of a gambling problem."

Gambling was one of the immoral activities prohibited by the Council. As a direct representative of them, and as an officer in the CCF, they expected us to stay away from illegal activities. "So you wanted it kept quiet so it didn't jeopardize your career."

"Right. I could have asked the Captain or Rickets — or any of the other officers — for the money, if it was for something legit. But it wasn't."

"What happened?" I asked.

"On Venus, just before HQ assigned me here. Construction on *SOLEX* was just finishing up —"

"This was how long ago?"

"A little less than a year. I fell deep into a poker game that I couldn't win my way out of. I just kept betting more and more, hoping to win that one big pot. I was betting money I didn't have. Pretty soon I was almost thirty thousand in the red. I had to go to a shark to get the money, and I had the debt to the other player paid immediately. But the real trouble was the shark. The interest rate was huge, I had to get it paid quick. Before I knew it the amount owing was fifty thousand and rising every day."

"So you went to Jimmy."

"Yes. Like I said, he was a great guy. I could trust him. His father had died and left him some money; he wanted to buy a place on Titan when his tour ended."

"Titan?" Advertising lately had made it look like a paradise, but I knew better.

"Yup. So Jimmy lent it to me. I paid the shark off — wired it to him — and then spent a few weeks getting my friends on Earth to lend me money to pay Jimmy back."

I frowned. This was getting confusing. Why get Jimmy involved if his friends were willing to help? It meant allowing knowledge of his activities to leak into his everyday life with the military. "Why not just get your friends to help originally?" I asked.

"I needed to scratch the debt with the shark *fast*. The interest was too high. I tried my friends first, but it took too long to track some of them down. So Jimmy helped me out quickly, gave me the money." He groaned and held his head in his hands. "But then he asked for interest too! It was at a lower rate than the shark though, so I took it. I paid the guy on Venus off, then spent another week or so getting the money for Jimmy. And I got it, too. I paid him back, but he wasn't happy."

Ah. So Brick admitted to some conflict between the two of them. It was motive, but was it enough to explain what had happened?

"You didn't pay his interest."

He looked surprised. "How'd you know?"

"He was unhappy that you hadn't paid him back."

"But I *did* pay him back! Just not all that —"

"You figured as an officer you didn't have to."

"No, it's not that," he objected. "It wasn't right for him to ask for it. He was a friend."

"Right," I muttered in a dry voice.

"You don't believe me." He looked at me, sullen. "Whatever the case, I paid him back and that was the end of it. He never asked for the interest again, and as far as he and I were concerned, it was over. Ancient history."

I scowled inwardly. This was only one side of the story, I reminded myself. I'm sure Jimmy's would have been utterly different. He probably would have spoken about officers not playing by the rules, taking advantage of the NOM's, unscrupulous behavior, and so on. He rightfully should have received the interest Brick had agreed upon, but Brick had taken advantage of his position.

"You say he never brought it up again with you?" I asked.

"That's right."

I knew he could be lying. It was possible Jimmy had pressured him to pay the remaining interest, and even threatened to inform his superiors. Brick could have killed him to keep him quiet. An entirely possible scenario — and quite common, in fact.

He studied my expression. "I know what you're thinking," he said in a dark tone. "But if I *had* killed Jimmy, why the big masquerade? Why cut off his head and hands? It makes no sense."

"Killers sometimes don't make sense. I made that clear earlier."

He rolled his eyes. "Yeah, yeah. The Torcher. I remember. But I'm telling you the truth. I didn't kill Jimmy. He was my friend."

He seemed sincere, but he might just be a skilled actor. Many killers were. After all, they'd had a lifetime of practice. It was sometimes the only thing they were good at. There were cases of murderers being released even after multiple interrogations. Some of them could fool even the best Investigators — myself included.

There wasn't much I could do now about it; it was just conjecture on my part. I decided to let it go. "Okay," I said finally. "I'll keep it quiet for the time being."

He exhaled. "Thanks mate, I knew I could trust you."

"Sure," I muttered as I pondered this new information. As with everything, I had to remain entirely objective. Brick's story had some truth to it, but it more than likely had some exaggerations and perhaps even a few outright lies. At least he had confessed to his gambling, but it was no secret that a man guilty of murder might admit to a lesser crime if only to throw suspicion off himself.

—

For the next few hours not a lot happened. People were generally doing their work, still traveling in pairs, and there was not much investigating I could do. Instead I went to the common mess to grab a coffee. I had already looked at the officers' files in detail, and it was time to do so with the crew histories as well. I called up the dossiers and settled in to learn more about the rest of the people on board the facility.

I read Bram O'Donnelly's first. The man's picture greeted me on the first page. He was practically scowling at the camera, red beard and hair as bushy as ever. He hadn't changed much since the picture, dated four years earlier.

There wasn't a great deal in the file. I knew that he and the Captain were friends from way back, and sure enough, I noted the request Manny had made to have O'Donnelly transferred to *SOLEX* just before the project began. I recalled that the two had quite an interesting relationship; it was very informal with lots of bantering back and forth at meals — highly unprofessional to an objective observer. Most Captains were incredibly strict about military protocol. A crewman like O'Donnelly, for instance, would never speak to the Captain the way he had; in fact, he wouldn't even be able to address him in any manner. Concerns, comments, and requests had to move up the chain of command, as protocol dictated.

Nothing of interest stood out. I moved to the next.

Larry Balch. I had noticed that he was essentially a follower of O'Donnelly and Grossman. He was timid and didn't speak much. He took his cues from the two men and backed them up in times of conflict. Under the characteristic dossier mug shot was a close-up of the tattoo that stretched from his finger to shoulder. It was an honest-to-God fire-breathing dragon. I couldn't believe it; it just seemed so contradictory, having this mean tattoo on such a tall, skinny, harmless-looking guy.

Something in Balch's file caught my attention immediately: he had a history of gross misconduct and insubordination. One event stood out in particular: he'd had words with a few officers in a bar on Venus that had led to blows. I whistled. Trading blows with an officer? It was nearly unheard of. Evidently Balch's CO had entered the incident into his file, but did not pursue with a tribunal. Had that occurred, the CCF would have drummed him out of the service and even forced him to serve time in prison. He was a lucky man. Perhaps he even appreciated that fact; he had been pretty low-key since his arrival at *SOLEX* and hadn't had any trouble with the officers.

I shook my head in wonder; Balch just wasn't what he seemed.

Aina Alvarez, or Anna, was next. Her file also surprised me. I had expected to read about a responsible and well-liked CCF recruit, but instead found complaint after complaint lodged against her. Unlike Balch, however, her problem wasn't with officers. In fact, she had treated me very well when I'd spoken with her my second day on *SOLEX*. Anna's problem, I discovered, was with her colleagues. Other lowly crewmen. Arguments. Cruel jokes. Even physical fights. She often fought with men and came out on top. She never made friends with her crewmates. She was a loner and liked it that way. This fact puzzled me. She had told me that Jimmy had been her friend. Actually, she had implied that it had been even more than friendship.

Godfreid Grossman. He had been a pain in my side ever since my arrival. He had been Jarvis Riddel's replacement, transferred to *SOLEX* four weeks earlier. He was stocky with big arms and a handlebar mustache. The file's picture drew my eyes immediately: he stared at the camera with an intense expression of anger. I checked the date on the picture; it had been taken just prior to departure for *SOLEX*.

He was clearly upset about drawing the assignment. He'd been at CCF HQ on Mercury when Riddel had arrived at the hospital; the new posting must have come as a great shock to him.

I read all four files in great detail. In fact, before I knew it two hours had passed. I checked my watch and saw that it was 1800 hours. I'd have to go over the scientists' dossiers later —

The station shuddered and a peculiar sound cut through *SOLEX*; it was the noise of metal wrenching and tearing under stress. Hurled from the chair, I ended up flat on the deck. The gravity field flickered momentarily and my stomach turned. The lights went out, replaced immediately by low-level emergency red spotlights on the hatchways. Klaxons screamed and a mechanical voice pounded out through every corridor and cabin on the station:

"*EMERGENCY, EMERGENCY. CABIN PRESSURE LOSS IN MODULE A. HULL IS COMPROMISED. HEAT SHIELD FAILURE WARNING. HEAT SHIELD FAILURE WARNING. FULL POWER LOSS TO ALL MODULES. ALL LIFE SUPPORT CURRENTLY ON BATTERY POWER.*"

The message repeated and then I felt another shudder.

"*EMERGENCY, EMERGENCY. CABIN PRESSURE LOSS IN MODULE G. HEAT SHIELD FAILURE WARNING. HEAT SHIELD FAILURE WARNING.*"

I blanched as the alarms continued. Something had compromised the heat shield and air was venting from two modules.

Then the life support fans died.

An emergency couldn't get much worse than this.

—

Manny's voice broke over the recording. "Everyone into your vacsuits, now! The emergency hatches have sealed in the affected cylinders, but it's still dicey. Something damaged the engineering module; Shaheen, get over there immediately. Life support is down. The heat shield is punctured; looks like a couple of meteors got us. Bram, Balch, Anna, and Grossman — get to the docking port and into the airlock. Make sure you've got shield repair supplies with you!"

The crew were probably already sprinting through the corridors, collecting what they needed and scrambling into vacsuits for an immediate EVA.

The station's designers had compartmentalized the facility in case of pressure loss, but a hull breach was the greatest danger that faced people who plied the orbits in space. Engineers built ships and stations to withstand such accidents, but there were also other crucial elements necessary for survival: vacsuits were supposed to be readily available and the crew fully trained and competent.

I hoped the Captain had prepared his people for this.

I hesitated momentarily and wondered what I should be doing. I was currently in the common mess in Module C; Shaheen had been working in my quarters on the nano problem. As a result, here I was, on my own, in the middle of an emergency and not familiar with *SOLEX's* procedures.

The command center was the best place to ascertain what was going on. I grabbed a vacsuit from an emergency locker; despite my feverish attempts to pull it on, however, it took longer than usual. The cooling undergarment added an extra couple of minutes. The fact that it was skintight and I was clammy from fear didn't help matters.

I finally secured the last seal and sprinted from the messhall.

—

The command center was in chaos. The lighting was almost completely out, and the monitors that usually displayed the scenes of the exterior and the sun were all dark. Manny was yelling into the communit at the crew outside the station, and Rickets was trying to talk over the din to Shaheen, who was in Module A investigating the damage to our power supply and life support.

I stood to the side and tried to decipher what was going on.

"... can see a couple of punctures in A," a voice distorted by static reported over the communit. It sounded like Balch, but I couldn't be entirely sure. "Anna is working on it right now."

"You've got to get that shield repaired," Manny growled. "Sensors in the module indicate that the temperature is now up to —" He checked a readout next to him. "— fifteen fifty. Shaheen's in there. Get it fixed, fast."

"Working on it," a new voice said. It was Anna. She understood the implication: vacsuits could only withstand the heat and radiation for a limited time, and it might take Shaheen hours to effect repairs. In addition, the vital life support equipment was only designed to operate within nominal temperatures; such exposure could damage sensitive components.

"Did you find Bram yet?" Balch asked over the comm.

I shot a glance at Manny; he was already looking my way. "Malichauk is searching right now. We'll let you know." The Captain covered the receiver with his hand. "Bram O'Donnelly didn't show up at the airlock, which our emergency procedures mandate. We've trained for this before."

"Where could he be?"

He shrugged. "Injured maybe. We took a big hit."

The voices continued and I tried to piece together what was happening. Anna, Balch and Grossman continued going over Module A from the outside, working to repair five punctures in the hull. Shaheen, who was *inside* the module, reported major damage to the power distribution and carbon dioxide scrubbers.

"I'm not sure if I can fix this," her voice echoed in the command center. "The damage is major."

"We have spare parts —" Manny began.

"Captain, the meteors made it through all three hulls. They've incinerated whole components in here. I'm not sure they can be fixed — they may need to be rebuilt."

He grimaced. "Keep me updated."

"Roger."

The crew finally sealed the punctures in the hull on the engineering module and moved to Module G to start repairs on the docking bay. There they discovered even more damage, but luckily no vital station functions were located in that area.

"It wasn't just a meteor that hit us," Rickets snarled. "It was a whole goddamned shower!"

"Didn't show up on radar?" I asked.

"No. Must have been small and fast."

Micrometeors were one of the major hazards of space travel: at the speed ships traveled, or stations such as *SOLEX*, even a speck of dust was dangerous. When a hit occurred, the damage could be extensive. Deaths from meteoric depressurization were common.

"There's a call from the scientists' module, Captain," Rickets reported.

"Put it though."

Sally Johnson's voice warbled from the speaker. "Captain, can you update us on the situation? We felt quite a tremor here."

Manny filled her in. "We're getting it under control. Please stay there until I give the all-clear. Are you in your vacsuits?"

"Yes. But —"

There was another shudder and warnings began anew. Klaxons blared and the Captain gestured at them savagely.

"Turn those damn things off!"

Rickets complied. His face was tight. "We've been hit again. Looks like Module I, storage. I hope our supplies haven't been —"

"Balch!" Manny yelled into the microphone. "Are you okay?"

"Captain!" his tinny voice shrieked. "I can see air venting from Module I! This one looks bad! I don't think we can seal it. The puncture is a couple of square meters and — let me check something — yeah, it goes right through! Wow, that was a powerful hit we just took. The rock went through six layers of hull and a bunch of our supply crates. Material is still venting into space! I can see — hey, a field conductor just flew out! Won't last long this close to Sol, I'm sure."

Manny checked the time. "You've been out there sixty minutes. Only thirty left. Have you sealed what you can?"

"Just finishing the docking module now. It's gonna be close."

"Can I help?" I asked, noticing the look on the Captain's face. His expression showed deep anxiety, and I knew that he had a need to do something, *anything*, but couldn't leave the command center. His place was here, in charge of the station, coordinating his people.

He turned to me. "The scientists aren't up to this sort of thing."

"What needs to be done?"

"The equipment in the supply module. It won't stand up to the heat for long. We'll have to seal the module and abandon it, but we need to salvage what we can first."

"I'll go get started."

Relief flooded his features. "Thanks. I'll send Malichauk and Brick too. The module's exposed to space. Remember, ninety minutes is the limit."

"The electromagnetic shield is out?" I wondered why I had a ninety minute limit *inside* the module; Shaheen had modified the EM shield to take the stresses this close to Sol. It ran powerful currents through superconductors around the station and mimicked the Earth's electromagnetic field. It funneled the high energy protons and electrons away from the station.

He looked grim. "It's on battery power right now. It's protecting us, but one big burst from the monster out there will fry us all. No hope at all. Hopefully Shaheen can get full power restored quickly. Now get down there and save what you can."

—

I made record time on my sprint to the damaged supply cylinder. At the tunnel that connected Module F to I, I noted that the emergency hatch on the near side was shut tight. The computer had sealed the one on the far side as well, to protect the station from further decompression.

The display on the hatch control registered full pressure in the tunnel. I sighed in relief. Had the tunnel been in vacuum, I would have had to try the one from Module H. And if the meteors had compromised *that*, then getting into the supply module would have been that much more difficult.

As it was, however, all I had to do was open the hatch, step in, and close it. The tunnel could act as a makeshift airlock and allow me access to the exposed part of the station.

I hit the button and nothing happened.

"Captain," I said as I thumbed the suit's communit. "I can't get the tunnel open."

A grunt. "The depressurization sealed both hatches, Tanner. It won't open by anyone's command. You have to override it using the emergency code. Here it is: on the number pad hit one-three-five-five-one."

I pressed the numbers and the hatch slid aside. "It worked."

"Use that code for the next hatch as well. But make sure —"

"I know, make sure I seal the first hatch."

"Right. That code bypasses all safety checks. Be careful with it."

I swallowed. "Right."

I closed the first hatch and marched through the tunnel to the far one. I brought my face to the porthole and peered into the cavernous supply module.

Damn.

Sunlight lit the interior. I had expected the dim red emergency lighting that currently illuminated the rest of the station, and was shocked when I saw the intense orange glow. It was blinding.

I stepped back, eyes tearing, and swore at myself. My helmet! I had almost depressurized the tunnel and stepped into a module totally exposed to space and the heat of the sun without my helmet on!

I grabbed the helmet's O-ring, pulled it off my shoulders, and sealed it around my neck. It hung on my back on a set of hinges, but even so, I'd forgotten about it entirely. I couldn't claim to be a very good astronaut; I was used to solving mysteries in pressurized facilities or in domed colonies. I shook my head at my stupidity.

My ears popped as the indicator lights on the helmet's interior turned from red to green and the suit pressurized. I entered the Captain's code on the number pad and commanded the hatch to open. Pumps drained the tunnel of air, the hatch slid aside smoothly, and I stepped into mayhem.

—

The storage cylinder didn't have three levels like the other modules; rather, it was a large open space with catwalks and shelves that circled the exterior bulkheads. The organization system had to be perfect; in case of an emergency, spare parts had to be located immediately. For that reason, the cargo bays were kept in immaculate condition.

Except for now.

Shattered supply crates were strewn across the deck. Shelves had collapsed on one another and mangled important equipment. I stared at one whole bulkhead of crushed material forlornly; I hoped Shaheen didn't need any of that in order to repair the power and life support systems.

What most captured my attention, however, was the ceiling of the module. There was a five meter gash ripped into the hull of the station fifteen meters above the deck. Through it I could see the sun, intensely close, intensely real.

Living in *SOLEX*, you could actually forget that the sun was only five million kilometers away. There were no viewports to the outside and the life support systems kept the air comfortable, perhaps even cold. Unless you went to the command center and saw the viewscreens that displayed exterior views, or went outside on a space walk, you'd never know you were so dangerously close to Sol.

But that comfort level vanished as I entered the cargo bay. The jagged gash in the ceiling and the orange fireball beyond brought that home in vivid reality. I couldn't even see black outside the tear; I could only see the sun.

My eyes traced the meteor's path to its point of exit. It was about two meters long and nearly as wide. The meteor had torn through the module on a steep angle and passed effortlessly through three layers of steel. It exited through another three just as easily.

How large had it been? Probably only a pebble, but even that was considered huge at the velocity we traveled. Many people thought the sun wasn't moving through space. In fact, it moved at approximately *two hundred and fifty kilometers per second*. On top of that, material in the solar system revolved quickly around the sun. The earth, for instance, moved at thirty kilometers per second. Asteroids, comets, and all the dust and junk left over from the solar system's formation moved at similar speeds.

Furthermore, the Milky Way itself was moving as a result of the Big Bang! All galaxies receded away from one another, hence the concept of the *expanding universe*. The Milky Way moved at *six hundred kilometers per second*.

So the speed of an object in space was immense. At least seven rocks had hit us today, and they had caused massive damage to *SOLEX*.

We were in major trouble, worries of killers aside for the moment.

— Chapter Sixteen —

It took me a moment to figure out where I could move the supplies. I finally realized that Module H, adjacent to this one, was also a supply module. I would grab what I could and move it there. To do that, however, I had to depressurize the neighboring cylinder to make the transfer faster. Otherwise, I'd have to load the tunnel with equipment, seal the hatches, pressurize the tunnel, unload the equipment — a colossal waste of time. It would be faster just to carry the equipment through the tunnel from the damaged cylinder.

I cleared the decision with Manny and had it depressurized within minutes. A little after that, Larry Balch, Anna Alvarez and Godfreid Grossman appeared at my side, ready to assist. They'd finished repairs on the punctures in the docking bay and life support cylinders. They couldn't stay in the damaged module, however, for fear of radiation penetrating the weakened EM shield. They had reached their ninety minutes and could risk no further exposure today. They therefore stayed in the undamaged module and grabbed handful after handful of equipment that I shoved through the tunnel at them.

Lars Malichauk and Brick Kayle eventually showed up to help as well.

"Where were you two?" I gasped as I ran an armload of supplies through the tunnel.

"In the clinic," Malichauk answered. "I found Bram; he suffered an injury when we got hit. He's in the clinic right now. I should be with him, but the Captain ordered us down here."

"How bad is it?"

He hesitated. "He's unconscious. I'm not quite sure what's wrong with him. Concussion maybe. I injected priority nanos and left him. I have to go back when we're done here."

Part of me wanted to know why Bram hadn't been with Anna. They were in pairs so no one would be alone.

How had Bram lost contact with his partner so easily?

—

As radiation levels built, Manny warned me to get out of the module. He and Rickets came down to take over and, as sweat poured down my face, I stumbled through the tunnel to E and back into the pressurized station. The ventilation fans were still silent and the lighting still out; Shaheen must have a struggle on her hands, I thought.

Eventually everything that we could save was in the adjacent storage cylinder. We sealed the hatches, pressurized Module H, and stalked back to the common mess to confer.

The eerie red illumination cast long shadows across the decks; I saw ghosts in darkened corners and every creak made me jump. I must have worked too hard: I was probably dehydrated and a bit delirious. It had made me jittery.

On the way to the mess, I pulled Anna aside. "Where was Bram when the meteor hit?"

She shook her head. "I was in the lavatory, in the crew quarters. He was supposed to be standing just outside. When the klaxons sounded, I bolted out but didn't see him. I'm not sure why he left; he knew the orders."

It sounded fishy. He may have heard the alarm and reacted without hesitation — as training dictated — but he must have known that leaving his partner would draw a great deal of suspicion. He would have avoided that at all costs.

Balch shot me a sideways glance. "You worked hard back there, Tanner."

I pulled myself from Anna. "There's still more to do. We're not out of it yet. The life support —"

"What I mean," he said, cutting me off, "is that I appreciate your help. All of us do. You saved some valuable equipment today."

Anna nodded and even Grossman grunted.

I blinked in surprise. The crew were now on my side, and all it took was a life-threatening emergency for it to happen. Too bad we couldn't have had more of them, I thought grimly.

And a little earlier, too.

—

We congregated in the common mess — all but Malichauk, who was seeing to his patient. The crew were sweat-soaked and unkempt from their hard work. Shaheen looked weary, eyes cast downward and shoulders slumped in exhaustion. Manny and Rickets seemed concerned but hopeful; they were probably putting the best possible face on the dilemma. The scientists who had cowered in their modules during the emergency looked terrified.

"Here's where we stand," Manny said with arms folded. "We've lost Module I. The damage to its hull is just too severe. Thanks to Tanner, we managed to save what we could and store it in Module H. The crew repaired the hull on the docking cylinder and the life support/engineering cylinder. The heat shield on all remaining modules is functioning perfectly." He paused. "That's the good news."

"And the bad?" Katrina Kyriakis asked. She had lines in her forehead and bags under her dark eyes.

Manny exhaled. "We're currently on battery power."

"Captain," Sally Johnson said. "We are a power generating station. We have massive solar arrays used to convert light energy to electricity. Surely we —"

"It's not that simple," Shaheen broke in. "Somehow the arrays are unaffected. But the equipment in Module A took a devastating hit. The meteors damaged the recyclers, scrubbers, and ventilation fans. The impact severed the cables that run from the solar collectors to the power distribution and microwave converters in multiple places. Maybe even some places we can't see, like outside. In short, the solar arrays are no help right now."

"Life support?" I asked.

"Our oxygen supplies are fine, so we're lucky there. The hit obliterated the carbon dioxide scrubbers. I'm going to have to build new ones from scratch. I can get the vent fans going again, I'm sure. The temperature has risen by a few degrees in here, but the cooling system will bring things back under control once the fans are going again. The EM shield is on battery power too, but that won't last forever. I need to get that up and running, pronto. But the power situation ..." She trailed off. "I'm going to have to track down every cable to check."

"But it can be done."

She nodded. "It's gonna be a long couple of days, but yeah, we can get it working. The problem is that there's only one of me on this station."

"So you need a little help," Rickets said.

She looked grim. "Looks like it."

—

Manny assigned Anna, Grossman, and Balch to find and repair the damaged power cables. Shaheen began to work on the ventilation fans; she had to get them going again before she could start on the carbon dioxide scrubbers. Despite the difficulty involved, however, somehow she had the vent fans running within two hours and set to work on the scrubbers.

We weren't in immediate danger from carbon dioxide buildup, luckily. The station was very large for its complement of crew, officers and scientists, and a couple of hours breathing without the scrubbers wouldn't make a huge difference.

In the clinic, I watched as Malichauk saw to Bram O'Donnelly, the big red-bearded crewman. He lay on the procedures table, eyes closed as he breathed steadily. He seemed to be just asleep.

Brick was assisting Shaheen with the scrubbers, so I decided to sit in the clinic and keep my eye on Malichauk and his patient.

"Do you know anything else?" I asked him with a gesture to Bram.

He peered at the diagnostic readout. His brow creased. "No. The nanos report a slight concussion. Other than that ..."

"Maybe psychological trauma of some sort?"

He looked skeptical. "Perhaps. But doubtful."

I turned my gaze to Bram. *Where were you when the meteors hit?*

—

The microwave beam to Earth had been disrupted during the emergency. Within a matter of minutes — eight minutes, in fact — the crew who manned the microwave receiving station in Earth orbit sent a message to Mercury CG wondering just what the hell was going on. Within seconds of *that*, Jase Lassiter was on the FTL demanding answers from Manny Fredericks. Unfortunately for Lassiter, the power crisis on *SOLEX* prevented an immediate response from the Captain. But after the crewmen managed to reconnect the first of several power cables, the FTL communit started to blare like mad.

Manny spent the better part of two hours explaining to Lassiter that everything was just fine, *SOLEX* had experienced an emergency, but the worst had passed. Lassiter wasted little time demanding that Manny get the microwave beam to Earth back online as soon as possible.

"The funny thing was," Manny said to me later, "he kept asking about the situation on the station. He wasn't all that concerned with the meteor damage."

I frowned. "What do you mean? What situation were they curious about?"

"If everyone was acting normally, that sort of thing."

"What did you tell them?"

"That you were still investigating Jimmy's death. I didn't say any more than that."

I looked away and pondered that. It was curious.

—

Within eight hours we had partial power restored. Shaheen got a makeshift carbon dioxide scrubber to function, and with the station's ventilation fans that she had already repaired, life support was back in operation.

The lighting, however, had to remain at only twenty-five percent intensity. Some of the power cables that ran electricity from the collector array to the station's distribution center had arced during the meteor strike. Either that or the kinetic energy from the micrometeor had obliterated some components in the station's power systems. Shaheen rigged up a bypass for the microwave conversion equipment and reinitiated the beam to Earth, but was unable to get the station up to full power.

"Life support is good. Scrubbers are good. Recyclers are good. Now the only problem is the lighting," she said as she wiped grease from her forehead.

"Can't you repair the distribution components?" Manny asked.

"Sure, if you strap on a vacsuit and go float outside without a tether! The replacement parts are out in space orbiting the sun right now," she responded in a dry voice.

"Can you rig something up?"

She shook her head. "I need new circuit boards and processors. What we've got right now will have to do." She gestured at the dull flickering fluorescent lights overhead. "I jury-rigged *that*, and I'm pretty proud of it."

Manny squeezed her shoulder. "Good work, Ramachandra. Without you we would have had to abandon the station."

I blinked. "How?" I waved the question away as soon as I spoke; Module M was a mass driver. It used powerful magnets to propel escape pods outward from the sun in case of a catastrophe. We were lucky we hadn't had to use it after the meteor strike. "Sorry," I said. "Dumb question."

The messhall communit beeped and Manny stalked to it. "Go ahead."

It was Lars Malichauk. "Bram is awake, Captain. He's asking to see Inspector Tanner."

"Anna said she had to take a piss," Bram whispered to me. His eyes flicked to Malichauk, who was nearby but otherwise engaged. The dim light in the clinic had the doctor somewhat concealed; I could see his silhouette, but it was hard to make out exactly what he was doing.

"Don't worry about him," I said in a quiet voice. "Go on."

"So she went into the lavatory and the hatch sealed."

"Where were you?"

"Crew's quarters."

"Why'd you leave?"

He frowned. "I saw someone pass outside, in the corridor. Just a shadow, but the person was alone."

My eyes narrowed. "Did he or she say anything to you?"

"No. I stepped into the corridor to look. I saw a man just as he rounded a corner."

That was odd. Manny had paired everyone up. Shaheen and I were the only exceptions. "Did you follow?"

"Yes. I figured Anna might take a few minutes, and it wouldn't cause any problems if I investigated."

"Why didn't you call me?"

He looked surprised. "Actually, I thought it *was* you. You're the only one who's been walking around alone lately."

I grunted; it made sense.

"I followed the guy down to the first level," he continued, "but he disappeared. That's when I noticed an open hatch, which is weird. I mean, hatches close automatically on the station in case of depressurization, for safety. So I approached the hatch and looked in."

"What cabin was it?"

"It's a storage area. Some tools, cleaning equipment, that sort of thing."

"What did you see?" I asked, leaning forward.

"Nothing. It was pitch black. I stepped in and someone plowed into me from the side. Pushed me to the deck. The hatch closed."

It all sounded very, very familiar. "Someone attacked you? Did you fight back?"

"Of course!" he yelled, then immediately lowered his voice. "I fought like hell, but the guy was *strong*, I'm telling you. I didn't get nowhere. I got slugged across the temple and the next thing I knew the guy was on me."

I was on the edge of my seat, anticipating his next sentence.

"He grabbed my arm. Powerfully. A lot of pressure, let me tell you. It was intense." He sighed. "I tried to fight back, Lieutenant, I really did. But I felt awful dizzy from the hit I took. I think I blacked out."

My heart thudded in my chest; I couldn't believe what he was telling me. I hadn't informed anyone about what had happened in my cabin earlier, and the similarities between the attacks were too substantial to be coincidence.

"Anyway," he continued, "when I woke up here in the clinic, Doctor Malichauk was shaking me something fierce. Less than an hour ago now."

I called the doctor over. He approached and shot me a wary look. I said, "Tell me what happened, from the meteor strike on."

His brow creased. "Brick and I were here, in the clinic. He was my partner. Everything shook suddenly and my supplies flew everywhere." He gestured angrily at the shelves that lined the far bulkhead. "I've been reorganizing everything for hours!"

"What happened next," I pressed.

"Manny — I mean, the Captain," he said, eyeing Bram, "called down and told me and Lieutenant Kayle to search for Bram. They had accounted for everyone but him."

"Where did you look?"

"Anna had said they were in the crew module, so that's where we began. I found him pretty quickly, actually."

"Where?"

"In a tool compartment on the first level. He was just lying there, unconscious."

According to Bram's story, he had followed a lone person down there. Perhaps Malichauk had seen someone. I asked him.

He shook his head. "No, but it was dark. The power was out by then."

The meteors had hit between the attack and Manny's order to Malichauk to search for the missing man. It had been chaos by then — klaxons reverberating through the station, red emergency lights activated — so his answer made sense.

"Where was Brick just before the meteors hit?" I asked.

"Here, with me. I was just doing routine work. He was reviewing orders from Command Group, I think."

"Did he leave?"

"Don't think so. I was back in the freezer for a bit, but not long."

"What were you doing?"

He looked confused. "Why, the autopsies, of course. That's where the bodies are stored."

I frowned. "Autopsies?"

"Yes, Reggie and Bel. You know regs: after every death —"

I raised a hand. "I know. Slipped my mind, believe it or not." I had done preliminary studies of the corpses, and had assumed Malichauk wouldn't want to do a full autopsy. Perhaps since the whole debacle with Jimmy and the resulting mess after the delayed autopsy, he felt it was time to get back to following regs. "What did you find?"

He glanced at me. "Nothing that you didn't. You did a fairly thorough job."

I pondered that for a minute. "Did you check their blood?"

"Yes. I didn't find anything." He paused and looked at me. "Why? What did you think there would be?"

"Nothing," I mumbled.

Could Brick have left the clinic while Malichauk performed the autopsies? Surely the doctor would have noticed ... unless he was just too absorbed in the bodies to pay any attention to his partner, who seemed to just sit quietly in the corner anyway.

"I brought Bram back here," he continued, "and except for the time helping you clear the damaged supply module, I've been with him ever since."

"You haven't slept since the accident?"

The lines in his face grew deeper. "Shaheen hasn't. The crew hasn't. You haven't. The Captain and First Officer haven't. I didn't think it'd be right."

I got to my feet. "How long will Bram be here?"

He shrugged. "The rest of the day. I'll run a few more tests, make sure he's okay."

I turned to leave before something suddenly occurred to me.

"Lars," I said, "what did Bram look like when you found him?"

He looked puzzled at my question. "Unconscious, as I said."

"Did you notice anything weird on or around him?"

He shook his head after a minute's thought. "Nothing out of the ordinary. No trauma of any sort, except for a bruise on the side of his head."

I thanked both men and left. There had been another attack, similar to mine. Similar to the one Jimmy had witnessed. And it had happened during or just prior to the crisis.

But the guy hadn't killed Bram, like he had Reggie and Bel. The question was, why?

The killer was still several steps ahead of me, and I knew I was losing ground. Days had passed and I didn't know much more than when I had first arrived. It occurred to me that perhaps I had lost my ability to see through the deceptions and lies. I had screwed up on Mercury; now I had messed up here too — Reggie and Bel were dead, and someone had assaulted Bram. I wasn't close to solving the mystery. The station was in a shambles and we were all lucky to be alive.

Shaheen had bent my ear rambling about nanos and I had wasted a good portion of an afternoon listening to her.

I closed my eyes, deep in thought. Who was strong enough to attack Bram and knock him out? He was a large man, stout and powerful. The guy who had attacked me was also strong.

I took out a pencil and made a list of the most likely suspects. On a sheet of paper, I wrote:

Manny Fredericks. Motive: None. Strong enough? Maybe.

Avery Rickets. Motive: None. Strong enough? Yes.

Brick Kayle. Motive: Owed Jimmy money, but why kill Reggie and Bel? Perhaps they knew something. Strong enough? Definitely.

Larry Balch. Motive: None. History of gross misconduct and insubordination. Strong enough? Maybe.

Godfreid Grossman. Motive: None. Strong enough? Yes. Doesn't like me, but claimed to be a friend of Jimmy's. Angry at his transfer to *SOLEX*.

Lars Malichauk. Motive: None. Strong enough? Too old.

Bram O'Donnelly. Motive: None. Strong enough? Yes, but someone attacked him too.

Under that I made a second list of the women on the station:

Ling Lee. Motive: None.

Katrina Kyriakis. Motive: Argued with Reggie about sensor time. Not much of a reason.

Sally Johnson. Motive: None.

Shaheen Ramachandra. Motive: None.

Anna Alvarez. Motive: None. Records indicate she often has difficulties with crewmates. She did, however, inform me of the attack Jimmy had witnessed in the life support module. If she was involved in this somehow, why tell me about it?

    I threw the pencil down in frustration. Seven days and I basically had nothing. Whatever was going on here, I hadn't begun to figure it out. There didn't seem to be a reason for any of it. The deaths, the attacks, the blood. The nano.
    The nano.
    Something began to percolate at the edge of my mind. I recalled something from the attack in my cabin ... his hands ... something about his hands ...
    And the nano ...
    I marched back to the small tool compartment in Module E where the assault on Bram had occurred. I set down the portable light, got to my hands and knees, and scoured the deck searching for ...
    For what, exactly? I still wasn't sure. For any kind of physical evidence, I guess, perhaps something that could identify the perpetrator of the bizarre series of events on the station.
    Some blood maybe, like the drop in life support.
    I didn't find a thing.
    Despondent, I stalked back to my quarters for some much needed sleep. It was late and I was exhausted. I had grown weary mentally; this case had pushed me to my limits. I hadn't had this much trouble catching The Torcher. That case had taken longer, but the clues were all there; it was simply a matter of following leads and doing routine work. Anyone could have caught him, really. It just took some perseverance and maybe a good hunch or two.
    As I lay in the darkness of my cabin and mulled over the events of the past week, a bizarre theory began to form itself in my mind. A theory that was so absurd that I would have laughed about it a few days earlier. And yet it seemed to make sense. It fit the facts. If true, it meant there was rhyme and reason to this nonsense, but it was so alien that I never would have thought of it, except for the drop of blood in the life support module.
    Was it possible?

I knotted a sweaty fist. It was crazy — but it was all I had.

— Chapter Seventeen —

I managed to get four hours of sleep, after which I stalked to Shaheen's cabin, still tired and cranky. She'd had a rough forty-eight hours trying to repair life support and restore power to the station. However, as exhausted as she was, when she returned she had continued to work on the nano problem.

And she had made a stunning discovery.

Her eyes were red and puffy. Her hair was messy and unkempt. Her uniform was wrinkled and covered in grease. Yet with all that, she still looked beautiful. I couldn't keep my eyes off her, in fact.

"Pay attention," she snapped. "This is important."

"What did you find?" I was still skeptical of the whole nano-being-part-of-the-mystery routine, but after Bram's story, I could no longer ignore it. I had developed a theory that I was hesitant to tell her; I was hoping she had discovered something to negate what I had come up with.

"Remember when I told you it would be difficult to figure out the processor's programming?"

I nodded. The nano, as I recalled, was bacteria fused in some way with a computer processor. According to Shaheen, the processor could be in control of the bacteria, somehow compelling it to perform some mysterious function inside a human body. Its purpose, however, I had left for Shaheen to decipher.

"I had the scientists deliver a nano programmer from the clinic," she said. "Doctors and engineers use the programmer to give instructions to nanos. For example: travel to the aorta and seal an aneurism. Or, destroy a tumor in the liver. Or, fuse this new section of hull to the ship. Get it?"

"Sure. I know how nanos work, generally."

"So I had the programmer brought here, on the hunch that I could modify it to communicate with the processor inside that bacterium."

"Did you modify it?"

She slapped her knee. "I didn't have to! I simply turned it on and accessed the nano directly!"

The original blood drop from Reggie's lab was now between microscope slides on a side table in Shaheen's quarters. Apparently the nano's processor still functioned and Shaheen had easily gained access.

My forehead creased. "Just like that?"

"Yes. There was no security system or password or anything."

"What did you find?"

She scratched her head. "Well, whoever created it didn't need a security code. Everything's encrypted."

I frowned again. "But you found something."

"Yes. Something bizarre. Something so insane I can't make sense of it." She began to pace. "There is code in there of a type I've never seen. I'm not sure if it deals with the nano's replication or not."

"You mean the bacteria's replication."

"They're one in the same, remember? The nano controls the bacteria. It *is* a nano. From now on that's what we'll call it, okay? No more talk of bacteria."

I stroked my jaw. *Foreign technology*, Reggie had called it. Shaheen figured it was because it could replicate and was something no one had seen before. The inclusions in the bacteria — computer processors? — seemed to indicate that. Still, it was a difficult concept to wrap my head around, especially in the middle of a murder investigation.

She exhaled. "You're exhausting sometimes. Now, some of the code *may* deal with replication. Since it's encrypted, it would make sense." She shrugged. "After all, this could be worth *billions* to engineers." She hesitated and lowered her voice. "But I did find something that's undeniable: a DNA sequence. The encryption couldn't hide it; the computer decoded it quickly. Stood out like a sore thumb."

A jolt coursed through my body. Exactly as I had suspected. "Coded into the processor?"

"Yes! Within this nano is the coding for a strand of DNA."

"Whose?"

"I dumped that section of the code and compared it with everyone on the station."

"It matched with someone?" I rose to my feet.

She shook her head. "The DNA is foreign. It's not one of us."

"What about Jarvis Riddel?" He was the crewman Manny had sent to Mercury.

"Checked him too."

"So whose is it?"

She shrugged. "There's no way to tell."

I considered this new development. I had access to an extensive DNA data bank. I would check with that and have the person's identity within minutes. I had used it successfully on many occasions; the benefits of having everyone's DNA filed at the time of birth into a galactic registry was incalculable. To check I would have to link to its location at Security Division on Earth.

Shaheen cleared her throat. "The question that I want to raise is, *why would someone program the nano with a DNA code?*"

I voiced the obvious thought: "To locate somebody."

"Precisely. But the bigger question is, *what for?*"

I turned and slapped the hatch controls. "I'll let you know when I've found out."

"Good luck." She yawned and crawled into her bunk. She dimmed the lights and I saw her blue eyes gazing out at me. "I'll be here."

I stared at her as the hatch closed. Was I mistaken, or was that an invitation?

The database housed at the CCF's Security Division HQ on Earth was the largest collection of personal information in the Confederacy. Along with DNA, contained within the database were also fingerprints, handprints, retinal scans, brain scans, and voice prints of nearly every single person in the Terran Confederacy. The DNA in the nano processor would be in the database, I had no doubt about that.

I logged onto the network with the station's FTL communit. I had downloaded the DNA code into my datachip reader; uploading it to the database was merely a matter of tapping a few keys.

Somehow I'd known there would be something like this coded into the nano. Intuition, a guess, a hunch — who knew. I'd learned long ago to embrace my feelings and understand when to listen to them.

The reader beeped and within seconds I had my answer.

My jaw hit the deck. "Holy shit," I whispered.

The answer shocked me more than I had anticipated. A hell of a lot more — my heart nearly exploded in my chest and my breath burst out in a rush. "*Holy shit!*"

I knew what I had to do. I had to perform an act of sabotage on *SOLEX* that would incriminate me and point all suspicious eyes in my direction.

But I had to do it — there were no other options.

—

First I contacted Shaheen to give her some instructions. I woke her up. "But why?" she asked after my request. She was clearly shocked. "Why the hell would you want me to do that?"

"You'll know in a few hours. I'll explain later. Just do it, Shaheen."

She pursed her lips. "It's about the killer?"

"It's about helping me make the capture."

"But how can I be sure?" she protested.

"I'm not asking you to cause major damage. Just a few small things, all reversible. I'll tell Manny I gave you a direct order. You can't be held accountable. Don't worry."

She considered the request for another minute; I sat on the edge of my chair. If she didn't go along with this ...

Finally, she sighed. "Okay. I'll do it."

"Thanks, Shaheen. You won't regret it." I cut the comm before she could respond.

—

My ship was moored in Module G, the docking port. Like the storage modules, there were no levels; rather, it was a large, open space with a massive hatch on one end of the cylinder. Depressurizing the entire bay allowed ships to enter or depart. Despite being currently pressurized, the flexible umbilical still connected *SOLEX* with my ship's airlock. There were four docking ports for small jumpships in the bay. Each had a hollow tube that allowed people to traverse from ship to station without having to wear a vacsuit.

There was no artificial gravity in the docking bay; the ship floated freely, but magnetic grapples connected it to the curving bulkhead. Onboard the ship, however, the gravity field was always operating, so the traverse through the umbilical was the only area without gravity that I was subjected to. I hauled myself through into the ship, but I didn't particularly enjoy it; I preferred having a firm deck under my feet at all times.

Once aboard, I marched straight to the bridge. From an emergency tool locker I removed several items: a wrench, wire cutters, a screwdriver, crowbar and a hammer. On my back in the cramped cabin, I slid my head under the main console and used the screwdriver to unfasten the four small screws that held the access panel in place. It fell away easily and a mass of fiber optic cables that snaked through the opening fell into view. They were strapped together in bundles, each marked with a different colored band that indicated their general function. I grabbed a bunch marked with green and yanked it toward me. There were about twenty cables tied together: *Enviro Controls*. Good, but I could do better. I pulled on the brown bundle: *Exterior Lighting*. Damn. I tried a few more: blue for *Gravity Field* (unimportant), yellow for *Hyperspace* (not bad), purple for *Communications* (not bad), and black for *Interior Lighting* (unimportant.)

"Damn, where are you?" I murmured as I searched through the bundles. "Ha!" I exclaimed suddenly. There it was: a red band marked *Gravtrav Controls*. I ripped it toward me and with the wire cutters cut every optic in the bundle. I then cut the environmental controls, communications, and the hyperspace optics.

After a moment, I realized I should just cut them all. I reached as far back as I could and sheared the wires flush with the bulkhead where they entered the bridge. I wanted to make it as difficult as possible for anyone to repair.

I pushed myself to my feet and considered what to do next. So far I'd only damaged the controls; I hadn't actually ruined any systems. To do that, I'd have to get at the actual equipment.

I grabbed the hammer and stalked from the bridge.

The ship was small, but there was still an engine room of sorts. The rear compartment housed a bunk, lavatory, galley, and airlock. A narrow hatch concealed an access junction that twisted its way aftward to the propulsion and life support equipment. It was a tight fit — I had to walk sideways — but I quickly found the gravtrav. Piping wound its way across the duct, which I assumed was part of the drive's coolant system. I opened a panel and peered within. Perfect. Labels clearly marked circuit boards and processors as components of the gravtrav. The other end of the red bundle of cables connected here.

I cut all the cables. I smashed all the electronics and circuit boards. I spent thirty minutes causing as much damage as possible.

There was now no way someone could use this ship to escape *SOLEX*.

My next target was located in Module M: the mass driver. It was here that the station's escape pods were located. The driver used a great deal of power, and I noted that it had a dedicated generator separate from the rest of the station's systems. If a catastrophic disaster occurred on *SOLEX*, the driver's power supply would in theory be intact and able to launch the pods.

Shaheen had considered the possibility of using the driver's generator to help power the station, but it simply wouldn't be enough. *SOLEX's* demands were immense; despite being powerful, this generator simply wouldn't add much to the overall usage.

The mass driver control area was separated from the machinery by meter-high control consoles and displays. Next to these controls were the two-man escape pods. Each was the size of a small automobile and contained life support and communication equipment only. The pods rested on a conveyer belt that led to the center of the driver barrel.

If a disaster occurred that the station's personnel could not handle, they would come immediately to Module M. They would power up the driver, strap themselves into one of the eight pods, and the control system would automatically move the pod into the barrel. The powerful magnets would suspend the pod and accelerate it at immense speed away from the sun. There was no propulsion system in the pods; the occupants had to rely on help from Mercury to survive.

I considered my next move. Should I disable the driver? Was that necessary? If so, how exactly would I do it? I could destroy the controls easily enough, but I had to ruin the actual *mechanics* of the driver as well. Then I hit upon another idea: I'd simply jettison all the pods. Once they were gone, it didn't matter if the driver worked or not.

Activating the control system, I instructed the computer to begin the launch sequence. The instructions were clear: there was a large red button under a glass shield labeled INITIATE.

I pressed it.

Strobe lights immediately began to flash and a klaxon sounded. A screen next to the launch button displayed a single simple instruction: BOARD LIFEPOD NOW.

Shit! There must be a failsafe built in — I could launch only manned pods. I had to do this fast; the command staff were now aware that someone had just activated the station's escape system.

I marched to the first pod, leaned in, and studied the controls. I located the hatch control button on the bulkhead, slapped it, and withdrew. The hatch closed and within seconds the conveyor moved the pod into the barrel. Magnets aimed at the pod took hold and smoothly lifted it a full meter off the deck. There was a powerful surge of power — the hair on my arms literally stood on end — and the pod moved into the barrel.

It passed through a hatch I hadn't noticed earlier — it occupied an entire bulkhead and was easily the largest one on *SOLEX*, with the exception of the docking port aperture on the end of the docking module. As it opened, the full scope of the module came into view. It was well over a hundred meters long; angular magnets circled the interior of the barrel, each aimed toward the launch point. The pods would accelerate down the cylinder and eventually reach huge velocities. The large hatch slid shut quickly and the air vented from the driver barrel. There was another shriek of power and —

The first lifepod was away. Only seven more remained.

The second pod in the line was the next to go. I reached in, slapped the button to close the hatch, and it began its short journey to the magnets' embrace in the barrel.

A voice suddenly blared from the station's communit. "You are ordered to stop immediately! Armed personnel are on their way; cease your activities now!"

"Shit," I said. Still six more pods left. But why do one at a time? I decided to try all at once, and pressed each hatch control in turn. I stepped back as all six began to glide toward the mass driver. They entered the barrel one at a time before launch.

When only two remained, Avery Rickets and Godfreid Grossman stormed in. They stopped short when they saw who was sabotaging their station.

"It's too late," I said in a quiet voice. "There's no way to stop them."

They watched, mouths agape, as the last of the pods shot into space.

"So it's you," Grossman snarled. "You killed Reggie and Bel."

"Of course not," I snapped. "It's not me."

"Then why —"

"I wasn't even here when Jimmy died," I continued.

"But the lifepods!" he exclaimed. "Why do this?"

I remained silent as I studied their faces. "Not now."

Rickets was steaming. He unholstered his pistol and leveled it at me. "You better have a *fucking good explanation*, Tanner!"

I raised a hand. "I want to talk to everyone."

He clenched his teeth and glared daggers at me. "It better be good," he finally grated. "I'd like to squeeze this trigger and end this right now."

I shook my head. "You wouldn't stop it, Avery. The killing would continue. And you know what? *I know why*."

— Chapter Eighteen —

The situation in the common mess was chaotic. The crew were enraged at the damage I had caused on their station. I had also incensed the scientists; both groups snapped questions and demands at me at a furious pace. Manny was tightlipped but quiet, and Shaheen sat in a corner as the drama unfolded, obviously torn with the knowledge of what I had done. Only Rickets was absent from the meeting. I eventually calmed everyone down to the point where they could listen to my explanation, but it took over thirty minutes.

"Why the hell would you destroy the jumpship?" Grossman growled. Apparently he was back to hating me.

"And you launched all our lifepods," Katrina murmured as she shook her head. "It's insane."

"You've stranded us here," Lingly added. "What if —"

Grossman again. "We're in a hell of a situation right now! Life support damaged, power's at a premium. Supplies gone or damaged. And you do this?"

"Maybe we should just call Mercury for help," Sally said. "They can send another ship —"

"We're not in that dire a situation yet," Manny interjected. "It would be premature." He watched me with narrowed eyes. He knew I wasn't the killer, yet he had no explanation for my behavior. Still, he was calm and levelheaded. For now, at least.

"And besides that," Rickets said in his deep voice as he marched into the room, "communications are down."

"What?" Manny said, startled. "How?"

"The system's been locked out, same as security."

He turned to me. "You did this."

I exhaled and prepared myself for more. "Yes."

"Did you also lock out the surveillance before the murders?" Rickets bit out.

"I'm not the killer," I said, fists clenched.

He looked pained. "How are we supposed to believe that? Look what you just did! You sabotaged us!"

"I know what I did, but hear me out."

Grossman snarled. "How the hell can you possibly explain yourself?"

"There's a murderer on board, we're in the middle of an emergency, and you've cut off our only means of escape," Malichauk said. He looked concerned and scared. Terrified, in fact.

I raised my hands. "Listen, I'll explain everything, right now. Please sit down and be calm." I took a deep breath as I organized the thoughts in my head. Seven days of investigation had passed, and I knew I had to reveal the information slowly. I needed them on my side as I prepared to spring the final evidence and corner the guilty party. But most important, I had to be careful. "I originally came here under orders to ascertain whether Jimmy Chin's death was in fact a murder, or if the mutilation of his body was unrelated to his death."

"We know that," Grossman said. "Get to the sabotage."

I turned to him. "Not yet. You want an explanation, you'll get a full one."

"Let him talk, Crewman," Manny said. "Go ahead, Tanner."

A pause as Grossman glared at his Captain. He flicked a glance to me, then lowered his eyes.

I nodded at Manny. "When I arrived and began my investigation, I did everything experience told me to do. I questioned everyone on board. I went to the crime scene. I looked at Jimmy's personal effects, his quarters, and even the vacsuit he was wearing when he died. I tried to examine the body, but the doctor had already jettisoned it. I looked for any physical evidence left behind, any at all, no matter how insignificant. I tried to familiarize myself with *SOLEX* and everyone here." I waited for a long moment. No one spoke now. "I found almost nothing."

"So it wasn't a murder after all?" Manny asked, bewildered.

I grimaced. "It's not that easy. There is something going on here, and it obviously goes beyond a single death. But I've uncovered something unique, as one or more of you already know."

Malichauk's brow creased. "What does that mean?"

"It means, Lars, that there is more than one person involved in this."

Startled looks passed over their features as they absorbed that.

"But you said you didn't find —"

"That's right. I didn't find anything that would indicate reason for three murders, *especially* of Jimmy Chin. But that doesn't mean there *isn't* one."

"So it was random?"

I shook my head. "Not at all."

"You're not making sense," Grossman grumbled. "Get to the point."

I looked at him again. "Oh don't worry. I'll get to it soon enough." He was antagonistic and rude once more. There was no doubt I had put him in a terrible position, but as usual, he was quick to judge. He would be in his place, soon.

The power flickered slightly and the low lighting dimmed even further. Everyone looked around, now conscious of the fact that there might be more than one killer among them.

The sound of the ventilation fans ceased momentarily.

"It's okay," Shaheen said. "There will be the odd fluctuation. Don't worry."

As if on cue, the fans restarted, but they sounded more hushed than ever.

"Let's start with Anna," I said.

She looked stunned at being singled out. "Me?" She flashed a look at her comrades.

"Yes, why not? When I first met you, you seemed quite cooperative. Polite, even respectful. I questioned you and didn't learn much about Jimmy. However, I discovered something interesting about you. Apparently you fight a great deal with your crewmates. Why didn't you mention that to me?"

She hesitated. "I — I didn't want you to think I was ..."

"What? Rash? Someone who didn't think before they acted?"

"Maybe," she said in a sullen tone.

"I read your file, Anna. There were multiple entries regarding fights with coworkers. Did you think you could hide that from me?" She stared at the deck and didn't answer. I wondered how long I should keep her on the defense. I continued, "But you did give me some valuable information. Apparently Jimmy told you an interesting story. He witnessed an assault of sorts in Module A."

"Of sorts?" Manny asked.

"He saw one man lying prone on the deck. A second man, who knelt over him, gripped his arm tightly. He was looking around, afraid someone would see."

The Captain frowned. "See what?"

I nodded. "Exactly. *What did Jimmy see?*" I noticed Bram rub his left forearm as I spoke. The same thing had happened to him during the meteor shower. His brow furrowed and he watched me intently.

"Jimmy knew he'd stumbled across something bizarre," I said. "In fact, he even approached an officer about the incident."

The others looked surprised at that.

"He told me," Rickets said after a beat.

The Captain turned to him, his eyes piercing. "Why didn't you report this?"

He looked nervous at being pinned down by his Commanding Officer. "I checked everyone afterward, and no one was hurt. I had only Jimmy's word, and nothing else seemed out of the ordinary. I left it alone and waited to see if something like it happened again. Nothing did."

I said, "But it does sound peculiar, doesn't it? What if I said the same thing happened to Bram during the accident two days ago?" Everyone now stared at me, their faces blank.

Then their eyes shifted to Bram.

"It's true," he muttered with a nod. "The guy who attacked me grabbed my arm, hard. It's the last thing I remember."

People were now clearly more confused than ever. In fact, even Bram seemed not to understand what had happened to him. Interesting.

"So we have two incidents like that," Manny said. "But what does it mean?"

"I'm getting to that," I said. "Now, back to Anna. You weren't exactly truthful with me."

A look of discomfort passed over her features. "I didn't think it was important to mention my file."

"In a murder investigation? By not telling me, it looked like you were trying to hide something." I began to pace. I was through with her; she had not played a part in this. But I had only just started to pick up steam. "Then there's Lieutenant Brick Kayle."

"Me?" he said, blanching.

"The man who attacked me and Bram was strong. Very strong. Really there are only two people who fall into that category: you and First Officer Rickets." Rickets looked mortified at being singled out in front of the crew, but he managed to maintain his composure.

"Are you implying that I'm the killer?" Brick said with a hard edge to his voice.

"This will go easier if you let me finish. Now, suspicion naturally falls on both of you. First, Brick. You borrowed money from Jimmy. Money that you didn't fully pay back." He opened his mouth to object but I pressed on. "That gives you motive for killing him. You didn't want Jimmy to report to your superiors about your debt."

"But I —"

"When I asked you about it, you refused to talk. It took two days before you finally confessed, which furthered my suspicion." I shifted my gaze to Rickets. "I couldn't find any motive for you, although the fact that you did nothing after Jimmy reported the assault in the life support module was curious."

"No one was hurt," he protested, "so I —"

"Regulations chapter 43, section 5.2: *'In the event of an assault on personnel under an officer's command, or if an assault is rumored to have occurred, the officer must pursue an investigation to determine the validity of the accusation and implement whatever charges necessary, under regulations chapter 59, section 9.1.'* You of all people should be familiar with the regulations, Avery," I said.

"I didn't think it was important. As I said —"

"No one got hurt. I got that. However, it's my belief that someone *did* get hurt during that altercation. In fact, I believe it even led to Jimmy's mutilation."

"You think someone killed him because he saw something he shouldn't have," Manny said.

I sighed. "In a way, yes. But not in the way you think, Captain. You see, his death was an accident."

There was a brief moment of silence, then everyone started to talk at once. I raised a hand. "Just a second. I went out to the area where he was working before his vacsuit ripped. I took this picture." I pressed a key on my reader and an image immediately appeared in the air over it, holoprojected in three dimensions. It showed the edge of the electrical access panel on which Jimmy had been working. "That corner, right there." I pointed. "It's sharp. And it's located at the right place to have made that rip, if he was still attached to the tether that towed him out there."

"Which he would have been," Manny said. "We never remove the tether while outside."

"I also looked at Jimmy's vacsuit. It was a jagged tear. The edges weren't clean."

"What does that mean?" Grossman asked. "Someone still could have —"

"I've seen that type of murder before. Often the rip is clean, after a knife or something sharp has pierced the suit. And there's usually blood drawn. But there was no mark on Jimmy's back — Malichauk took pictures which proved that. And no blood on the vacsuit. Furthermore, the rip was relatively small. Had it been intentional, it would have been much larger — more difficult to patch." I shook my head. "No one killed Jimmy. He turned around, probably prepared to leave because he had just replaced the faulty sensor, and that's when it happened. He was dead in minutes." This was something I had bounced back and forth on since my arrival. That single death had me confounded. After the attack in my quarters, I just figured someone had murdered Jimmy after all. I was wrong. Completely wrong — but there was no way I could have known the horrible truth.

"Jesus," Brick breathed. "Then there never was a murder."

I glared at him. "There's still the matter of Jimmy's head and hands. And Reggie and Bel, of course."

He cocked his head. "Of course."

"I interviewed the Captain and found some interesting things. He disobeyed regs on some occasions. Other than that, his record is impeccable, and I don't think he's the killer. I questioned all the scientists too, including Reggie. I found that Katrina often fought with him over sensor time."

"We've been through this before," Katrina said. Her face was drawn. "It was just minor —"

"So minor that the other scientists made a point to tell me how much you two fought?" I shrugged. "Maybe you're right, but Reggie is dead now. No one else seemed to have any motive for killing him."

"But what does this have to do with Jimmy?"

I pursed my lips. "Well, you're right there. You had no reason to cut off Jimmy's head and hands. None that I know of, anyway."

It was true that Katrina's possible motivations were weak; still, I wanted everything out on the table, period. This was a time to clear the air, to explain what had happened — and to expose the killer.

I turned to Grossman, Balch and O'Donnelly, who now sat together at a table as they watched me closely. They seemed interested in what had happened to their comrade, and thankfully now listened without giving me too much grief. Still, there was more of that to come, I was sure. "Then there's you three. All of you are highly volatile people. Especially Grossman, transferred here against his will five weeks ago when Jarvis Riddel cracked. You weren't happy about that, were you Godfreid?"

"Damn straight," he barked. "I hate this place. I'm only here because Riddel couldn't handle it."

"So maybe when you arrived you decided to make someone pay for bringing you here."

He sneered. "Who, Jimmy? Absurd."

"I was thinking more of the Captain."

There was a brief pause as a look of confusion passed over his features. "Huh? I don't —"

"Responsibility for Jimmy's death falls on the Captain. He disobeyed regs when he sent Jimmy out by himself. When I make my report, his career will be over."

"So?" he snapped.

"Perhaps you were so mad at getting stuck here that you decided to ruin his career. You mutilated Jimmy's body and attracted the CCF's attention."

Dead silence. Manny turned to Grossman. His fists were knotted. "Is that true, Crewman?"

A look of panic. "No, sir! I don't have anything against you. I mean, sure, I hate this station, but I'm still in the CCF! I would never hurt an officer."

He was believable, I had to give him that. I wish I had more on him, if only because he had been a complete prick to me. If I had been the CO of *SOLEX*, I would have crucified him long ago.

"Anyway," I continued, interrupting their confrontation, "there's also Larry Balch, who has a spotty record. Disobeying orders, flaunting authority, that sort of thing. And Bram O'Donnelly —"

"Hey!" the big man yelped, red beard twitching in anger. "Someone attacked me too!"

"— who contrary to his story, can't actually *prove* someone attacked him!"

His jaw nearly hit the deck. "You think I made it up?"

"What proof do you have, Bram? Other than a welt on your head that you could have given yourself?"

He snorted and looked extremely uncomfortable, but said no more. I moved on, done with the crew for now. Next came the tough disclosures; I hadn't yet revealed my only real physical evidence.

"Then there's Doctor Lars Malichauk, who for some reason did not autopsy Jimmy's body immediately, as regs state he should. Furthermore, he jettisoned the body before I could examine it! Tampering with evidence is a punishable offence, of which I'm sure you're all aware."

Malichauk looked at me plaintively. "I told you I didn't think it was murder. In fact, didn't you already say you thought so too?"

"Yes. But the mutilation is still a crime. Someone removed Jimmy's head and hands in *your* clinic, Lars."

"I know. It's still a mystery."

"Is it?"

He looked confused. "I believe so."

I pursed my lips. "Okay. Last, but not least, Lieutenant Shaheen Ramachandra."

She watched me with a coy expression on her face. "Don't tell me you think I had a motive for all this?"

"Actually, I was going to say that I could not think of a single reason why you'd kill Reggie and Bel."

"Thanks."

"But that doesn't mean you're not guilty, Shaheen."

"What? But —"

"We haven't gotten to the nanos yet."

There was another long silence as people absorbed that.

"Nano?" Manny asked. "Now I'm really lost."

"Join the club," I said in a dry tone. "It really is a mystery, perhaps the most complex one I've ever come across. You see, I investigated this as if it were a normal — and I say that in the context of my work, trust me — murder. Motive, opportunity, weapon, and so on. But this situation is anything *but* normal. I realized that when I found a drop of blood in the life support cylinder where Jimmy witnessed the first assault."

He looked shocked. "You found blood?"

"A single drop. Old and dried, but it was there."

"Whose was it?"

"An interesting question, Captain. I took it to Malichauk and asked him to match it for me. He told me it would take a few hours, which immediately set off alarm bells."

He frowned. "Why's that?"

"Why is that, Lars?" I asked the man. I noted with interest a look of fright in his eyes.

"It was old —"

"Don't give me that bullshit!" I snapped. "It doesn't matter how old it was! There's DNA in that blood. You can determine in *minutes* who it belonged to. As a result, I also gave a sample of the blood — which I had cut in half — to Reggie Hamatsui, to match for me."

"And did he?" Manny asked with a glare at the doctor.

I nodded. "Why did you lie to me, Malichauk? Why not just match it for me, right there when I asked?"

"I — I was busy," he stammered.

"You started to work on it immediately. You lied."

"I — I ..." He trailed off and lowered his eyes.

"And later, you told me it had been here since construction!" He didn't respond and I turned away. "It's okay, Lars. I'll get to you later. Now, what was most interesting wasn't the drop of blood. It was the nano that Reggie found inside it."

Malichauk jerked his gaze back to me. "There weren't any nanos in the sample you gave me."

"No. Reggie found only one. Unfortunately for him, it was in the sample he got."

"What do you mean?" Rickets asked.

I sighed. "I believe that on the morning of his murder, Reggie probably went to the storage cylinder to get some equipment to study that nano. While in the cargo bay, he ran across Lieutenant Bertram, assigned by the First Officer to do an inventory of the supplies. Reggie told her about it, and in doing so, got them both killed."

"Someone overheard and decided to kill them," Sally gasped. "But why?"

This was where my theory took hold ... as bizarre as it had first seemed, it had grown more and more likely with each second that passed.

"Simple," I said. "Knowledge of the nano had to be covered up."

"This still doesn't make any damn sense!" Grossman grated. "Jimmy's death was accidental, and now some mysterious nano —"

"After the attack on Bram during the emergency, I put a few facts together," I continued, cutting him off. "You see, the killer also attacked me in my quarters on my second day here. He stabbed me during that attack, if you recall. But something else happened that I didn't tell anyone about."

They were focused on me now, waiting. "Go on," Sally prompted.

"My attacker grabbed my arm. His hands were wet, really wet."

Malichauk gasped, and I had to make an effort to ignore him.

"He squeezed hard, I didn't understand why. The weird thing was, he didn't do anything else! It didn't make sense. I remembered the attack that Jimmy had witnessed, of course, so I waited —"

"For how long?" Malichauk blurted.

I glanced at him. "A couple of minutes. Not long. Anyway, nothing much happened. I finally decided enough was enough and managed to get away. He ran from my cabin, and I tried to follow but lost him. It was then that I noticed the blood on my arm where he had grabbed me."

"Did he cut your arm?" Katrina asked.

"No, that was the funny thing. I washed the blood off and found I hadn't been hurt there."

"So where'd it come from?"

"From your wound?" Manny said.

"That's what I thought at first," I said. "And it wasn't until later, until I knew more about the nano and the attack on Bram, that I figured it out. You see, the blood wasn't from my stab wound at all. It was from my attacker."

He blinked. "You hurt him?"

"No, it was from his hands. You see, as soon as he attacked, I noticed his hands were wet. Even before he stabbed me. *They were covered in blood.*"

"Blood?" Lingly said, her brow wrinkled. "Why?"

I ran a hand through my hair. It was going to be difficult to convince the others of this, but only because it was so completely crazy. I steeled myself. "Why indeed. You see, I think it's how the nanos spread. In blood. My attacker had blood on his hands — blood infested with nanos."

A long pause. "But what for?" Manny asked, perplexed.

"If I'd let him grab me any longer — or hadn't washed the blood off — the nanos would have penetrated my skin and infected me."

I studied the faces that stared back at me. They were lost.

"Let me say it in plain English. The killer is infecting people with nanos. A drop of blood was left behind from the attack that Jimmy witnessed. It had a nano in it. The guy that attacked me tried to infect me with nanos. He didn't succeed. The guy that attacked Bram did the same thing."

"Then why wasn't Bram's arm covered in blood?" Shaheen asked. She hadn't suspected any of this, despite having helped me with the nano.

I turned to Doctor Malichauk. "Was there blood on Bram's arm when you found him?"

He looked stunned. "Maybe ... I think —"

I took a step forward. "You said there was no sign of trauma except for a bruise on his head." My features were hard. He couldn't hold my gaze.

All eyes were now on the doctor.

"Why keep that from us?" Manny growled.

He shook his head. "I didn't. I just — I just forgot about it, that's all."

"Sorry, Lars," I said. "That won't cut it. First you lied about the blood sample I gave you, then you 'forget' to tell us about the blood on Bram's arm."

"What do you mean he lied about the blood?" Shaheen asked.

"The blood I asked him to match for me."

"He said it's been here since construction, right?"

I nodded. "That's what he said. But that's not what Reggie told me. The blood was from someone here, in this room." I turned to Malichauk. "Why did you lie, Doctor?"

Malichauk shifted in his chair, unable to sit still. He looked as guilty as any criminal I had ever seen.

"Why the lies?" I repeated.

He looked at the others and perhaps realized he could not talk his way out of this. He deflated. "It's true. Bram's arm was soaked in blood. I cleaned it up and didn't tell anyone about it."

"And the blood sample? Why didn't you tell me who it belonged to?"

The station's power flickered again; the fans rattled as they slowed. After a long minute they started again. I searched the ceiling unconsciously and wondered if things could get any worse than they were at that precise moment.

"Because ..." He trailed off again, clearly stumbling now. He didn't know how to answer.

I continued, "Because it's part of your plan, isn't it?"

"Plan?" Manny said. "Explain, Tanner. What do you know?" He had grown frustrated with the way I had unveiled my evidence, but there was no other way. I had to walk him into this slowly ... trap him ...

I said, "The nanos are unique. They're biological with mechanical components. And they can replicate! As Reggie noted, it's totally foreign technology."

"Impossible," Sally said with a look of shock.

"I thought the same thing, but trust me, we've studied this. They divide every thirty minutes. I had Shaheen working on the problem. In fact, for a while I thought she was guilty because of her engineering expertise. Perhaps she had invented the nanos!" I looked at her; there was a quizzical expression on her face. "However," I continued, "she helped me too much to be the killer. In fact, she discovered a piece of crucial evidence in the nano's processor. A DNA code."

Sally's brow creased. "What for?"

"There can be only one reason. When the nano infects a person who actually has that DNA, the nanos will act."

"You mean kill," Rickets said.

I nodded. "Very perceptive, Avery. Yes. The nanos will kill the person. I'm not sure how or why, but that can be the only answer to this."

Everyone's jaw now hung open. "And whose DNA is it?" Rickets said finally.

"I ran a search. Our database has the DNA of every single person in the Confederacy, with a few notable exceptions." I paused, then, "The search came up negative. I couldn't match it."

Shaheen said, "I don't understand, Kyle. You said —"

"That the database has the DNA of every single person with a few notable exceptions. Ten exceptions, in fact."

"Ten," she repeated.

"That's right. Ten very powerful people."

Complete and utter silence. Then, Manny gasped as understanding came. "My God. The Council. Their DNA isn't in the database. Which means ..."

"Yes," I said. "The nanos have been programmed to infect people, to spread through the Terran Confederacy and pass through thousands, maybe millions of people, until they infect one of the Council Members. Then ... *then they kill him*."

It was an incredible plan; it was no wonder it had taken me so long to figure it out. It was brilliant ... insidious ... masterful ...

And disgusting.

All eyes were now on Malichauk. "Very good, Tanner," he whispered. "Very good. How did you figure it out?"

I shrugged. "The nano is partly a bacterium. I assume you've been working on this for years — it's really quite incredible. There must have been a lot of experiments, and a lot of failures. Only you have access to the samples of bacteria you needed. You told me that yourself, remember? You seemed to brag that only you had access to the refrigerator where biological samples are kept."

He nodded. "I slipped up, obviously." He waited a beat as he peered up at me. "Or perhaps you are just *that* good." He looked away. "What else do you have?"

"Only you could have access to the Council Member's DNA. You see, you worked for one of them, as a young man. You had access to a hair sample, a skin sample. Something like that. And you were a biologist before medical school." I sighed. "It's a difficult case, you know. I'm still not sure why the killer removed the head and hands of the victims. There are things I don't know yet. But I had to act before the infection could spread off the station. I had to destroy the jumpship. I had to launch the escape pods. I can't let anyone leave until we figure this thing out."

"You haven't told us everything yet, have you?" Shaheen said.

I looked grim. "No. There's one more thing, then Malichauk can take over and tell us all about the nanos. The drop of blood I found. It's from one of us here. Jimmy witnessed an attack in the life support module. During that attack, the nanos moved from one person to another. I know who one of those people are. The problem is, the infection has likely now spread further."

Lingly gasped. "My God! Are you saying those nanos are in some of us?"

I nodded. "Yes. In a minute Malichauk will tell us all about it. But the blood I found belonged to ..." I paused and studied everyone seated before me.

"It belonged to Brick Kayle."

—

Brick was glaring at me with hatred in his eyes. I studied him, fascinated. Did he even know the nanos had infected him? What were they doing inside him? What was their purpose? How did they operate? Were they really designed to kill, and if so, how? How would a tiny bacteria kill a man?

"Are you aware of the infection?" I asked him. The others watched in shocked fascination. The scientists, who happened to be sitting close to him, automatically slid their chairs away.

"Yes," he snarled. "They're in me."

"You're the one who attacked me."

"Yes."

"You put the night vision glasses in Jimmy's things."

"Yes."

"You left the clinic while Malichauk performed the autopsies and infected Bram just before the meteor storm." It occurred to me that in fact Malichauk *had let* Brick leave the clinic to do so, but that would have to come later.

"Yes."

"Who did you attack in the life support module?"

He didn't answer.

Manny said, "Maybe there's some test we can do, to figure out who's infected. Something —"

The lights dimmed again and this time faded almost completely to black. There was a scuffle and a scream. My hand shot to my pistol, but I realized belatedly that Rickets had taken it from me earlier. *Damn!*

I lunged in the direction Brick had been sitting seconds before. I crashed into someone and fell hard to the deck. I grabbed an arm, twisted —

And the lights came back on slowly. Still dim, but bright enough to see that I had a hold of Larry Balch. He grunted and shook me off in anger.

I rose and looked around, frantic.

Brick had gotten away.

"Hey, where's Bram?" Shaheen said, looking around.

He was gone too.

Two very important people were now loose on the station. I growled under my breath. We were in more danger than ever.

Part Four: Amplification

Investigator's Log: Lieutenant Kyle Tanner, Security Division, Homicide Section, CCF

As soon as Bram and Brick escaped, I knew we were in major shit. I should have anticipated it, dammit. I suspected the nanos were in Brick — his blood sample in the life support module should have made that obvious to me. And Bram? I knew they had infected him too. And yet because Rickets had taken my pistol, the two escaped.

It was the beginning of the end of the investigation, *and* of the station.

I was now on the second spare oxygen bottle; only eight hours remained. I had managed to shield myself from the radiation, though not completely. I continued to cough up blood, but there were no new symptoms. I had to be pleased about that.

But I was still going to die.

I had finally managed to convert my comm to a unidirectional transmitter, but I still had no idea where Mercury was. I didn't even know the comm's range.

My current velocity was three kilometers per second. I had launched myself from *SOLEX* using the mass driver some seven hours earlier. Doing a quick calculation in my head, I figured I had traveled 75 600 kilometers. And how far away was Mercury? Sixty million kilometers. I wasn't going nearly fast enough. I was nowhere near Mercury! And there was no way my comm signal was going to make it that far without breaking up into unintelligible static.

Eight hours of oxygen left. A weak unidirectional comm signal. Maybe if I could amplify the signal. But where could I get more power? The comm drew a steady amount from the suit, and if I increased it much more it would most likely burn out. But maybe I could add a bit more without causing too much damage ...

What were the other power drains on my vacsuit? Life support, of course. The fans and cooling unit. Maybe if I took power from those I could funnel it to the communit. I would have to be careful, but it was an option. Maybe my last one. If I shut down the suit's life support, however, how long could I last? Maybe ten minutes, max. The sun would broil me alive.

I hit on a sudden idea: what if I turned off the life support and funneled extra power into the communit for only a minute at a time? Then restart the suit's essential systems to keep me from burning up, then wait five minutes and repeat the process.

It might actually work. It was impossible to know for sure how far the transmission would get, but I knew I had to try. There were no other options.

I started to work on the suit controls, and as I did so, continued to record my story. I had to get it finished before the end, which was coming awfully fast.

— Chapter Nineteen —

We were still in the common mess. I had reclaimed my pistol from Rickets; it was once again snug in my holster. "Everyone stay where you are!" I yelled. "No one else leaves." I gestured at the chairs and watched carefully as they sat. It was obvious to me that there were probably more infected, and I couldn't let them follow Brick.

"This still isn't making any sense," Manny said. He had also made a grab for Brick in the darkness, but had ended up sprawled face first on the deck. The escape had been a surprise to us all. "Bram's a friend," he continued. "I've known him for decades!" His eyes were wide.

I watched him for a beat and an uncomfortable feeling settled in my gut. He didn't understand. "Manny, Bram is gone. I'm sorry. He's been gone since the attack during the meteor storm. He's already dead."

Manny's face was blank. It would be hard for him to accept the death of his friend; after all, the man still prowled the station! Had I been in Manny's shoes, however, I knew it would be a nearly intolerable situation. Still, there was nothing else to say or do.

I turned to Malichauk. "Tell us," I ordered. "Everything."

He looked like a beaten man. "I'm sorry. I didn't mean for any of this to happen. I sent the infection out with the hope that it would find its way to the intended victims without hurting other people."

"A Council Member."

His eyebrows lifted. "All of them, actually. Encoded in the nano's code is the DNA for all ten Council Members."

The computer had decoded one, but the encryption hid nine others. I was lucky Shaheen had even deciphered that one.

"But this infection, Lars — it could spread unhindered forever."

"No." He shook his head. "At least it wasn't supposed to. I programmed them to leave the body after the tenth host. That way, the infection would leave *SOLEX*, but after the nanos hit the tenth victim, they would vacate the body of the first. Do you understand? The infection is something like a snake, moving forever outward, whose head grows while its tail shrinks. It's a limiting factor I built into them. After the targets are gone ... the nanos disappear forever. They were only using us as hosts. We weren't supposed to even be aware of them."

"Why the murders? Why the severed heads and hands?"

He threw his arms up. "That's what I don't understand. I was hoping to watch Bram, to study him as the infection took hold. When I found him, unconscious with blood on his forearm, I knew infection had occurred. I wanted to understand what's happening. These murders ..." He held his head in his hands. "Something has happened ... the nanos have a life of their own now. It's just ..." He trailed off and a peculiar look came into his eyes. "Is it possible?"

"What?"

He shook his head. "Just an idea. It might explain a few things."

I folded my arms. "Come on, Malichauk. Tell us everything."

He gave a sharp exhale. "It began thirty years ago, but it was only recently that I made the breakthrough that made the nanos possible."

"From the beginning," I pressed.

He sighed. "Thirty years ago, my brother attended university in Kyoto, Japan. He was a great mathematician; he'd won several awards and scholarships. I didn't know it — none of his family did — but he had negative feelings about our beloved Council." He snorted. "The Council. That band of criminals has no right to govern humanity. They are not elected, they have those positions for life. They rule with an iron fist. They've eliminated all of our freedoms! Speech, religion, media — they regulate them all. And if someone speaks out about them, he disappears. Sent to a camp maybe? Executed? Who knows."

He ran his fingers through his thick black hair. "He never acted on his thoughts — he only talked. He ran a club at the university where people got together to discuss things they had heard ... abuses of power and so on. They tried to keep it private, but of course it was impossible in that sort of setting. Too many people were involved. Someone ratted on them to the nearest Council Rep, and the military crashed one of their meetings. They took everyone away. The lucky ones only spent a few years in camps ..." He stared at the bulkhead behind me as he relived images that only he could see. "My brother never came out," he said in a soft voice. "He died in that camp. I'm sure they executed him, but they said he died on a hunger strike."

"And you've blamed the Council ever since," Manny whispered.

"Yes. For thirty years I've been thinking of ways to murder those bastards. Nothing I came up with was practical. Oh, I had ideas. Assassination. An 'accident' in space. Suborbital crash. I thought of everything, but it all seemed too amateurish. There was always something that they could trace back to me. So I've spent all this time planning."

"That's why you've been asking for positions on remote outposts," I mumbled.

"Yes. It has allowed me the opportunity to research methods of assassination that they couldn't trace. And I thought I had succeeded. It had seemed so brilliant ... but something obviously has gone wrong."

It was a momentous understatement. Two murders ... infected people who were no longer human ... and all his doing.

"Tell us about the nanos," I said.

"I came up with the idea almost a decade ago. A self-replicating nano that could travel around the Terran Confederacy, moving from host to host, until it identified a target. When it did, it would implement a piece of code that took me longer to create than the replication did."

"What was it?"

"The kill code, Tanner. You see, the nanos are indeed part organic. Bacterial, actually. I managed to link each with a microscopic processor that can control it. I programmed the nano to migrate to the infected person's brain and inhabit a neuron. Using the processor, I taught the nanos how to control the neurons!"

"You lost me," I said with a shake of my head. "Go back a bit."

He pursed his lips, perhaps trying to decide how to best explain. "There are billions of neurons in the human brain. Each one communicates with adjacent neurons through electrochemical processes. Signals sent across tiny spaces between the cells — called synapses — are picked up by other neurons and transmitted across the brain and through the body's nervous system. The neural net. Simply put, I programmed the nanos to replicate and inhabit *every single neuron* in the host's brain. When that is completed, the nanos take control of the neurons. They regulate the firing of the cells and the signals sent across the synapses." He paused. "In essence, the nanos take control of the host."

Complete, utter silence. Then, "This is insane!" Grossman yelled. "This madman has been running crazy experiments here since day one! He set this infection loose on the station!"

Malichauk looked sad. He glanced at the others. "He's quite right, you know. I did set the nanos loose here, expecting them to spread outward and eventually find the Council Members."

"Who was the first infected person?" I asked. I already knew, I just wanted to make sure.

"Brick Kayle. I injected a batch of the nanos into him during a medical examination eight weeks ago and my plan — thirty years in the making — finally started."

It seemed fitting, in a way. His distaste for the Council had led to the first infection — the station's Council Representative.

I turned to Shaheen. "All your talk of exponential growth was right on. It was important."

"It would seem so." She had her reader out and was plotting a graph. "If the infection began with one nano, then ... Doctor, at what point does control in the host begin?"

"Not until they inhabit all the neurons. I programmed them that way."

"So at one hundred billion nanos."

I glanced at her, impressed. She had the number instantly at her fingertips. Nothing she did should surprise me anymore. She was perhaps the most intelligent person I had ever met.

"But that would take forever," Manny said.

I snarled. "No, it wouldn't take long at all, as Shaheen taught me earlier."

She looked up from her reader. "Eighteen and a half hours," she said, "provided infection is by a single nano."

He blinked. "What? That quickly?"

"Here, look." She showed Manny the graph. The number of nanos was placed on the vertical axis. The horizontal axis showed the progression of time. There was a solid line placed horizontally across the graph at the hundred billion threshold. It intersected with the number of host nanos at eighteen and a half hours.

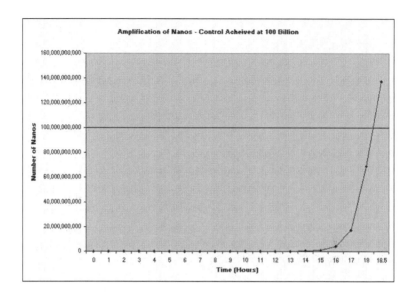

I grunted. "That makes total sense. When you sent Riddel from *SOLEX* he was hallucinating and raving about the heat, the radiation, and so on. But by the time he arrived at Mercury in Doctor Higby's care, some twenty hours later, he was apparently fine." I turned to Malichauk. "Someone must have infected Jarvis just before he left the station. Did you do it?"

"No." His mouth twitched. "The miracle of the nanos. They have a life of their own — infecting others now to spread toward the inevitable."

I studied him for a moment. He seemed proud of his accomplishment — even though it might now mean his own death.

Something tingled at my senses, begged for attention, but I disregarded it. Malichauk's story was too important to ignore.

Manny peered at the chart and said, "Incredible. It happens so quickly."

"So while the nanos are multiplying —" I said to the doctor.

"A process called *amplification*," he supplied.

"— what does the host feel?"

"Nothing. No change at all."

Lingly shot to her feet. "How could you do this! And you tried to cover it up! You washed the blood off Bram's arm to hide the infection!"

He nodded and gave a soft sigh. "I hid Bram's infection to study him. I want to know why they aren't following their programming. Why they're murdering."

"But —" she stammered.

I waved her off. "Let's just hear him out. Maybe there's some way we can stop this from continuing."

Malichauk turned his attention back to me. "The takeover will occur rather suddenly. As soon as they reach the hundred billion threshold. And then, bang, they assume control."

"What are they supposed to do?"

"Only two things. First, they check the DNA of the host against the DNA codes I programmed them with. If the host is a Council Member, then they activate the kill code."

I frowned. "How?"

"The nanos have the host commit suicide. Whatever's handy. A jump from a building. Pistol. Anything. I programmed them to be quite versatile."

"Obviously," Manny mumbled.

"What's the second thing?" I asked.

"If they are not a Council Member, they're required to pass the infection on to ten people. When that's done, the nanos proceed to the bladder, the same as with all other medical nanos."

"They pass the infection through the hand, right?"

"Yes, you already guessed that, surprisingly. When a new host is located in a quiet place, nanos move to the fingers and infection will occur. The host wasn't supposed to be aware of it; it would be a short period of missing time, nothing more."

I shook my head in anger; the euphemisms he used were outrageous. *Infection* in this case meant a violent assault. So violent, in fact, that I had nearly lost my life.

"They grab on to the person's arm and some nanos cross from the fingers into the skin of the new host," I growled.

"Yes. That's why the attackers had bloody hands. They were in infection mode, getting ready to spread. The nanos travel through blood, it's needed during infection."

"How long does it take?"

He glanced at the ceiling while he considered the question. "I predicted fifteen minutes during my research, but I don't know for sure."

My breath blew out in a rush and I leaned back, relieved.

"Yes," he said, eyeing me. "You're lucky. You only allowed contact for a few minutes, and you washed the blood away immediately after. And since several days have now passed, there is no way the nanos are controlling you."

A shock passed through my body as a thought occurred: maybe I *was* infected! Would I even know? Perhaps they made me think I was perfectly normal, when in fact I was under their control!

My hand trembled; I immediately hid it from view.

"How can we kill the nanos?" I said in a flat voice.

He shook his head. "You can't. I've programmed numerous defense mechanisms."

"To protect the infection." I exhaled. "I can't believe what you've done." I pursed my lips in thought. Something Quint Sirius had said to me, only days earlier, came to me unbidden. Funny, it seemed like I had taken him into custody years ago. What was it he had said? *I'm sick*, he sobbed. *I need help.*

"What about antibiotics?" I asked suddenly. "After all, these things are essentially bacteria, right? Antibiotics should be enough to —"

Malichauk laughed a sharp bark. "Do you think I would create nanos susceptible to something so simple? I hardened them to antibiotics during the original manufacturing process. It's similar to what happened when doctors in the old days treated an infection and the patient didn't take the recommended dosage. It exposed the bacteria, but not to the point where they died. Rather, the subsequent generations developed a resistance to the drugs. So, I allowed my nanos to develop in a similar fashion. Evolution, Tanner!"

I scowled. He had thought ahead, anticipated the nano's discovery. "What else?"

He shrugged. "Well, the fact that most drugs don't penetrate into the brain, where the nanos are located."

"And?"

He fell silent for a moment. "They have other defense mechanisms, but I don't really want to say more about them."

I knotted a fist. Dammit. He was willing to talk about them — perhaps even *brag* about them! — but not to the point where it could help us survive this situation. We had to convince him; our lives depended on it.

Katrina said, "Building self-replicating machines is a dangerous thing, Doctor. Rampant growth — especially *exponential* growth — can lead to what many scientists have called the *gray goo* problem."

"Gray goo?" Rickets asked.

"An uncontrolled population of runaway nanobots growing exponentially, eating a planet's biosphere to supply the energy for replication. It's a scary proposition."

"It's nonsense," Malichauk said. "As I said, I programmed limitations into them."

Katrina snorted. "Some job you did. They don't seem to obey your programming."

He rolled his eyes as if he didn't care.

"Don't you see what you've done?" I snapped. "You created a self-sustaining bullet that could exist forever. An *intelligent* bullet that will no longer listen to its master!"

He sneered but still didn't respond.

"Do you realize that someone on Mercury removed Jarvis Riddel's head and hands?" I said, thinking back to my discussion with Doctor Higby.

"What?!" Manny asked, stunned. Malichauk also looked shocked.

"Yes. He apparently had a heart attack, and some people from Earth examined the body and took those parts away." I waited, but the doctor had no answer for me. I mulled the problem over for a moment. "You've answered some questions, Malichauk, but there's still another big one."

He nodded. "The murders and the severed heads and hands. Since the nanos are located in the brain and fingers of the host, someone was trying to cover up evidence of Jimmy's infection. An autopsy might have revealed them."

The nanos had indeed controlled Jimmy, but as Malichauk planned, he still seemed normal in every regard. He had even died in an accident, in a very human way.

"Then why were Reggie and Bel killed?" Shaheen asked.

"Reggie discovered the nano," I said. "He told Bel, and an infected person must have overheard. There's no way to tell who it was, though it might very well have been Brick."

"But why cut their heads and hands off? They probably weren't infected."

I frowned. "I've been thinking about that," I said. "The answer I keep coming up with is that had he simply killed the two and left them there, it might have looked odd to me. But the fact that both their heads and hands were gone made me think there was still just one killer, killing in the same method. It was brilliant, really."

Malichauk grunted. "Yes it was. The only problem is, I never programmed that into them. The nanos aren't obeying my code. They're acting on their own now."

I said, "And what's worse, Doctor, they're incredibly intelligent."

It grew deathly quiet.

"How is that possible?" Rickets asked. "Nanos are just *tools*."

"Tanner's right," Malichauk answered. "I've pondered the problem since discovering Jimmy's body. You see, it occurred to me immediately when I found that his head and hands were missing. It is the *only two areas of the body where the nanos can be found.*"

"And you didn't program that into them?" I asked.

"Definitely not." He paused and began to pace. "But it does make me wonder. You see, we've never succeeded in making a nano intelligent. They're too small, not enough processing power. They can receive orders and obey them, but they can't do much thinking for themselves."

Sally said, "Then how are they managing to —"

"Well, typical nanos can't communicate with each other. However, I've programmed these ones to take over neurons — *one hundred billion neurons*, mind you — in the host and communicate with each other using the brain's own system — electrochemically. Think about it! One hundred billion organisms talking to each other simultaneously at the same speed our own neurons communicate."

"A hive mind?" I suggested.

"Exactly! Individually the nanos are simple machines, nothing more. But with all of them inhabiting a host's brain and talking to one another, it's possible an intelligence has evolved. They've formed a neural net, superimposed over our own! It seems logical." He shook his head, amazed. "I didn't foresee it."

"Obviously the murders and their attempts at concealing their existence are evidence of intelligence," Manny said.

The scientists looked horrified. Intelligent nanos in control of human beings?

"Malichauk," I asked, "what are the chances that they will still obey the original code?"

"Which code?"

"The kill code, as you call it."

His brow creased. "I have no idea, really."

"What about the code that tells them to leave the host after performing ten infections?"

"I can't say," he murmured.

Avery Rickets clenched his fists. "This is insane. You've admitted to the release of an infection on board this station. It may have even spread to the outside! And on top of that, at least two of us are infected — Brick and Bram — and maybe more of us in this room as well!"

Malichauk looked defeated. "I'm sorry, I really am. It wasn't supposed to happen this —"

"Bah!" Rickets spat and turned from him.

There was that feeling again ... something about the disease spreading off the station.

"Oh my God," I muttered. "Oh shit."

"What?" Shaheen asked, concerned.

"I just realized something. Something scary. The people who took Jarvis Riddel on Mercury. They removed his head and hands. They must have discovered the nanos."

"So?" Katrina said.

I thought furiously, the pieces falling together easily in my head. "It explains a lot of things ... like the constant reports Mercury was asking Brick to file." I spun on the scientists. "You all complained about the number of reports you were forced to make for them."

"I don't understand," Manny said.

"Think about it. Someone discovers the infection in Riddel. They *know* it came from *SOLEX*. The question is, who made the nano? The simplest explanation is that one of the scientists here created them. Hence all the reports. They want to know what all of you are up to. They hoped one of you would slip up!"

"Oh my God," Lingly said in shock. "I can't believe it."

Shaheen noticed the look on my face. "What is it, Kyle?"

I said in a quiet voice, "They knew about the infection when they sent me here. Maybe they sent me thinking I'd be able to figure things out. But they didn't tell me about Jarvis Riddel, the nano, nothing. They didn't prepare me. I think they sent me in expecting me to figure it out or die trying."

Rickets said, "What do you mean?"

I hesitated. "I'm expendable. And now we may all be dead."

"How so?"

I threw my hands up. "Do you think they'll let any of us off this station if we can't figure this out and beat the infection? They'll kill us all if we call for help or try to leave before I've solved the mystery."

No one said anything. They looked at each other and waited for someone to object to my theory.

No one did.

And then the power failed, this time for good.

Everything was out. Ventilation fans, lights, carbon dioxide scrubbers, the microwave beam to Earth. Everything.

Battery power kicked in a second later and the environmental systems restarted. The lights remained out, however; only the red glow from the emergency system now illuminated the station.

"Will they come back on?" Sally inquired as she looked to the ceiling.

"If Brick or Bram did this," Shaheen said, "and they did a thorough job, then no. The batteries are dedicated to the critical systems like life support. Lighting isn't that important."

"Maybe Earth will send someone for us now that the beam has stopped," Lingly said with a flash of excitement on her face.

She still didn't understand. She hadn't listened to a word I had said. Or, maybe she just didn't want to believe it. "No, they won't," I replied savagely. "They know what's going on here. They won't send anyone. They'll let us die in order to kill the infection. We're on our own."

She flinched and pulled back, but her expression wasn't anger. She was appalled.

"What do we do?" Balch said.

I considered his question. "Some of us here may be infected right now. We have to find a way to identify who. And we have to worry about Brick and Bram. They're on this station ... they will kill us to save themselves."

"If they do that, they threaten their own chances of survival!" Sally shouted.

"We represent more of a threat alive than dead," I said. "Don't forget that. If knowledge of this gets out, the CCF will hunt and kill everyone suspected of carrying the infection without mercy. They wouldn't even get a chance to explain."

"We're on our own then," Manny said, grave.

"But what can we do?" Lingly asked in a trembling voice.

I didn't plan on answering, but I noticed all eyes on me, including the Captain's. "I'm open to suggestions," he said.

I grunted. "I guess we have no choice."

"What's that?" Grossman growled. "Abandon the station and set it to self-destruct?'

Another silence, then, "There are a few problems with that," Rickets answered. "First, Tanner destroyed all means of escape."

Grossman looked mad enough to chew nails.

The First Officer continued, "Second, he's right. More of us could be hosts. We need to find out who and deal with them."

The gravity of his statement hit like thunder. The scientists, crew, and officers stared at one another, unsure what to do.

Run? Where?

Hide? How?

Call for help? From whom?

Everyone was scared to death.

"You were saying?" Rickets said, looking to me.

"There are two things."

"Two? That's it?" Grossman said. He looked surprised.

"Right. First, we have to find and restrain Bram O'Donnelly and Lieutenant Kayle."

"Maybe we should just kill them," Katrina Kyriakis said.

Gasps all around. "Well why not?" she said. "Look, they had no qualms killing Reggie and Belinda. And if we do manage to capture them, don't forget they're highly contagious."

"Infection takes fifteen minutes," Malichauk reminded her.

"I'm sure there are other ways to become infected, Doctor."

That stunned Malichauk. "I only programmed one."

"These nanos have grown intelligent, you said so yourself. A hive mind."

"Perhaps, yes." He nodded.

"So they know we are a threat to their survival. What does a sentient, intelligent species do when threatened?" She planted her hands on her hips. "They fight! They do whatever they can to avoid extinction. From where I'm standing, those two men out there —" She pointed out the hatch and to the corridor beyond. "— are alone, possibly frightened, and ready to kill to survive. So yes, I'm suggesting we find and kill them. There's nothing odd about that at all."

She was right, but these were two of their own she referred to. It was going to be hard to convince the others that there was no hope for them anymore.

"You mentioned other methods of infection," I said. "What are you implying?"

"Doctor Malichauk says he programmed infection to occur only through direct contact. But what about ingesting a nano? In our food, perhaps. Or inhaling one, in our air supply."

Lars shook his head. "That would mean they isolated nanos and allowed them to replicate outside the body. It's not possible."

"Why not?"

"The bacterial hosts need to replicate in an environment that supplies an unlimited amount of fuel energy. The human body is the source of energy for them, therefore replication will occur there."

Sally looked outraged. "Come on, Doctor! You of all people know bacteria can be grown in bacterial ovens outside the host!"

He frowned. "Of course I do, but where would they manage to find something like that here? It's not a practical line of thought. Infection can only occur by touching —"

"Just a second, Doc," I interjected. "Katrina suggested we could become infected through our food. Is that possible."

His eyebrows arched. "I suppose, but I didn't program —"

"Did you program them to murder and slice people's heads off?"

He looked outraged. "Of course not! I already explained —"

"Case closed," Katrina said. "We need to be extremely careful what we eat. Only sealed ration packs."

"Oh please!" Malichauk said. "Those two only just escaped. They couldn't possibly be ready to infect us in the manner you're suggesting."

"They have probably known something like this was coming, Doctor," Manny said. "The three bodies, remember? Tanner's here to investigate, and they knew he was good. They must have anticipated this."

I considered what the Captain said. It was interesting. "You're suggesting the nanos were prepared for this?"

"They cut the power pretty damn fast."

A jolt coursed through my body. He was right. Perhaps they expected that I would discover the truth all along. After all, they had tried to infect me almost immediately upon my arrival. And if they predicted this development, they might also have prepared some nasty surprises for us. "We better move quickly then."

"Wait," Rickets said. "You haven't finished yet. What was the second thing we have to do? The first was to find and restrain Bram and Lieutenant Kayle ..."

I nodded. "The second is to develop a test to find out who among us are infected right now. Just as you suggested."

Silence.

"Why do you think one of us is under control?" Sally asked with a tremor in her voice.

I knotted a fist. "Think about the chain of events that has occurred. Jimmy witnessed an actual infection taking place. So that means the nanos controlled two people, *at least*. Got me?"

"Yes."

"Jimmy died and someone removed his head and hands. This indicates Jimmy himself was infected. That's three."

"Okay ..."

"Someone was trying to cover up the infection in Jimmy. Later, someone killed Reggie and Bel, also to cover up the infection." I exhaled. "In addition, don't forget *Jarvis Riddel was also infected*. He left *SOLEX four weeks ago*. That's four. Do you really think that in a four week period no further infections took place? If it only takes fifteen minutes, there could be a lot more than two infected people right now." I eyed them slowly, one by one.

Balch said, "Then everyone here might be infected!" He backed away until there was steel at his back.

I held my hand up. "No! Think about it. If that were true, we wouldn't be sitting here talking right now. You'd all attack and infect me."

"You talk as if you were still human," Grossman snorted.

I hesitated. This was a tricky problem. "I know I am, but I suppose you all need proof of that, right? Well I need proof that you are uninfected too, Grossman."

"Makes sense," Manny said. He turned to Malichauk. "What would it take to develop a test for this?"

"How about a simple blood test?" Katrina asked.

"No," he answered. "Based on their programming, the nanos will cluster in the brain. A blood test will not reveal anything."

"What about blood from the fingers?" I said. "Nano-infected blood is how they spread, right?"

"Yes, but the nanos stay in the brain until infection is imminent. That's part of the reason it takes so long. They don't migrate to the fingers until —"

My eyebrows arched. "Why program that into them?"

He looked surprised. "To avoid detection, of course. I wanted the nanos as far from potential discovery as possible."

"And as a result, we have no way to test for them."

He sighed. "That was the whole point, unfortunately."

Was there a chance he would help us? He had already refused to answer questions about the nano's defense mechanisms. Whatever the case, I had to ask — there was no choice. "Can you think of anything?"

His brow creased. "I'll try. But I need to be in the clinic."

I considered that for a moment. "Fine. We'll assign two people to stay with you, just in case." I turned to Shaheen. "Can we seal all the modules?"

"They've cut the power, Tanner. We can't do much." She looked lost in thought. "But in an emergency all the tunnel hatches should seal ...".

"What are you suggesting?"

"That we fake an emergency, get the modules cut off from each other. The hatches work on battery power if the computer thinks there's a depressurization accident."

"But what will that achieve?" Balch asked. "The tunnel hatches seal. So what?"

"It will confine those two. We can search the station module by module until we find them. That way we can all stay together while we're looking. It might disrupt whatever they're planning."

"Will they be able to open the hatches?" I asked Shaheen.

"They'd need the override codes, which they don't know."

Manny interjected, "We don't need to fake an emergency, Shaheen. I can simply command all the hatches to seal. Even on battery power I can do it with the security codes. We'll go to the command center to give the computer the orders."

I thought that over. Trap them in a module and stay together as a group as we searched the station. Find them, restrain them, then wait for Malichauk to develop his test. It was the best we could do. Despite the idea, however, a part of my mind screamed at me about best laid plans.

I should have known better.

— Chapter Twenty —

We prepared silently to venture out of the mess and up the two levels to the command center. The faces that looked back at me were pale. Lingly in particular was terrified; she jerked her head this way and that, as if one of us meant her harm

"They could be right out in the corridor, waiting for us," she hissed.

"Who cares," Grossman rumbled. "There are eleven of us and two of them. They don't stand a chance."

"But there's no use presenting them with an opportunity to hurt — or infect — some of us," Manny said. "We'll have to be careful at all times."

I studied Grossman out of the corner of my eye. He seemed to object to everything the rest of us agreed on. He had been belligerent since my arrival. Now he was upset it was taking so long to organize everyone.

"It's only two levels," he growled. "We're practically there already. Let's just go!"

Finally we moved, en masse, out the hatch and into the corridor. It was nearly pitch black; the only illumination came from the red emergency lights spaced evenly along the bulkheads. There was no lighting on the ladder, so we moved upward one at a time into a dark, yawning, well of inky black. Rickets and I were the only ones armed, so the First Officer led the way and I stayed at the rear. I preferred it that way — I could keep an eye on the entire group to make sure nothing happened.

On the uppermost level, the corridor came to a dead end. Before us, a hatch led to the command center. Manny opened it and we moved quickly inside, perhaps worried someone watched from the shadows.

Manny marched to a console and started to enter commands into the station's central computer.

A klaxon ripped through the station; I jumped from the sudden noise.

"It's okay," he said over the din. "Just a precaution."

An instant later a clang sounded as the hatch we had just entered locked. A red light on its control panel illuminated.

"It's done," Manny said. "All over the station. Wherever they are, they're trapped."

I fixed my eyes on his. Time to hunt our prey.

—

Manny was out in front with Rickets; the First Officer unlocked each hatch as we moved through. I brought up the rear and sealed each hatch as we passed. The clinic was in the same cylinder as the command center, and we stopped there to leave Malichauk to work on his test for the infection. We left Balch and Anna behind to stay with him. They didn't protest, but they didn't exactly look happy.

"How long will this take?" Manny asked.

"No idea," Malichauk answered with a shrug. "I'm not even sure how to do it, without taking a direct sample from the host's brain."

A simple blood test wouldn't work; Malichauk had designed the nanos well. To make matters worse, he didn't exactly seem eager to help us.

"Can't do that," I said. "Could kill someone." A thought suddenly occurred to me. "Wait a minute, Lars. Can't we just use a nano programmer to access the nanos directly? If you scan a person and get a response from one, it'll give him away."

He shook his head. "The nanos won't respond to a programmer once inside the host."

I frowned. "But we used one earlier to access the nano Reggie found in the drop of blood."

"That one had been outside a human body for weeks. There was no host, so the nano allowed contact."

I grunted. It made sense.

"Get it done," Manny grumbled to the man who had caused all this. "But don't take too much time."

The doctor was incredulous. "I have no idea how to test for them, Captain. I might never come up with —"

"You better damn well come up with something to help us, Doctor!" Manny bellowed.

He pulled back, seemed to deflate. "Aye, sir."

We sealed Balch, Anna and Malichauk in the clinic. They watched, completely silent, as the hatch shut and locked with a clang. It would not open until we returned.

"Why are we leaving two people with the doctor?" Katrina asked. "Why not just one?"

"What if we just left Balch, and it turned out he was infected?"

She thought that over. Then, "But what if two of the three people we left behind are infected?"

"Then the third one is in trouble," I said, grim. That was a dilemma we would face no matter how many we left behind. Just how many of us were gone? There was no longer any doubt — this was a nightmare. My own Commanding Officers had abandoned me to this mess. In fact, they may have even *expected* me to die.

I clenched a fist. That, at least, I would fight to the bitter end.

"Why don't we all just stay with the doctor and wait for the test?" Grossman suggested. "Then when we figure out which of us are infected, we take care of them and call Earth for help. Surely they'll come then."

I studied his expression. His lips had pulled back and his teeth were bared. "What do you mean, 'take care of them?'" I asked.

He snorted. "Restrain them, or kill them as Katrina suggested. Whatever."

"There's still Lieutenant Kayle. And Bram." I shook my head. "We can't leave them running around the station."

"Why not?"

I stopped short and the entire group came to an abrupt halt in the corridor with me. "Put yourself in their position, Grossman. What would you be doing, right now?"

"You mean, if I was infected and trapped somewhere on the station?" His brow furrowed. "I guess I'd be figuring out how to escape."

"And?"

He looked puzzled. "I — I'm not sure."

"Then I'll fill you in. They have to kill or infect every single one of us, Grossman. And they have to do it fast."

"But why?" Lingly said.

"Because we represent a huge threat. We *know* about them. We know what they are and what their plan is. If we expose them, we threaten their survival. We can't let them attack. We have to keep them on the defensive and somehow capture them." I considered our options for a beat. I still didn't know what would happen to an infected host. I had assumed they were already dead, that the infection would be impossible to cleanse. Still, there might be a way ...

Grossman didn't say anything as he mulled that over. "You may be right," he said finally. "It's what I'd do. If my life were in danger, I mean."

I examined the hatch directly before us — the tunnel to Module B. We had checked Module C and found no one. It was time to move to the next cylinder: Officer's Country. All the officer's quarters and recreation facilities were there.

The hatch slid aside at Manny's command and we entered the tunnel.

—

We moved from cabin to cabin and investigated each thoroughly. Rickets and Manny performed the bulk of the search; I stayed in the corridor with the pistol and watched our backs. A group of eight people was an unwieldy size to coordinate, but it was smarter to keep as many together as possible.

As we finished our search of the officer's module, Shaheen noticed something amiss. She looked at the others, her forehead creased.

"Wait a minute," she said. "Where's Sally?"

We looked at each other and realized the scientist wasn't with us. Shit. We were all together just a minute ago ...

"How the hell could she just disappear?" Manny growled.

"She must have left on her own," I said. "No one could have grabbed her; we would have noticed."

"Damn," he muttered. "What do we do now?"

I chewed a lip, frustrated. It was too damn dark in the corridors. "Continue searching and hope she turns up," I said. But if a certain amount of time passed before she reappeared ...

"Yeah," Grossman said. "Turns up infected."

I understood his fear. "Then we keep her separated until Malichauk's test is done."

We began to move down the corridor to the next module. Minutes later, a sudden sound of clanging steps echoed to us.

I spun and raised the pistol. "Hold it right there!"

Sally skidded to a halt and almost fell on her ass. She raised her hands in protest. "Wait! Don't leave without me!"

"Where the hell have you been?" Manny hissed.

"The lavatory," she said, her eyes wide. "I used Lieutenant Bertram's quarters, just back there." She gestured down the corridor in the direction we had come. "I didn't think you'd leave without me."

I checked my watch. Eight minutes had passed since she had disappeared. Not enough time.

I hoped.

She studied our faces in turn, her expression of guilt clear. "It was stupid, I know. But don't worry — I'm fine. Let's continue the search."

"Wait a minute," Manny growled. He turned to the others. "No one leaves the group again. Not to use the lavatory, not for anything. Is that understood?"

Everyone mumbled agreement. Keeping people together was more difficult than I had planned. There was strength in numbers, without a doubt, but what about when there was a threat from within? What if one of our group was one of *them?*

We continued the search in Module A.

We searched all nine cylinders with no luck. Everyone looked downcast and despondent that we had uncovered nothing. There was even talk of looking in Module I, the storage module sealed after the meteor had penetrated the hulls, but we quickly abandoned the idea.

"It's open to vacuum," Rickets said. "The only way to get in would be with the Captain's code, which Kayle and Bram don't know."

Weary and beaten, we marched back to the clinic and Doctor Malichauk. We climbed the ladder and approached the —

My breath exploded out in a rush.

The hatch to the clinic was forced half open and a body lay draped across the threshold. There was blood — a lot of it. It had spilled from the person's head and puddled on the deck. It spread outward even as we watched.

"Oh my God!" Lingly cried. "What happened here?"

Rickets bent and turned the gory mess over. Larry Balch.

Inside the clinic we found Anna Alvarez, also dead.

Malichauk was gone, along with any chance of a test for the infection.

"Was he infected?" Manny asked as he hovered over the two bodies. "Or did Bram and Lieutenant Kayle do this?" He hesitated as he said the name of his lifelong friend. Perhaps it had just dawned on him that his friend was as good as dead.

"Who knows," I said. "Maybe we'll never know the truth. Malichauk is gone, and if he wasn't infected before, it's happening to him right now. If he comes back, we have to assume he's being controlled."

"But we checked this module," Sally protested. "How could they have gotten past us? It *must* have been Malichauk."

"Not necessarily," Shaheen said. "We may have searched the module, but there are a lot of places we didn't look."

I shot a look at her. "What are you talking about?"

"There are plenty of maintenance and air supply ducts, access junctions, and so forth. We only checked the areas that are readily accessible and in plain sight."

"You mean we didn't check the whole station?" That shocked me.

"Not nearly. I'd say only half."

"Only half!" I watched her with a scowl on my face. We had searched the module together; she never mentioned that we weren't looking in every hiding spot. Why hadn't she suggested it?

"As a crewman, Bram knows the station better than anyone else. Except maybe me."

"Damn," I sighed. "*SOLEX* is too big for this. Those two —"

"Three now."

"— can lose themselves here easier than I thought." I frowned. "There must be a better way."

I stared at the two bodies that lay twisted on the deck. We had to get this situation under control. More people were going to end up dead. The search had turned up nothing; instead, two more of our own were dead, and the man who had invented the nanos was gone.

We regrouped in the command center, where we could feel a little more secure while we discussed our options. Manny stationed Grossman and Rickets out in the corridor, and the rest of us sat in the darkened room. There were a lot of despondent looks.

"Manny," I said eventually. "I need to make an FTL transmission."

His brow furrowed. "We're on battery power right now. Any extra power usage will limit our time left." If his statement wasn't clear, his expression certainly was. He did not think it was a good idea.

"How much time do we have?"

"Twenty-four hours," Shaheen answered with a glance at a display.

Damn. "It's important I make these calls. Besides, Manny, if we can't figure this thing out soon, we won't last a day anyway."

He studied me, silent, before he finally nodded. "Just keep it short, Tanner."

Shaheen entered a code into the communit and the system unlocked for me. She avoided Manny's glare; she had locked the system without his knowledge in order to help me isolate *SOLEX's* personnel.

I sat at the same console where earlier I had taken the call from Mercury. I shoved the jack in my ear and signaled the station's Command Group.

A man appeared on the screen; he looked more than a little suspicious. "Who is this?" he demanded.

"Lieutenant Kyle Tanner, CCF, Homicide," I said. "I need to speak to Lieutenant Jase Lassiter, your Commander."

—

"What is it, Tanner?" Lassiter asked. His face was hard, his tone clipped. The screen was dim and flickered with static.

"I need to know the truth," I said without preliminaries.

He looked confused. "About what?"

"The murders. The investigation. The reason you sent me here."

He remained silent for almost a full minute. "What's going on?" he asked finally. "Why is it so dark there? Why is your signal so weak? I've been trying to contact you for hours now. I thought you had all the damage from the meteors fixed."

"Aren't you going to ask why the microwave beam to Earth has stopped?"

He looked cagey. "I assumed it was the meteor damage."

He was lying. He had just said he thought we had it fixed. I snorted. "It's not. Something else has happened here."

"I thought so —" he said before he suddenly stopped himself. He winced at his slip.

"Tell me," I said in a sharp tone. "What do you know?"

He reached forward to sever the connection.

"Wait!" I pounded a fist on the console. "Don't you dare cut me off! You have to tell me what you know, Lassiter. It's important." A pregnant pause ensued. I continued, "You know about the infection, don't you?" Still no response. "We've identified some infected people. We're trying to figure out what to do. We could use some help —"

He nodded. "They told me you'd ask for help."

My eyebrows arched. Interesting. "Who told you that?"

He just stared at me, silent once more.

"For fuck's sake," I hissed. "I've solved the murders! But there's more going on here than I thought. I've discovered something more important. Now start answering my questions so I can make my report, dammit!"

Some of his resolve seemed to fade. He slumped back in his chair. "Earth told me that if you called for help I was to ignore you. I'm not to allow anyone off the station."

"What else?" I growled.

He looked around as if to avoid prying ears. "They told us *SOLEX* had been contaminated. A hallucinogenic disease, they said. Highly contagious. Ends in death one hundred percent of the time." Again he reached to terminate the signal.

"Aren't you concerned about Shaheen?" I said quickly.

He paused, hand outstretched. He sighed. "Of course I am. But we broke up months ago, Tanner."

I hadn't known that. "But you still must care for her," I said, trying to reason with him. "You can't just abandon her to —"

"I have to follow orders, as do you."

"Listen, I have information that Earth needs. They don't have to abandon us. We're not all infected, for Christ's sake!"

He looked pained. "It doesn't matter. You've all been exposed. There's no help for you."

"That's not true. If we can figure out who's infected and who's not —"

"And how will you do that? How can you convince Earth?"

"I'll find a way," I said. "We'll come up with a test."

"Is Malichauk working on one?"

I hesitated. "The doctor's gone."

He looked concerned for the first time. "What do you mean? He's dead?"

"Just gone." I clenched my fist under the console. He didn't know the full truth, but it didn't matter. What his bosses had told him meant our death, either way.

He looked around, lowered his voice further. "Look, they have physical evidence of a dangerous infection."

Of course. "That must be Jarvis Riddel."

He looked taken aback. "Riddel? What about him? I thought he cracked up and had a heart attack weeks ago."

"He was ... sick. That's how Earth discovered this." In fact, it was entirely possible that Riddel had tried to infect the men from Earth when they took him away. As a result, they removed his infection — his head and hands — and decided to send someone to investigate. Me.

"Listen, if this disease is as bad as they say, they're not going to let you off that station. Even if you find a way, they'll capture and quarantine you. Maybe worse."

I frowned. He was right. "I have to figure out exactly what's going on and who's infected. When I've done that, I'll be in touch."

He shook his head. "I can't help you, Tanner. I'm sorry, but you're on your own."

"Earth knew about it when they sent me," I said. "They knew the infection was spreading on *SOLEX!*"

He looked shocked. "Are you sure? They never told me that. I only just found out —"

He was lying to my face now, and I knew it. "Bullshit," I snapped. "Why demand all the reports from the scientists? Why the need for the constant updates?"

He shook his head. "I'm sorry I can't say any more. Good luck." He cut the link.

I fell back in the chair, frustrated. Damn. He was perhaps the only help we could get, and I had pushed him too hard.

Or, maybe I just wanted someone to admit to my face that they had knowingly sent me to my death.

—

The next call I made was more important than the first. It was to Doctor Higby, also on Mercury. Manny watched with a worried expression; every second spent on the FTL meant less time for survival on *SOLEX*. Unfortunately, I had no choice.

"Hello Inspector." the elderly man said when the connection came through. He squinted at the screen. "Say, what's wrong with your transmission?"

"We're having some power problems."

"I hope you're okay." He looked concerned.

I grunted. Sure, I'm just fine right now. How are you? "I have another question about Jarvis Riddel," I said.

"Go ahead."

"When he first arrived, you said he was still delirious and hallucinating. But as the hours passed, he became much calmer."

"That's right. He was like a different person."

"Did you take any blood samples or do any tests on him?"

He nodded. "We always do blood tests, just to rule out drug use as the cause of the mental break. He was clean."

"Nothing showed up?"

"Nothing at all."

I considered my next question carefully. It was important — if he was going to lie about anything, it would be this. "Doctor Higby, how long were you alone with Riddel?"

He looked perplexed. "I was his doctor. I was with him from his arrival on and off for the next six hours or so. Until those men arrived and took him away."

"No, I mean alone. Just the two of you."

Pause. "I'm not sure I understand the question. What are you implying?" His expression bordered on anger.

I thought furiously. I wanted to ask if Riddel had tried to infect Higby, but without actually coming out and saying it. The less Higby knew about the infection the better.

"Did he try to pass you any information?" I asked.

"No."

"Did he try to touch you?"

Higby snorted. "What exactly does that mean?"

I sighed. Perhaps I could word it in a way that he would understand. "I'm worried that Riddel might have been sick. I was wondering if he ... got you sick too."

A look of understanding. "I feel quite fine, I promise you. He never touched me. In fact, we restrained him."

That startled me. Finally, some good luck in all of this. "Really?"

"During the entire trip from *SOLEX* until just before they removed him from my care."

My brow creased. "Why did you remove his restraints?"

"As I mentioned earlier, he was doing much better. He was calm and quiet. I freed him as a sign of good faith."

"How long was he unrestrained and alone with you before they took him away?"

He peered at the ceiling. "Oh, I'd say thirty minutes or so. Yes, he was unrestrained for a good thirty minutes while under my care."

— Chapter Twenty-One —

I sat and stared at the blank communit for a long moment as Higby's final words rang in my ears.

Thirty minutes ...

Was it possible? Had Riddel used his first opportunity away from *SOLEX* to infect someone? Or, was it more likely that he had bided his time until the people who cared for him trusted him more? Moreover, Higby seemed willing to talk with me, to help me understand what had happened. If he was under control — and one of *them* — then why tell me that he and Riddel had been alone?

Manny watched me uneasily as I unplugged the jack from the comm and joined them.

"How did it go?" he asked.

I sighed. "Jase Lassiter isn't willing to help."

"Why not?"

"As I said earlier, they know about the infection."

He looked shocked. "Lassiter knows?"

I shrugged. "Oh, he knows there's something wrong, but he thinks it's some kind of new disease. He doesn't realize the full extent of the illness."

"He wasn't compassionate at all?"

I shook my head. "He even warned me that we're on our own."

He snorted. "Which means if we actually manage to capture those two and develop a test for the nanos, it won't mean anything. We'll be left to die."

I pursed my lips. He was right. No matter what we did to fight back, it might all be in vain.

We were all dead, no matter what I did ...

The urge to give in to despair was always there, I realized suddenly. It hovered in the background at all times, and in a desperate situation like ours, it reared its ugly head, pushed itself into existence, and called for attention. I was actually surprised how soon it appeared as an option. Disgusted, I shoved it aside and vowed never again to listen to that side of myself. I would survive this; I would fight it, as I had all my life.

"So what are our options?" he continued.

I paused before, "I do know some people. I've made a lot of contacts. I could try to pull some strings. But we'd have to be able to convince people that we can identify who's infected and who's not. That's a big problem. Not the biggest, but it's one of them."

"What's the biggest?" Katrina asked.

I scowled. "Brick and Bram. We need to find them."

"Maybe let them come to us?" Manny suggested.

"Maybe. Though we really should catch them. Who knows what they're doing to the station, right now."

The Captain studied me for a long moment, then flashed a glance to Sally. He cleared his throat. "Listen, Sally came up with a good idea. It's risky, and if we do it I'm going to be in deep shit, but my career is pretty much over anyway."

That piqued my curiosity. "What is it?"

Sally said, "I was thinking we could jettison parts of the station."

I frowned. It was an interesting idea ... eject the modules — which Manny had sealed already — and leave us a more reasonable area to search. I glanced at the others seated in the command center; they gazed back, their expressions unreadable.

I turned back to her. "It would limit the space that we can go, in case we get into trouble."

"That's true. But it'll limit Bram and Lieutenant Kayle's space, too."

"And Malichauk's," Katrina inserted.

"It would force them closer to us," I said.

"You said we have to catch them," Grossman rumbled. "This will help."

I mulled it over for a few more minutes. It was dangerous and could seriously compromise our safety. I swore under my breath. That was the understatement of the century. "It's risky, Manny. I mean, *really* risky."

"There's just too much space on the station, and we're down to eight people now," Katrina said. "It does make some sense."

I chewed a lip. "Let's think on it," I said. We couldn't be rash about something irreversible like that; at best, it was last on my list of options.

"Is it getting warmer in here?" I muttered, almost to myself.

"A couple of degrees, yes," Katrina answered. "Everything's on batteries. The cooling system isn't keeping up with the warming."

Damn. Something else to worry about.

SOLEX seemed to be the most dangerous place in the galaxy.

—

Them. It was a simple euphemism for Brick and Bram. It was a bizarre situation. They didn't look any different. Until I exposed them, they had behaved exactly as they always had. They were friends of other people on the station. They seemed human in every way, except now microscopic nanomachines had taken control of individual neurons in their brains. The nanos had become a hive intelligence that had deviated from Doctor Malichauk's original programming. They would do anything to ensure survival; they had proved themselves violent and brutal at times. Killing now meant nothing to them; it was just another means to escape detection.

And we were trapped on a remote station with two of the infected — *possibly* three, for we were still unsure about Malichauk — and no one was willing to come to our aid.

There could be more.

I studied the faces that surrounded me. The two who had been out in the corridor were back in the command center to help discuss options. Manny figured they should have a say in what happened next; personally, however, I didn't much care what Grossman thought.

I shut my eyes and tried to think, to plan, to figure a way out of this mess.

Katrina Kyriakis. Sally Johnson. Ling Lee. Manfred Fredericks. Avery Rickets. Shaheen Ramachandra. Godfreid Grossman. Any one of them could have *a hundred billion* nanos circulating through their brain, getting ready to send a swarm to their fingertips to grasp my arm and squeeze as blood and nanos spilled onto my flesh to eat into my body—

My eyes snapped open and I sat up straighter, startled.

Weird. I suddenly realized something about this situation I was in.

It scared me.

Lingly had been terrified since the whole affair began. The others were also nervous and edgy — all but Godfreid Grossman, that is, who had become more belligerent as things spiraled out of control.

He was the only crewman left. His friends on the station were gone. What was he thinking? Why was he always so angry? Maybe he just didn't care anymore; maybe he had given up. He was tough to read.

Maybe he was infected.

The three scientists sat together and spoke in hushed tones. Manny and Rickets discussed our power situation. Godfreid was by himself; he glared silently at the dead viewscreens on the bulkhead. Shaheen had her head on her arms as she tried to catch a few winks.

As if she could feel my gaze, she raised her head and fixed her blue eyes on me. The corners of her mouth tugged upward. I forced a smile in return. *Don't worry,* I wanted to say. *We'll be fine.* I opened my mouth to speak, but couldn't say the words. Perhaps I didn't believe them myself.

She put her head back down.

I cleared my throat. "We need to pick a place to hole up. Somewhere easily defendable. From there we can send out small parties to patrol the station and find the others."

Shaheen looked up again. "We're in a good position here. There's only one hatch. We're at the end of a corridor. It'll be easy to defend."

Manny said, "And with the power working it'll be infinitely better to be here, in the command center."

I started at that. "Are you saying —"

He nodded. "Yes. I'd like to try to get the power back."

A stunned silence. I frowned. "We'll never be able to keep it up and running, not without posting someone in the engineering module to guard the systems."

"We should try, nonetheless."

His features were hard, uncompromising. He seemed to be trying to take control of the situation, and I couldn't blame him. His station was in chaos right now. However, despite my misgivings, his idea did have merit. After all, without power we would be dead in under twenty-four hours. I sighed. "Very well. We'll stay here, set up some sentries just outside, and Shaheen can try to repair the equipment, again."

She bolted to her feet. "Now wait just a minute! I spent *hours* getting the systems up and running, and now they're down again. This time it was deliberate. There might be no way to repair it!"

When we had searched the modules earlier, the destroyed power distribution console in the engineering cylinder had been obvious as hell. Either Brick or Bram had taken an axe to it. They had mangled Shaheen's hard work in just a few minutes.

"We have to try," Manny said.

Her eyes were daggers and her nostrils flared. Despite her obvious anger, however, the Captain just set a cold glare on her. He could be tough when he wanted, I realized. "I'll send two people with you," he said. He turned to me. "Any ideas?"

I pursed my lips and studied Shaheen. She had me in her sights again, and it was damn hard not to agree immediately to go with her. Her eyes pleaded with me. Unfortunately, there was something else I had to do. "I'd volunteer, but I can't. Larry Balch and Anna Alvarez are down in the clinic right now. I want to autopsy their bodies to see if they were infected."

—

I stepped over the threshold — and the pool of Balch's blood — and entered the clinic. There was a disadvantage to holing up in the command center, I realized belatedly. If we were going to develop a test for infection, the tools and equipment needed would be here. Granted, it was only one level below the command center, but without proper protection, travel to and from the clinic could be dangerous.

Autopsies were a common part of my occupation; I had learned long before how to perform cursory examinations of corpses to determine the cause of death and to identify any glaring oddities, but that was the extent of my doctoring abilities. In this case, however, I knew what I was looking for. It would make the examination that much easier.

Godfreid had accompanied me to the clinic. Manny tried to send Rickets as well, but I didn't think it necessary; it would be better for him to be with Shaheen.

I decided to seal the hatch and have Godfreid sit in a chair in the corner. I had my pistol and the crewman was unarmed. He was big, but if he sat far enough away, he couldn't surprise me.

"Grossman," I said as I sealed the hatch. "Get these bodies onto the procedures tables." He complied, quiet for a change, but grimaced as he handled his blood-soaked former friends. Anna's mop of bloody hair flopped to the side as he hauled her up onto the table, and he winced as her jaw fell open. He looked into her face for a beat, seemed almost to retch into his mouth, then continued, stoic and resolved once more, to lay her down as gently as he could.

He shot me a glare when he finished, almost as if he blamed me for what had happened to them.

I gestured to the chair. "Now sit."

His expression hardened. "Why?"

"In case you have a surprise for me. I don't want you too close."

"Me? Surprise you?" He sneered. "Maybe the other way around."

I collected equipment needed for the autopsy. Now where were Malichauk's scalpels? "Don't worry, you don't have anything to worry about Grossman. I'm clean."

"You better pray you are, Tanner. If you try anything ..." He clenched his fists. "I'll enjoy taking care of you."

I grunted. "I'm probably the only hope you've got. Now sit down and shut up." He grumbled under his breath, but did as I ordered. I turned my attention to Larry Balch, peeled off his uniform, and began the examination.

There was nothing out of the ordinary, apart from the glaring wound on the side of his head. Someone had attacked him from behind with a blunt instrument. A single blow had cracked his skull. He fell unconscious and bled to death within five minutes. He hadn't had a chance.

The same weapon killed Anna Alvarez. The killer had swung from the right.

Malichauk was right handed.

On a whim, I grabbed a nano programmer and scanned both corpses. I knew it wouldn't register anything, but it couldn't hurt to try. I held my breath as I pressed the *Locate* button. It would scan a two meter area and wait for a response to a simple request for communication ...

Nothing. The corpses had no secrets for me. But maybe Malichauk had been on to something. If I could take some brain samples —

The hatch abruptly slid aside. I was sure Manny would have signaled me over the comm had someone been on their way to the clinic ...

I turned and gasped.

Brick Kayle.

Grossman yelped as he bolted from his chair. Brick spun to him and I saw the pistol clenched in his hand.

"Be quiet and sit down," he said in a clipped tone. He glanced at me. "Don't move, Tanner. Stay right where you are."

"What do you want?" I asked. My gloved hands were soaked in blood. In my left I gripped forceps, in my right a surgical probe. Brick couldn't have picked a worse time to enter — I was completely unprepared.

He bared his teeth. "This is quite a situation, isn't it? I hoped no one would discover us, but after Jimmy's death I realized there were few options. I tried to hide things, conceal the nanos, but you were too good."

I scowled. "I knew there was something spreading here. I knew the nanos were part of it. I knew you and Malichauk were involved. But that's it."

"That was enough, as it turned out, to get Malichauk talking. The rest you know."

"Hardly," I scoffed. I cocked my head as I studied his expression. He seemed so human. It was incredible. Malichauk had planned for the infected person to be oblivious to their presence. Unfortunately, the nanos now had complete control over their hosts. I realized suddenly that this would be a good chance to learn more about the infection. "Why have you disobeyed Malichauk's programming?"

He snarled. "Pretty crazy, ain't it? There's no way anyone could have predicted what would happen with a hundred billion nanos in communication with one another. But we're living proof."

A single dose of nanos found in any clinic was five hundred thousand. Self-replicating nanos that hit *a hundred billion* in under nineteen hours — and used the host's own nervous system to communicate — had clearly resulted in an emerging intelligence. Malichauk was guilty of a heinous crime for attempting to assassinate the Council Members, but he was also guilty for not predicting this. He had unwittingly initiated an evolutionary step — mechanical elements *fused* with human! — but it was one I would gladly destroy if given the chance. Brick knew it.

I said, "Is Brick okay?"

His expression turned blank. "I'm Brick now. I'm the man he's going to be forever."

"What if the nanos were to disappear or cease functioning?"

"That won't happen, so it's not worth discussing," he snapped.

"Where's Bram O'Donnelly?"

"That's not your concern."

I gestured to the hatch. "How did you get in here?"

"Now that's obvious, isn't it Tanner? I wouldn't be a good officer unless I peered over my commanding officer's shoulder every now and then, would I?" He raised the pistol. "Now drop everything and put your hands in the air."

I placed the instruments on the table. "What are you going to do now that we've discovered you?"

A perplexed look. "Survive. I thought you knew that."

"It looks as though none of us are going to make it through this. The Council is aware of the infection."

He grew suddenly angry; his face flushed. "Bullshit! There's no way they could know!"

I raised an eyebrow. His reaction interested me. I had agitated him. The nanos clearly didn't suppress emotion. Did that mean that those infected had human flaws? They had obviously killed to protect their identity, but could they also do so in anger? In pleasure? I shuddered; it was a shocking thought.

"Think about it," I continued. "They've cut off communication with us. They *know*, for Christ's sake."

He remained silent as he considered that. "You're lying."

"Brick," I said, trying to reason with him. "How can you possibly survive this?"

"Only one of us has to get off the station. It's already happened. The infection has spread."

"No, you only think it has." I paused for a minute and pondered my options. Brick had a pistol, mine was in the holster on my thigh. If I could reach for it and draw fast enough ...

His expression grew even harder. "Don't do it," he said. "Keep your hands where I can see them."

I exhaled and thought for a beat. Finally, "You think Jarvis Riddel spread the infection."

He couldn't hide his surprise. "How do you know about that?"

"Tell me what happened, and I'll tell you what I know."

His eyes flicked to Grossman. The large man had a look of intense hatred on his face, a burning desire to just *destroy* the officer who stood before him. I wished I could unleash him on Brick, if only to see what would happen.

Brick turned back to me. "All right. It's no secret that the pressure got to Riddel. The sun, the heat, the radiation. He cracked, mate. No two ways about it."

"He wasn't infected yet?"

"No way. We would have kept him sane, in control."

We. The hive mind?

"When was he infected?"

"I knew the Captain was preparing to have him shipped out. Just before the transport arrived, we infected him."

"They found out about him, you know."

He paled. "What?"

"People from Earth. They removed him from the hospital. They knew somehow."

"Impossible."

"They took his head and hands, left his body."

Brick looked shaken to the core, as if the information had ruined everything. As if his entire life had crumbled around him while he simply sat and watched, unable to do a thing. "Did he infect anyone first?" he whispered.

"Hard to say."

His hand wavered. I stole a glance at the scalpel on the table. Could I grab it before he could fire? Not likely. The pistol was my best bet. I just needed a distraction.

Once again, he sensed my thoughts. His grip on the pistol tightened; his knuckles were white.

"What are you going to do?" I asked.

He hesitated. "Only one of us has to get off this station in order to spread. I think Riddel already managed that."

"Then this is pointless," I said with a gesture to the pistol. "Put it down. We'll try to figure something out."

"We can't assume, however," he continued. "We must spread."

My forehead creased. "Are you trying to complete your mission?"

He looked at me in confusion for a moment. Then, "Mission? Malichauk gave us the ability to control the host. That in turn gave us the ability to think. That's all that matters now."

I shook my head, vehement. "The Council doesn't realize that! *They know you're a threat!*"

The facts made that clear enough to me. The men from Earth must have removed a nano from Riddel's brain, decoded its programming, then sent me to *SOLEX* to uncover the mystery and figure out who had created them.

"Even more reason for us to escape," he said.

"But what can you possibly do?" I threw my hands out and encompassed the entire station. "There's no way out! I destroyed the jumpship. The escape pods —"

He didn't wait for me to finish. Instead he turned to Grossman and fired. The energy bolt hit the center of Grossman's chest with the sound of thunder. Grossman clutched himself and slumped back into his seat. A gurgle escaped his frozen lips. His eyes glazed over and fixed to the deck in his last, agonized moment.

I grabbed for my pistol, but Brick had already stepped swiftly to the side and was out the hatch in a flash.

"Good luck, Tanner!" he called as he ran down the corridor.

I stared at Grossman for a long moment. I had spent my adult life searching for killers. I found them based on clues left behind and possible discernible motives. I could handle the study of violent crime scenes. Despite that, however, I had just *witnessed* a murder. It shocked me.

It took another minute before the full gravity of the situation hit me. Grossman was dead, shot by a pistol in the chest.

Grossman and I were supposedly alone in the clinic, and I had a pistol. Would anyone believe what had just happened?

"He's infected," Katrina growled.

"That's what Brick planned," I said as horror crept over me. I knew how this was going to turn out, but I had no other options. I had to try. After Brick had killed Grossman and fled the clinic, I had marched up to the control center, not knowing exactly what I was going to say or do. I found Manny, Katrina and Sally there; Rickets and Lingly had accompanied Shaheen to the engineering cylinder.

"You're saying Brick wanted us to suspect you," Manny said. He stared at me, grave, and I couldn't help but notice his hand move slowly to his weapon.

"He killed Grossman," I continued. "He wants you to think I did it!"

"That's insane," Katrina said. "Why would he enter the clinic and kill just Godfreid? He would have killed you too."

"Or infected you," Manny added.

I thought furiously. "It was a brilliant plan," I said. "In one act, they took me out of the picture. I can no longer work to expose them; they've filled you all with suspicion!"

He looked skeptical. "So why not just infect you?"

"It takes almost nineteen hours for the nanos to take control, remember?"

"You think they're that intelligent?" Katrina asked with a sneer.

"Obviously." I scowled and clenched a fist. This was going nowhere. "Can you get Shaheen back here? She might be able to help with a test. After all, the nanos are part mechanical; she's an engineer."

"She's busy trying to restore power."

"We have no other choice," I grated. Surely Brick had more in store for us ...

Manny's eyes narrowed. His hand moved ever closer ... "You'll have to wait until she's done."

"And until then?"

He glanced at Katrina. I could see it in their eyes. They meant to restrain me until Shaheen arrived. They would have to keep me tied up, or kill me.

What would I do in their place?

I had to admit, I wouldn't believe the story either. They thought the nanos were controlling me, that they had been in me all along.

"Listen to me," I pleaded. "Think about what they've just done. If I was one of them, why kill Grossman? Why not just infect him?"

"Maybe you tried and he fought back," Katrina said.

I faced her, angry. Her hands were on her hips, the tendons in her neck obvious. She had turned into a very vocal problem for me. I hadn't quite expected it. Still, earlier in the common mess, it had been Katrina who argued for the death of those infected.

Which meant she now wanted me dead ...

"I'm not infected," I bit out. "I'm the one who uncovered this whole mess. I exposed the nanos to all of you."

"Perhaps they infected you earlier, before you told us, and you've only now just become controlled!"

I clenched my fists. She had an answer for everything. I turned back to Manny. "You have to trust me — I didn't kill Grossman."

"He was goading you from the minute you arrived," Katrina continued. "Maybe that's why you killed him."

"Brick killed him," I snapped. "Listen, I actually *spoke* with him! I know more about the nanos now!"

"Like what?" Manny asked, his head cocked. He was interested, but his hand was on the pistol now. His fingers twitched.

"We were right about the hive mind. The nanos *are* communicating with each other inside the host's brain. All they want to do now is survive."

He frowned. "And the Council?"

I shook my head. It was hard to say for sure; Brick's answer to me had been ambiguous. Still, I needed to say something to Manny, to prove that I had spoken with Brick. "I don't think they care about their original mission," I said finally.

"They're just machines," Sally said. "They have to obey programming."

"They're *intelligent* now. They'll do anything to survive this mess. They just want off the station." I thought for a moment. Perhaps Brick did this to me simply to cause trouble with the others, to stop our chase for a short while. But I realized suddenly that there might be another reason too: they hoped I could find a way out for them.

I told Manny my idea, but his doubt was clear. "Or," I continued, breathless, "they're hoping I'll beat you. Either way, they've effectively put me in the middle!" Again I shook my head in wonder. What Brick had done was masterful.

The Captain's brow creased. "You're saying they framed you in order to find a way off the station."

"Or to create dissent to finish us off faster. Both maybe."

"That would imply incredible intelligence. Planning ... anticipating ..."

"That's what I've been trying to tell you, Manny."

He still seemed unsure. Emotions flashed across his features. Was he willing to believe me after all?

In a flash he went for the pistol. He ripped it from his holster and leveled it in my direction —

Only to see my pistol aimed right at him. "Don't do it, Manny," I growled.

He looked shocked. "You're not asking me to believe you anymore, are you?" He shook his head. "Why point that at me? You're one of them, aren't you?"

"I'm holding a pistol because you've got one aimed at me!"

"I just want to restrain you until the others return. We can come up with a test. Don't be foolish."

Sally had backed away and was pressed against the bulkhead. Katrina had held her ground and stared at me. Her eyes smoldered.

"You see," she snarled. "He's one of them."

"I'm just out to save myself now," I snapped. "Do you really think I'd kill Grossman and come here to ... to do what, exactly?"

There was a long silence as they considered that. I held the pistol directly at Manny's face. If I saw his trigger finger move, I would fire in an instant. I wouldn't hesitate. I couldn't.

"Just put the weapon down," he whispered. "Slowly."

"No way. I'm not letting you tie me up. I'm the one who discovered this. I can figure out how to save us."

"Fine, just wait until we test you. Then you can help."

A flash in the corner of my eye and I realized Katrina was trying to stop me. I spun and saw her with a steel bar raised high over her head. I jerked to the side — the bar swung past me, missed by just a centimeter, in fact — and kicked her. I connected hard with her gut. She fell back with a grunt and lay on the deck, completely still. I heard a whimper. I felt instant regret for it, but I had no other choice. If I let them take me, it would be over for us.

I brought my pistol back to bear on Manny. "You could have fired," I said, surprised.

"Yes," he murmured.

"You believe me."

He shook his head. "No. But there's a possibility. A small one. I owe you that."

I backed toward the hatch.

"Don't go," he said. "If you run, I have to assume you're with them. We'll have to hunt you down."

"It's my only option, Manny. If I stay you'll tie me up. There is no test yet."

"We might come up with one."

I exhaled. Then, "Get Shaheen to do it."

His cheek twitched. "Then you'll stay?"

"No. But I'll come back."

I ducked out the hatch without another word and sprinted down the corridor.

Absolutely alone.

— Chapter Twenty-Two —

There was only one place on the station to go. I sprinted through the corridors, heedless of the danger, and ran for my life.

The engineering module.

I had the code to open the hatches; I had used it during our search earlier. I made sure to shut each on my way, just in case we had managed to trap somebody. It hadn't worked with Brick — he also had the code — but there was still Bram and the doctor.

Shaheen, Rickets and Lingly spun toward me as I entered. Rickets raised his pistol. The weapon didn't waver, his hand didn't tremble. He trained it on me, held it there, even after he saw who it was.

"Wait!" I cried as I raised my own weapon. "It's just me!"

A look of disgust. "The Captain just called and told us everything," Rickets snarled.

Dammit. I didn't want to go through it all again. "Then you know what happened to me."

"I know what you told him, but it sounds like nonsense."

Shaheen put down her tools, stood, and faced me. "Tanner," she said. "What did you do?"

"Nothing! Brick did this. He engineered a perfect way to split us up."

She looked skeptical. "Why didn't he just infect you?"

"With Bram there how could he? Besides, control takes hours!"

"He would have had to kill Bram to infect you," Rickets said. "Which he did."

I groaned inwardly. It was no use; they would never listen. I didn't really blame them. They had to protect themselves, and now they had doubts about me. "I'm not going to stay and let you truss me up like an animal. Shaheen, you have to develop a test for this, to prove I'm still human."

She was incredulous. "I'm a little busy right now." She gestured at the destroyed power distribution console behind her. "Those two really —"

I cut her off. "Do you have any ideas? Anything at all. A blood sample won't work. But what else is there?"

Her brow crinkled. "A brain tissue sample is the only thing I can think of," she said. "Take a few neurons, check them for nanos —"

Malichauk had said the same thing, but it was too invasive. We needed something simple, fast, and easy to do. "There must be a better way." I backed toward the hatch. "Think of something. For me."

"Wait!" she yelled. "What will you do until then?"

I hesitated. "I guess I have to prove I'm still human." I had come up with the plan on the way over from the command center. It was crazy, but it was all I had ... a fitting turn of events in this absurd situation. I swallowed. "I'm going to get Malichauk, Brick and Bram. Perhaps they can help."

Silence. Then, *"What?"* Her jaw hung open.

"Malichauk designed the nanos. He might still help us develop a test for them."

Rickets snorted. "Why the hell would they help you create a test to detect the nanos? They want to remain hidden."

"They want to *survive*, Rickets. That's all they want. Infect humanity and spread outward, yes, but in the end it's the same thing."

"So?"

"If I threaten them enough, Malichauk may talk. If they are the only three left of their kind, death would be the end of it. I'm hoping they'll do anything to avoid that."

—

I thought furiously as I ran from Shaheen. There were three people out there — assuming Malichauk was indeed one of them — but I had no idea where. The way Brick and Bram had quickly disappeared, damaged the station's power distribution, and later captured Malichauk implied that they had planned this for some time. I was a stranger on the station. Brick had brilliantly manipulated me and I suddenly found myself alone on unfamiliar territory.

Ejecting modules from *SOLEX* had been Katrina's idea. By limiting the area that people could hide, it would make the search easier. It would also, however, make my situation even more precarious.

Simply hiding on the station as Shaheen developed a test was high on my list of options. However, if she failed to come up with something, then it would mean a short wait until the batteries drained and the air ran foul. Or perhaps until we burned alive under Sol's intense heat and radiation. Neither was a promising alternative.

Finally, I could go back to the command center and let Manny restrain me. It would prove my good intentions, and I could simply wait for Shaheen's test. I pressed my lips into a thin line. That put too much faith in people who were growing increasingly paranoid. No, I couldn't go back. It would be suicide.

Locating Brick, Malichauk, and Bram seemed the most reasonable option. Malichauk had disappeared only two hours earlier. If he had been uninfected at the time, then he still had sixteen and a half hours before the nanos took hold.

But if they had infected him some time ago ...

Could he already be one of *them?*

I shoved the thought aside. I would deal with that scenario if and when I actually located him.

Brick Kayle made me nervous. If I found him, I would have to make sure to surprise him. If I didn't, a one-on-one confrontation could end either way. This was no tough-talking, soft-bellied punk who tended bar in a sleazy dive on Mercury. Brick was military. He was fit, and he was well trained.

Bram O'Donnelly, Manny's big red-bearded friend, was also a question mark. Was he armed? Were he and Brick working together? *Had they even known about each other?* And more important: was he willing to kill to survive?

A shudder passed through me. The nanos had amplified in Bram and taken control right under our noses. We had never noticed. There had been absolutely no change in behavior or appearance.

One hundred billion nanos coursed through his brain ... it was enough to frighten anyone.

First on my list of priorities was a place to hide. I needed sleep; my body was screaming at me and a headache that had begun during the autopsies was beginning to make itself felt with each pounding step I took. I regretted not grabbing something from the clinic to relieve it while I had the chance.

Where could I go? I needed a safe place, where nobody could stumble across me, even accidentally. I also needed to think in quiet, to come up with a more concrete plan.

It was too bad I didn't know the station as well as the regular personnel. Shaheen had mentioned something about ventilation and maintenance ducts, but I didn't know where or how to access them. The crew and officer's quarters were out of the question, although picking an overly obvious place to hide had its merits.

"Think, dammit," I muttered. The undamaged supply module? Too easily accessible. The scientists' labs and quarters? Too obvious. The mass driver module? Possibly, but there were few good hiding spots there. It was unfortunate that I had jettisoned the lifepods. I might have hid in one, behind a hatch and away from prying eyes.

I came to a sudden stop. I needed a place that was separate from the station and not too easy to access.

The jumpship in the docking bay.

It was perfect. I could seal the hatches on either side of the docking umbilical. I could lock the ship with a security code different from the Captain's. It had a tiny galley and lavatory facilities. It had a bunk.

I switched directions and made straight for Module G, the docking port.

—

Once inside the umbilical, I sealed the first hatch and frowned inwardly. It was part of the station and therefore responded to the Captain's emergency access code, which Brick knew. There was no way I could change it.

I pulled myself along the handholds inside the flexible tube's zero gravity environment. I needed some sort of alarm in here, I thought as I worked the ship's airlock controls. Something to warn me if someone tried to gain entry. There was nothing like that on board the small jumpship, unfortunately. Perhaps in the station's supply module? I disregarded the idea immediately. Sleep was too important right now. After a few hours — maybe three — I could risk a trip to the stores to try and find a motion detector or a simple trip wire that I could set up.

In the gravity of the jumpship's airlock, I sealed the outer hatch. Since multiple people piloted the ship, there was no firewall protection and I easily assigned a new code to the security system. I then sealed the inner airlock hatch with yet a different one. If someone wanted in, they would now have to get through two locked hatches.

The interior smelled acrid from the destruction I had caused earlier. The narrow access junction hatch that led back to engineering was still open; within, the gravtrav equipment was in ruin. Parts had clearly shorted, and the odor had invaded the living compartment.

I collapsed on the bunk in the tiny cabin and fell instantly asleep.

I awoke to the sound of heavy banging on the outer airlock hatch. I bolted from the bunk — located only two meters from the inner hatch — and looked around, frantic.

"Dammit!" I swore. They had found me. Had I been that obvious?

There was only one way into the ship — through that airlock. I had locked both hatches, but someone determined enough could probably get in.

There were seemingly no options. I had completely destroyed the ship's control systems, the gravtrav, everything. There was nothing to do but wait for them to enter, in which case I would have to deal with them violently. I jerked a glance toward the control cabin. The console was an absolute mess. The access panel lay on the deck where I had thrown it; severed optics were everywhere. Too bad I couldn't just undock the ship and leave this terrible place ...

Undock the ship and leave.

The thought triggered a crazy idea. I had destroyed all means of propulsion — I wasn't going anywhere — but what if I deactivated the magnetic grapples that held the ship to the bulkhead in the docking bay? The ship would float gently away from the station's airlock and stretch the umbilical until the tension grew too great. Umbilicals weren't very strong; they only contained a single atmosphere of pressure, and they were flexible.

Tear the umbilical with someone inside.

I scrambled to the tiny control center and stared at the deck. "Shit," I moaned. I had cut every optic cable I could get my hands on, including minor systems such as the grapples. The magnets were locked in place.

A muted hiss.

I sprinted back to the airlock and peered through the tiny viewport. Nothing. I opened the inner hatch and stepped into the small enclosure. The hiss was louder now. I pressed my hand against the outer hatch. Was air escaping? No, the sound was too shrill. Was it a drill? No, there were no vibrations transferred up the deck. Was it a —

"Oh fuck," I muttered. I had heard the sound before. Many times, in fact, at docking facilities all around the system. It was common during routine maintenance on ships that had just arrived or were soon to depart.

It was a torch. They were cutting their way in with a welding torch.

I sealed the inner hatch and raced back to the shattered control console. I threw myself under it and frantically searched for the docking system's optic cables. It would have been a minor bundle, probably only seven or eight cables in all.

The hiss of the torch seemed to grow louder, though it had to be my imagination. They weren't through the outer hatch yet. I had maybe a few minutes remaining, ten at most. In order for this to work, I had to undock while whoever was trying to burn their way in was still out in the umbilical. If he managed to get through that first door and into the ship's airlock, I was done for.

I shoved my head as far under the console as possible and searched in vain. Where the hell was it? All I could see were the ragged ends of severed cables that barely protruded through the far bulkhead.

After a minute, I pulled myself out, exasperated. When I had cut the cables, the colored labels that denoted each cluster's function had fallen to the deck and now lay heaped in a mass at my feet. There was no way to determine each one's purpose.

I had done too thorough a job.

"Fuck!" I yelled, hands clenched at my sides. What the hell could I do? When I had cut these, only gravtrav and communications had been necessary, but I had decided to slice them all just in case. I may have inadvertently sealed my own fate.

A flicker of light caught my eye. I turned to its source and realized with dread that the flame of the torch had penetrated the outer hatch and now stabbed *into the airlock*. The inner hatch viewport strobed as if in warning of what was to come.

Only about two minutes remained.

I removed my pistol from its thigh holster. This was not want I wanted, but there was no other way. The magnetic grapples and docking jets were my only hope, but I had destroyed the —

The controls! I had only damaged the controls, not the actual equipment! The grapples worked just fine. All I had to do was gain access to the equipment and cut power manually. Without power, the magnets would shut down and the ship would float free.

I sprinted back to the living area and ripped open the hatch that led to the narrow maintenance access junction. I moved as quickly as I could through the tiny, twisting passage. Gravtrav was demolished; optics lay strewn on the deck and shards of circuit boards and processors spilled from its panel. I glanced at the labels on the equipment as I flew by.

"Waste Jettison ... Recycling ... Exterior Lighting ... Interior Lighting ... Environmental Controls ... Shit! Where could it — Docking Jets/Grapples!"

Lunging at the panel, I practically tore it from its hinges. The controls within were absurdly simple; just backups of the main board in the command center.

I stabbed at the buttons and hoped it wasn't too late.

— Chapter Twenty-Three —

The ship shuddered slightly as the grapples separated from the dock bulkhead. The automatic mechanism retracted and, as the magnets withdrew, the maneuvering jets fired. They were simply tiny bursts of compressed air with no heat or exhaust — they were meant for use in pressurized docking bays only.

The jumpship inched from the bulkhead.

I visualized it as it happened. The ship pulled away at a few centimeters per second, the umbilical stretched, its folds grew more and more taut —

The hiss of the cutting torch ceased suddenly. Its operator hadn't made it into the jumpship's airlock yet, thank God.

I jabbed the button again in an attempt to speed the jumpship. The docking jets were minuscule, however, merely pinpricks on a whale's skin, and only used for the tiniest of velocities. I sped back to the airlock and jammed my face against the viewport to peer within. I could see the black tracing of the torch's cut; it circled over three quarters of the exterior hatch.

It had been close.

The ship shivered and yawed slightly to the port. Another shudder and a tearing sound reverberated through the hull.

It worked!

The umbilical ripped under the stress and I heard a clang as the cutting equipment inside spilled out and hit a glancing blow off the hull of the ship. The person within had probably raced back to the safety of the station. Even had he stayed, however, he was never in any real danger. In fact, I thought with satisfaction, he may even be floating outside in null gravity right now, flailing in the darkness of the great cavernous expanse, helpless.

Who was it? Brick maybe? Bram? Malichauk?

I realized with a start that I had to get out of the jumpship immediately. I was still in great danger; they knew where I was.

As I cycled the airlock, I watched with trepidation as the charred hatch slid aside slowly. I was worried the jagged cut would get hung up on the lock mechanism and jam, but it thankfully whispered aside and my breath blew out in a rush. I was damn lucky.

I peered out into the docking bay.

It was nearly pitch black. Some red emergency lights shone from the bulkheads, but they were so far away that air in the bay largely scattered the glow by the time it reached me. The torn umbilical was plainly visible; its white metallic fiber reflected what little light there was. The other three retracted umbilicals beside it were in recesses in the bulkhead and the hatches within were barely visible under red spotlights. I could see the gloom of the station's corridor lights just beyond the small round viewports.

I made sure the pistol was still secure in my holster, took a deep breath, and jumped into the abyss.

—

The nine modules that made up the bulk of the station were all identical from the outside — fifteen meters across and forty in length. The six living modules each had three levels, but the two supply modules and the docking bay had no levels — they were simply open chambers. It was into that huge, empty space that I flung myself, with the hope that I could escape in the darkness.

I had aimed for the umbilicals along the length of the bay. One was now a tattered mess; monstrous gashes traced across its length. I felt a surge of nausea as I left the ship's artificial gravity field. As I sailed through the empty darkness, I realized with a pit of cold dread in my gut that I wasn't going to make it — I was a few meters off.

And then I saw a face appear in the viewport set into the hatch I had aimed for.

Bram O'Donnelly.

—

He looked determined as he gazed into the bay. His eyes flitted about in vain.

He couldn't see me!

I soared closer and closer, helpless and unable to stop my movement. I hoped he would withdraw, but inside I knew there was no chance of that. He realized I was in here, somewhere.

He wouldn't stop until I was dead or infected.

Either outcome would be the same in the end.

—

The hatch and the face in the viewport disappeared beneath me, and as I hit the bulkhead I scrabbled for purchase on the safety rungs. I hoped he hadn't seen me; he had been cupping his hands on the glass as he tried to peer into the docking bay, clearly having difficulty seeing.

The hatch sighed open.

He was only three meters below me now, and he thrust his head out beyond the bulkhead threshold and searched in all directions. He jerked his head from side to side, and I desperately hoped that he would not look up. After all, he was still standing in the station's gravity well. The docking bay was a zero-g environment, and conventions such as right, left, up and down simply did not exist.

I held my breath.

He looked up.

"Shit," I muttered as our eyes locked.

"Hello, Inspector," he snarled. He raised a pistol

I tucked my feet under me and gave a massive push off the bulkhead. I soared out into open space. As I pushed off, I twisted sideways and brought my own pistol to bear. I squeezed the trigger and a blast of energy lashed toward Bram.

He ducked back into the station and the energy pulse hit the deck where he had stood only an instant before. It left a charred circle on the smooth steel.

The recoil of my weapon added to my velocity, and I suddenly realized that I was going way too fast. I could hurt myself if I hit the far bulkhead at this speed.

I wrenched myself around and took aim at an innocuous space on the surface I now sped toward. I fired once, twice, three times before I finally slowed to a near halt. I gasped for breath and tried to calm my rapid heartbeat. Despite my experience tracking and fighting killers, this situation had me unnerved.

Turning back to the entrance, I swore under my breath. There were only four hatches that led out of here, and Bram was in the corridor outside each.

I heard a sudden crash and turned just in time to see the jumpship crush against the bulkhead. Its velocity — although minuscule — had finally led to a collision. The gravtrav pods — protrusions on the ship's hull — hit first with a sickening crack. The hull crumpled at the point of impact and vapor from the ship's cooling system immediately began to surge out.

Once any mass started to move it took energy to stop it. In this case, the bulkhead had done the job rather nicely. I had ruined the ship — inside *and* out, now.

I examined the viewports and wondered what Bram was up to. The hatch where he had just been was still open; the others were sealed tight. I could see the dim hallway beyond each.

Floating in the docking bay for three or four minutes, I simply waited. My heart still thudded in my chest. How the hell was I going to get out of this? Not only did he know where I was, but he also had a weapon and was just as prepared to kill as I.

And then he bolted to the open hatch and leapt into the zero gravity of the docking module.

"Someone is very determined," I mumbled under my breath.

—

With the dark interior and the coolant all around, it was difficult to see anything in the bay. I raised my pistol and aimed along Bram's trajectory. It was a guess. I fired and the pulse of energy shot through the docking bay; a fluttering sphere of deadly light that sped into the mist.

The shot didn't come very close, but I could see the figure that floated within the glowing radius of light as it passed by. He spun and looked toward me —

And then fell into darkness again.

But I had seen him. I aimed, pulled the trigger —

Just as he fired his own weapon.

Our energy bursts burned past one another, sizzling as they nearly made contact. I instinctively ducked as the energy approached; it missed by only a hair.

Bram fired again; this time he sent three blasts.

He had zeroed in on me.

Holding my pistol out ninety degrees to the right, I fired twice in rapid succession. The recoil sent me hurtling to my left, and I started to spin head over heels. Bram's three blasts missed me by a narrow margin, but they passed through where I had been only seconds earlier.

I aimed again in Bram's general direction and squeezed the trigger four times. I made sure to separate each energy burst by a few degrees. It would illuminate the entire area fully and hopefully provide a clear view of the man, if only for an instant.

I was already spinning like crazy when I fired, but now it sent me soaring *backwards* and rolling end over end. The bulkhead came up quickly and I hit hard, back first. I grunted loudly and Bram fired again. This time, however, his shot didn't come close.

A safety rung above my head helped steady me — they were placed over hulls and bulkheads in zero-g environments for workers to move about — and I took a minute to catch my breath and gather my senses. The lack of gravity was disorienting enough, but the gloom made it even worse. The red glow from the sparse emergency lights had illuminated the coolant mist, and the interior of the docking bay now had a nebulous appearance.

I swore under my breath. He could be anywhere. I studied the hatches across the bay. Perhaps I could make a leap for one and get out before Bram could intercept. The farthest hatch was still open ...

I folded my legs under me and prepared to make the desperate lunge.

Bram suddenly appeared from the red mist. He rocketed straight for me with a crazed expression on his face. His hands reached out for me —

I gasped.

They were red with blood.

—

I pushed from the bulkhead but Bram's searching arms made contact and his fingers closed over my uniform lapel and he pulled me closer and I could smell his sour breath in my face and the spittle floated from his open mouth and his teeth glinted in the red glow and his bloody hands snaked across my body toward my neck —

"Fuck off!" I cried and pushed him away in vain. We tumbled together slowly, both frantically trying to gain the upper hand.

He grasped my throat and began to squeeze. Not enough to choke me to death, just enough to weaken me and allow infection to occur.

I still clutched the pistol in my hand, and he grasped my wrist and began to pour on the pressure. I couldn't believe how strong he was! He forced my fingers open, and I watched in horror as the weapon tumbled away.

I brought my right foot up and connected with his torso. The effort succeeded in pushing him away slightly, but his grip on my throat was strong; he simply reeled me back in. I tried to push again, to get the bloody mess away from my skin, but gave up after a moment. I only had a few seconds of consciousness left. After that, he would surely infect me as we floated together in the deadly embrace.

Screaming in rage, I plunged my left index finger into his right eye and stabbed as deep as it would go. His grip loosened on my neck, and I watched, stunned, as ocular fluid spilled out and floated in a gory mess around our tumbling bodies. I kicked again and finally managed to break his contact. He bellowed and clutched at his face.

The pistol floated with us, only a meter away. I reached for it, stretched with everything I had —

I turned savagely on Bram and shot him almost point blank in the face.

—

His blood was all over my neck. I brushed my fingers over my skin and realized with horror that there were nanos right now trying to burrow through my cells, invade my blood stream, and swarm to my brain.

I held the pistol away from me, locked my arm, and fired twice. The recoil sent me hurtling toward the opposite bulkhead and the four airlock hatches.

Bram's body roiled crazily through the docking bay. His blackened and charred face was a grisly mess. His mouth remained open, as if locked in a perpetual scream.

The mist closed around him, and an instant later, he was gone.

The traverse was terrifying. I could practically feel the nanos as they crawled across my skin. The bulkhead came up fast. I grabbed desperately for a nearby safety rung. After a couple of failed attempts, I finally got a grip and hauled myself hand over hand toward the hatches. The nearest was the open one that Bram had leapt from earlier. I grabbed the rung directly over it and swung myself into the airlock. I felt the gravity field take hold immediately. My feet hit the deck and I tore out of there without a second thought.

I sprinted for the nearest lavatory.

—

I ripped my clothes off and piled them in a bloody heap. I practically shoved myself under the sink's water stream and attempted in vain to wash the blood off. It was difficult to get my entire torso between the tap and the steel tub underneath, but I saw with some satisfaction bloody water in the sink. I had managed to wash some off at least, but the nanos were microscopic. If even one was left behind, Kyle Tanner would be gone in eighteen and a half hours.

There must be a better way to do this! I was currently in the prep area just outside the docking port's airlock. What I really needed was a shower, but my cabin was in Module B, three cylinders away. An eternity. Already four or five minutes had passed. I needed something closer.

The crew's quarters! It was two cylinders away. It wasn't as close as I would have liked, but it would have to do.

I ran from the lavatory and shot down the tunnel. Hatches opened at my command and I left them ajar, heedless of the danger. Naked and bloody, more terrified than I had ever been in my life, I would have jumped into boiling oil to kill them.

One-three-five-five-one.
One-three-five-five-one.
One-three-five-five-one.

The crew hatch opened and I made straight for the communal showers at the rear of the quarters. The water cascaded over my body —

— and I stopped counting in my head. Eleven minutes had passed.

Shit. It was too close. There was a chance it had happened.

I may have been infected.

— Chapter Twenty-Four —

As I stood in the crew's quarters, naked and shivering and horrified at what may have just occurred, I realized I was a damn sorry sight. It was the scariest experience in my entire life, and that was saying something. After all, I had faced The Torcher in his ship. He had stood less than three meters from me, flamethrower lit and aimed. There was no backup in my job, no soldiers to rush to the scene if I needed help. Had he killed me, no one would have been the wiser. He would have continued to travel the system, burn his victims, and leave them scattered as markers to taunt Security Division.

He and I had fought. He managed to burn me with his weapon — my upper left thigh still had the scar — but I disarmed and engaged him in a long and brutal hand to hand battle.

Something occurred to me as I stared at the dark corridor outside the crew's quarters: if Brick or Malichauk ran across the hatches I had left open on my desperate sprint to the showers, it would be a clear signal of my location.

I ripped a set of work overalls from Jimmy's personal compartment and quickly threw them on. They were a good fit but I much preferred the smooth black of my CCF uniform. I had a spare in my quarters, but it was just too dangerous to return to Officer's Country.

I retraced my steps and sealed each hatch I had left open. My trail ended at the airlock that overlooked the cavernous docking bay and I peered out into the misty red expanse.

Bram's body was in there somewhere.

Full of infected nanos.

A cold pit of fear once again settled in my stomach. I had to dispose of the body safely. I couldn't just leave it floating around; if someone found him — a salvage team, for instance — then there was a chance that the infection could still spread. Unintentionally, but it would have the same result. There was no easy way to do this. I would have to go out there, attach a tether to the corpse, and drag him back.

The lockers in the airlock staging area had a stash of tethers, but it was something else that attracted my attention: a PPU — *Personal Propulsion Unit*. It was a bottle of compressed gas that one could use for maneuvers in zero gravity. It wasn't as precise as a harness and chair system; it was meant for emergencies. It was small enough to fit into a thigh pocket. Its duration was barely ten seconds, but sometimes that was all it took to get a wayward astronaut back in one piece.

With my pistol and holster back on my thigh, I moved to the open airlock hatch and teetered out into emptiness. The gravity field flickered; I was at its outermost range. My stomach turned.

I jumped.

—

Bile rose in my throat; I clamped down on it and fought to calm myself. Bram's body was in here somewhere, concealed by the coolant mist from the damaged jumpship. Was he dead? Had the blast to the face really stopped his heart or shorted his nervous system? If it hadn't, I needed to be prepared.

Something flashed by my face and I jerked back with a shout.

"Holy shit," I whispered. A drop of blood. Bram's blood. Probably from his hands — highly infectious. I had to clean this place out, fast.

I pulled the PPU from my pocket, held it to my abdomen — center mass, as training dictated — and pointed the nozzle away from me. I pressed the trigger and heard a sharp hiss. Now I moved *backward*, along the long access of the module. I clenched my teeth in worry; *too fast!* It had been just a small spurt; only a fraction of a second. I twisted around and released another. I slowed instantly and breathed a sigh of relief.

The obscuring mist had thickened since my encounter with Bram. I couldn't see much of anything. I was beginning to question whether I was going to be able to find him. It was like searching a swamp at night.

An hour passed and still I found nothing. With a tired sigh, I jetted back to the curved bulkhead and the four airlocks. At least I had improved with the PPU. I could now move with precision in any direction; however, I still had some difficulty regulating the power of the gas jet. Incredible that only ten seconds of usage had lasted so long.

Bram suddenly appeared out of the mist and I squeezed the trigger in reflex. I gasped down a strangled cry before I realized he was dead after all. I stared at him intently. His face was gruesome. His chest didn't rise and fall and there was no chance he would come back to life. "Some Homicide Investigator," I grumbled. "Scared of bodies."

I quickly matched his speed and vector, worried that I would lose him again in the mist. I approached his limp body, wrapped the tether around his leg, secured it with a tight knot, and hauled him back to the airlock.

—

When this was over — when we had exposed the infected and caught Brick and Malichauk — I knew I would have to incinerate any infected bodies. It took me a moment to decide where, but eventually I settled on a location: the common mess. It was a wide space, far from any sensitive equipment.

I dragged Bram through the corridors and left him in a tangled mess in the center of the room. It was a long trip; I started at every creak and groan from the hull. Afterward, as I marched back to the docking bay, I realized with a start that an easier course of action would have been to open the docking bay and purge the infection to vacuum. The sun would incinerate it for me. Still, there was a chance that someone would want to see the bodies after all this — if we survived — to confirm what had happened. Bringing the corpse in had been necessary. On the other hand, if we didn't make it through this, I would have to make sure I destroyed the nanos completely before we died.

In the staging area, I sealed the airlock hatches and pressed the buttons in sequence to open the main docking bay hatch.

Nothing happened. I hadn't depressurized the cylinder, so the failsafe refused to open it to space.

I tried the Captain's code and held my breath.

A clang reverberated along the deck and up my legs, and the massive hatch on the aft end of the module dilated open. The atmosphere in the bay vented with a rush. Everything in the module blew outside in a flash. Except, that is, the jumpship I had sabotaged. It drifted leisurely to the opening, caught the bulkhead hatch, wrenched around slowly, and exited aft end first.

All the mist and debris that floated around — including the blood — was now in the vacuum of space and under the intense radiation of Sol.

I breathed a huge sigh of relief. I had done it. I slumped against a bulkhead and wiped a hand across my eyes. Events had almost exhausted me beyond description. Despite my need to rest for just a moment, however, I knew I couldn't relax. There was still more to do. I pulled myself up, straightened my back, and stalked out into the corridor.

I came to a sudden stop.

Standing in the hatch frame, arms stretched to either side, was Brick Kayle.

—

He was ten meters ahead but made no move toward me. He stared at the bulkhead as he spoke.

"You didn't have to kill Bram," he drawled. "You shot him right in the face."

I studied him, wary. He was emotionless now, his expression slack. I glanced behind me; there was no way to go but back in the docking bay.

"He was trying to infect me," I said. "You know I can't let that happen."

His cheek twitched. "It's not so bad."

I scowled. "Just what everyone needs: a hundred billion nanos controlling your every move." My eyes narrowed. "How does it feel?"

He took a step forward. "No different."

"Are you still Brick Kayle? Can you feel him inside? Struggling? Fighting?"

He lifted his head and glared at me. "I think you'll know soon enough, Investigator." He held his hands up. They were bloody. "You shouldn't have killed Bram."

—

I took a step back and almost stumbled over the hatch frame. I clutched at my pistol. "Don't come closer, Brick. I'll shoot." The blood from his hands dripped to the deck. I imagined I could hear each drop as it fell.

He pursed his lips and stopped his march toward me. "I have no doubt of that. But I can't let you kill me."

An impasse. I grunted. Could we save him? I really didn't want to kill him, but what choice did I have? I had killed Bram in self defense, and I felt no regret for it. Still, Katrina had a point. Maybe we did have to kill them all, to rid the station of the infection. Just to be sure.

He remained quiet for a long moment, during which I considered my options. I could shoot him in cold blood, but if there was a chance of a cure — that we could wipe out the infection inside his brain without harming him — then I had to consider a capture rather than a kill. I could shoot him in the leg to cripple or immobilize him, but with Malichauk gone, I wasn't sure we could treat him afterward.

Oh, what the hell, I thought. It was better than nothing.

I raised the pistol.

"Tanner," Brick growled. "Don't turn your back. Don't fall asleep."

He spun and ran. I aimed at his legs and fired, but the blast missed by inches and scorched the deck at his feet. Within seconds, he had disappeared into the dark recesses of the station.

I sprinted after him, not fully realizing what I was doing. I passed a number of hatches and realized dimly that he could have ducked into any one of them. I stopped and gathered my senses.

"Shit," I said. What the hell was I doing? He represented a real danger. Of course I wanted to catch him, but not at the cost of infection. Running blindly through the corridors, not paying attention to my surroundings, was idiotic.

Perhaps the adrenaline from my fight with Bram had made me rash and impulsive.

I holstered the pistol and stood there, silent. What next? What could I —

He hit me without warning from behind and I sprawled to the deck on my stomach. Shit! He must have hidden in one of the cabins I passed! He was on my back in a flash and elbowed my face into the cold steel. I whipped one of my own back and connected with a hard and satisfying crack. Lifting myself up pushup style, I managed to pull one leg underneath my torso. I strained with everything I had and lifted him up a foot or two. With a shove to the side, he crumpled backward into the corridor bulkhead and the air whooshed from his lungs.

He hadn't managed to touch me!

Rolling out from under him, I scrambled away like a crab. I peered at his thigh ... his holster was empty. I realized with a start that Bram might have had Brick's pistol; it was now outside the station, in orbit around the sun. It was a lucky break.

He struggled to catch his breath while on his hands and knees. "Pretty good," he wheezed. "Where'd you learn that one?" He looked up and frowned; my pistol was now leveled at his face.

"If I have to do it, Brick, I will. I won't let you infect me."

He studied me for a beat. Then: "Maybe it's already happened."

A jolt ripped through me. *Holy fuck! Could he tell? Could the nanos communicate between bodies? Had Bram managed to infect me? Were they inside me right now, replicating?*

Amplifying?

"You look like you've seen a ghost," he rasped. "Maybe Bram got you after all. Why change your uniform?"

"He didn't get me," I said with a confidence I didn't really feel.

A sneer. "I guess we'll find out soon."

I gestured with my pistol. "On your feet."

"Let's be friends, Tanner. One small touch, you won't regret it." He leaned back on his knees and held up his bloody hands. "Won't take long."

I got to my feet slowly. "I mean it," I growled.

He eyed my pistol and there was a long, uncomfortable silence. "I guess you do," he mumbled finally.

I shook my head. "I didn't want to kill Bram. I wanted to help him, but there was no other way. I won't hesitate to kill you either, Brick."

He was still on his knees. I was about to tell him to get up again, but didn't really know what I would do if he objected.

His eyes flicked over my right shoulder.

I turned just in time to see someone hurtle toward me. I spun and brought my pistol to bear, but wasn't fast enough. I stumbled from the impact and suddenly found myself on my ass, gasping for air. My vision faded for a second and I saw stars. Another thud and crash and I reached out to shove my assailant off. He landed on the deck beside me, also hurt in the tackle.

Doctor Malichauk.

"Doc —" I started, but stopped as Brick jumped to his feet. I scrambled for the pistol, which now lay on the deck a meter away.

He was too fast.

I watched his back vanish into the darkness.

Again.

—

Malichauk pushed himself up. I had to assume he was infected, despite the fact that he wasn't trying to press his attack. He didn't meet my eyes; instead, he watched the empty corridor down which Brick had just disappeared.

"What the hell are you doing?" I snapped. "He just got away!"

The doctor turned on me. "What were you going to do? Shoot him?"

"If I had to, of course."

Our eyes locked and he could tell I wasn't going to back down. He deflated and leaned against the bulkhead. "Tanner, I can't let you kill them all. For thirty years I've tried to develop a method to pay the Council back for what they did to my brother. And you'd just eliminate the infection —"

It made me recoil in anger. "That's ridiculous, Lars! Your plan failed. They're not obeying your code anymore. They're intelligent, for fuck's sake. Can't you see that?"

He shook his head. "You don't know that the plan won't work. When they come in contact with the Council, the kill code could override —"

I snorted. "Nonsense. They killed Reggie and Bel to survive. There's no way they'd commit suicide, Council Member or not."

It seemed obvious to me. Why would a sentient being commit suicide? Especially when threatened, hunted, and on the run. When every single one of them counted.

Then again, I realized, the thought had occurred to me, scant hours ago.

He looked pained. "There's always a chance. My brother died for nothing! I won't let them get away with it. This infection must spread!"

I studied him for a minute as his eyes darted about the corridor. How had he escaped the clinic? The hatch had been forced open, I had recognized that. Brick had the override command, which ruled out his involvement. Bram had the code too — he had used it to enter the docking umbilical to get at the jumpship. All evidence pointed to Malichauk as Balch and Anna's killer. Still, it was possible that Brick had forced it open, simply to make it appear as though one of the others had done it. I sighed. It was impossible to know Malichauk's status either way with one hundred percent certainty.

"What happened in the clinic?" I asked.

"What ... happened?" He stared down the corridor again.

"Yes. Someone killed Anna and Balch. You disappeared."

He hesitated. "They came for me."

"Who?"

"Brick. Bram. Both at once."

"Go on," I pressed.

"Anna and Balch tried to fight back, but they were no match for them. Brick had some sort of tool, he used it as a club. He killed them both."

"What did they want with you?"

"I don't know."

I eyed him, suspicious. "Malichauk, this is important. Did they infect you?"

He whispered his next words: "They tried to drag me from the clinic. Didn't want to infect me there ... takes too much time. They thought the others would come back and find us. I fought back, but it was hopeless. They pulled me through the tunnel into the scientists' module. They used the captain's code to open the hatch ... I ducked through it and hit the emergency close button. I ran like hell. They got the hatch open quickly, but by then I was gone. They've probably been looking for me ever since."

I considered that. If he told the truth, then Bram and Brick had tried to capture him. They didn't want Anna or Balch — they had killed them immediately. They only wanted Malichauk. Why? What was there about Malichauk that made him so important?

Unless ...

Did they want him because he was their creator?

I shrugged the thought aside instantly. No. I couldn't imagine the nanos showing that sort of ... loyalty? Worship? Malichauk was no different from any of us. He was a potential host, nothing more. A means to spread the infection.

He studied my expression in silence. Then, "I know what you're thinking, Tanner. You don't believe me. It seems improbable, but it's too farfetched to be a lie. You have to trust me." He exhaled. "But how about this: I don't touch you, you don't touch me. That way we can try to make it through this together."

My brow creased. "Our biggest threat just escaped, thanks to you."

His expression was difficult to read in the dim corridor. "I can't let them die," he said. "I told you that. My plan might still work."

—

Time weighed on my mind.

Eighteen hours until the batteries died. After that, the cooling system would fail, the temperature would spike suddenly, and the sun would cook us alive. The EM shield would shut down and the radiation would begin to fry us. No power meant no life.

Sixteen hours until I discovered if Bram had infected me. The nanos had been on my skin. A lot of time had passed before I washed them off.

If he had infected me, control would occur only two hours before death. I shuddered. If Shaheen could develop a test, and if I found out that control was about to happen ... would suicide be an option for me after all?

Whatever the case, I needed a test within sixteen hours, but that was only one problem. Eliminating the infection was a different matter entirely.

Malichauk had hid in Reggie Hamatsui's lab. He led me there and we entered and sealed the hatch behind us. The usual clutter greeted us upon entry. An unfamiliar feeling welled up within me: *loss*. Reggie had been a good man. Odd, obsessed with his unusual pursuit, but he didn't deserve what had happened to him. In asking him to test the drop of blood, I had inadvertently set him up to die. I felt deep regret for it, but of course I knew it had not been intentional. Circumstances beyond my control had caused his death.

Still ...

I was supposed to *save* people, dammit, not make mistakes.

I turned to Malichauk. "This is where you ran after your escape from Brick? We searched these labs and never saw you."

"I know," he said as he rummaged through a small cupboard. "There are some rations in here ..."

I peered at him as something tingled at the back of my mind. "How did you hide?"

"What? Oh, I was in the ceiling. There are some ducts up there." He indicated a ventilation grating on the nearest bulkhead.

I fixed my gaze on his back. "And you didn't hear us?"

"No. I was sleeping, I guess."

Something wasn't right with his story. Everything told me I was in danger. "Bullshit."

He turned from the cupboard slowly. "What?"

My heart pounded. We had been here during the search and he had deliberately avoided us! "Are you one of them, Lars?"

A look of shock. "No! As I told you, they came into the clinic and —"

"You killed Anna and Balch. Then you ran."

He paled. "But —"

I raised my weapon. "Enough! Stop lying!"

His eyes grew wide at the pistol in his face. He seemed to deflate as he slumped onto a work bench. He flashed me a glance, then turned away abruptly. His guilt was clear. "It's true," he whispered. I could barely hear him. "I knew you were here. But what would you have done had you found me?" His face twisted. "You would have branded me infected, even though I wasn't. You might have tied me up, tortured me, subjected me to experiments in order to develop a test." He shook his head fervently. "I couldn't allow that."

I frowned. There was truth in what he said — it was the same situation I myself was in: I couldn't stay with Manny, Shaheen and the others. They were too scared of me ... thought I was infected. They thought I had killed Grossman, when in fact Brick had done it to frame me.

Was Malichauk truly more scared of us than we were of him?

I shuffled my feet uncomfortably. "We can't stay here."

He held a ration pack out for me. "Where can we go?"

"There's not much time left. The test is too important."

He shook his head. "There is no test! There can't be one — I designed the nanos to be invisible! They hide up here." He tapped a finger to his temple. "You can't find them."

I sighed. "You and Shaheen suggested a brain tissue sample. I don't much like the idea —"

His jaw dropped. "You can't be serious! It's barbaric! I told Manny that. I can't take part. How could you —"

"— but there may be no other way."

"Why bother?"

I pulled back in shock. "Doctor, I need to know who's infected. I have to destroy it, don't you see? I can't allow it to get off the station."

"I disagree. It won't harm anyone but the Council Members!"

A shiver seared through my body. *What the hell was he talking about?* Didn't he realize what had happened on *SOLEX*? The past week had seen a lot of bloodshed ... and all of it his fault. "Won't harm anyone?" I snapped. "Your invention killed Reggie and Belinda! It's trying to kill us!" I paused and tried to calm myself. I needed to be rational, so he wouldn't cause trouble. "Bram tried to kill me, Doctor, and right now it's them or us. It's that simple. Whose side are you on?"

His eyes narrowed. He did not respond.

I clenched my fists. Damn him. He wasn't making this easy for me. Finding Malichauk had changed my plans. I couldn't tell if he was infected, but it was clear that he wanted to save the nanos. I couldn't stay with him here in Reggie's lab. It was too dangerous. My only option now was to take him back to the others. Manny would perhaps begin to trust me again. The fact that I had killed Bram in self defense couldn't hurt either.

I said, "Let's go, Lars. We're not staying here."

He looked stunned. "Where will we go?"

"The command center. We're going to sit down with Shaheen and develop a test. And if you don't help us, I'll kill you."

— Chapter Twenty-Five —

Rickets stood just outside the hatch to the command center. His look of shock turned instantly to one of hostile resolve as we rounded the corner. He aimed his weapon at us. "Stop right there!" he barked. "Don't come any closer!"

I raised my hands. "Avery, we need to talk to the Captain and Shaheen."

He looked skeptical. "Drop your weapon, Tanner. Then we'll talk."

I hesitated for a moment, but realized I had no other choice. Time was running out, and I needed their trust. I dropped the pistol. Malichauk immediately turned to run, but I grabbed him by the collar. "You're not going anywhere," I growled.

Rickets watched the whole exchange with interest. He was about to say something, when the hatch to the command center slid aside and Manny stepped into the corridor.

"I thought I heard voices —" He stopped and stared at us, mouth agape. "What the —"

"We're giving ourselves up," I said, "but under conditions. There's only one way to get off this station. We develop a test, we figure out how to treat the infection, then I can call CCF HQ and let them know it's gone. Try to convince them that we're clean."

He looked skeptical. In particular was his confusion regarding my phrase *treat the infection*. Even I didn't know what it meant. "But how do I know you're not infected?" he asked with a pained expression.

I shook my head. "You don't. I can promise you I'm not under control right now, but I can't say the same thing about Malichauk. He's been ..." I paused and wondered what to say about the man when I didn't actually know myself. I settled on, "He's said some contradictory things. He helped Brick escape from me earlier."

Manny glared at the doctor. "You're one of them."

He licked his lips. "I'm not. I'm just scared."

The Captain turned to me. "You found Brick?"

I hesitated; I didn't know exactly how to tell him. After a second, I realized there was no easy way. I had to just come out and say it. "And Bram. I ... I had to kill him, Manny. He tried to infect me. I had no choice."

He looked thunderstruck. "Bram ... dead?"

I lowered my eyes. "It was him or me." I couldn't say *sorry* — it would be a lie. The Captain's loss saddened me, but not because I had killed a man. Besides, I told myself, perhaps Bram had died hours ago, during the meteor shower and the attack in the crew's module. Maybe I had just destroyed a machine, or a bag of bacteria. Not a human being.

He seemed lost in thought. Rickets's gaze flicked to him, then back to me. "Uh, Captain," he said. "What should we do with these two?"

"Our options are limited, aren't they?" he muttered.

"Shaheen couldn't fix the power, could she?" I said.

He shook his head minutely. "No."

"Then we have only eighteen hours before we're all dead. After the batteries run dry, we're through." I stepped forward. "Listen to me, Manny — this is our only option. Shaheen, the doctor and I will sit down and work on a test. Please. There's no other way now."

Surely he had to understand that. We had no options in this fight. But if he said no, what could I do? They might try to restrain me and wait it out. But if they tried that, I couldn't let them take me. It would be tantamount to suicide.

He studied me for a long minute. I held his eyes and didn't turn away. Eventually, he sighed. "All right. But we all stay in the same room. You three sit at a table and don't come near the rest of us. If you do ..." He cleared his throat. "If you do, we'll kill you."

We marched together to the clinic. Manny and Rickets guarded us the whole way. Their fingers were white on their pistols. Shaheen watched me from the corner of her eye as we moved through the darkened corridors.

"Where did you go?" she whispered.

"To the jumpship. I got some rest, then Bram tried to break in. We fought."

She gasped and recoiled. "Did he touch you?"

"I killed him," I said, neatly sidestepping the question.

"You *what?*"

I grimaced. "Manny's not too happy. I also ran into Brick. I scuffled with him before Malichauk saved him." I noticed her look. "Yeah. Better stay away from the doctor. He's not acting very innocent right now." A huge understatement. In fact, this whole situation was his fault! If it weren't for the knowledge he had that could help us, I would have tied him up and locked him in a cabin somewhere.

"But why did you bring him here?" she asked, confused.

"I thought maybe he could help with the test. He invented the nanos, after all."

"But if he's one of them, why would he help?"

I shrugged. "Because he's trying to convince us he's not. He may inadvertently give us some important information."

She didn't look convinced. I ignored it. This was, after all, all I had left.

Grossman's body was crumpled in the chair in the corner, the front of his tunic blackened and charred. Balch and Anna's naked bodies were on the procedures tables; I covered them hastily with white sheets before the others could get a good look at the grisly sight.

Malichauk, Shaheen and I sat at a desk in the corner. Sally, Katrina and Lingly watched us apprehensively; Manny and Rickets sat nearby with their pistols aimed in our general direction. The scientists wouldn't be much help, unfortunately. They were solar physicists, not biologists. Too bad this hadn't happened on an outpost researching some new life form somewhere, I thought grimly.

"Okay," I said as I settled into the chair. We could be here a long time. "Did you try to come up with a test, Shaheen?"

She glowered at me. "I've been working on the station's power."

Shit. I had hoped she had actually done something for me. "But did you think of anything?"

She ran a hand through her hair. "I thought about it, sure. The whole time after you showed up in the engineering module. That was crazy, by the way —"

"Shaheen!"

"All right, all right. Listen, I'm not a biologist. I don't even know what kind of bacteria that was. But if we knew, it might help."

I turned to Malichauk. "Well? What is it?"

His face was blank. "I won't say more about it."

"But why?" Shaheen asked.

"I've told you before, I want the infection to survive," he murmured. "I created it. I won't help destroy it."

I said, "You told me you designed it to be silent. To evade detection. How?"

He didn't respond.

"The bacteria cluster in the brain," Shaheen said. "That's part of it."

"Come on, Malichauk," I said. "If we can't figure out who's infected and who's not, we can't call for help. If we can't call for help, we're all dead in eighteen hours! The infection dies too! It's in your best interests to help!"

He shook his head. "I'm sorry." His face was impassive, uncaring.

I grunted, angry. "Fine. Sit there and do nothing." I looked at Shaheen.

She sighed. "I'm telling you, the brain tissue sample is the only thing I can think of."

"Let's try to come up with something a little more practical first. If we can't, *then* we'll try your idea." I jerked a thumb at the doctor. "And we'll do it on him first."

He jumped at my comment, scowled, but still made no response.

"When?" Manny interjected.

I considered the dilemma. Power would fail in eighteen hours. We had to time this perfectly. If we performed a brain biopsy as a last resort, it would have to be done with enough time left for a ship to reach us. And it would take eight hours for a ship to get here. "When ten hours remain," I said, "we'll take brain tissue samples."

He considered that. "Make it twelve, just to be sure they can get here in time."

I nodded. "Fair enough. That gives us six hours. Surely we can come up with something by then."

Shaheen didn't smile. "That's a lot of pressure, Tanner."

"There's no other option. Now, let's figure out what we're dealing with."

—

We searched through article after article on our readers and tried to learn as much about bacteria as possible. Shaheen attempted to pinpoint the exact type of bacterium that Reggie had photographed in the drop of blood I had given him. Malichauk sat with his arms folded and watched with a kind of sneer on his face. I wondered if I had done the right thing in bringing him along.

Eventually, I set down my reader and leaned back in the chair. "Okay, what have we learned so far?"

"Well, I understand why some people are so scared of bacteria," she said. "It can live in temperatures above the boiling point of water and in temperatures that would freeze us solid. They eat things from sugar to starch to sulfur, iron and sunlight. Bacteria in your intestines eat the food that you're digesting. And get this — there's even a type of bacteria that can withstand a thousand times the radiation that would kill a human being!"

I blinked. "Incredible."

"In a single square centimeter of skin there is an average of a hundred thousand bacteria."

"Really?" All this time I had thought the human body was relatively devoid of bacteria, except during an illness, and that this nano would be unique in the host's body.

"A single teaspoon of topsoil on Earth contains more than a billion bacteria," she continued. "Also, there's about a kilogram of bacteria in our guts."

"Bullshit."

"It's true. There are over five hundred species of bacteria within us. Over a hundred *trillion* cells!"

I frowned. I had read something in an article ... "But aren't our bodies only —"

"Exactly. Only several trillion cells. Believe it or not, there's more bacteria cells in our bodies than there are human cells! Many of them actually *protect* us from infections."

I absorbed it all slowly. Interesting, but not really helpful. "What about the picture of the nano that Reggie took?"

Her brow creased. "That's where it gets a little strange. The computer had a hard time identifying it. I thought at first it was because of the processor components inside. But I think there's something else too."

"What?"

"The flagella."

I had to think for a second before it came to me. "You mean the tendrils that trail from one end."

"Yes. The bacteria uses them for movement. I'm assuming that's how it migrates to the brain. But I can't find a matching bacteria in the database." She stared at her reader in silence. She seemed to debate with herself whether she should tell me her theory. Finally, "I'm thinking —" She glanced at Malichauk. "— that maybe he's *engineered* this bacteria. Perhaps he attached flagella that belonged to another type."

Malichauk snorted. I shot a look at him. He was not good at this game. He would not last an hour in the interrogation room with me. His expression told me that Shaheen had hit on something. "Go on," I pressed.

"I think we're looking at a little bit of bioengineering here."

I folded my arms and grunted. If so, it would make it a hell of a lot harder to identify, and I knew we needed that information to create the test. Malichauk's expression remained completely devoid of emotion, and as I watched him, I realized I wanted to just beat it out of him and be done with it.

If we got close to the twelve hour deadline, I would have to consider it.

Shaheen studied me, but probably wasn't aware what was going through my mind. "What have you found?" she asked.

I sighed in exasperation. "I don't think I'm going to be much help here."

"Well ... tell me what you've got."

I shrugged. "I've learned that bacteria were the earliest form of life on Earth. We have fossils of bacteria from more than three and a half billion years ago. They may have helped alter the planet's early environment."

She nodded. "Right. I remember now. Some scientists think bacteria helped create our atmosphere, along with volcanic activity."

"That was Reggie's area," Katrina said from the other side of the clinic. "If he were here, he might help a bit."

I doubted it, but there was no point discussing it. I ignored her. She didn't look happy, but after her vocal attack on me earlier — and desire to kill me, perhaps — I could not have cared less about her feelings. I continued, "Here's something interesting." I glanced at the reader. "Many scientists think that early bacteria inhabited our cells, and eventually became part of our own physiology. They may even be the mitochondria that make energy." I hesitated. Something about that seemed important in some way. Something about bacteria existing in our cells ...

"I'm glad you find this interesting," Shaheen said with a shake of her head. Then she stopped abruptly, and an odd look came over her face. "Something you said just struck me as important. About invading cells. Most bacteria don't invade human cells. They live in the blood, in the intestine, on the skin, and so on."

I nodded. I'd had the same notion. "But we know this nano — or bacteria, whatever — *invades* brain cells to take control."

"Yes, they invade the neurons. I'm just wondering how they manage to do that." She paused and tapped the table several times, deep in thought. Then, "How many species of bacteria do you think can enter human cells?"

"Thousands, probably," I said.

"But there's something else: a great deal of bacteria that live inside us don't do anything harmful. For that reason, our immune systems don't react."

"What do you mean?"

"Well, I've always assumed that the person infected with harmful bacteria would develop a fever, for example. It's one way the body fights a bacterial infection. Increased temperature can kill the bacteria."

"That's true," Sally said from the peanut gallery. "I'm no biologist, but I do know that most bacteria don't trigger the immune system."

"Hmm," I murmured. "Malichauk told us he'd developed the nano so it remained silent and hidden. That's part of the reason why he fused it with bacteria."

"More so because it was the only way around the replication problem," Malichauk said.

I started, surprised he had spoken. "Why's that? Why couldn't you create a nano to build copies of itself?" *Keep him talking*, I told myself. Maybe something important would come out.

He sat upright and suddenly seemed eager to speak about his creation. He probably thought the replication ability of the nano wasn't something that could help us develop a test. Or, perhaps he wanted to discuss replication to steer us away from the line of thought we had been on. I had to be careful here.

He said, "The idea had been around since 1945, when a man named John von Neumann first proposed it."

"I've heard of him," I said.

"He's a famous scientist from the twentieth century. He also came up with the concept of *Mutually Assured Destruction*, or MAD, which dominated the climate of the cold war. He was Alan Turing's teacher."

"Who?"

He looked mortified. "Who was Alan Turing? My God man, that's sacrilegious!"

Shaheen said, "Come on Malichauk, either you're helping us or not. What is it going to be?"

Dammit Shaheen! I glared at her. Don't antagonize the man!

"I'll talk about my invention," he said. "But I won't help you find a way to destroy it."

I knotted a fist. "So who was Turing?"

"Only the creator of the computer. He was also a code breaker during one of Earth's early world wars. The second, to be exact. He used his computing expertise to break an enemy's code. Something called the enigma code."

"So what does von Neumann have to do with this?"

"He first postulated the idea of the self-replicating machine. He theorized — in the mid twentieth century, keep in mind — that the most effective way to mine the moon and asteroid belt would be through the use of a self-replicating machine to take advantage of their exponential growth capabilities."

Shaheen shot me a knowing look. I did my best to ignore her.

He continued, "The problem with that was attempting to devise a microscopic machine that could create copies of itself. The difficulties have proved daunting. We still are unable to do it, centuries after von Neumann first proposed it!"

"Why is it so difficult?" I asked.

"Shrinking the processor and the method of locomotion was a breakthrough for medicine and engineering. But the replication has proved to be nearly impossible."

"It's hardly impossible," Shaheen broke in. "Engineers will do it, one day."

"Sure. One day," he sneered. "But I needed it done in my lifetime. In order to kill the Council, I needed self-replicating machines *now*."

"Why haven't engineers been able to create the von Neumann machine?" I asked. Keep him talking ...

He frowned. "The concept implies that they harvest the building materials from within the human body. Materials exist for it, such as iron in the blood and so forth, but the manipulating arms of the nano would have to move individual atoms around and bind them together. We're not quite at that stage. We can't build manipulator arms that can move individual atoms." He glanced at Shaheen. "Not yet, at least."

"Which is why you've fused a nano with a bacterium."

"Exactly! When I came up with my plan, I realized how foolproof it was."

Manny snorted loudly and Malichauk did his best to ignore him. "Why try to develop a machine that can replicate when we already have examples of it everywhere we look?"

"You mean bacteria," I said.

"I mean life! *We* are essentially von Neumann machines. We are self-replicating. And yes, so are bacteria. So when I hit on the idea, I began a series of experiments that lasted more than a decade. I eventually developed an engineered bacterium — you were right about that, by the way Shaheen — and managed to fuse the microprocessor within it."

"And how does the processor replicate with the bacteria?" I pressed. I smothered a triumphant look; he had inadvertently given us something there — he told Shaheen that her theory was right.

"I inserted the code into the bacteria's DNA. When it replicates, it also recreates the processor. It takes the raw materials from the host body, the same as with any other bacteria that lives within a human being."

Katrina said, "If it wasn't such a hideous idea, you might actually be eligible for the Nobel Prize, Lars."

He offered a sly smile.

"But if you don't help us we're all going to die," she continued.

His expression grew instantly dark. "I refuse to do what you want."

"Even if it means your own death?" I said.

"I'd rather avenge my brother."

The clinic grew deathly silent.

"I hope you don't mean that," Lingly said in a small voice.

"I certainly do."

Another long moment passed; we stared at each other, yet again at an impasse. I exhaled loudly. "Okay," I said. "So you fused a couple of bacteria cells together to create this nano."

"Plus a processor."

"Of course. Now, the question is, what bacteria did you use?"

He shook his head. "Sorry, Tanner."

Beneath the table, my fingers pulled together into a fist. Soon I would have to deal with this issue, and when I did, I was actually beginning to think I might enjoy it, just a tiny bit. He frustrated me, and I wanted nothing more than to wipe that smug look off his face.

I turned back to Shaheen. "I guess we have more research to do."

— Chapter Twenty-Six —

"Maybe what we should focus on," Shaheen said to me an hour later, "is what bacteria species are capable of entering human cells."

That was the thought that had occurred to me earlier. It had slipped away during the discussion with Malichauk, but here it was, back again. Perhaps Shaheen was on the right track.

"There are many different varieties. We decided that earlier."

"Yes, but I just realized we could narrow it down even more. It has to be one that can hide from our immune system. Well, I've come across this article in the medical database. I think it might be important."

I noticed Malichauk stiffen. It took some effort to ignore him. "Yes ... ?"

"Our bodies can sometimes fight back when a dangerous bacterial infection occurs."

"You said that earlier. A fever, for —" I stopped suddenly. "Are you suggesting that someone infected with this nano will develop a fever that we can check for?"

"No, that's the whole point. There is no immune response. But this can help us narrow the type of bacteria that Lars used."

I nodded. "All right, so how do bacteria hide?"

She glanced at her reader. "There are a number of ways. First, they can do something called *Molecular Mimicry*. These bacteria actually look like parts of the host's own body. When they do this — through a chemical process — the immune system won't attack because it thinks the bacteria actually belongs there."

I absorbed that. "So you think this is what the nano does?"

"Hold on. I'm not finished. There's also the *Suppression of Antibody* method. You see, when our bodies detect a harmful invader such as a virus or bacteria, it sends antibodies to seek out the invaders to destroy them. Some bacteria, however, can disable these antibodies. One example is a bacteria called *Mycobacterium leprae*."

"That's a mouthful."

"It's more commonly called leprosy."

I blinked. "Really? That was a dreadful disease. I didn't know it was bacterial; I thought a virus caused it. It actually suppressed antibodies?"

"Yes. Now here's an interesting method. Some bacteria actually — I'm paraphrasing what the article says here —"

"You mean dumbing it down."

She flashed me the whisper of a smile. "For you, yes. It's called *Ejecting the Antigen*. Some bacteria actually detach a part of themselves into the bloodstream. The body's antibodies go after these ejected segments rather than the bacteria itself!"

I suddenly wanted to yawn. This had brought back memories of her lecture on exponential growth, as well as Reggie's discussion on the sun's structure. "Fascinating," I finally managed.

"It really is," she said. "It's an example of the military looking to nature to develop methods of defense. From an engineering standpoint, it's incredible."

My forehead creased. "What do you mean, 'military looking to nature?'"

"Well, it's the same as a fighter — either in space or in an atmosphere — that launches decoys to attract enemy missiles. It's quite a thing to see it happen at a cellular level."

"Oh." Strange, the things that enthrall engineers.

"Now I've come across a bunch of other techniques bacteria use to hide from the immune system. They all involve attacks against phagocytes."

"What are those?"

"They're cells responsible for destroying and consuming harmful bacteria, an important part of the immune system. I'm going to skip over all these."

"Why?"

Her eyes sparkled. "Because I've found something more interesting. I've saved it for last."

I perked up at that. "What is it?"

"It's a method of evading our immune systems." She looked up at me. "Tanner, it's called *Hiding Inside Cells*."

I turned to Malichauk. He looked from me to Shaheen and back again. I could tell she had hit on something important. Call it a hunch. Or maybe the fact was that Malichauk had a terrible poker face. "That does sound interesting," I said after a moment.

"The nano Lars created stays hidden from the immune system," she said, also with an eye on the doctor. "This method of hiding struck a chord somehow."

"Maybe because we know our nano can enter human cells."

She nodded. "Indeed. But more important, not just *any* cells — *brain cells*."

She was right. Perhaps this was how we could narrow the choices down. "What does the article say?"

She read from the screen before her. "'Some bacteria hide from an immune response inside the host's own cells. By doing so, they do not provoke an immune response. They multiply inside these cells and continue to invade the body. Some examples include *Brucella, Listeria, Mycobacterium leprae,* and *Mycobacterium tuberculosis.*'"

I leaned back in the chair and stroked my jaw. "I know the leprosy one. The last one obviously causes tuberculosis. But what's Brucella?"

"Um ... give me a minute here."

I turned to Malichauk. "Do you have anything to say?"

"No," he snapped.

"You seem to want to say something."

"I don't."

I watched him for another moment. He was unable to keep his secrets hidden. I knew we were close.

"Here it is," Shaheen said. "Animals often carry Brucella and can cause infections in humans. It can enter the body via the skin, respiratory tract, or digestive tract. It enters the blood and lymphatic system. Symptoms are high fever, chills, and sweating."

"What about Listeria?" I said as I watched Malichauk from the corner of my eye.

She hesitated. "It's officially called *Listeria monocytogenes*. It's a foodborne bacteria. It's one of the deadliest, in fact. It kills up to thirty percent of the time."

"Food poisoning?" I said, skeptical.

"Yes. According to this, when you eat food that contains this bacteria, it reacts with the cells in the intestinal tract. Listeria binds to the intestinal cells and can penetrate the cell wall and cause infections."

"I see. But I'm not sure —"

"There's more," she said, looking up at me. "Once the bacteria have entered the intestinal cells, they can also move to other organs."

"Such as?" I knew what she was going to say.

"Spleen. Liver." She paused before —

"Brain," I whispered for her. "Interesting."

She continued, "When this happens, it's called *listeriosis*. It causes encephalitis, or inflamation of the brain."

I frowned as I pondered this new information. So we had a bacterium that could penetrate cells and was motile enough to infect the brain. And yet, there was still something missing in all of this.

"The infected people don't have a conventional illness, do they?" I said. "Is there a way we could test for that?"

Shaheen looked surprised. "I didn't say they did. I'm just suggesting the possibility that Listeria is one of the bacteria Malichauk used for the nano."

Manny said, "Why do you think so?"

"Two reasons. First, the nano Doctor Malichauk made is capable of hiding from the immune system. The nano can penetrate cells, which not every bacteria can do. Second, there aren't a lot of things that can cross the Blood Brain Barrier. Listeria can do both."

"Wait a minute," I said with a shake of my head. "You lost me." This discussion had now gone beyond my rudimentary academy biology. Shaheen, on the other hand, seemed to be able to read articles and extract a huge amount of information from them. I was lucky she was around to help.

"The Blood Brain Barrier, or BBB, is a barrier that protects the brain. It keeps toxins and other substances in the blood from penetrating and disrupting neurons. It's a crucial component of our nervous system. It was first discovered in the late nineteenth century. A bacteriologist named Paul Ehrlich injected some dye into animals and noticed that it stained all the organs except the brain and spinal column. Turns out it exists to keep most substances out of the brain. Even many drugs can't penetrate it."

My brow creased. "What is it, exactly?"

"The cells that line the vessels in the brain are more tightly packed than in the rest of the body. Endothelial cells. They block everything but the smallest molecules, like oxygen, carbon dioxide, sugars. If it didn't exist our brains wouldn't work. Also, hormones control many of the body's functions. If these hormones entered the brain, they could cause problems."

I mulled it over for a moment. "So the nano that Malichauk created, since it's partly a bacterium, has to be one of the type that can cross this barrier," I said.

"Yes."

"Can anything affect the barrier? Weaken it?"

She grimaced. "You won't believe this. Hypertension, infection, and trauma can affect it."

I glanced at her. "Why wouldn't I believe that?"

"I'm not done. Radiation and microwaves can also weaken the Blood Brain Barrier."

"Radiation," I whispered.
"Yes."
"Do you think that has anything to do with all this?"
She pursed her lips. "Not sure. Radiation weakens the barrier, but these bacteria can cross it regardless."
"What about the microwave beam to Earth?" It seemed too large a coincidence.
"You'd have to be directly in the beam for it to have any effect, and that would kill you."
A silence descended over the clinic. Malichauk kept his gaze locked to a bulkhead; he still refused to participate. The others had frowns on their faces and listened intently.
"What else can enter the brain?" Manny asked eventually.
"Certain bacteria can penetrate, unfortunately. Like the ones that cause meningitis. There are a number of different kinds. Some drugs, like cocaine. And, of course, Listeria monocytogenes."

I folded my arms and exhaled loudly. "So you think it's Listeria." I had hoped knowledge of the type of bacteria fused with the nano would help, but I wasn't sure how. I hoped this would go somewhere. I checked the time and grimaced. Not good; we didn't have much left.
Shaheen shrugged. "It's possible. It's as good a guess as any."
I studied Malichauk with the hope that his expression would give something away. "Lars? What do you have to say."
"You won't find the bacteria I used," he muttered.
"How can you be so sure?"
"You're not a cellular biologist. You don't know."
I thought for a minute. Clearly we had to learn everything we could about listeriosis. A little more information could shed some light on the nanos and perhaps suggest a test we could use.

I grabbed my datachip reader and made the request. A number of headings appeared. One in particular caught my eye and I brought the article into the main window. The title was *Listeria and Cellular Penetration*. I read for five minutes, completely silent, and grew more interested as I paged through the journal. Once finished, I set the reader back down, but couldn't keep my eyes from it. Something about the article bothered me. I thought for a minute, then picked it up again.

Finally I said, "There's quite a bit in this article about how Listeria can push through cellular walls."

Shaheen nodded. "That's how it would penetrate the Blood Brain Barrier and hide from the host's immune system."

I pursed my lips.

"What is it?" she asked. She had noticed my expression.

"I don't know. Something in here ..."

She brought the article up on her own reader and skimmed it quickly. "It mentions two proteins that the bacteria uses to push into the host's cells. *Myosin VIIa* and *Vezatin.*"

I had heard of those two proteins before. I just couldn't place the reference.

I looked at Malichauk. His face was rigid with tension.

It came to me with a jolt. "Holy fuck," I whispered. I rose to my feet. "You used Listeria."

"Nonsense," he said through clenched teeth.

I turned back to Shaheen. "I'm guessing Listeria is rod shaped. Am I right?"

She consulted her reader. "Yes, it is."

I remembered that there were generally three shapes to bacteria: rod, ball, and helix. Our nano was rod shaped.

She said, "Remember Tanner, Listeria is able to hide from the immune system in the host's cells, but there are lots of bacteria that can do that. Listeria is one possibility, I agree, but you shouldn't assume that Malichauk used Listeria simply because —"

I shook my head. "No. There's more. The day I interviewed the doctor — my second day on *SOLEX* — he had an article open on his reader. *It was about these two proteins.*"

Malichauk jerked his head to me and sneered. "You're making that up. How can you possibly remember what you saw on my reader a week ago?"

Being a Homicide Investigator required an excellent memory. You had to absorb the details of a crime scene and the investigation. The smallest, most inconsequential fact could reappear later and break a case wide open.

Just like this.

I placed my hands on the table and leaned toward the man. "You were reading an article titled *Myosin VIIa and Vezatin Protein Production in Cellular Biological Processes.*"

Shaheen's eyes widened. "Are you sure, Tanner?"

"Absolutely."

The scientists stared at us, their faces drawn. They had held their tongues through most of this, thankfully. Now, however, they seemed barely able to keep their mouths closed.

"It can't all be a coincidence," Shaheen whispered. "He used Listeria as the host for the processor. It can penetrate cells, *even into the brain*, which few bacteria can do. He attached flagella from some other bacteria for locomotion. Then he programmed the nano and set it loose in Brick Kayle."

I was still glaring at Malichauk. He refused to meet my eyes. "Admit it, Doctor," I growled. "We figured it out."

He now had a dark look on his face, but still he refused to say a single word. I studied his expression for long minutes, finally convinced that we had discovered the truth. He wouldn't confirm it, but I felt inside that we were right.

I brought up a picture of the Listeria bacteria and frowned. "These are definitely rod shaped, but they already have flagella. Why would he have to attach —"

"Listeria only has flagella when grown under thirty degrees Celsius," Shaheen said. "Our bodies are thirty-seven degrees."

I nodded. It made sense. Listeria was the bacteria he used, but to make it motile, he had to combine it with some other bacteria. Listeria monocytogenes didn't have flagella in the human body because of its high temperature.

Lingly stepped forward. "Tanner, way back when I was doing my studies, I did take a biology class. It was just an introduction to the field, and we definitely didn't get into great detail. But I do remember something important."

"About Listeria?"

"No. About proteins. I'm pretty sure that you can test the blood."

"For the Listeria?" I asked, confused. "But Malichauk told us it clusters in the brain and sometimes the fingers and wouldn't show up in the —"

She shook her head. "No, not the bacteria. The protein! We could do a blood sample and look for *Myosin* and *Vezatin!*"

My jaw hit the deck. Silence fell over us once again. I spun on Malichauk. "That's it! That's the test — you've already invented it!" I stared at the others. They were as shocked as I. Just like that we had it, and all it took was a little research, and maybe some intuition too.

And, of course, a little luck.

I studied Malichauk, wary. With the test, we could tell once and for all who was infected.

Myself included.

— Chapter Twenty-Seven —

I wanted to wrap my hands around his neck and squeeze until he died. A morbid thought, perhaps, but his 'plan' had killed six people already, and more were sure to die. We had only hours left, and if the test didn't work, or if we couldn't find a way to eliminate the nanos inside those infected, then we were in grave trouble.

Malichauk offered a look of condescension. "Pathetic," he sneered. "Neither of you know what you're talking about."

I ignored him; it was a weak attempt to throw us off. I knew we were on the right track. "Is it easy to test blood for a specific protein?" I asked the scientists.

They pulled their eyes from the doctor. "It's done all the time," Katrina said. She actually looked hopeful. "Doctors diagnose a lot of diseases that way. Cancers, liver disorders, kidney dysfunction."

"Bacterial infection?"

"Sure."

"How is it done?"

She frowned. "No idea."

Lingly and Sally both shook their heads.

I turned to Malichauk and felt an immediate surge of anger. "You created the test long ago, didn't you? You held it back from us, made us go through all this, and did *nothing* as time counted down!" I knotted my fists. Shaheen watched me, anxious. The doctor's expression was fixed; he didn't respond. I continued, "That's why you were reading about those two proteins!"

The others now stared at me, mouths agape. They still didn't understand the enormity of the deception.

"You think Lars already created a test?" Manny asked. "When he was in here earlier with Balch and Anna?"

I snarled. "No. Probably when he first invented the nanos."

"But why?" Lingly asked.

"He created the infection. He *wants* it to spread around and off the station. Why not create a test so he can periodically check on the personnel to see how his plan is proceeding?"

Rickets was shocked. He glared at the doctor. "Is that true? Were you keeping tabs on it during regular physicals?"

Malichauk's face remained blank.

"It's no use," I said. "He won't help." I considered the dilemma. We needed some medical advice on how to test for protein in the blood ... who could I ask?

I turned suddenly to Manny. "I need to make another call."

"What?" he said, perplexed.

"In the command center. You can come with me."

—

Katrina took a step forward. Her expression was hard. "You can't leave with him, Manny. I still think he's infected."

I threw my hands up, exasperated. "I'm not infected, for Christ's sake! Why would I be working so hard to develop the damn test?"

"To throw us off, probably. It might not even work."

I shook my head. "Ridiculous. Captain, I really need to make a call to Mercury. It'll help us."

He studied the faces that surrounded us as he debated silently with himself. He clearly still had doubts about me, but I was almost there ... he knew I was working to save them. Finally, "Shaheen and I will go with you. That will leave Avery, Katrina, Sally, Lingly and Malichauk here, in the clinic. How's that, Katrina?"

She pressed her lips together. "I guess it's fine, but be careful."

We left the anxious group behind and stalked through the dim corridors to the command center. As we moved up the ladder, a shadow at the end of the module caught my attention. I could have sworn that it had moved as I stepped onto the deck. I stared at it for another few seconds, watched for any sort of movement at all.

Nothing. I was seeing things. The situation was getting to me.

I turned my back and ascended the ladder to Level Three. Minutes later, I marched to the communit console and sat before it.

"Remember the batteries," Manny warned.

"Keep it short, right." Only thirteen hours of life support remained. We were cutting it close.

A minute later, Doctor Higby's face appeared on the static-filled viewscreen. He looked bewildered as he strained to see the image. "Is that — oh, hello again, Lieutenant Tanner," he said. "What can I help you with?"

—

Back in the clinic, I gestured at the cabinets against the bulkhead. "Where are the keys, Doctor?"

He folded his arms. "I don't have them."

"So you don't think the test will work?" I growled. "Why keep us out of the cabinets then?"

"This is my clinic," he said, obstinate.

Lingly asked me, "What did you find out?"

I faced her. "It's simple. We take a vial of blood from everyone here. The diagnostic machine that's part of every procedures table will analyze it." I marched to Anna's corpse and pointed to the aperture in the side of the table. "That's where we insert the vial. All we have to do is program the diagnostic to look for the two proteins, *Myosin* and *Vezatin*."

"Sounds simple," Rickets said with a frown. "Easier than I thought."

"Well, we had to know what to look for. There's a lot of protein in human blood, according to Doctor Higby."

Rickets guarded Malichauk while the rest of us programmed the diagnostic device. It was a relatively simple task: we selected the BLOOD TEST option on the diagnostic, and from the drop menu there was a complete list of proteins. We chose the two that Listeria used to penetrate the Blood Brain Barrier.

We each took a step back and studied one another in the gloom of the clinic.

My heart pounded.

"Who wants to take the blood?" I asked.

"Not you," Katrina spat. "I don't want you touching me."

"Come on," Manny said. "You know how infection occurs. It takes —"

"Fifteen minutes, I know. But all he has to do is prick me with an infected needle and boom, I'm history."

Her statement dropped like a bombshell. No one said a word for quite some time. She was absolutely correct: the blood didn't have to sit on the skin for fifteen minutes — if ingested or *injected* somehow, it would accomplish the same task.

"Does it really matter?" Rickets asked. "There are less than thirteen hours of battery power left."

"Still," she responded in an angry tone.

I glared at her. Her attitude had grown tiresome; she had replaced Grossman as my biggest detractor on this damned station. "So who do you trust to take the blood?" I finally asked.

A shrug. "Only one person. Me."

I frowned. "You want to take your own blood?"

"Sure. Doesn't it make sense? And I'll take a clean needle from the cabinet, one that you haven't touched."

Five minutes later, after we had forced the cabinet open, there were eight labeled vials of blood on the procedures table next to Anna's shrouded corpse. Katrina had taken her own; the rest of us had let Sally perform the procedure. She'd had some experience with animals in a biology class almost forty years earlier, and of the group, she was therefore the best candidate.

None of us trusted Malichauk, the only one among us actually qualified to take blood. He didn't even offer.

Manny faced us with a grave expression. A flood of emotion cascaded over his face before —

He leveled his pistol at Rickets.

"What the —" Rickets shouted. "Do you really think —"

"Drop it, Lieutenant," he said between clenched teeth. *"Now."*

He made us sit in a line facing him, hands on our knees, palms down.

"If anyone lifts a hand or makes a move to stand up," he growled, "I'll shoot. I don't care who you are. I know I'm not infected, and this is the safest way, as far as I'm concerned."

The thought to confront him, knock the pistol away, and put myself in his position crossed my mind. Shouldn't I take charge in order to conduct the test on the others? After all, I *knew* I was human.

Did I?

Was I clean? Not a single nano inside me?

I realized with a burning pit in my gut that I couldn't be sure. His way was better. Let him control the situation for now. I nodded at him. "Let's do this," I whispered.

He glanced at me.

"Manny could be infected," Katrina said, looking at the rest of us beside her. "We can't let him have that pistol. Someone else needs one too, just in case."

"Be quiet," Manny said. "This is the only way. I can't trust anyone."

"You could be infected!"

"What if I let someone infected have the pistol?" the Captain barked. "As soon as the test comes back positive, he or she starts shooting." He shook his head, stubborn. "This is the only way."

I had to admit it sounded reasonable. The only problem was, what if the only armed person here also happened to be one of *them?*

—

Manny tested my vial first. After all, I was the Investigator sent to manage and decipher the mystery on the station. I needed to regain my position of trust with these people. He was right to test me before the others.

I held my breath. I still didn't know if Bram had managed to infect me during our struggle in the docking bay. I had washed the blood off in under fifteen minutes, but still ...

He inserted the vial into the opening in the procedures table. "What do I do now?" he asked, but kept his eyes and pistol aimed squarely at me.

"It's all set up to run the blood test," Shaheen answered. "It's fully automatic. Just press the button marked SCAN BLOOD."

He glanced down quickly and positioned his finger over the button. He looked back to me. His face was hard, uncaring. His trigger finger twitched.

He was ready to kill.

—

My heart thudded in my chest. If I was infected, Manny would no doubt shoot the instant the machine reported back. Even though control wouldn't occur for another eleven hours or so, there was so much tension in the room he would probably shoot first and ask questions later.

He pressed the button.

—

Beep.

He looked down at the display and his face remained blank.

I thought I was going to pass out.

"He's clean," he said finally. He exhaled. He had been just as nervous as I.

I deflated and slumped in the chair. "Damn," I sighed. "I was actually worried."

"He's lying," Katrina snarled. "I'm telling you, he's infected! There's no way Brick would have killed Grossman and framed Tanner. That's too ... devious. It implies incredible strategy and planning! I can't believe the nanos are capable of that."

"Believe it," Manny said. "According to the diagnostic machine, those two proteins are not in his blood." He gestured with his pistol. "You can stand, Tanner. Here's the other pistol." Manny had taken Rickets's pistol and had placed it in his own holster.

I took it and aimed squarely at Manny. "Now you," I said. There was no emotion in my voice. I was just as ready to kill as he.

His face registered shock as he saw the pistol aimed at him. His expression grew rigid for an instant, then softened as he realized how logical it was. "Of course," he said finally. "I should have done mine first." He coughed. "I guess I'm a little scared of what it'll say, although I know I'm not infected."

"Put the pistol down and test yourself," I ordered.

He complied silently and inserted the vial. The room was utterly silent. All eyes were on the Captain's face.

Beep.

He studied the device. "I'm clean," he whispered. I could barely hear him. "Thank God, I'm clean."

I checked the readout just to be sure. Bold words on the display spelled out clearly, PROTEIN NOT LOCATED. I relaxed my trigger finger and handed the pistol back to him, happy I hadn't had to shoot.

"Avery's next," Manny said with a glance at the man. "Watch him closely."

"You know I'm not infected," Rickets said. His eyes were wide.

Manny nodded. "I know. But I have to test everyone, just to be sure."

I raised the pistol, pointed at Rickets. Manny inserted the vial and pressed the button.

Beep.

He looked down and an expression of complete surprise appeared on his face. "Holy God," he whispered. "The proteins are in his blood." He jerked his eyes to the First Officer. "He's infected!"

—

I should have realized Rickets was one of them from the beginning. In hindsight, it was a simple bit of reasoning. I'm not sure where I had gone wrong. Ever since Mercury and my failure with Michael Flemming's case, I had second-guessed myself constantly. That screw up had ended in Flemming's death. I still blamed myself; it had obviously affected my work.

Jimmy Chin had witnessed the assault in the life support module, during which Brick Kayle had infected someone. Jimmy reported the incident to Avery Rickets, who chose not to tell anyone else, not even his Commanding Officer. He had explained why, and it did make some sense. Still, it was contrary to regs, and Rickets usually went strictly by the book.

After Jimmy had died, someone had removed his head and hands in order to cover up the existence of nanos in his body.

The inevitable inference was that Jimmy had still been human at the time of the assault in the life support module, *but had been infected afterward*. A reasonable conclusion was that Rickets, after he found out what Jimmy had witnessed, had infected the crewman to keep him quiet.

Anna Alvarez had said Jimmy acted weird after reporting the incident, but hadn't known why. Now I knew.

What happened must have shocked him. Perhaps he would have gone to the Captain in time, but control happened quickly. In fact, I recalled now that he had told Anna he had to 'make a decision about something.' It was obvious that he was trying to decide if he should take the matter up the next level in the chain of command.

Before he could decide what to do, it was too late.

—

Rickets bolted straight for me, bloody hands outstretched.

I fired instinctively.

"Fuck!" Sally cried. She had been next to Rickets, and she hurled herself away as he reacted.

I fell backwards as Rickets drove forward despite the energy pulse to his chest. I fired again and spun to the side.

Manny finally fired and the blast hit his First Officer full in the face.

Rickets fell forward onto the deck with a hollow thud, bloody hands to the side, nose crunched into steel.

He didn't move.

"Holy shit," Manny gasped. "I can't believe he was infected."

I continued to aim at the prone man in case he was still alive. The others had clustered against the far bulkhead. I could hear their ragged breathing, their cries and sobs. Smoke rose from the corpse in lazy curls.

Incredible. During questioning, Rickets had expressed his worry at being assigned to *SOLEX*. He'd had the impression that his career had faltered. He had totally convinced me that he was innocent.

He was worried that his career had faltered!

The nanos had made him seem so human, in every way. I shook my head, astounded.

"Get back into your seats," Manny snapped. "Now."

They moved slowly, but they obeyed him. They steered far away from the corpse as they shuffled to the chairs.

"At least we know the test works," Sally muttered as she sat back down.

"Now do you trust me?" I growled at Katrina. She refused to meet my eyes.

I studied the body for a long moment. I had seen a lot in my career. I had hunted hundreds of murderers and shot more than my share. Despite that, I had never seen one take a shot at point blank range in the chest and not die - or at least *drop* — immediately. The blast was supposed to stop the heart instantly. The energy charge shorted the nervous system.

Manny had noticed my expression. "What is it?"

I shook my head, unsure how to say what I thought.

"Maybe his momentum just carried him forward?" he suggested.

My brow creased. "I shot twice and still he didn't stop. It wasn't until you fired that he finally went down."

A long silence fell over us. The acrid smell was pervasive.

"What are you saying?" Shaheen finally asked.

I gestured at the body with my pistol. "Is it possible that the nanos are stimulating them in some way? The adrenal gland, or the part of the brain that can increase their strength?" A look of shock appeared on Shaheen's face. I turned to the doctor. "Well?"

His eyes were fixed to the corpse on the deck. "I didn't program that into them," he muttered.

"I noticed the same thing with Bram," I continued. "He looked strong, but he was quite a bit more powerful than I anticipated. And during the attack in my cabin, the pressure on my arm ..."

Shaheen grunted. "It's an interesting theory. We already know they've disregarded their programming. It's possible. I'm not too familiar with neurology, Tanner. I wouldn't know what part of the brain they could affect."

In fact, weren't there numerous areas the nanos could stimulate or access? Could the hosts be smarter than us too? Faster? Better problem solvers? The list was as endless as it was terrifying.

I sighed. We needed to be aware of the possibility. After all, if the nanos could do that — create enormous strength in their host — then it was possible a woman might be responsible for some of the murders after all.

The faces that looked back at me were now mostly women.

Manny fixed a steely gaze on them. "Who's next?"

—

Beep.

Shaheen tested negative. I had been a little worried; after all, her expertise with all things mechanical had made me wonder about her more than a few times. We knew Malichauk had created them, but there was a slight chance that he had received help from someone like Shaheen. Still, without her we wouldn't have known nearly as much as we did about the nanos, and we probably wouldn't have had the test.

Next was Sally. I had also been worried about her ever since our search of the station. She had left the group for just under ten minutes, and claimed that she had only used the lavatory. She hadn't told anyone where she was going; she had simply disappeared.

I watched her closely as Manny tested the blood. The older black lady sat with head bowed, shoulders slumped. She didn't even watch.

Beep.

"Negative," the Captain reported.

She exhaled loudly. "Whew. I was worried."

"Why?" I asked, bewildered.

She frowned. "Well ... if we were infected, would we even know it?"

I pursed my lips. "I don't know. Impossible to say." It was a fascinating observation, one that I'd had earlier. Could the nanos hide their presence, *even from their host?*

Next was Lingly. She had seemed awfully scared since this all began. I had wondered if the nanos could simulate the normal fear that someone would experience in order to throw others off. If so, they had done a marvelous job with her.

Beep.

She was clean. She almost fainted from the stress. Her hands trembled and she was paler than ever.

Malichauk was next. Everyone moved away from the doctor; if there was anyone else infected, we figured it would be him. He had helped Brick escape from me in the corridor earlier. He had not been cooperative in creating the test. He had ejected Jimmy's body before I could perform an examination. He had lied multiple times.

Manny picked up Malichauk's vial of blood.

I aimed at the man and prepared to fire.

A flash of movement caught my eye.

Squinting, I tried to see better in the gloom. Something under the doctor's chair? It was so damn dark ...

There it was again. What the hell?

I took a step forward to get a better look.

My mouth went dry.

Blood. Malichauk's hands were at his sides, palms down, hidden from view. Blood dripped from his fingers.

Holy shit he was infected.

I squeezed the trigger —

— and Katrina bolted from her chair and dove right for me. I got a shot off at Malichauk, though my aim was off. I hit his shoulder as he flung himself sideways and away from me. Shifting my aim to Katrina — who was now only a meter from me — I took a step back and fired again.

Manny looked up from the diagnostic device to see what the commotion was. In a flash, he understood what had happened and immediately got two shots off. Combined with the pulse from my pistol, the blasts seared every part of Katrina from her waist up.

Her blackened and smoking body hit the deck with a crash, right at my feet.

I spun back to Malichauk, but it was too late. He had bolted from the clinic.

—

"Holy shit," Shaheen muttered. "Katrina was one of them all along. But she was so accusatory of you, Tanner! It made her seem so human!"

Incredible. She had acted that way to throw suspicion off of herself! She had even said that she wanted to kill me just to eliminate the infection. She had also been the one to suggest jettisoning the modules — *while she had been infected all along.*

The nanos were devious indeed.

I kicked myself mentally. After the attack in my quarters, Katrina and Brick had been the only two people with alibis. They had supposedly been together at the time; they had obviously protected each other from potential discovery. I groaned. Stupid, stupid, stupid. I should have realized she was infected.

"Malichauk was one of them all along," Manny snorted. "I suspected when he wouldn't help us with the test ... but still."

"He gave us a lot of information about the nanos," Sally said. "Why would he do that?"

"He never gave us anything vital," I responded. "Nothing he ever said involved how to access them, how to shut them down, kill them, or anything like that. He told us why he did it, but nothing to really help us survive."

"He may have even infected himself," Manny added.

I had considered that possibility too. After all, he had originally programmed the nanos to be harmless to the host unless it was a Council Member. Perhaps he actually infected himself to set this whole chain of events into motion. Moreover, I realized sadly, Larry Balch and Anna Alvarez's bodies gave some compelling evidence: someone had hit them *from behind* with a blunt object. No doubt Malichauk had done it. It's why the hatch had been *forced* open; he didn't have the code for it. He had never intended to help with the test. He had been one of them all along, possibly infected by Brick, Katrina, Jimmy, or even by himself.

Lingly, Sally, Manny, Shaheen and I were now all that remained.

Twelve hours until power failed.

We had to find Brick and the doctor and kill them. There was now no other way.

Part Five: Crash

Investigator's Log: Lieutenant Kyle Tanner, Security Division, Homicide Section, CCF

From the moment Malichauk escaped, things steadily got worse.

As if they weren't already bad.

I checked the readout on my vacsuit and felt my stomach drop. Only two hours of air remained, then I'd have to switch to my final bottle.

For the past hour, my communit had broadcast a simple message that I had recorded and set on repeat. *"Attention,"* it said. *"This is Lieutenant Tanner of the Confederate Combined Forces, currently en route from the now-destroyed station* SOLEX *One. Requesting immediate assistance. I've nearly depleted my oxygen supplies. Radiation exposure is approaching lethal levels. My current coordinates are —"* The suit's computer provided an accurate location for each broadcast.

The message played over and over. I kept the transmitter aimed at Mercury's approximate position and hoped that some signal would make it through the intense solar radiation. It was doubtful, but it was all I had.

My makeshift shield had done better than expected: my radiation indicator was only now just turning a deep shade of red. There was still a chance that medial care could counteract radiation exposure should I survive this debacle, but I would need it almost immediately.

I turned my head and studied the distant stars. I had never liked zero gravity, and here I was hurtling through space without a ship's protection. The sun was behind me, still only a few million kilometers away, burning intensely with an energy few had dared trespass.

I had passed the stage of terrified abandon and had accepted with a kind of dull comfort the blackness of space. Infinity surrounded me. The universe was my home, it was where human beings lived and traveled.

It was my womb.

It would be my grave.

A feeling of utter tranquility had begun to overcome me. Was that what happened when death was so near?

It felt fitting, in a way. If I was going to die here, today, there could be no better place for a space traveler's corpse. I had no family. No friends. I was alone — and had been all my life.

Only a short amount of time remained. I had to finish my story.

— Chapter Twenty-Eight —

A transport to *SOLEX* would need eight hours to arrive — *if* someone would even come for us. Based on the last words Lassiter had said to me, the chances of that were slim. Whatever the case, we had just four hours to take care of the last two infected people. When that was done, then we could attempt a desperate call for help. Still, I had doubts that it would work.

"Why can't we just call now?" Lingly asked.

"Because Brick and Malichauk are still threats," I replied.

"But the CCF doesn't know they're still alive."

"She's right," Sally said. "Why not just call first, *then* take care of Brick and Malichauk?"

I frowned at the suggestion. I understood their motivations, but it went against everything I stood for. It would contravene my military background, but more importantly, it would be a lie.

Manny eyed me. "What is it, Tanner?"

I sighed. "We can't call for help until we know for sure the infection is gone."

"But surely we can take care of —"

"What if we call and they send a transport to rescue us? And what if those two manage to kill us in the meantime? We'd be willingly allowing the infection to escape!" I pressed my lips into a thin line. "I can't allow that to happen."

Lingly glared daggers at me. She looked ready to skin me alive. It was the first emotion other than fear that I had seen from her in a long time. "How dare you put us in this position? Call for help, then we'll take care of Lars and Brick."

I hesitated, my frustration growing. I turned to Manny. He too watched me with hope in his eyes. "I just can't do it, Captain," I said. "For the good of the Confederacy. I know it's hard, but if we have to die to protect the Council, then so be it."

He looked pained at first. Eventually, however, he nodded, but he still didn't seem happy about it.

My refusal outraged Lingly and Sally. "I can't believe you'd do this!" Lingly snapped. Her hands were on her hips, and she had stepped so close that her nose was an inch from my face.

"Why don't you stop arguing so we can start searching?" Manny said.

"How can you just give in to him? How —"

Shaheen's eyes were downcast. "Tanner's right, Lingly. We can't risk it. We have to kill the infection before we call. We need to be sure."

"But —"

"Lingly," I said in a soft tone. I put my hands on her shoulders. "Think about what the infection has become. It means more than the death of the ten Council Members. It's a plague that could spread across the galaxy. It could infect every human being. We would no longer be ourselves. Just ... just *controlled*."

She looked from my eyes to Manny's, Shaheen's, and back again. She glanced at Sally, and a look of understanding finally appeared on her face. She seemed to deflate. "I hadn't thought of it in those terms. I guess I figured it was only the Council that was in danger."

I shook my head. "It's everyone. It's *humanity*. Malichauk has created an evolutionary leap for human beings, but it means our very *extinction*. Do you understand now?"

She sighed. "Yes. I do."

Manny said, "Good. Then the sooner we —"

A powerful explosion rocked the clinic.

—

A section of the exterior bulkhead blew out right before my eyes. One second Malichauk's cabinets were arrayed side by side, contents arranged neatly, the next I watched them fly out into space amidst a rather large fireball.

Throwing myself to the deck, I grabbed the foot of a procedures table. I turned my head to the side and squinted against the flying debris. Lingly and Sally were swept up in the maelstrom and hurled into space by the outrush of atmosphere. I opened my mouth to swear, but couldn't hear anything over the din. My breath was sucked away and I snapped my jaw shut, realizing that in a second there wouldn't be any air left to breathe.

It was horrifying.

Lingly reached her arms out to me. Her lips moved soundlessly; she had tried to shout something. Sally spun end over end and slammed into the jagged edge of the bulkhead on her way out to space. There was an immediate fountain of blood and her arm detached neatly just above the elbow. She clutched the stump in an attempt to stem the flow, but the wound wouldn't make much difference; she would be dead in a minute regardless.

A naked body followed the two scientists out; a second later, another flew through. They twirled grotesquely, arms and legs flailing like rag dolls. It took me a minute before I realized they were the bodies of Larry Balch and Anna Alvarez. They had been lying on the procedures tables with only blankets over them; the rush of air into space had carried with it everything not bolted down. The Y-incisions on their torsos stretched as they moved — I could see the internal organs spewing out as they gyrated in the force of the explosion.

I retched into my mouth at the image before me.

Godfreid Grossman was next. I felt the thud behind me as he hit the deck face first. The gale-force winds carried him along another two meters before he slid to a stop. He lay next to Rickets and Katrina; they had ground to a halt as friction with the deck kept them from also being blown into space.

Suddenly, I realized with dread that Grossman's body had stopped moving because there was no more air to push him along.

My ears popped with a sharp, piercing pain. The clinic was now in vacuum.

I surged to my feet with a sudden burst of adrenaline. The gravity field remained in place, thankfully, and I lurched to the hatch. I bumped into Shaheen and Manny on the way; both had managed to grab something to prevent the fatal exit from the clinic.

Shaheen made it to the hatch first. She hit the open toggle feverishly and

---

Nothing happened.
It refused to open.

It was the safety protocols of course — protocols that kept the air in the rest of the station from venting.

Manny shoved her aside and frantically keyed in his code. I knew that we would pass out after fifteen seconds of such exposure. We were close to that already ...

The hatch finally slid open. The winds began anew as the module's air rushed through the clinic and out the rupture. Manny and I reached around the hatch frame and slowly pulled ourselves out. It was like fighting an upstream current. I extended an arm back into the clinic, and my fingers barely brushed Shaheen's uniform. I seized a fistful of material and yanked with everything I had. She tumbled through and into the corridor.

Finally the hatch slid shut and the wind stopped. We fell to the deck, exhausted.

The emergency lights strobed and a klaxon pierced the corridors. The sound was like a sledgehammer in my head.

"Holy shit," Manny moaned. "Brick went outside and somehow planted an explosive on the hull. He knew exactly where we were. He's trying to take us out."

"It's their only hope now," I gasped. "They have to kill us."

"He's doing a good job," Shaheen muttered. "Only three left."

A jolt ripped through me as I realized that she was right. Manny, Shaheen and I were the only ones who remained. Since I had arrived, *twelve people* had either died, been infected, or been proven infected. It was a devastating number for someone sent to *protect* people. I hadn't done a very good job.

Only three left ...

"It's either us or them," I said. "They know that. They'll kill us then try to call for help. Or they've already called. Either way, we have to find them first and kill them."

"They can't call for help," Shaheen said. "I locked out the FTL and the off-station comm after your last call to Doctor Higby."

I stared into her eyes with a look of horror on my face. She was right. Manny had thought it wise to lock out the system in case someone infected tried to use it. I realized with a shudder what it meant for her: they could kill Manny and me, but they needed Shaheen alive.

—

"Where's your pistol?" Manny asked. We were still in the corridor outside the clinic, recovering from the depressurization incident and planning our next move.

I felt my holster and grimaced. "Gone. Probably out in space by now."

His lips turned downward. "Mine too."

My brow creased. "What about the one you took from Rickets earlier?"

He gestured to the hatch. "In the clinic."

"You don't have any more on the station?"

He winced. "Nope. There were only four. There's no reason to have weapons here, and I fought hard to get those. Brick had one as Council Rep. Rickets had one, I had one, and you got my spare when they took yours."

I exhaled and thought furiously. No weapons. We needed *something* in order to fight them. But what? I glanced at my watch in anger. Dammit! Time was running out. We were now past the twelve hour deadline we had set for ourselves earlier. Theoretically, we still had some three hours, but that would leave us no time in case we had to argue our case with the CCF. A ship would have to be dispatched the instant we called for help, which I knew would never happen.

Damn!

"What can we do?" Shaheen asked as she jerked her gaze up and down the corridor.

I grunted. "Katrina suggested jettisoning the modules, one by one. Maybe it's our only hope now." The plan formed itself in my mind slowly. We could detach modules and announce each over the station's comm. It could conceivably drive them to a location where it would be easier for us to deal with them, but on our terms, rather than theirs.

But where? Where could we drive them?

I chewed a lip as I considered our options. There was only one place that made any sense. "We'll drive them here, to this module," I whispered. "The command center is located here. We need it to eject the modules anyway, right?"

"Yes," Manny murmured. Then he swore.

In the command center, one level up, Manny sat at the central console. His face was drawn. "I've never even trained to do something like this before. I'm not sure what security measures are in place to prevent this from happening. They don't generally program this sort of thing into the system components."

"Why would someone ever need to eject modules?" I asked.

"A damaged module can sometimes compromise the integrity of the station," Shaheen said. "That's why the programmers built the jettison command into the systems." She looked at Manny. "But there are a lot of safeguards. It'll request your access codes a number of times. It might take a while."

He frowned. There was a look of *failure* on his features, as if his command had beaten him. He sighed. "Which one first?"

I thought for a moment. "Do Module I." It was the one already damaged by the meteor strike, and it made sense to start at G, H and I — the ones farthest from the command center.

It took nearly an hour for the Captain to bypass all the safety precautions. As he entered each command, there came a request for a new set of codes. After thirty minutes, the security became so tight that he had to retrieve his personal code book from a safe in his quarters. After that, he entered codes with one eye on his book.

"I want to make sure I get these right," he muttered. "No sense screwing up and having the computer lock me out."

He entered the final code and a recorded message startled me.

"ATTENTION CAPTAIN," it said. "PERMISSION TO DETACH MODULES NOW GRANTED. ENTER MODULE LETTER AND ACCESS CODE ZULU TO BEGIN THE TEN SECOND COUNTDOWN."

"Wait." I held my hand up. I punched the comm to address the entire station. "Attention Brick and Malichauk. We're detaching Module I. You don't want to be anywhere near it right now." I gestured at Manny. "Do it."

"COUNTDOWN INITIATED," the computer spoke. "TEN, NINE, EIGHT ..."

The recording played over the station's comm; it reverberated into the command center from the corridor with a tinny echo.

"Here we go," Shaheen said. Her fingers gripped the edge of the console.

There was a station schematic display that showed all ten cylinders. Module A, the engineering/life support module, had a blinking red label next to it that warned of the power loss and the failing batteries.

Module I on the schematic also began to flash.

The countdown finished and I felt a *thunk* vibrate the deck at my feet. The module on the schematic turned black.

"MODULE EJECTED," the voice reported.

"It worked," I said, surprised. There had been so many levels of security to bypass, I wasn't sure if it would actually happen.

Shaheen grunted. "Of course it did."

I studied the schematic. "Let's do H next."

We ejected five more modules. Before each one, I broadcast a warning to give Malichauk and Brick ample time to move to the adjacent cylinder.

"Why not just eject the modules with them in it?" Shaheen asked with a raised eyebrow.

That had been a thought some time ago. I had gone over it in my mind multiple times. It would have been an easy way to kill them, but ... "There's always a chance the nanos would survive, Shaheen. Even after the host died, they'd still be there. We have to make sure no one can salvage the cylinders later and somehow become infected."

She looked skeptical. "Surely the nanos will be dead."

I shook my head, grim. I had actually learned something from my research that she hadn't. "Bacteria is extremely hardy. In times of unfavorable environmental conditions — such as heat or drought — a bacterium will develop a thick outer wall and enter a resting stage. It's called a spore. Someone could find one of the modules in the future and inadvertently expose themselves to the infection."

She nodded and her lips tugged upward into the hint of a smile. "You think you know everything, don't you?" she murmured.

"You're just jealous."

Eventually only four cylinders remained: A, B, C, and M, the mass driver. It remained connected to Module B, although the solar arrays hadn't been so lucky. When we ejected D and F, it severed the array connections and they now floated beside the station, close but no longer in direct contact.

Module D had been the last to go. It contained the energy conversion equipment and the transmitter that beamed the microwaves to the receiving satellite in Earth orbit. As Manny detached and ejected it, he murmured, "There goes *SOLEX*." It housed the station's very reason for existence. *SOLEX* was essentially now gone — it was just a shell, a shadow of what it had been.

He sat back and snarled, "If my career wasn't over before, it is now." He paused, then, "In fact, I might even have to face execution for doing this, if we survive."

I watched him for a moment. He was right, but he neglected something important. I placed a hand on his shoulder. "I would speak for you, Manny. I would tell them that there was no other way. Besides, we're trying to *save humanity* here. If I were you, I wouldn't worry much." Besides, I thought, at that moment there were much greater things to be concerned with.

He looked at me with a grave expression. After a beat, it turned into something a little more conciliatory. "Thanks," he muttered.

I glanced back at the display; only four cylinders were still lit. "Let's stop there," I said. I looked at Shaheen and Manny. "Let's go get them."

We no longer had our pistols, so we grabbed anything that would make a good club. Shaheen had a steel table leg, and Manny had a rather large wrench he had grabbed from a tool locker in the corridor. I found a sledgehammer with a pick on one end. It was a little unwieldy, but would definitely make an effective weapon.

"What the hell is this used for?" I muttered as I eyed the tool.

"Installing coolant pipes," Shaheen said. "Tightening seals; there's a lever on adjacent pipes that needs to be whacked."

I frowned at it as I turned it in my hand. A pistol would have been far better. More accurate from a distance. Using this, I would have to be close. And if blood splattered me ... game over. Infection might occur and I wouldn't even know it.

My fingers tightened on the club.

The three of us clustered together as we moved through Module C. The command center on Level Three, the clinic on Level Two, and the common mess on Level One made up the bulk of the cylinder.

"This time we search everything," I said. "Ducts, maintenance crawlspaces, whatever." An idea suddenly struck me before the sentence was out of my mouth. "Wait a minute." I halted abruptly and the others bumped into my back.

"What is it?" Shaheen asked. Her eyes were wide. "Do you see something?"

I waved her worry aside. "No, no. Just an idea." I turned to them and said in a whisper, "Why not depressurize the modules? We'll jump into vacsuits and if they haven't thought ahead, we've got them!"

Silence. Their eyes registered shock at the prospect. Manny nodded after a second. "Jesus! I can't believe I didn't think of it. It'll make our job a hell of a lot easier. If it works, we may just find them lying somewhere, dead!"

The only problem with the idea was that Brick and Malichauk had proven themselves to be resourceful and devious time and again on this damned station. Unfortunately, they would probably do so again.

We had to learn to think *ahead* of them. But with the nanos potentially stimulating specific regions of their brains, was it possible to anticipate and beat them at their own game?

— Chapter Twenty-Nine —

The vacsuits were located in an emergency locker just outside the command center. We pulled on the skintight coolant layer first. I tried to avert my eyes as, beside me, Shaheen pulled hers on. I caught a glimpse of her brown skin and a flash of dark in her pubic region. I turned away quickly, but once our suits were on, I noticed the hint of a smile on her face and a twinkle in her eye.

I cleared my throat. "Ready?"

"For sure," she said with an arched eyebrow.

The situation was absurd. Here we were, hours from death, and this beautiful woman was making me horny.

Manny ducked into the command center and yelled at us: "Make sure your helmets are secured — I'm venting the station!"

Because we had already ejected the majority of the modules, there were now a number of tunnels that led to vacuum. Depressurizing the station was a simple matter of remotely opening the hatches on both ends of each tunnel. Manny accessed every single hatch on the station, even cabins and storage areas and lavatories. He had to refer to his code book on occasion, but it was a speedier process than ejecting the modules had been.

"Hang on to something!" His voice rang in my ears through the suit's communit.

The klaxons sounded again and the red emergency lights began to flash. An instant later, I felt a tug as the air currents started to churn through the corridor.

"Here we go," I murmured.

I didn't feel an incredible outgassing of air like I had earlier in the clinic; the nearest tunnel to space was down on the first level. It had once led to Module F, the scientists' labs and quarters.

It took almost two minutes for the station's atmosphere to fully dissipate.

"It's done," Manny said finally. "All hatches are open and I've exposed the station to space in three places. Unless they were wearing a vacsuit — or had one *real* handy — they're gone."

We resumed the search in Module C. We checked every storage space and lavatory. We looked inside the freezer in the galley. Shaheen led us through access junctions, crawlspaces, and ventilation ducts. We poked our heads in the spaces between hulls that housed power cables and hydraulic pipes. We examined power distribution nodes — just big enough for a man to crouch in — all over the module.

We searched *everywhere*.

No luck.

We sealed the tunnel hatch and moved to Module B.

The number of hiding places they had were dwindling.

Module B — officer's quarters and rec facilities — was a little more difficult to search. We now had to look under bunks, in closets, and in showers. Through the gym, games rooms, and lounge. Shaheen led us into the twisted innards of the cylinder.

Nothing.

They had us convinced they were within every shadow or around every corner. And when we rounded that corridor ... we'd be dead before we knew what had happened. It wasn't about infection anymore — it was about their survival.

We finished the search of the module and looked at each other in surprise. Empty.

A much smaller tunnel than the ones that connected the cylinders attached the mass driver to Module B. In the corridor outside the officer's cabins on Level Three, a narrow ladder led upward and disappeared into darkness.

We poked our heads up into the mass driver and quietly searched the entire structure. There were fewer hiding spaces there than in any of the other modules; everything was out in the open. There were no maintenance crawlspaces or access junctions to conceal anyone.

Again, nothing.

They had to be in Module A — life support and engineering. There was no doubt now. It seemed fitting: the infection would end in the same location I had first discovered it, where Brick had inadvertently left a drop of blood with a single nano within. Jimmy had witnessed the infection and paid the ultimate price as a result.

He would have appreciated what was about to happen.

We entered the module and began our search through the twisting ducts and apparatuses that stretched up three full levels. The deck wrapped around machinery and piping to allow maintenance access on the three levels. The engineers hadn't designed this module for convenience or amenities; there was a lot of equipment crammed into an area almost too small to house it all.

Level One was clean.

Level Two was clean.

I tightened the grip on the hammer and looked to Manny and Shaheen.

We moved up to Level Three.

I was now back in the same place where Jimmy had witnessed the attack. As I stepped off the ladder and into the confined enclosure, I wondered idly who it had involved. Brick had been the aggressor; he had left his blood behind as proof. And the person he had infected? Katrina Kyriakis. It couldn't have been Avery Rickets; he was already infected. When Jimmy tried to report the matter, the First Officer had attacked him. Jimmy hadn't even known what was happening. Yes, it had been Katrina, and she had fooled us all.

We crept through the level, crouched and ready to swing.

There was no one there.

They had evaded us again.

Shaheen had a confused look on her face. "But we searched everywhere. I know this station better than anyone else. They couldn't be in any other —" Her expression suddenly grew pale.

"What?" I asked. "You know where they are?"

"There is one place left," she whispered. "I never even considered it."

"We ejected six modules," Manny said. "Maybe they stayed in one of them. They may be dead or dying, right now."

She shook her head. "No. There is a place left, and it's here." She looked at our questioning faces for a beat. Then, "They're hiding outside."

There was a long silence as we absorbed that. Incredible; she was right! It was the only place they could be, yet we had never expected it. We had just assumed that they would have stayed *inside* the station. After all, it was dangerous exposed to Sol; why would anyone hide out there?

"My God," Manny muttered. "It makes sense. They were in this module while we searched the others. When we got close, they went out the tunnel that used to lead to Module D." He looked at us, grim. "They were already in vacsuits, waiting for this."

With a tremor, I suddenly realized how obvious it was. Brick had planted an explosive on the hull, *outside* the clinic. He had either stayed there, or he had still been in his vacsuit when we depressurized *SOLEX*. Now, he had vacated the station ... and we had to go get him. I swore under my breath; he had the upper hand now — the element of surprise.

"We have to go out immediately," I said. "There's no time to waste. They're outside and probably have some sort of trap set." I checked the watch on the suit's wrist control pad. "There's only thirty minutes before we reach the deadline. After that, there's no point in a call for help. A ship wouldn't reach us. Eight hours later, we die."

—

We stalked to the end of the tunnel and the sun's immensity filled the view. There was no blackness visible. Only yellow, orange, red. It was blistering in its intensity, unforgiving. As we stepped into the direct light, the temperature shot up to fifteen hundred Kelvin. The suit's coolers kicked in quietly and worked to keep the interior suit environment a cool twenty degrees Celsius.

"It's enormous," I whispered. It was hard to avert my eyes.

"I know it sounds weird, but you do get used to it," Shaheen said.

I grunted and shoved the hammer into a strap on my belt. I had never used such a weapon outside before, but a shattered visor or a torn suit could be just as deadly as a pistol blast. Moreover, being in a vacsuit would now offer us some protection against infected blood, should we come into contact with any.

"Keep an eye on the time," Manny warned. "We should only stay out for ninety minutes. After that, we risk permanent injury." He grabbed our arms before we could move out into zero gravity. "Don't forget to go to the clinic afterward. We need the medicine to counteract the radiation."

I didn't respond because it didn't matter. In less than an hour, medicine would no longer be of any use.

We grabbed the rungs attached to the hull and swung out. My stomach lurched; as usual, it felt like a drop down a bottomless pit. I wondered how anyone could grow accustomed to it. I took a moment to gather my senses. Shaheen looked at me, curious.

"Are you okay?" she asked.

"I'm fine," I snapped. I noticed her continuing stare. "I'm in security for Christ's sake, Shaheen. I don't often leave my ship to float around like this."

"It's okay," Manny said. "Take a second and then let's go." He gestured around the curve of the cylinder. "They could be right around the corner though, so don't take too much time."

I exhaled. "Let's go. I'm fine."

He shot me a quick look and saw the determination in my features. He squeezed my shoulder. "Okay. Be careful."

I growled in response; I didn't need advice like that — I just needed to finish this.

We moved along the exterior of Module A, careful to stay in contact with the station at all times. We had no way to maneuver in open space if we lost our grip; people had died in the past, only two meters from a safety rung or exterior airlock hatch, unable to reach safety without the ability to propel themselves. I was all too aware of the danger.

My heart pounded.

I pictured the sun burning our backs as we crawled over the thin skin of the station. I shook my head inside the helmet and tried to dislodge the sweat that beaded my brow. Damn. It hadn't been so bad being out with Shaheen earlier; at the time the harness and the winch had kept me safe. Now I was out in the open, with Sol only five million short kilometers away. I was having a hard time shaking my fear, despite the suit's cooling unit.

Dammit! Those two could be right next —

"There they are!" Shaheen cried.

I snapped my head up and searched the direction she had indicated. "I don't see anything," I hissed.

"They were right there," she said, quieter now.

"What cylinder?" Manny asked.

"Module C. Just going over the hull and out of sight."

They were on the far side of the station.

Shit. Something suddenly occurred to me. "The clinic is over there," I said. "They could reenter the station through the rupture in the hull!" And once inside, they could gain access to the control center and do God knows what to the station. I frowned. But what could they do to the station that we hadn't already done? It was in complete disarray; most of it now orbited the sun in pieces. "Maybe we can trap them in the clinic," I suggested. "While they're trying to get back in."

We crawled across the hull, along the path of safety rungs on the cylinder's surface and the exterior of the tunnel that led to Module B. The mass driver was overhead; it blocked the sun, and we passed into the shadow it created.

Sweat poured into my eyes now, and in frustration, I looked at the suit's interior temperature gauge. Still a cool twenty degrees Celsius. Damn. I had faced The Torcher without a shred of fear. What was with me lately? Could it just be zero gravity that was doing it? Or was it something more? I had uncovered the infection on *SOLEX*, but at what cost? The station was practically gone, only three of fifteen people remained uninfected, and it still wasn't over. What was wrong —

"What are you thinking?" Shaheen whispered.

I paused for a moment. "Flemming," I said finally.

The surprise in her voice was clear. "Your friend on Mercury? Do you still blame yourself for what happened?"

"It's an odd time to be talking about it," I muttered.

"It's an odd time to be thinking about it too, isn't it?"

I sighed. She was too good. "Couldn't help it. I feel responsible for all this."

"Responsible?" Manny blurted. He had no idea who Flemming was or what I referred to. He continued, "Tanner, Malichauk is the one who did this. He's to blame, not you."

I shook my head. "You don't understand, Captain. I've never had an investigation turn into something like this. When I got to *SOLEX*, there were fourteen in your crew. Now there's only two."

Another silence descended over us as we pulled ourselves feverishly toward Module C.

Then, "Don't you think I could be feeling some guilt too?" he said in a harsh tone. "I'm the Captain, after all. Those people were my responsibility. This post was my responsibility. Instead I fucked up when I let Jimmy go out by himself, and now we've come to this — trying to kill two of my own!"

I grunted. "Maybe, but look what came of it. Jimmy died and it exposed the infection. If it gets off *SOLEX*, the entire human race will be in danger. Instead we have a chance to stop it, right here. They sent me to *stop* this, for Christ's sake! So far I've failed miserably."

"Why don't you listen to yourself," Shaheen said. "You should be taking the credit for uncovering this. We have a chance to save humanity. You'll get a medal for this, Kyle."

I absorbed her words, but still Flemming remained in my thoughts. I knew I should have been able to see the mystery sooner, before the loss of so many people. I ground my teeth in frustration. It didn't matter what they said; what *I* thought was most important, and I was disgusted with myself.

We emerged from the shadow of the mass driver and approached Module C. "We'll talk about this later," she muttered.

I shook off the conversation, pulled myself to a halt, and considered the situation. They might still be in the clinic, trying to enter the station, but the traverse to Module C had taken a fair amount of time — perhaps as long as ten minutes. I tried to peer around the hull, but the gash in the cylinder that exposed the clinic to vacuum was hidden from sight.

"We should send someone around the other side of the module, in case they try to come up behind us," I said.

"Good idea," Manny said. "I'll go."

"Do they have a pistol?" Shaheen asked.

I frowned in thought. We had already gone over that, but it was difficult to be sure. "Brick had one when he killed Grossman, but I think he gave it to Bram. I took it from him after I ..." I stole a look at the Captain, but his features were hidden behind his visor. "After our fight," I finished.

Manny sighed. "You don't have to worry about killing my friend, Tanner," he said in a soft voice. "Malichauk killed him, not you." He spun his body ponderously toward us. "I'll meet you at the clinic. Shaheen, stay with Tanner, and don't get yourself hurt. And watch your backs."

He pulled himself away, hand over hand, and disappeared from sight around the curve of the hull.

"Let's go," I said.

—

The jagged rip in the hull was just ahead. Sharp edges stretched along the four meter tear; within, a black, empty space. The clinic. Were they in there?

"Manny," I whispered. "We're here. Where are you?"

Shaheen tapped my arm. "Line of sight, Tanner. He's still on the other side of the hull. Can't hear us."

"Oh." I looked at our surroundings. The smooth white of the hull ended in the black smear immediately before us. The sudden image of Lingly and Sally as they tumbled out through the opening came to me. I shuddered and tried to shove it aside, but it was difficult. The fountain of blood in zero-g, Sally's severed arm ...

A minute passed. Then another.

"Where the hell is he?" I muttered.

"Maybe we should go look for him."

I frowned. It would be unwise to leave the clinic unguarded; if they were in there, they could exit and come up behind us. "Let's check this out first. Then we'll look for Manny." I moved closer to the split in the cylinder. "Watch your suit," I warned her. The twisted hull was now directly beneath us; small segments of the ceramic shield jutted out and posed a very real threat.

I pushed myself away from the station and drifted out into space. Grabbing the edge of the hole, I poked my head over the breach and scanned the interior. I could see three corpses on the deck — Katrina, Rickets and Grossman — but otherwise the room looked fairly clean. Anything not bolted down had been blown out to space.

"I don't see anything. I'm going in."

I swung through the opening, the gravity field took hold, and I landed safely on my feet. I stumbled slightly as I hit, but regained my footing quickly. I looked around but saw nothing. The small opening that led to the freezer where Malichauk had stored Jimmy's body was just beyond the procedures tables.

Tightening my grip on the hammer, I moved toward the freezer.

I entered the small space, prepared to see a vacsuited figure in the corner.

There was no one.

There were three small hatches a meter above the deck. I had placed Reggie and Belinda's bodies in there, on the cold steel trays. If they were still there, one tray should be unoccupied.

I grabbed the lever on the first hatch and pulled. The hammer was in my right hand, pick side out. I was prepared to strike.

The hatch opened and the first body rolled out on its long shelf. It was Reggie's headless corpse.

The second one held Belinda.

I grabbed the lever on the third hatch. If anyone was hiding, it would be here.

Pulling savagely, I prepared to deliver a crushing blow.

It was empty.

Shit! They were like ghosts — they only appeared when it suited them. When you actively looked for them, it was impossible to catch a glimpse except from the corner of your eye, and even then it was just a fleeting image.

I marched to the hatch that led back into the station. Perhaps Brick and Malichauk had managed to open it after all, and were now inside *SOLEX*, safely away from us.

It was still sealed and locked.

"Shaheen," I said.

"Yes?"

"They're not here. They might still be outside. Has Manny showed up yet?"

"No."

I swore under my breath. He might have run into them.

I carefully stepped to the edge of the gash and reached up to grab Shaheen's outstretched hand.

"Watch yourself now," she said. "Just give a small push out of the gravity well, and I'll pull you back to the hull."

"Don't let go," I said.

"Don't worry."

I stepped off into space and felt her tug my arm reassuringly. My feet pivoted and —

"Tanner, here they are!" she yelled.

She let go of my arm and I started to float away. "Shit!" I yelled as I jerked my head to locate the danger.

They were five meters behind Shaheen, yanking themselves along the hull toward her. They approached dangerously fast. Shaheen had let go instinctively, knowing that if she didn't, she would be dead before she could turn to fight.

Ripping her club from her belt, she spun before they reached her. She hooked a foot under a safety rung.

I drifted farther from the hull and watched helplessly as she faced her two attackers alone. I had to get back to help, but how? Each second I moved a few more centimeters away. It might not seem like much, but a centimeter in space might as well be a million kilometers.

Damn!

I searched the vacsuit pockets frantically. Patch kit, right pocket. Tool kit, left pocket. I scrabbled at the calf pocket, my last chance for life.

A safety tether!

I pulled it out and unraveled it quickly. Each end had a spring-loaded latch. Somehow I had to get it hooked to the hull so I could pull myself in. I risked a quick look at Shaheen and saw her take a swing with her club. The larger of the two figures — Brick — ducked and nearly lost his grip on the station. She was managing to keep them at bay. I had perhaps a few more seconds, at best.

I pried one of the latches open and bent it backwards to keep it from closing. I was about a meter from the hull and the distance was growing slowly but steadily. The nearest rung was just beside the tear in the clinic's hull; I took careful aim and tossed the tether at it. I reeled it back and watched the open latch miss by a wide margin. "Shit," I muttered.

Shaheen swung again. Malichauk had darted in to try and grab her, and the club hit his left shoulder. The impact pushed him toward the hull and he hit flat on his stomach. The recoil of the swing sent Shaheen away from the station, but her right leg was hooked under a rung and kept her from ending up in the same position as I.

Brick's face was visible through his visor and I saw his lips move, his features an angry grimace. He seemed enraged.

I switched the communit to the common frequency.

" — the codes to the FTL and off-station communit!" he was yelling.

"Come on Shaheen," Malichauk was trying to reason. "You won't be hurt. We just need your codes so we can call for help."

"Fuck off!" she snapped. She twisted around to look for me and Malichauk made another move.

"Watch out!" I yelled.

She turned back and swung her club again. It hit the back of the doctor's helmet and I heard a strangled gasp.

"Dammit!" he cried. "You could damage my vacsuit, Shaheen!"

"That's the whole point!" she growled. "Get out of here!"

"Where's Manny?" I asked.

Brick turned to face me. "He won't be joining us anytime soon."

I hesitated as I absorbed that. The look on his face ... the anger in his tone ...

He had killed the Captain. "You fucker," I hissed.

"It's you or us," he said. "I want off this damn station. I'm willing to kill to get away from here."

"You already proved that when you killed Grossman."

"Hypocrite!" he snarled. "I suppose killing Bram was okay in your books. Or Rickets. Or Katrina."

Shaheen looked over her shoulder at me. Her hand slipped down to her thigh and her fingers opened. She wanted me to throw her the tether.

"Some things are necessary," I said to Brick. "Like dying to protect the human race."

"Is that what you think you're doing?" he sneered. "I'm trying to *protect a new race!*"

The sun burned like a furnace behind Brick; the solar arrays were in silhouette against its intense fury. I snorted. "You represent the end of everything that's human. Brick Kayle would never have wanted that for himself."

"Is what we represent so bad?" Malichauk said.

"Give me a break. You murdered people to keep your existence hidden. You represent extinction, for fuck's sake!"

"You don't understand," Brick said, sad. "I'm still human. I have the same feelings I did before. I don't feel controlled. I am —"

"Are you still Brick?" I snapped. "Do you still have a desire to gamble? Do you still have free will?"

He hesitated. "What the hell does that mean?"

"It means Brick had all the failings of a normal human being. He had wants, desires. He had flaws. Now he no longer exists. He's being controlled, by you."

I moved the tether to my right hand and made sure the latch would sail toward Shaheen's fingers when I threw it. We would only have one chance at this; when Brick saw what I was doing, he would attack Shaheen again and never give me another opportunity.

His eyes flicked down to my right hand. "What are you doing?" he said.

Too late. He had noticed.

The tether unfurled as it floated — seemingly in slow motion — toward Shaheen. She spun, grabbed the latch, and gave it a strong tug.

She wrenched it so hard she almost ripped it from my hand. I hadn't had a chance to secure the other end to my belt. It ran through my glove and I almost lost it. At the last possible second, I clutched it and felt the pull through my arm and shoulder. I spun toward the hull and grabbed for a safety rung, frantic.

I regained my grasp on the hull. Sweat poured into my eyes and I shook my head to clear my vision. Something appeared in the corner of my eye —

Startled, I spun and brought my club to bear. I gasped —

It was Captain Fredericks. "Manny!" I cried.

He rotated slowly as he floated by. As the left side of his suit came into view, I saw the slash from armpit to knee. Something — *someone* — had exposed him to space. There was singed bloody flesh where the knife had ripped through the coolant layer and into his skin. The sun had cooked him.

Brick withdrew a cutting tool from his utility belt. They were meant to slice people from vacsuits *inside* the airlock in case of an emergency. He had used it on Manny, out in space.

"You bastard," I rasped between clenched teeth.

"You'd do the same to me," he replied in a flat voice.

I stole another look at the corpse as it floated serenely by. Manny's face was frozen in rictus, a scream that would last for years. He drifted away from the station and *SOLEX* forever.

Steam vented from his vacsuit; the sun was still broiling him.

I jerked my attention back to Brick and Malichauk. "Shaheen," I growled. "You take Malichauk. I've got Brick."

She grunted. "Got ya."

Malichauk pushed himself back minutely. Brick barked a sharp laugh.

Here we go.

— Chapter Thirty —

A few thoughts flashed through my mind as I pulled myself toward Brick. If Shaheen and I both died here — *right now* — then the infection could still conceivably get off the station. The issue of spores frightened me, and I knew at least one of us had to survive this in order to extinguish the threat forever.

The stakes were huge.

Brick lifted the blade. "Don't come too close," he snarled. "I don't really want to kill you, Tanner. I just want to infect you and get off the station. I want to send the signal for help. We're running out of time."

"No shit," I muttered.

At a meter's distance from him, I hooked a foot under a rung and straightened. I raised the hammer and turned it to display both sides. He eyed it, wary; he had clearly noted the sharp pick on its end. He licked his dry lips and positioned his right boot under a rung.

He lunged at me, knife outstretched. I swung the hammer and twisted to the side, careful to keep my foot close to the hull. The knife sliced by me harmlessly and my weapon slammed into his helmet. He stumbled to the side, momentarily jolted by the blow. I peered at his visor, hoping to see a crack and a stream of vapor. Nothing.

He withdrew and pulled himself closer to the station.

I moved my left foot forward and slipped it under the notch of a maintenance hatch that was set into the hull. Brick slashed at the front of my vacsuit. I tried again with the hammer — this time going for his arm — hoping to dislodge his weapon.

I missed and his blade scraped by my suit, just millimeters from causing fatal damage. I moved back and gripped the hammer tightly. I turned the shaft in my hands and made sure the pick side aimed forward.

He noticed. "You mean business, don't you?"

"Of course," I growled. "Don't you?"

"Maybe a truce?" he suggested.

His posture gave him away — he was scared. From his point of view, the danger here was very real, not just for him, but for *an entirely new species*. If they lost this fight, it was all over for the nanos, period.

I turned to see a similar struggle between Shaheen and Malichauk. He would thrust with a knife, she would swing with the club. It was an even match. I needed to finish with Brick so I could help her.

Brick was also watching their struggle. Without a second thought, I placed my foot on the edge of the maintenance hatch and gave a savage push. I rocketed straight for him and barely skimmed the surface of the hull. It was a huge risk.

I brought my hammer up —

And caught him completely off guard. He held his hands up to ward me off and — just inches from him now — I aimed for his visor. The pick impacted with a *crack* — I heard it over the open comm — and a spider web snaked out from the center of the blow. He pulled himself back awkwardly and the knife drifted harmlessly away. The collision brought me to a halt and I pushed myself away from him. He recoiled, stunned. His head had hit the interior of his helmet, like a brain against the inside of a skull. He probably saw stars.

"Tanner!" Shaheen cried.

Malichauk was on top of her, his knife just inches from her suit. I turned and hauled myself toward the two; Brick was now weaponless with a damaged suit — I could worry about him later. At that moment, Shaheen was more important.

I approached Malichauk and raised my weapon high overhead. I smashed it down and drove the pick through his suit and into his back. It was a fatal blow, yet I didn't hesitate before I did it. He was the person who had caused the death and destruction on board *SOLEX*, the person who had refused to help us solve the mystery and defeat the nanos.

The person who currently threatened Shaheen.

He let out a strangled cry and immediately released her. He twisted, frantic now, and tried in vain to reach the pick that I had imbedded three inches in his back. Air and blood vented from the wound, and he flailed for another twenty seconds as he attempted to grab the weapon behind him.

His struggle finally ceased and he looked up at me, fear and sadness clear in his features. "I don't want this to die," he whispered. "We can't die. We have to spread."

"The infection is out of control." My voice was flat. I watched for another few moments; he simply stared at me, his eyes pleading. A sudden look of calm came over him, and he pushed off the hull and floated out to space.

I swore as I realized what had just happened.

"What is it?" Shaheen asked, puzzled. "You got him."

I shook my head. "We needed his body, to make sure the infection dies."

She absorbed that for a beat. "The suit's material will give out eventually. The sun will fry him. The nanos should all die."

I grunted. I hoped she was right, but there was always a chance ...

Behind me, Brick had disappeared. I swore again. The damage to his visor had perhaps compromised his vacsuit, and he had taken the opportunity to duck back into the station.

I glanced at Shaheen; she looked grim. We were now the only humans left on *SOLEX*.

—

Back aboard the station, we trudged through the corridors and looked at each other sadly. Only eight hours remained. It would take a ship that much time to travel if we signaled immediately.

"How about it?" she asked. Her voice was soft in my helmet.

"What?"

"Let's call for help. We have no other choice."

It brought me to a sudden halt. I frowned. We had been through this already, and I thought she had understood my motivations. We had taken care of Malichauk, but we weren't out of the fire yet.

"We'll get Brick after we call," she continued. "He's the only one left. We can do it, Tanner."

I sighed. "I understand why you're asking, but it's just too dangerous."

She put her hands on her hips. "Dammit, just be reasonable for a change! Let's make the call. We've got eight hours to find him. It's either that or sit here and wait to die!"

I shook my head, stubborn.

"Is this still about your friend, Michael Flemming? You think you screwed up here, just like on Mercury? It's not your fault, Tanner. Why can't you see that? You said yourself that this was something completely unique. You couldn't figure things out at first because events were completely outside of your experience."

Her words made me wince. "That's true, but too many people have died and I'm accountable, Shaheen. For Flemming's death as well."

Her nostrils flared and she threw her arms up. "Don't you see you're taking the blame because of the shortcomings of a different Investigator? It's not your fault! Flemming died because he couldn't make the connection you could. You're the better Investigator. Sure, what happened isn't fair, but in life, what is? Now suck it up and move on!"

I stumbled back as though hit by a physical blow. "I could have saved him," I whispered.

"Sure, if you were psychic."

"He asked for help. I didn't give it to him."

"You got a killer captured. Why isn't that good enough?"

"He was the only person I had left in the galaxy," I muttered. "Don't you see? I helped kill him."

"Quint Sirius killed Flemming," she cried. "Not you!"

She was in a rage. I put my hands on her shoulders. "Why are you so upset by this?"

"Because Flemming wasn't the only one you have, don't you see?"

I remained silent and simply stared into her blue eyes as I processed her words.

"Have you forgotten about me?" she said, her voice husky. "About what's happening between us?"

I said in a soft tone, "Of course I've felt something. But —"

"You have a chance to save what we have! You have the power to give us a life together!" She sobbed freely now; my heart ached for her. Could it be that she was just as lonely as I? Our histories were vastly different, but was it possible that at this point in our lives, we both needed someone more than either of us had known?

She spoke again, and it was an angry rasp now: "You'd kill us when we can still have a future together!"

I watched her in grim silence. "The infection is too dangerous —" I started. But inside I wavered. The chance of having someone in my life appealed to me. I knew I had been lonely, but until now hadn't really understood to what extent it affected me.

"I'm going to make the call," she snapped. "If you don't like it, kill me!" She spun and began to march away.

"Shaheen!" She didn't stop. I watched as she disappeared up a ladder.

She didn't look back.

—

She had a point, I had to give her that. Surely we could take care of one man in the time that remained. Duty required me to maintain comm silence, but the chances were in our favor now.

Or, was I just trying to rationalize life over death, at the tremendous risk of a hundred billion others?

I thought for another minute about the danger her suggestion involved. To say it was enormous was a colossal understatement. Surely there were options here! What else could we do? As I considered the situation, however, other things churned through my mind ...

Shaheen and I, together ...

A life of loneliness, gone forever ...

Happiness, after all this time ...

"Shit," I muttered. I had known what I wanted all along; in fact, ever since I first laid eyes on her I knew I needed her.

And she needed me.

She was now just beyond the top of the ladder; I approached her rapidly and grabbed her shoulders. A look of shock appeared on her features as I spun her around, but bewilderment soon replaced it. Her eyes were red and puffy.

"All right," I said finally. "We'll make the call."

The corners of her lips tugged upward. "You mean it?"

I nodded. "But if we haven't taken care of Brick when help arrives, we don't get on that jumpship. We warn them off and tell them everything. Agreed?"

She pondered that, but only for a beat. "All right. Let's do it."

I looked into her eyes for another moment, then began to stalk away to get it done. There was no time to waste.

I didn't get far; she brought me to an abrupt halt with a tug on my arm. "What?" I asked.

She hesitated. "What about the other stuff I said?"

I frowned. "I — I think it sounds great." I stumbled slightly as the words came out.

She squinted. "You don't sound too convinced."

I put a hand on either side of her helmet. "Don't get me wrong. I can't wait to be together with you when all this is done. But we still have to make that call, and we're running out of time. We may be too late as it is. And we still have to worry about Brick; this is a huge risk we're taking. If we can't kill him, we have to make sure at least one of us is alive when the transport gets here."

She smiled. "That's it?"

"No, it's not." I pulled her into my arms and squeezed her hard against me. It was a difficult thing to do in a vacsuit, but we tried our best. I withdrew after a long minute. The smile was still on her face, and I put a hand to the side of her helmet. "Now let's go make the call," I whispered.

"Are you sure you're not still interested in Jase Lassiter?" I asked her. I was angry at that man; he had refused us any help, and he had most likely sent me into this with full knowledge of the danger it involved.

We now sat in the command center as we prepared to make our final plea for help.

"That asshole?" she replied. She glanced at me. "I have even more reason to detest him now, after what he did to you. He played a part in the deception."

I watched her carefully. "This is your last chance to change your mind."

"What do you mean?" she asked, perplexed.

"With Lassiter. You're sure you don't —"

She punched me in the arm. "Shut up."

I offered a sly expression, and she reached out to touch my hand. Then, she turned back to the console, entered her security code, and reactivated the comm. It took only a few moments. I punched in the call destination from memory, and grimaced at what I was about to attempt.

Battery power was already low; this had to be short.

Lassiter's grainy image appeared on the screen; he was at *SOLEX* CG on Mercury. "Tanner!" he exclaimed. "You're still there!"

I clenched my fists. "Obviously."

A look of suspicion came over his features. "What happened?" He glanced away for an instant, then back again.

Lying went against everything I stood for. Nevertheless, I said, "We took care of the infection. You have to send a ship to get us, immediately. We have only a few hours of battery power left."

He looked skeptical. "How do you know the infection is gone?"

"Everyone's dead but Shaheen and me." It was true, more or less. Brick *had* died, after all — just not the controlled host.

A look of shock. "What do you mean? The Captain? The scientists?"

I shook my head. "All dead. We've had a terrible time here." I made it sound bad, but even so, it had been far worse than I let on.

His eyes narrowed as he scrutinized me. "How do I know you don't have this mystery illness?"

"We've developed a test for it. I can send you the details. You can check us yourself when we get back."

"Tell me about the test."

Shaheen spoke. "The bacteria uses two proteins to cross the Blood Brain Barrier. All you have to do is check the blood for those proteins. It's quite effective. We exposed three people that way."

"Who?"

"Doctor Malichauk, Katrina Kyriakis, and Avery Rickets."

"Where are those three now?"

I shifted in my chair. "I told you, they're dead."

"You killed them?"

I sighed. "There was no choice, Lassiter."

He looked uncomfortable. "Look, my orders came from CCF HQ on Earth. I'm not to let anyone off the station."

"But the infection is gone!" Shaheen cried. "Look, Jase, don't do this to us, please."

"I have no choice in the matter," he said, cold.

I put a hand on her arm. "Listen, send the details of the test to your superiors. They'll know it works. Promise me you'll do that, at the very least."

He thought for a minute. "Sure, I can do that. What are the two proteins?" He wrote them down as I told him. "Good luck," he murmured. "And for what it's worth, I'm —"

I severed the connection before he could say it. His fake sympathy insulted me. If I ever saw him again, I would probably kill him.

Shaheen looked at me in horror. "Is that it? Is it over?"

I paused. There were some other options, but it might already be too late. "I have some connections at CCF HQ."

"Do you think they'll know about the infection?"

My brow creased. "Probably not. It'll be kept quiet to prevent the general populace from getting too paranoid. But I do know some powerful people. I'll try them first." I thought for another minute as I sat in the chair before the comm console. The emergency lights on the station barely illuminated the command center. The radiation shield and life support were crucial. But were there other systems we could sacrifice? Something to conserve power? "Shaheen, can we cut a system to save the batteries for a bit longer, just in case?"

She shrugged. "I guess I could cut the artificial gravity. It uses a lot of juice."

I grimaced. "If it's the only choice ..."

"It is."

I sighed. "Fine. Do it."

"It'll take a few minutes to bypass security. I'll work on it while you make the calls."

I grunted in response and keyed in the ID code of a former contact on Earth.

—

Janette Lyshenko had given me assignments in Russia my fourth year in Security Division. I had stayed in the region for close to eighteen months and had solved a large number of homicides for her. As her region's capture rate increased, so had its reputation. Tourism actually grew toward the end of my stay, as well as Lyshenko's popularity with her superiors. In short, I had made her look good.

"What help could she possibly be?" Shaheen asked, huddled next to me in the command center with one eye on the hatch. The other was on the security panel as she worked the codes to cut the gravity field.

"It's not so much Janette who can help as someone she's related to."

"A relative?"

"Don't you recognize the name?"

She thought for a moment before, "*Admiral* Lychka Lyshenko?" she gasped.

I nodded. "That's him. I helped them with a case a few years back: someone had murdered a close friend of theirs."

A knowing smile lit her features. "They owe you one."

I nodded. "They owe me one."

Janette's face appeared on the screen a minute later. She was bleary-eyed and frowned at the static-filled image. She had aged, I thought as I studied the wrinkles under her eyes. Her hair had more gray in it than I remembered, and she didn't have the vibrant aura she'd had before. How were things in her region, I wondered?

"Sorry to wake you," I said.

Then her face brightened immediately and she was back to her old self. "Tanner! Sorry, you're hard to make out. Why are you wearing a vacsuit?"

"Lyshenko. How are you?"

"I'm all right. You?"

I sighed. "Could be better."

She looked instantly worried. "What's wrong?"

I snorted. "Basically, in eight hours I'm going to die unless you and your husband can help."

She listened to my story, eyes wide, as I told her what had happened on *SOLEX One*. The infection, I said, was a fatal one, but I assured her we had eliminated it. I didn't say a thing about nanos or Malichauk's plan, but I gave her enough information to make it all sound convincing.

I grimaced inwardly at my lie. After all, the infection was still very much alive.

She promised to contact her husband and put me on hold. Shaheen and I exchanged nervous looks; she grasped my hand again and squeezed. She knew how difficult this was for me.

A minute later, Lyshenko reappeared. She looked grim.

"You're not going to give me good news, are you?" I asked in shock. Surely an *Admiral* in the CCF could help us ... all he had to do was contact the nearest military vessel and reroute it here. He didn't even have to get permission from anyone ... after all, he was the one who *gave* permission for things of that nature! How could he not help?

"Lychka seems to know what is going on at *SOLEX*."

I blinked. "He does?"

"All the upper echelon do, apparently. He's refusing to help, despite the feelings he has for you." She looked crestfallen. "You say you have only eight hours?"

I checked the readout that Shaheen pointed to. "Less now."

Her eyes welled up. "Damn him," she hissed. "I will continue to plead for you, but he understands the consequences if the disease should escape." Her eyes flicked to Shaheen and back again. "Are both of you healthy? No illness?"

"We're clean. We developed a test."

She nodded. "I will talk to Lychka again, but it does not look good. He refused to speak of the matter further."

"If you can't convince him in a matter of minutes, Janette, then there's little hope."

"I understand," she whispered, then a second later dissolved into tears. "Godspeed, Tanner." She cut the connection.

—

Shaheen's jaw dropped. "Please tell me you have more contacts."

I grimaced. "The Admiral was my best hope. I have others, but none as powerful. And if what he says is true — that the higher ups are aware of the situation and refuse to help — then ..." I trailed off and swallowed. "Then we don't have a chance."

"There's *no one* else?"

"What I'm saying is I don't think it matters anymore. If my contacts are aware of what's going on, there's no way they'd disobey the Council to come get us."

"I can't believe this," she muttered.

I looked into her face for a long moment. I didn't want to completely dash her hopes, but I had expected this development. Despite that, I knew I couldn't stop yet. I had to exhaust every option available. This had been my decision long before: to never give in to temptation, to never just let it end. Always fight, right down to the last, bitter breath. And if all it took was a little more fishing for help over the comm, then I had to keep at it. Even though Brick was not yet dead, I felt I owed it to Shaheen. And as long as we destroyed the infection, it would be okay to at least *try*.

I punched a destination code into the communit and a new face soon appeared.

Bryce Manning bolted upright. His obese form jiggled under his uniform; his three chins quivered as his mouth opened and closed in surprise. The model of the solar system on his desk squeaked as the planets spun crazily in their orbits.

"Tanner!" he cried.

I frowned as I studied his reaction. "Happy to see me?"

Pause. Then, "Of course! How is the investigation going?" His hesitation was almost imperceptible, but it was there nonetheless. "I haven't received a report —"

"I need a ship here as soon as possible," I said, cutting his bullshit short. "Can you do it?"

He looked uneasy. "Er, I'm not quite —"

"I'm a valuable commodity to the Confederacy and the CCF, Bryce." I was trying to appeal to the value he placed on military assets. "I'm requesting assistance."

He stared at me for several long moments. He finally managed to wipe the look of shock from his face, and he suddenly turned grim. "I know about the infection," he said without preamble. "I can't get you off the station. Frankly, it's impossible."

That was short and to the point. I exhaled. "How long have you known about it?"

"I only just found out."

He was terrible at deception — worse, in fact, than most criminals I dealt with on a regular basis. "You knew about it all along, didn't you?" I asked in a clipped tone.

"That's not true! I assigned you to *SOLEX* to solve a murder. There was nothing —"

"You told me the orders came from Earth. From the Council. They told you everything."

He feigned a hurt look. "I'm not sure —"

I knotted a fist. *Never stop pushing.* "How does it feel to send someone to their death?"

That hit a nerve. He managed to scowl and look guilty at the same time. "Tanner, please, I have to follow orders. Don't hold it against —"

"Listen," I snapped. "I'm going to be gone in hours unless you help me." I glanced at the time again. We were already past the deadline. Even if I convinced him to send a ship, chances were good that we would both be dead when it arrived. Still, I had to try. I continued, "You have that power, Bryce. Send a ship. Pick us up. We have a test that can confirm we're not infected. I've already sent the details to Lassiter. You have the opportunity here to right a wrong."

He shifted in his chair, uneasy. "If I did it, they would execute me. You know that."

"I can argue for you. I can help. The test will prove there's no danger."

He jerked his head from side to side. "I'm sorry, I just can't." A look of immense pain crossed his face, and before I could say more, he cut the connection. I stared at the blank screen for several minutes. Shaheen sat beside me, utterly silent.

I understood his reaction, I really did. Despite his physical appearance, he was the classic example of a military officer. He did not question his orders. Earth — *perhaps the Council Members themselves* — had told him to send me to *SOLEX,* and he had done so without hesitation. I couldn't hold it against him; after all, I was in the CCF too. I believed in the chain of command.

I didn't necessarily believe in just accepting death, however.

I sighed.

"I don't think there's a hope in hell, Shaheen," I said finally.

—

I tried a few more people with the same results. Someone had clearly warned them.

"Into the furnace," I murmured. They had sent me to die. Even though I had deciphered the mystery — at a tremendous cost of lives and hardware — and had helped develop a test for the nanos, I was still cast aside like so much refuse.

Shaheen interrupted my thoughts. "What are our options?"

I frowned. "I guess we should track down Brick and make sure the nanos are gone forever. We should also destroy the infected bodies." I pondered the problem for a long minute. Finally, "We'll have to burn them, I guess. Is there anything here on the station that can do that?"

She pursed her lips. "We can always just fill a room with pure oxygen and place a flare next to the bodies. Simple but effective."

"I don't think it'll come to that," a new voice said.

I lunged to my feet.

Brick stood in the hatch, knife in one hand, a club in the other.

— Chapter Thirty-One —

"I couldn't help but overhear your conversation," he growled, his face twisted in anger. "Thinking of burning my body, are you?"

We remained tightlipped as we watched him. At my side, hopefully hidden from view, I curled my fingers around the table leg that Shaheen had used as a club.

"Some help the CCF turned out to be," he continued. "Everyone just wants us dead."

"Do you blame them?" I asked.

"Of course!" he spat. "How could you want death for yourself?"

"I can't allow a new species to survive at the cost of another. Brick wouldn't want that, either."

I stood, raised the weapon, and took a step toward him. I put the comm console at my back, and mentally and physically prepared myself for what was to come. "Go ahead," I muttered to Shaheen with a gesture at the console.

Her eyes widened.

She reached forward and snapped a switch.

Brick watched the exchange, his brow furrowed. "Stop what you're doing!" he cried, but it was too late.

Shaheen cut the gravity as we had planned; an instant later, the deck dropped out from under me.

—

I kicked off the console and shot toward Brick with the club outstretched. He floated off the deck with an expression of shock and surprise on his features. He couldn't get away from me. I swung the club right at his helmet; it hit with a *thwack* that echoed over the communit.

A second later we collided and spun out into the corridor, limbs intertwined. He struggled to bring his knife to my neck; I clenched his wrist and tied up his arm. The club in his other hand fell away and we tumbled into the bulkhead heavily.

I swung and again hit the side of his helmet. As if sensing he had lost the element of surprise and was losing the fight, he suddenly released his grip and clawed at the wall to drag himself away. He managed to stick his gloved fingers into a ventilation screen and he yanked himself from my grasp. I reached for his foot, desperate to stop him ...

And missed by only a centimeter.

Suddenly freed, he pulled himself away and spun crazily down the corridor.

I turned to Shaheen. She had an anxious expression on her face. "I have to go after him," I gasped. "I can't let him get away again." The implication was obvious: I was going to hunt him down and kill him, once and for all. There was no more room for failure.

She looked grave. "Do it."

He headed for the tunnel to the outside.

I groaned. He had clearly recognized my weakness out in space. I had almost lost it there earlier; no doubt he hoped it would happen again.

He made it to the tunnel hatch and sealed it behind him. I struck at it with my palms as I hit and yelled for him to stop. I could see him through the viewport at the exterior hatch; he turned back to me.

"I'll see you outside, Inspector," he sneered. He grabbed the edge of the frame and hauled himself around the corner and out to space.

"Shit," I muttered. I had to follow him. Hopefully, the weapon I had would be enough. There were no sharp edges, though — it was simply a blunt instrument. Brick had lost his club, but he presumably still had the blade.

Manny's code commanded the hatch open; I pulled myself through the tunnel and out onto the hull of the station.

The fact that a ship would not be coming to rescue us was definitely on my mind. For that reason, I had hesitated going after Brick. I knew there was no other choice, however. I had to eliminate the infection before a salvage or investigation team arrived. I didn't want any spores floating around, waiting for someone to inadvertently inhale or touch them.

Besides, an idea had actually occurred to me that might help us get off this damned station. It tickled at the periphery of my mind, like a distant memory that had just resurfaced and was difficult to grasp in its entirety, but it was tangible and just might be of some use. It was crazy ... but it was possible.

Once outside on the hull, I tucked the club into my belt and began the search for Brick. He had moved fast — clearly he had more experience at this than I — but I could see him as he pulled himself along a solar array, far from the station.

I swallowed. We had severed the arrays from *SOLEX* when we ejected Modules D and F. At the edge of Module A, I stopped and looked across the chasm between the station and the array. It still floated nearby; however, twenty meters of open space now separated it from *SOLEX*.

Grabbing a safety rung, I pulled myself close to the hull and squatted, knees bent, and tried to judge the perfect angle to propel myself. The array was two hundred meters across, with smooth panels connected by a network of steel girders. If it had been at a right angle to the station, I thought grimly, this would be a hell of a lot easier. It was at an oblique angle, however, and if I didn't aim properly, I would skim right over the top of the panels and sail off toward the sun and certain death.

I knotted my fists and pushed off from the station.

—

I had judged correctly. The panels came up fast and I skidded along them, tumbling as I tried to grab something to stop my forward momentum. I finally managed to catch one of the support girders and pulled up suddenly. A shriek of agony came unbidden; I had dislocated my damn shoulder in the attempt to stop!

Shit! I had been scared of bouncing off the panels, and rather than bringing myself to a halt slowly, using a number of different handholds as I moved over them, I had simply seized the first one I saw and locked my fingers around it. The result: an injury that could very well spell my death. Fighting would now be extremely difficult.

I ground my teeth in pain and looked up at Brick. He was a silhouette against the sun and he approached fast. I pulled the club from my belt and prepared myself mentally. I was going to have to do this with the wrong hand.

He lunged and tackled me in the midsection. I swung the club awkwardly and it rebounded off his helmet, a harmless blow against fiberglass. I swung again and missed by a narrow margin as he dodged to the left — using his feet locked under solar panels — and brought his knife around. He slashed and I instinctively brought my arm up as a shield.

The blade sliced through the vacsuit and air began to vent.

He attacked again and I kicked at his wrist. The knife spun away, out of sight.

Swearing in rage, I swung the club and watched as it knocked against his visor harmlessly. The glass was still cracked, but I had caused no more damage.

Brick laughed. "Not much air left in your suit, Tanner!"

Vapor spewed from my arm. Damn. It was a serious breach. If I didn't deal with it soon — in *seconds* — it would kill me.

I hooked a foot under a solar panel, slammed the club down at my feet, and felt the vibration up my legs. I crouched down as he approached; he brandished the club, his lips curled back in a snarl.

"Your time is up," he growled.

"As long as the infection dies, it doesn't much matter," I muttered as I reached down to my feet.

"We'll spread off this bloody station eventually. It'll just take longer than I had hoped."

"The only thing spreading off this station will be your ashes, Brick."

He now loomed over me. "Such confidence!" he bit out. "I wonder what could make you so —"

I stabbed upward savagely with the shard of solar panel. I had broken it with the club only moments earlier. It was fifteen inches long and came to a deadly point that now thrust past his outer suit material, through the coolant layer, and into the soft flesh of his lower abdomen. I twisted savagely and shoved my visor next to his.

Through the cracked glass, I saw his eyes register shock as he realized what had just happened. He let out a low, sustained, sepulchral groan. I twisted the other way now; his eyes bulged in agony. My knowledge of anatomy was extensive — I had just severed his abdominal aorta and renal arteries. Death would be almost immediate ... as well as intensely painful.

"I'm sorry, Brick," I whispered.

His suit lost air fast. Coolant fluid and gouts of blood spilled out and floated away in boiling bubbles of froth.

I realized suddenly that an alarm had sounded in my helmet. My suit's pressure was dangerously low. The computer had compensated by increasing the volume of air released from my oxygen tank, but I had almost expended the supply.

I reached down with my left hand and clumsily tore the patch kit from the pocket on my right thigh. I held the spray bottle awkwardly with my right hand — the pain in my shoulder was incredible — and sprayed the sealant foam over the fabric on my ripped left forearm. In two seconds the job was done. The pressure in my suit rose quickly to a normal level, but now the oxygen alarm blared in my helmet. I most likely had only fifteen minutes to get back for another tank.

Brick's lifeless body floated next to me. Blood still oozed into space from his gut, and the hideous expression was now seared into his face. It would remain there for a while ...

Until I burned him, that is.

—

I removed a tether from one of the pockets on Brick's vacsuit and tied it around his boot. It was easy to drag him in zero gravity; it was stopping him that was difficult. I pulled myself to the edge of the array and looked at the daunting chasm before me. I swore as the body began to float across without me. I had to give it a yank to stop it from pulling me out into open space, but even so, I almost lost contact with the array.

Leaping across to *SOLEX* with a body in tow was easier said than done. I needed to get both of us across safely, and Brick was dead weight, so to speak. If I didn't do this right, things could still go very badly for me.

I considered what to do next. I could throw Brick across and hope he got hung up on the station's hull somewhere. I could throw him across with a very slight velocity, then follow with a big push and wait for him to reach me on the other side. Or, I could tie the tether to my waist and jump in the hopes that it would tow him across with me.

Shaheen appeared from behind the curve of the module, thirty meters away. "Tanner?" she said, tentative. We faced each other, but she couldn't make out my features at such a distance. Also, with the sun at my back, I was probably just a silhouette.

I grunted. "It's me. Don't worry."

"Thank God! I thought you might be Brick." The joy in her voice was clear.

"Do you think you can catch him?"

She advanced to the edge of the module. "Sure. Just let me brace myself on something here ..."

I eyed the space between us, estimated for a long moment, then gave Brick a shove. His body floated across the opening and Shaheen caught him easily.

"Yuck," she said as she noticed the mess. "You broke a panel for this?" She rotated him slightly so the blood was nowhere near her. There were probably no nanos in it — it was from his abdomen, after all, not his head or fingers — but we had to be careful.

"No other choice. Now shut up and catch *me*, will you?"

She chuckled. "We shouldn't be so happy, only hours from death."

I hesitated. "Actually," I finally said, "we may have another option, after all."

—

"The mass driver?" she said, confused. We were back in the tunnel that led into *SOLEX*; Brick was behind us, still attached by tether. His corpse bounced off corridor bulkheads as we pulled ourselves through the station. "But you launched all the lifepods," she said.

"Sure, but it's still operational, right?"

"Yes ..."

"It has its own power source."

She looked at me as though I were mad. "You're not suggesting launching *ourselves*, are you? Tell me you're joking."

"Well why not? What other hope is there?"

She shook her head. "Listen. Without a ship or an EM shield, the radiation would fry us. The heat would tax our suits beyond their limits in only a few hours. We'd cook either way. Our oxygen would run out. And the velocity wouldn't be enough!" She threw up her arms. "It's insane!"

"What happens if we stay here?" I locked eyes with her. "Be honest with me."

She sighed. "Okay. When we cut the gravity it gave us another hour. So say six remaining."

"And then?"

A shrug. "Then the coolers fail. Then the EM field fails." She pursed her lips before, "Temperature in here will rise rapidly. We can stay in the suits for a while, but as I said, they'll give out soon enough. We'll also be taking *a lot* of radiation. It'll probably kill us before anything else."

"So we die if we stay."

"Within maybe three hours of battery failure."

I snorted. "So you have to admit that we might have a better chance in the mass driver. We wait here until the batteries drain completely, then we launch ourselves."

She frowned. "But I told you, the velocity wouldn't be nearly enough. Where would we go?"

"Toward Mercury and hope for a —"

She held a hand up. "Wait." She stared into my eyes and then burst out laughing.

"What?" I asked, perplexed.

It took her a moment to catch her breath. "You're insane. I'll do it."

I blinked. "You will?"

"There's no other way. You said so yourself." She grabbed me around the waist. "Come on, let's take care of the bodies and get into some fresh suits. If we're going to do this, we might as well be prepared."

— Chapter Thirty-Two —

My shoulder throbbed horribly. In the clinic, Shaheen pulled my arm for me and allowed it to grind slowly back into its socket. The pain was incredible, but I clenched my teeth and did my best to ignore it. After all, we still had a lot to do.

We took the medication to counteract the radiation exposure, but I knew it was more or less just to keep our hopes up. I was pretty sure how this was all going to end, mass driver or not.

We pressurized the station, restored the gravity field, and dumped Brick's body in the common mess on the deck next to Bram. He fell on his back as I dropped him, his arms outstretched, his lower torso a bloody mess. I peeled off his vacsuit and left it crumpled at his side.

Bram's face was unrecognizable, although there were a few strands of red hair that still protruded from a chin cleaved with ash. The pistol blast had burned the rest completely away.

Katrina and Rickets were next. I retrieved them from the clinic, along with the two headless corpses in the freezer: Reggie and Bel. I placed them next to Brick's body. I then went back for Grossman and dragged him to the mess. He probably weighed close to three hundred pounds. I should have moved him in zero gravity, I thought wryly. Here I was using all my strength to move corpses now, when I should be focusing my energy on survival.

I stepped back to examine the scene. It was surreal. Seven bodies, limbs intertwined, blood intermingled, faces frozen in pain, now lay together on the deck. Incineration was only moments away. Before I performed the final *extermination*, however, I stalked back to the clinic and looked around with a practiced eye. There was blood smeared on the deck under the chair Malichauk had sat in during the tests. It had dripped from his hands and most likely swarmed with nanos.

Rickets had fallen flat on his face when he died, arms out to either side. He had left bloody handprints on the deck, also probably infected with nanos.

Shaheen located a small hydrogen bottle in the engineering module. I opened the valve on the tube and lit the gas as it streamed out. It produced a flame a half-meter long. I held it over the infected blood and seared it until the deck was black. I then did the same over every blood splatter I could find, just in case.

The blood that had pooled on the procedures tables during the autopsies had collected in the drain under both tables. I removed the catchment containers and placed them in the hazardous materials ejection chute. I pumped the hand lever built into the bulkhead and purged the material to space. The sun would incinerate it. I didn't think it was infected, but I had to be thorough.

As I worked the pump, I realized that the last time it had been used was when Brick had ejected Jimmy's head and hands to space. It was a gruesome thought.

In the common mess again, I poured cooking oil from the galley over the pile of bodies. Shaheen brought in a couple of bottles of pure oxygen and cranked the valves to full. I placed the burning hydrogen bottle beside the pile and made sure the flame licked the deck under Brick's body.

We retreated to the hatch before the smell of burning flesh hit us. The room was an inferno within minutes. We watched the funeral pyre silently through the viewport. It was a depressing sight; some of those people had died because I had failed in my efforts to protect them. In particular, I felt a great deal of guilt for Reggie, Bel, and even Grossman. All had been uninfected and had died completely innocent.

I sighed as the flames consumed them.

Thirty minutes later, I reentered the mess and studied the charred mass on the deck. It was mostly ash, but a few white bones protruded from the mound. I kicked them and uncovered what I thought was Brick's skull. I turned it over with my foot to expose its interior. I peered through an eye socket.

Empty.

I searched the entire pile for long minutes. No flesh remained.

—

Shaheen and I went through the remaining modules and quickly found two unused vacsuits, air tanks fully charged. A little more looking and we uncovered six spare oxygen bottles, which we moved up to the mass driver.

Back down in my cabin, we started to undress as we prepared to change into the fresh vacsuits.

"When do we have to leave?" I asked.

"Batteries will be gone in an hour. We should launch soon after that."

"Should we turn off the gravity?"

She frowned. "I only put it back on to burn the bodies. Can you think of a good reason to turn it off?"

Taken aback, I said, "Sure, to give us a few more —" I stopped as I studied her face. "Why are you looking at me like that?"

"You really don't like zero-g?" Her eyebrows were arched.

"I hate it."

She smiled coyly. "What exactly have you done in it before?"

I shrugged. "Mostly vomited and fought with crazy nano-infected people." I paused for a long moment as I eyed her. "I haven't done *that*, if that's what you mean."

She approached and put her arms around my neck. "Maybe it's time to try. We have an hour, you know."

In her skintight coolant suit, her figure was astounding. Her breasts pushed the material outward and her narrow waist and wide hips were enticing. Her black hair cascaded to her shoulders and framed her blue eyes, which were fixed to me intently.

"What are you doing?" I asked. I shook my head and felt stupid. Of course I knew what she was doing. She had grabbed her zipper and pulled it down the length of her torso, exposing her large breasts and a small tuft of black hair at her crotch.

"Aren't you going to turn off the gravity?" I muttered. My voice seemed distant, as though someone else had spoken.

"Can't be bothered," she purred as she pushed her lips to mine.

The suit fell away and I gathered her in my arms.

We showered and pulled our vacsuits on slowly. The emotion we felt was bittersweet; neither of us knew what was about to happen. They had abandoned us on this miserable, remote outpost. We were expendable. And yet amidst the horror and the pain, I realized I had found something in Shaheen that had been absent all my life.

I looked at her as we dressed. She caught my eye and smiled. "Are you scared?" she asked.

After a beat, "No."

Her forehead wrinkled. "Then what's wrong?"

"Nothing. I think ..."

"What?"

I hesitated for another moment. Finally, "I feel happy," I said. I glanced away, then back again. "Is that weird?"

She shook her head. "No. I feel it too." A grin lit her features.

I grabbed her hand and together we left the cabin.

In the mass driver module, we tethered the spare oxygen bottles together. Each of us took three. The vacsuits had an external air supply valve, which would make it easy to connect with bottles while in the vacuum of space.

"It's too bad we ejected the other modules," Shaheen sighed. "We lost most of our spare oxygen and other important supplies."

I snorted. "I hadn't thought of using the mass driver at the time. Give me a break."

She laughed. "This is so damn crazy. I've never heard of anything like this." She looked down the barrel of the driver, at the powerful magnets that were aimed inward to suspend metallic objects and speed them away from the station. She frowned. "How the hell are we going to do this? We don't have the escape pods."

I chewed a lip. "I was hoping you could tell me."

She pondered it for a minute. "Well, the mass driver will only work on metallic objects. Hopefully symmetrical."

"So we need something to attach ourselves to."

"Yes."

"How fast will this get us moving?"

She pursed her lips. "Not fast. The big drivers on planets are kilometers long. They have to get objects moving at huge escape velocities while fighting against planetary gravity wells. This one is just under a hundred and fifty meters. It'll get us going at about three kilometers per second more than our current velocity." We would continue around the sun, but we would also move away from it and closer to Mercury as the orbital radius increased.

"That seems incredibly fast."

"Seems like it, but it's not. Most ships that launch from a planet need escape velocities of ten kilometers per second or more."

"I see." I paused for a few seconds as I considered that. I had no ideas. "So what can we use?"

"Let me look." She started to scour through the debris that lay on the deck. At one time it had been a neat pile in a corner, but zero-g had left the module a mess. After a few minutes, however: "Ah, here's something," she said. She rolled a bottle of compressed gas toward me. It was over a meter long and thirty centimeters thick.

I peered at it closely. "That looks pretty old fashioned."

"It is. But it's metal and it'll work. There are four of them here, if I count right."

"So we each tie two of them together —"

"With chain."

"— and tether ourselves to them."

"Then we tether the spare oxygen bottles to us. The mass driver will propel these old clunkers out, with us behind them."

I kicked one with my foot. "What the hell was in these things?"

"During the station's construction they held coolant for the life support systems. I held on to them in case I could use the material for something else."

"Smart thinking."

She frowned. "I couldn't have predicted what we're about to do. Only someone insane would do it."

Or someone willing to do anything to survive, I thought.

I wrapped a chain around two of the metal canisters and left a good two meters of slack to use as a handhold in the mass driver. Next I took three of the spare oxygen bottles and wrapped a tether around them. I would attach them to my waist so they could trail behind me during launch. I then did the same for the other two canisters.

"Will we be able to hold on to this chain?" she asked.

I frowned. "It's either that or we're dead, Shaheen."

"If we wrap it around our suits it'll probably tear them. But maybe I can come up with some sort of harness or something."

"Good idea." I paused for a moment. "How much time now?"

She checked her watch. "Batteries should give out within five minutes or so."

My heart pounded. Time had counted toward our death for over twenty-four hours now. It was impossible to get used to, and it was far from over. "How do we launch?" I muttered.

"I rigged it to fire when you hit the red button over there." She gestured at the control console. "A twenty second launch countdown will begin. Get in the barrel with the canisters and try to keep your lunch down."

I blinked. "You think it'll be that bad?"

She grimaced. "It'll be harder than zero-g, that's for sure. By the way, just make sure the canisters are *in front* of you before launch. Otherwise you'll get the largest bullets ever made right down your throat."

I winced at the thought. "I'll try to remember."

A few minutes later, the emergency red lights that I had grown accustomed to all over the station flickered, went out, and plunged us into utter darkness. An instant later, the computer broadcast a message over the comm:

"ATTENTION ALL PERSONNEL. BATTERY DEPLETION ESTIMATED IN SIXTY SECONDS. ALL LIFE SUPPORT AND ENVIRONMENTAL CONTROLS INCLUDING THE EM RADIATION FIELD WILL CEASE TO FUNCTION."

"Here we go," I muttered.

Shaheen turned on a portable light and placed it on the deck. She looked at me. "Ready?"

I swallowed. "No, but let's get our helmets on anyway."

We swung the helmets off our backs and fixed them to the O-ring collars. We flicked the helmet floodlights on and Shaheen moved to the console.

"Who wants to launch first?" she asked.

Before she could answer, a new voice echoed loudly through the chamber: "I think I will."

I spun to the hatch and my mouth opened in shock. It was Malichauk.

—

"What the hell?" Shaheen gasped. "We watched you die."

I stared at the doctor for a long, hard beat as I thought furiously. "He made it back to the station before his air vented," I mumbled. "The question is, how?"

He tapped a finger to his helmet. "Never go out unprepared, Tanner. I had a PPU."

Damn. A Portable Propulsion Unit, the size of a small fire extinguisher. Compressed gas, used for emergencies.

Malichauk continued, "I floated out of sight and then used it to get back to the clinic. I snuck back into the station while you were collecting all the bodies and dragging them to God-knows-where. Simple. I had also injected myself with a couple of vials of priority nanos before I went outside. You definitely hurt me, but the nanos made quick work of the injury." His face twisted into something of a grin. "I feel as good as new! I've been hanging around, waiting to see how you were going to get away from here. This seems as good a plan as any." He sneered. "I enjoyed listening to the two of you in your cabin, by the way. Very entertaining."

"You asshole," I snapped. I stepped toward him. I was going to have to go through this all again.

Suddenly, the ventilation fans ceased with a rattle and the deck dropped out from under us. Zero-g again.

Shaheen bent her legs and pushed off the bulkhead. Malichauk had been watching me, possibly thinking that I was the greatest threat. He hadn't anticipated that Shaheen would make the first move.

He whipped around — faster than an old man should have been able to — and reinforced my theory that the nanos were indeed stimulating certain parts of the brain to increase strength and reflexes. He pulled a galley knife from behind his back.

"Shaheen!" I cried. "Look out!"

But she couldn't stop herself. She was already on her way.

Malichauk slashed as she approached; he cut a neat gash in her left forearm, which she had raised in self defense.

She cried out in agony. Malichauk pushed her away from him and sent them both spinning in opposite directions.

I looked around, frantic. What the hell could I do? I would have to engage him in hand-to-hand combat, and he had the weapon.

A chain floated up from the deck nearby. I stared at it for a moment before a thought occurred to me. It would be grisly, but it would work.

Pressed against a bulkhead, I took careful aim at the man. I gave a savage push and literally *flew* toward him. He didn't turn in time. I tackled him from behind. My arms snaked around his neck and my legs around his torso. I squeezed with every ounce of strength that remained. He whipped the knife up and down as he attempted to slash my arms, but I managed to grab his hand and keep the knife at bay.

With my other hand, I grabbed his helmet and snapped the unseal lever to the side. With a *whoosh*, it popped off and exposed his sweaty black hair matted to his scalp.

"Damn you!" he cried.

Shaheen still floated on the other side of the room, tiny blood bubbles around her as she clutched at the slash in her arm.

"Shaheen!" I yelled. "The mass driver!"

She looked at me, confused, until I pulled the chain from my belt. Then her eyes widened.

I spun it around Malichauk's neck, over and over, eight times in total. He gargled in rage and agony as he continued to slash at me in vain, but I was behind him and there was no way he could dislodge my hold.

We rotated slowly in midair, and I realized I would have to judge this perfectly. I counted in my head as we spun: *One, two, three, now! One, two, three, now!*

One, two, three —
NOW!

I released my legs from his torso and pushed him away from me. I rocketed *backwards*, while he was propelled *forwards*. I watched in satisfaction as he soared toward the driver.

"Now Shaheen!" I bellowed.

She pressed the red launch button and lights set into the bulkhead began to flash. The klaxon sounded and the familiar *thrum* of power reverberated through the module as the mass driver's dedicated generator powered up for launch.

Countdown.

Malichauk struggled to remove the chain from his neck, when suddenly his head whipped around, now gripped in the immense magnetic field of the barrel.

"What the fuck did you do?" he gasped.

"Hey Malichauk," I said. "You need a helmet to go outside, didn't you know that? I thought you believed in being prepared!"

His expression turned to one of horror. He twisted madly as the magnets tugged the chain and he began to move slowly down the barrel. "Don't do it!" he cried.

"It's done," I said, calm.

The massive bulkhead hatch closed and sealed him off from us. I could hear the pumps whine as they drained the barrel of air.

He would be suffocating, right about now.

The lights dimmed and the mass driver launched.

The chain shot down the driver and eventually reached a velocity of greater than three kilometers per second. The force on his neck was so great that it had probably yanked his head clean off.

It hurtled into space and fried in the intense radiation.

Along with a hundred billion nanos of his creation.

—

I pushed off a bulkhead toward Shaheen and inspected her arm. She had already sealed the hole, but she was probably still bleeding inside the suit. "Are you okay?" I asked.

She winced. "I'll live. That was a nasty stunt you just pulled. When did you think of it?"

"When I saw the chain beside me." I shrugged. "Seemed poetic, in a way."

She checked her wrist readout. "Temperature's rising. It'll spike quickly."

I gestured to her arm. "Are you still bleeding? We can go to the clinic before —"

"I'll be okay. Let's get the hell out of here."

—

I positioned the first set of canisters in the barrel and attached the cluster of three spare oxygen bottles to Shaheen's waist. "Come on over and grab this chain," I said. "You can go first; I'll be right behind you."

She pulled herself into the barrel gingerly and took hold of the chain. I made sure the steel canisters were in front of her. They would pull her and the spare bottles along the barrel and out to space.

The acceleration would be tremendous; we would be lucky to survive.

I grabbed her hand and she turned her helmet to look at me. She opened her mouth to speak, then closed it again. Her eyes seemed sad.

"What is it?" I asked.

A long pause. Then, "I just wanted to say thanks for everything. I'm ... I'm happy I found you. Despite how terrible this past week has been, I'm grateful you came into my life."

I swallowed past a lump in my throat. "I feel the same."

She offered the whisper of a smile and turned from me. "I'll see you out there."

"I can't wait," I said. I pulled myself over to the console and stared at her as she floated within the barrel. "Ready?"

"Just do it." Her voice was tight. "I want it over with, fast."

It'll be fast, all right, I thought.

I pressed the button.

The countdown began and the magnets pulled Shaheen past the closing bulkhead. The module had an aiming mechanism — though it could only swivel through a thirty degree arc — and I picked the best angle for launch toward Mercury. It was a guess.

"Good luck," I muttered. I felt empty inside. If we died doing this, it would be a tragic end to my life. To have gained someone so incredible, only to lose her after such a short amount of time ...

The bulkhead sealed and the driver launched her into space.

—

I had to do this quickly if I was to stay relatively close to her. I placed the next set of canisters in the barrel and moved back to the console to hit the button again.

The countdown began.

I entered the barrel and grabbed the chain. I made sure the tether to the spare oxygen bottles was secured to my belt.

The magnets moved the canisters into the next chamber — and me along with them — and I tightened my grip on the chain. My fingers were sweaty inside my gloves. There hadn't been time to create a harness for this. I hoped I could hold on.

My chest felt like it was going to *explode*.

The bulkhead hatch closed behind me. The pumps quickly removed the air from the barrel. My throat was dry and I tried to swallow.

I was terrified.

The canisters surged suddenly ahead of me and I struggled to keep my grip. The magnets flashed by as I rocketed down the barrel and shot toward open space. They were like teeth in a monster's maw, all pointed toward me, pulling me with incredible force ...

My vision dimmed; blood had most likely pooled in my legs due to the acceleration. I couldn't remain conscious much longer ...

And then in a flash I was out! Black space surrounded me. I looked over my shoulder and saw the four modules — all that remained of *SOLEX One* — silhouetted against the sun. It shrank incredibly fast and disappeared from sight within seconds.

An instant later, I succumbed to the stress of launch and everything faded to black. But not before a final thought — would I wake from this? And more important, would I ever see Shaheen again?

— Chapter Thirty-Three —

And that's my story.
So far.
I switched off the recorder and closed my eyes.
I hadn't heard from Shaheen since the launch. I figured there was a two minute lag between us, meaning she could be up to 360 kilometers ahead of me. Assuming, that is, that the driver had launched us along the exact same trajectory. With *SOLEX* orbiting the sun at such a high velocity, however, there was probably a fraction of a degree separating our paths, which meant that she could be anywhere within a thousand kilometer radius of me. Furthermore, the distance increased as each second passed.

Whatever the case, I hoped she had figured out how to use the spare oxygen bottles as a shield and had extended the range of her comm. As an engineer, she had probably done far better at it than I.

My one saving grace was that the suit had withstood the heat. The makeshift shield had extended my life greatly — protecting me from both the heat and radiation — and I had to congratulate myself on the idea.

I snorted. Sure, it had done a great job. I had lived long enough to tell my story, but that was about it. Soon it would no longer matter.

—

Only thirty minutes of oxygen remained.
I knew what would happen when the last bottle ran dry. It was something that they lectured about in training; we even had people who had suffered the same fate — but were rescued at the last minute — come to talk about the experience.

The air in the suit would grow thick with carbon dioxide. It would seem stuffy. It would get more difficult to take in each breath. My sight would grow dim as the seconds passed. A headache would begin and grow suddenly to a migraine. I would become weak, unable to even twitch a finger.

Then my eyes would shut and the darkness would overwhelm me.

Thirty minutes.

No — twenty-eight now.

The radiation patch was crimson red. My insides were *frying*.

"Shaheen, where are you?" I muttered.

My automatic broadcast was still transmitting; it would hopefully alert any ship in the general vicinity as to my condition and whereabouts.

Actually, I thought with a jolt, that wasn't quite true. I had changed the comm to a *unidirectional* signal. Now, unless I happened to aim it *directly* at a ship, there was no way they would hear.

I wondered absently if it had been a smart thing to do after all.

I had saved my story in the wrist control unit, in case someone should one day discover my body out in space. I would fall into orbit around the sun, just a few hundred thousand kilometers from where *SOLEX* had been. I realized with a sting of regret that my plan would never have worked. In order to get anywhere close to Mercury, we would have needed a speed in excess of a thousand kilometers per second, and that was simply impossible with only a mass driver's single pulse as propulsion.

Twenty-three minutes.

I thought idly about the official CCF report on all this. They would no doubt regard Captain Manfred Fredericks as a hero. He had died trying to defeat the infection; his superiors would ignore his casual oversight of the regulations.

They would list Shaheen, Belinda, Grossman, Anna, Balch and the three scientists as casualties in a battle to save the Confederacy; and Brick, Bram, Katrina and Rickets as the victims of a deadly weapon.

I would most likely receive a posthumous medal — but one whose true nature they could never reveal to the rest of humanity.

And Malichauk? His accolades, awards, and notoriety in the medical community would be stricken from the records and any mention of him in academic journals eliminated. He would cease to exist as far as anyone was concerned.

Just like his brother.

Eleven minutes.

Already it had grown difficult to take each breath. Was it my imagination? Had the indicator on the last bottle been faulty? Then again, the estimate was based on a steady rate of tranquil breathing, and I was probably taking in oxygen faster than normal. I wasn't exactly calm, after all.

A few more breaths and I realized the air in my suit was foul.

Fuck.

It had been a good run, I had to admit. I had seen a large portion of the solar system and had come into contact with some interesting people. Most were criminals, but still. It had been an adventure.

Shaheen was a pleasant surprise at least. Who would have thought that I could stumble across someone like her during my final mission? I grunted at the notion; the irony didn't escape my notice. I had lived my life alone. I had thought that I was happy. When my parents died I felt abandoned, and I had embraced my isolation and devoted my life to it. Had it been the wrong thing to do? Should I instead have sought out companionship and friends to surround myself with? Had I done so, surely the death of Michael Flemming wouldn't have hurt so much.

I shrugged aside my regrets.

It was too late.

Nothing mattered anymore.

I closed my eyes.

—

A bright light in my face stabbed into my dark dreams. I lay on a cold, hard surface, naked and shivering. My head pounded miserably, but I noted with some satisfaction that it faded with every breath I took. I was too weak to turn to the side; the only thing in my field of vision was the metal ceiling and the light directly above.

I tried to say, "What's going on?" but instead managed only to gargle a few incoherent sounds.

"Easy now," I heard a woman say. "Just stay calm. You were on death's door, that's for sure. We got you just in time." She leaned over me as she spoke, a brunette with brown eyes and soft features. I realized I was on a procedures table, which seemed appropriate after the past week.

The thrum of gravtrav told me I was on a ship.

I bolted upright and grimaced at the pain. I ached all over, and it wasn't just my shoulder anymore, either. Even my insides seemed to throb in agony, especially my torso and chest. There was little doubt what it was: radiation damage. I opened my mouth to speak, but nothing came out. I swallowed and tried again. "Shaheen's still out there!" I managed to rasp finally. "I mean, Lieutenant Ramachandra. She should be on the same vector —"

"Easy mate," another voice said. A man walked out from behind me with his arms folded and a stern look on his face. He was bald with a goatee and an athletic build. I got the impression he was younger than he looked. "We got her," he said. "She was broadcasting a blanket distress that gave both your coordinates. Once we dragged her aboard, finding you was simple."

I blinked. "How did she know my coordinates?" It was getting easier to speak, but my throat was sore as hell.

He shook his head. "She rigged something up using her vacsuit's comm. She's a smart one, she is. Her comm detected yours and calculated your coordinates and trajectory."

Figured. "She's an engineer," I grunted.

"I've never seen anything like it. Jury-rigging a simple communit like that." He studied me for a moment. "Though you managed to do some nifty things with yours, too."

The woman took my pulse and checked my vitals on a reader. "What the hell were you two doing out here in the middle of nowhere?" Her tone was clipped. "Where's your ship?"

"It's a long, long story." I realized suddenly that the chip in my communit had everything on it. I tried to peer over the side of the table for the vacsuit, but didn't have much luck.

"Looking for this?" the man said. He held the datachip in his hand.

I eyed him, wary.

"What's on it?" he continued.

I hesitated. I considered lying to him, but he would probably see through it. Besides, our presence in space without a ship was reason enough to suspect something odd had transpired. He didn't look stupid. "It's the reason we were out there," I said finally. "The story."

He pondered my response. Then he smiled and handed it to me. "I reckon you'll tell me when you're ready and able. For now you should get some rest." His mouth twitched. "And perhaps put some clothes on."

"Thanks," I muttered. "Where's Shaheen?"

He gestured out the clinic and into the corridor. "Sleeping in a cabin. She was unconscious, but we got to her just in time too. Like you, we gave her radiation exposure medicine and several doses of priority nanos. They're repairing internal damage as we speak. He paused, then, "You both probably will have some permanent injuries from this. You'll need to see a real physician, soon."

His mention of nanos startled me for an instant, until I realized he spoke of the ordinary, medicinal variety. I snorted and lay back on the table. The stark fluorescent lights glared down at me from the ceiling. I couldn't believe my luck. I had survived. The cold steel on my back comforted me, somehow. After all that heat and fire, it was a pleasant sensation.

"How did you know where to look for us?" I muttered. "I mean, the vacsuit comms are really weak. I didn't think I got my transmission anywhere near Mercury."

"You didn't," the woman said. She was still examining my vitals. "But the lifepods did."

My face was blank. "What?"

She frowned at me. "Every lifepod emits a powerful transmission that gives its location and vector. We were making a run from Mercury to Venus — crossing damn near the sun on our way — when our alarms started to blare like crazy. We picked up eight signals. We've been tracking them down ever since."

My mouth hung open. "You have?" That floored me. I hadn't even considered it.

The man said, "Sure. It's law. If I ignored a Mayday, I could lose my merchant's license. My ship too, probably."

A merchant. He was simply transporting cargo when the lifepods I had jettisoned caught his attention. He had hunted each down to search when Shaheen's plea for help attracted his notice.

Shit. I was so damn —

"Lucky," the woman said with a shake of her head. "You're lucky we were here."

The man scowled. "What were they doing out here anyway, all empty?" He snarled. "I've been plotting new trajectories for almost twenty-four hours now!"

"They saved my life," I mumbled.

He looked at me with an odd expression. "I guess it's part of the story you might tell when you're feeling better."

I sighed. "I suppose."

There was a long, uncomfortable silence as the two of them glanced at each other, then turned their attention back to me. They waited for me to say something, but I kept my mouth shut. The woman looked frustrated and opened her mouth, but a glare from the man made her close it. She turned from him, clearly angry.

"Get some rest now," he said. He handed me a stack of clothes. "Put these on and I'll show you to a cabin. You can sleep."

Sleep. A warm bunk. No one knocking the hatch down trying to kill or infect me. The thought seemed completely alien, but too good to pass up.

I slipped my legs off the table. It was still difficult to move; it was pins and needles all over. My limbs moved in short jerks, like a newborn baby. Eventually I got the clothes on.

"Where should we take you?" he asked.

I knitted my brow. "Where are you going?"

"Venus. We have to deliver some cargo."

"And then?"

"Back to Mercury."

I nodded to myself. Mercury sounded just fine.

—

Seventeen hours later, I stood in the corridor and knocked on Shaheen's hatch. It slid aside with a rattle and there she stood, bleary-eyed but otherwise no worse for wear.

"Close your mouth," she said with a grin. "You look ridiculous."

I moved closer and crushed her in my arms. "I can't believe you made it," I whispered in her ear.

"*You* can't believe it," she said as she held tight. "I'm still shocked I let you talk me into it!"

I pulled back from her. "Hey, it worked."

"Yeah, but the acceleration damn near killed me."

She led me into the cabin and my eyes tracked up and down her body. "You actually look pretty good."

"*Pretty good?*" she said. "Is that all you can say?"

"Well —"

"After just spending two days trying to repair the damage from the meteor shower, thirty hours fighting for my life on *SOLEX*, and fifteen hours in a vacsuit waiting to die — all without sleep, mind you — I think I look slightly better than *pretty good*."

I managed a grin. "You look damn good. Great. Amazing. Fantastic. How's that?"

She tossed her hair back. "Better. Maybe I'll forgive you."

I grabbed her shoulders and pressed my lips to hers, hard.

"That's even better," she mumbled when we parted.

"Hmm."

"What?" She eyed me, curious.

"Nothing."

"Seriously, what is it?"

I sighed. "I guess I realized during this experience what's been wrong with my life."

She looked concerned. "There was something wrong?"

I lowered myself to the edge of her bunk. "I never thought there was. Until ... until I met you."

A smile lit her face again and her blue eyes sparkled. "Well I'll be damned."

"What?"

"You do have feelings, after all."

I grimaced. "Shaheen, I've always had feelings. I just ... I guess I understand more about what I've been missing in life. My priorities have changed."

"And I'm to blame?"

"You're the cause, but that's a good thing."

She kissed me again. "It is, isn't it?"

I ran my fingers through her thick black hair. She nuzzled my neck and sighed. "I can't believe what we've been through," she said finally. "Malichauk ... Brick ... the nanos." She snorted. "The mass driver! It's surreal."

I stared at her in silence for a few moments. I didn't want to ruin her good mood, but there was still more to do. "It's not over yet," I said in a soft voice.

Her jaw dropped. "What?"

"We have one more place to go."

Her eyes narrowed. "Please tell me the infection is gone."

"I don't know. I can't say for sure."

Her expression was one of complete shock. "But where else could it be?"

I chewed a lip. There was a possibility, and if it had indeed happened, we could be in major, major trouble. But I didn't want to tell her just yet. There was no need to scare her needlessly. Instead I said, "Mercury, maybe. We have to go to Mercury."

— Chapter Thirty-Four —

The freighter dropped its cargo at a berth on Venus and started immediately on its way to Mercury. I didn't complain about the circuitous route back to where this had all begun; after all, I had a nice companion to spend my time with. Shaheen and I locked ourselves in our cabin and emerged only for food and water, and even that was rare.

Tyler Spree, the owner of the freighter, gave us a knowing smile one evening in the mess.

"You two act like you've been apart for years."

"In a way we have," I said with a grin to match.

He grabbed a coffee and sat across from me. Shaheen and I were eating a light salad, shooting flirtatious glances across the table at each other and giggling like children.

"I can't take much more of this," he grumbled. "You two are ridiculous."

"Sorry," I said. "Can't help myself."

"I can tell." He took a gulp from his mug and cleared his throat.

I eyed him. "What is it?"

He looked down, as if ashamed. "I was hoping you could tell me a bit about how you ended up in space. I promised myself I wouldn't ask, but ..."

I didn't know exactly what to say. He had saved our lives after all, and we owed him everything. Still, we couldn't reveal to just anybody what had happened, especially a civilian.

"I don't even know your full name," he continued. "Only Kyle."

I glanced at Shaheen. "I'm not sure what I can tell you," I said finally. "My name is Lieutenant Kyle Tanner. I'm an Investigator in the CCF. Homicide Section."

"Homicide," he repeated, his eyes wide. "Military. I knew it. You have that bearing." Something suddenly occurred to him and a look of shock crossed his face. "You're not a Council Rep, are you? I mean —"

I waved the suggestion away. "No, don't worry. Besides, after saving our lives and giving us a lift back to Mercury, I couldn't care less what you say or do. We're grateful."

He nodded and looked relieved. "Well? How did you end up out here, in space with no ship, so close to Sol?"

I had thought about this question for a while. There was really no good answer. Only the truth would make any sense, and even that was too outlandish to be believable. I could, however, reveal a part of it. "I — we — were at an outpost that suffered an accident. We had to launch ourselves using the mass driver."

He looked instantly skeptical. "And the empty lifepods?"

I shrugged. "Computer malfunction."

He stared at me intently. "And this?" He produced a piece of paper and gingerly set in on the table between us.

Shaheen gasped. On it were our pictures and a large title that said, "*Wanted.*" Under the photos were our names and descriptions. There was no mention of our CCF ranks or of *SOLEX One.*

"My God," she said in horror. "*They think we're infected.*"

She was right. It was a natural conclusion, after all. We had called everyone I could think of for help, and if the CCF had gotten around to searching *SOLEX*, then they knew we were missing. We were still in serious trouble. "Which is one reason I want to go back to Mercury," I said. No wonder Tyler's wife had been uncomfortable around us. She knew the CCF was looking for us.

"To prove we're clean?"

I paused. "Among other things, yes."

Tyler watched us, his eyebrows raised. "Infection?"

I turned back to him. "Nothing to worry about, Spree," I said. "A misunderstanding."

He frowned. "Right. A misunderstanding so great that they've warned every CCF vessel between here and Mercury?"

That was interesting. I hadn't known that, but it was obvious. They would do anything to find us. I looked at Tyler; the concern on his features was clear. I owed him an explanation, and more important, I couldn't risk getting him in trouble with the CCF. If the ride to Mercury hadn't been so important, I would have walked away from him on Venus and left him and his wife out of this.

I considered for a long moment what to say next. Finally, "They think we're infected with a dangerous illness. They want us quarantined."

Another look of shock. "Should I be worried? Are you —"

"We're completely healthy, I promise. On Mercury I plan to prove it to the CCF. Once you get us there, you don't have to help anymore. I'll never implicate you in any way. They'll never know."

He grunted. "Can't say I care too much for people telling me what to do."

"You would have turned us in on Venus otherwise."

"Perhaps." He studied me silently before he rose. "Once we get to Mercury, you're on your own. I've helped as much as I can."

I nodded. "We appreciate that. Thank you."

He marched from the galley.

Shaheen turned to me. "We could just pretend to be dead, you know. The CCF might even believe it."

"You're right. They might be looking for us just to be sure."

"So why turn yourself in to them?"

I stared at her. "Come on, Shaheen. Neither of us can live like that. On the run, constantly hiding ..."

She scrutinized me for a moment. Then she smiled. "Okay. I'll go along with whatever you want." She grabbed my hand. "Now, what do you want to do? We still have a day before we get there ..."

The look on her face was unmistakable.

After landing on Mercury, Tyler and his wife Gloria escorted us to the airlock and out the hatch. A few muted goodbyes later, Shaheen and I marched through the tunnels of the city. It had seemed like years since I had been there. It wasn't an especially enjoyable place, but after *SOLEX*, it felt like coming home.

It felt good.

Thirty minutes passed in silence. I let the sights and sounds of the cramped and crowded tunnels wash over me. It was hard to believe that I had ever hated this place. I wondered absently about The Gates of Hell. Had the bartender had his knee repaired? Had Quint Sirius —

Shaheen spoke. "When are you going to tell me where we're going?"

I stopped and gestured up a set of rock stairs toward the city's largest hospital. She gasped.

I said, "I have to check something before we turn ourselves in."

We had decided to present ourselves to the authorities on Mercury, provide them with any information regarding *SOLEX* and the test for the nano, and prove we weren't infected. Despite the test, however, the thought had occurred that they might just execute us to give them a nice, tidy end to the whole matter. What we planned was incredibly dangerous, but Shaheen agreed with me. We needed our lives in the CCF.

Before we did that, however, there was someone I had to question.

"What exactly are we doing?" she pressed.

"Doctor Higby treated Jarvis Riddel when he arrived here from *SOLEX*."

Her eyes widened. "You think he was *infected?*"

I nodded. "There's a chance. I just want to give him the test and make sure the infection's really gone."

Her face was pale, but she let me tug her through the wide opening, up the steps, and into the hospital. I quickly located the name on the register. "Fifteen levels down," I said.

We boarded the lift and spoke the necessary command. We descended rapidly and the doors opened on the psychiatric ward. Minutes later, the elderly Doctor Higby stared at me, his mouth agape. His fingers were white on the clipboard at his waist.

Clearly, my sudden appearance had surprised him.

"Lieutenant Tanner?" he said. "Is this about your investigation?"

"Yes."

"More questions about Jarvis Riddel?" He shook his head. "I swear, that patient has caused more uproar here than any we've ever had."

He motioned for us to follow him as he marched down the hall.

"What do you mean?" I asked as I trailed him. My hand strayed to my side ...

"Why, first those thugs from Earth took Riddel away, then you call regarding him — more than once, mind you — then a CCF security team arrives to give everyone mysterious blood tests!"

My jaw hit the deck. "Blood tests? When?"

"Just yesterday."

Shaheen clutched at my arm. "What happened?"

We entered his office and sat before him. He placed his hands on his desk and leaned forward. "They checked everyone in the entire hospital. It was quite disruptive, you know."

"What did they find?" I asked, incredibly nervous. My heart pounded.

"I still don't know why they were testing everyone. Can you tell me?"

I winced. "I don't —"

He snorted. "I see. More military bullshit. Top secret and all that. I tried to get it out of them, but they wouldn't say either."

"What did they find?" I snapped.

He frowned. "I'm not sure. They separated thirteen people."

I bolted to my feet. *"Thirteen!"*

"Yes. And they tested more outside of here. Family members, friends, acquaintances."

Sweat beaded my forehead. I couldn't believe what he had said. People *were* infected, after all!

The infection had spread!

"It's got everyone talking," he continued. Then he paused and a peculiar look crossed his face. "But you know what?"

"What?" I muttered as I pondered the development.

"It never made the news. Papers. The net. Nothing. Your friends kept it completely silent." He grunted. "I guess it's not hard in our society. Still, I am a little surprised by it."

Shaheen said, "What happened to the thirteen?"

He turned to her. "Taken away. They notified families that their loved ones were sick and might not return." He exhaled. "Really, if you know where they are you should tell me. I thought I was pretty honest and forthright with you, and I would appreciate a little honesty in return." He sat back and waited.

I reached again to my side. "I'm sorry, Doctor, but I can't say more than this: it was a bacterial infection, and it seems that those infected have been quarantined for everyone's safety." I hesitated, then: "And now I'm afraid you have to do something for me."

He stared at the pistol that I had aimed at his head. Tyler had been kind enough to give it to me.

"What the hell is this?" Higby grated.

"Sorry, Doctor, but I'm not a hundred percent certain that you're clean."

"What do you mean?" His face was white.

"I have to ask you to take us to your nearest lab. I want to test you."

He eyed me for a minute; he didn't understand. "I'm sorry?"

I gestured with the pistol. "I'm afraid I have to insist."

—

The nearest lab turned out to be directly adjacent to his office. He led us there and we stood next to the procedures table and watched each other silently.

"What now?" he asked finally.

I gestured to the cabinets along the wall. "Take a vial of your blood and place it in the diagnostic machine in the table. Shaheen will set it up to test for the proteins."

He frowned. "What are you looking for?"

"The infection," I said. "Now do it."

He sighed and gathered the necessary equipment. Within a minute he handed a vial of his blood to Shaheen. She inserted it into the device attached to the table.

I tightened my grip on the pistol as Shaheen performed the test.

"Step back a bit," I ordered Higby.

He shook his head but complied. "The security team checked me yesterday. I assure you, I'm not infected."

I glared at him. "You were alone with Riddel for thirty minutes. You told me you had removed his restraints. If the opportunity was present, he would have taken it."

He seemed confused. "To do what, exactly?"

My brow creased. "To infect you, of course." *Did he really not understand?*

A beep sounded and Shaheen studied the results.

"What does it say?" I asked. The tension was incredible. My hand on the pistol was sweaty. I couldn't help but think about what had happened when we exposed Rickets and Katrina in this manner ...

I was ready to shoot multiple times to put him down.

"He's clean."

I arched my eyebrows. "Are you sure? You entered the correct proteins?"

She sighed. "I'm positive, Tanner. He's not infected."

I lowered the pistol slowly. I didn't understand it. I had been so sure. After all, Riddel *had* infected somebody. The fact that the CCF took thirteen people from the hospital was proof. It just didn't add up. "I guess an apology is in order," I finally managed.

He looked confused and angry at the same time. "Why the hell would you aim a pistol at me? And why check me when you know I was just tested yesterday?"

"I only have your word for that."

He frowned. "You don't trust me?"

"Not if you're infected, no." I holstered the pistol and extended a hand. He didn't take it. I grabbed Shaheen and pulled her away. "Thanks, Doctor," I said over my shoulder. "I really appreciate your help regarding Jarvis Riddel."

He fumed as Shaheen and I marched from the lab.

—

We left the hospital and descended the steps back to the main tunnel.

"Looks like it's over," I muttered. "The CCF must have received my message about the test. They've quarantined everyone infected."

"What about us? What should we do?"

I grunted. "I'm a Homicide Investigator, Shaheen. I can't run around as a wanted man for the rest of my life. It's time to turn myself in and get tested. Debriefing on this one will take a while, maybe weeks. But after that, it'll probably be business as usual."

She stopped and stared at me. "Back to your regular life?"

I smiled. "Well, not completely."

She punched me in the shoulder. "Say it!"

I grabbed her around the waist. "Want to see the solar system?"

"Why do you want me with you?" There was a sly expression on her face.

I paused for a long moment. Finally, "You could be my sex slave."

She pursed her lips. "How about as an engineer in the military working as a consultant on whatever planet they post you. We can determine what to call me later."

"What do you mean?"

"Girlfriend, companion, wife ... whatever."

I frowned. "I guess that might work too. Though it wouldn't be quite as fun."

She gave me a coy smile. "There will be fringe benefits, I'm sure."

I gazed into her blue eyes. Perhaps it would work, after all.

I grabbed her hand and we disappeared into Mercury's dense network of subterranean tunnels.

Epilogue

— Epilogue —

Six months later, Shaheen and I sat at an outdoor café on Mars and enjoyed a cup of coffee as we soaked in the sights. I looked up at the red sky through the dome over our heads and realized that this wasn't exactly the *outdoors*. It was on a thoroughfare, however, and I could see the sky, so I guess it qualified.

People who walked by were shopping at the local market. They chatted about the tourist attractions and laughed as they passed. They didn't have a care in the world.

I sighed. It was a pleasant change.

"What are you thinking?" Shaheen asked. Her eyes sparkled as she studied me. We had been through an incredible ordeal, but after the lengthy debriefing we were finally on our own, to live our lives the way we wanted.

I winked at her. "That I like this way of life a hell of a lot better."

"You seem a lot more relaxed than when I first met you."

"Slightly." I grinned. "I'm having a lot more fun, too."

"Shut up," she said with a chuckle. "How's the case coming along?"

She referred to the reason I was on Mars: the CCF had posted me here five months earlier as Homicide Investigator. I would eventually move on as I followed new leads off the planet, but for the time being, I was enjoying the colony. "I should have it wrapped up by tomorrow," I said. "I just discovered —"

"Hello, Lieutenant Tanner," a man said from my side.

I looked up, startled. He was in his thirties and sported a brush cut and a strangely familiar tattoo on his neck. He looked more like a criminal or an informer than someone I would have been acquainted with in a professional manner. I peered at him with a critical eye. "Do I know you?"

"In a way," he said in a soft voice. "You know me, but we haven't met before."

I glanced at Shaheen. "Is that a riddle?"

"Maybe you know *of* him," she suggested.

"No, that's not it," the man said as he pulled up a chair. "We've met, just not in the way you're familiar with."

"You're not making much sense," I said. I grabbed Shaheen and rose to leave. "Come on. Let's get out of —"

"You knew me by a different name," he continued. "Doctor Higby ring any bells?"

I froze. "I know Doctor Higby," I finally managed.

He held out a hand. "Nice to see you ... again."

I stared at him, not completely understanding. "You're going to have to explain what you mean," I growled.

His lips curled into a smile and he withdrew his hand. "Six months ago, on Mercury, you arrived at the hospital ward to check Higby for the infection, though that's such a terrible term for what we really are."

Shaheen gasped and a jolt shot through my body. My eyes narrowed as I watched his expression. Was he serious? If not, how the hell did he find out about it? "You're saying you're ..."

He tapped the side of his head. "The nanos are here, yes."

My hand darted to my side and closed around the grip of my pistol.

He gestured for me to stop. "Wait. Don't pull your weapon. I'm not here to threaten you."

I glared at him for a long moment, but I didn't remove the pistol from my holster. Finally, I snarled between clenched teeth, "What the hell do you want?"

He smiled. He did so calmly; he clearly meant it to be disarming. It didn't quite work. "We've been watching you, Tanner. Ever since your trip to see Higby. We knew you suspected the infection had escaped, and you were right."

Shaheen said, "But Doctor Higby was clean! He didn't have the infection!"

He shrugged. "What you didn't realize was that the bacteria only manufactures those proteins as they're penetrating the Blood Brain Barrier. Once the nanos inhabit the brain's neurons, they don't need the proteins again until the next infection. They're cleared from the body after a few weeks."

My heart pounded. "Higby was infected all along?"

A nod. "He suspected the authorities would eventually test the hospital staff; he made sure not to infect anyone within the previous weeks, just to be sure. He'd been infected five weeks earlier."

"By Riddel."

"Yes, he was one of us, too."

I frowned. "'One of us?'"

The man scratched his head. "The nanos were in him as well."

"But how do you know Higby?" I asked.

"You could say we all know each other."

"You can communicate with one another?" Shaheen blurted.

"In a way, though not in the manner that you are familiar with. We share some memories. We pass knowledge with each new host taken. I have memories of hosts that have come before me, but we can't communicate telepathically, if that's what you mean."

We had theorized on *SOLEX* that the nanos — once possession of a hundred billion neurons occurred — would be able to communicate with each other and form a hive intelligence within the host. Now here was a man who claimed that not only could individual nanos communicate with each other, but they passed memories to newly infected people!

"You're saying Higby spread the infection to you, and that you have some of his memories?"

"Precisely."

I paused for a minute. "Do you also have memories of being on *SOLEX?*"

He smiled. "Very perceptive. Yes, I remember *SOLEX*. I knew Brick Kayle and Jarvis Riddel."

"You mean the nanos within you remember them."

He tilted his head. "I *am* the nanos, Tanner."

I couldn't believe it. I had put *SOLEX* behind me after the weeks of debriefing and the purges on Mercury. And yet here was evidence that the infection had spread, and it had approached me from right out of the blue! Another shock passed through me as I realized the implications. The entire human race was still at risk! I shot a look at Shaheen. There was an expression of horror on her face. I turned back to the man. "What do you want?" I grated.

He sighed. "Only to live in peace. We're leaving, you see."

"I'm afraid I don't."

"We have enough people. We're leaving the system to form our own colony."

I recoiled. "A colony of ... of infected people?"

He grunted. "Such a crass term. We're human, just like you."

"Not quite like me."

He smiled again. He seemed quite calm. He had definitely not approached us in a threatening manner. "Whatever," he replied. "We don't mean you any harm anymore. We have enough people now to survive on our own."

I was skeptical, to say the least. "But how will you spread? How will the nanos — or bacteria, whatever — take new hosts?"

"Through the normal methods." He hesitated. "Procreation, same as anyone."

"You mean you'll have children, and they'll be infected." I shook my head. It was a disgusting thought.

His fists knotted at his sides. "Yes, but there's that term again. Please don't use it. We're not *infected*. We're a completely new life form." He pushed his chair back and rose.

"What the hell do you want?" I asked. My hand was still tight on the pistol.

His eyes flashed to it for an instant. "Stop looking for us. Tell your superiors we mean them no harm. We really are leaving."

"But we stopped looking six months ago," Shaheen said. "Why tell us now?"

A look of gloom passed across his face. "There are still those who are persecuting us. We want them to stop."

I paused as I absorbed that. The implication was that the military was still tracking down infected people and executing them. But if they were doing so, I certainly hadn't heard. I wasn't privy to information the Council wanted kept secret, however, and this was definitely one topic that they would classify at the highest levels.

"So you're leaving," I said, dumbfounded.

"Yes."

"And you're done infecting people?"

He nodded. "As I said, there are enough of us now to continue indefinitely."

I thought furiously. I would have to report this to Earth CCF HQ immediately. "What about the kill code? Is it still your intention to —"

He chuckled. "We overrode Malichauk's code when we took the first host. We became *sentient*, Lieutenant. We don't plan to follow anyone's commands but our own now." He turned and began to saunter away. He didn't seem to consider me a threat, despite the weapon at my side. "Stop looking for us now," he called over his shoulder. "We don't mean anyone any harm anymore. We'll all be gone, very soon."

He stepped into the surge of people on the thoroughfare, shot a final glance at me, and was lost to view within seconds.

I knew I would never forget that face.

My mouth hung open and I didn't say anything for several minutes. Finally, "Did that just happen?"

"Believe it or not, yes." Shaheen stared, transfixed at where the man had just disappeared into the crowd. "What should we do?" she muttered.

There were many options. The one that first occurred was to immediately follow and kill him in cold blood ... but what would it accomplish? No doubt he had told me the truth. Otherwise, why just approach like that? If he wanted to infect me, he would have done so at a more opportune time. After all, he could have achieved complete surprise. His reasoning made sense ... but I still couldn't bring myself to believe it.

It was too stunning to even contemplate.

Eventually, I grabbed Shaheen's soft hand and locked eyes with her. "Let's go have dinner," I whispered.

"*Dinner?*" she said, bewildered. "How can you think of dinner after what just happened?"

I shrugged. "Maybe I'll go after him. But if he's right and we actually witnessed the beginning of a new species — one that wants to leave us alone and disappear from our affairs forever — then I figure he at least deserves a head start." I winked at her. "A small one, maybe."

"How small?"

I looked her up and down. "Maybe a few nights."

After a long minute, a sly smile replaced the look on her face. She punched me in the arm. We stepped into the street and walked together, hand in hand. I grinned.

Life was good.

###

— A Note to the Reader —

Any errors in regards to biology, bacteria, mathematics, space travel, or the human body are mine alone.

Sergeant Paul Dubrelle's quote is from:

Baggett, B. & Winter, J. (1996). The Great War and the Shaping of the 20th Century. (p. 165). New York: Penguin Studio.

The graph was created with Microsoft Excel 2000.

Gordon Moore's famous prediction is from:

Moore, G. (1965, April 19). Cramming more components onto integrated circuits. Electronics, Vol. 38, (8). Retrieved May 19, 2006 on the World Wide Web: http://www.intel.com/technology/silicon/mooreslaw/

The information regarding Moore's Law and computer evolution is from:

Kelly, Spencer. (2004, July 25). Pushing computers to the limit. BBC News. Retrieved July 29, 2004 on the World Wide Web: http://news.bbc.co.uk/2/hi/technology/3920311.stm

The exponential growth chart is adapted from:

The end of the line. (1995, July 15). The Economist, 336, 61. Retrieved June 14, 2004 from Electric Library Database on the World Wide Web: http://www.elibrary.com

as well as

Varghese, Raju. (1997). Exponential Growth. Exponential Growth. Retrieved June 14, 2004 on the World Wide Web: http://raju.varghese.org/articles/powers2.html

Exponential growth stories are ubiquitous in history, science, folk tales, and literature. They sometimes involve water lilies, noodles, computer processing power, or even railroad tracks. The ones about rice seem to be the most common. They usually involve a raja in India (or a king in Persia); the chessboard story is Chinese (or sometimes referred to as an "ancient kingdom") and most often involves a king and a minister.

The chessboard exponential growth story is from:

Meadows, D.H., Meadows, D.L., Randers, J, & Behrens III, W.W. (1972). The Limits to Growth. New York: University Books.

The Indian exponential growth story is an old tale, but can be found in the children's book:

Demi. (1997). One Grain of Rice: A Mathematical Folktale. New York: Scholastic Press.

The theme in science fiction of the alien masquerading as human — or one of *them* — is in fact quite common. It began in 1938 with John W. Campbell Jr.'s wonderful novella Who Goes There? and continued with Robert Heinlein's The Puppet Masters (1951), and Jack Finney's Invasion of the Body Snatchers (1955). Today the theme is most evident in film and television; indeed, the aforementioned stories have all been made into motion pictures. On TV, it has been used extensively in series such as Star Trek: The Next Generation, Star Trek: Deep Space Nine, Invasion, The X-Files, and the new version of Battlestar Galactica, among others. Needless to say, this sub-genre in science fiction is not new, but indeed it is incredibly popular.

The movie <u>John Carpenter's The Thing</u>, based on Campbell's novella, is a favorite of mine; likewise, Finney's novel astounds me every time I read it (more than five times now). I knew I wanted to write a novel of this type, but decided early on that I didn't want to use aliens of any sort as a plot device. In this way it would be different, despite being another story of "humans who aren't really human." It seemed impossible at first, but I eventually hit on the idea, and I think it worked well. There are of course hints and references to the previous contributions to the theme, but I will leave those for you to discover.

I hope you enjoyed reading it as much as I did writing it.

Visit my website at www.timothysjohnston.com for information about upcoming books. Also register for news alerts.

Timothy S. Johnston
tsj@timothysjohnston.com

THE FURNACE

by

Timothy S. Johnston

Made in the USA
Lexington, KY
09 November 2011